SCARS OF THE REVOLUTION

HARBOR OF SPIES ~ BOOK 3

MEGAN SOJA

For my own miracles - Natalie and Hope
May you always remember how precious you are to God, and to me.
I love you forever.

*And he said unto me, My grace is sufficient for thee:
for my strength is made perfect in weakness.
Most gladly therefore will I rather glory in my
infirmities, that the power of Christ may rest
upon me.*

— 2 CORINTHIANS 12:9

*The race is not to the swift, nor the battle to the
strong, but the God of Israel is he that giveth
strength and power unto his people.*

— ABIGAIL ADAMS, LETTER TO JOHN
ADAMS, JUNE 18, 1775

CHAPTER 1

BOSTON

JUNE, 1775

*L*ibby Caldwell peered at her reflection in the darkened glass of her bedroom window, hardly recognizing the woman that stared back at her. The flickering candle she held illuminated worry lines between her brows and shadows beneath her eyes. At twenty years of age, she should not look so weary. So worn.

She sighed, and the flame stuttered at the rush of air. The cheerful facade she'd worked hard to maintain felt just as flimsy, threatening to falter under the strain of the past weeks. Or perhaps it was much longer. Ever since Papa died two years ago.

Shifting her focus beyond her own image, Libby gazed at the first streaks of dawn that graced the horizon in soft hues of pink and orange. *My Sunshine*, Papa had called her. What would he think of her now, shrouded by such clouds of gloom?

She blinked and shook her head. Enough melancholy thoughts. Turning from the window, she reached for the apron that hung on a peg beside her chamber door. She tied it around her waist, having already donned her favorite linen round gown the color of a redbud's blooms. Then she pinched her cheeks, hoping to bring some of the same color to her overly pale face.

It should not matter how she looked, yet she could not help herself, knowing who dwelt downstairs.

Lieutenant Harrison had been quartering with them since last September, and try as she might to convince herself to ignore his presence, her heart continued to disregard all reason.

She frowned, a silent personal scolding. Lieutenant Harrison would never see her as anything more than the young girl she'd been when they first met six years prior. And that was for the best, for there could never be anything between them. He was a British officer occupying her town. Fighting against her countrymen. Never mind that he had been Papa's friend. That he had only ever treated her and Mama with respect and kindness. Or that he'd sought quarter in their home out of a desire to protect them.

Never mind how his handsome face filled far too many of her daydreams. Or that his deep brown eyes held a hint of sadness she wished she could be the one to soothe.

Her frown dipped lower. Dwelling on such things would not help her banish the misplaced affection she held for Lieutenant Harrison. And banish such feelings she would. She must.

Libby made her way downstairs, careful to tread lightly on the step that creaked. Mama would still be abed. Though Libby had never been one to rise early in the past, her sleep had been fitful of late, and 'twas better to be productive than dwell in the fog of questions and doubts that plagued her.

Passing into the kitchen, she stopped short at the sight of Mama, already tending the fire.

Her mother looked up with raised brows. "You're awake early."

"I could say the same for you, though even more so." She eyed the pot of porridge already hanging from the iron crane.

"One might think the quiet makes for better rest, but I've found the opposite to be true." Mama pushed a charred log farther into the hearth.

"Aye."

The quiet that hung over their home, over their town, was not of the peaceful sort. It held an eerie emptiness. A constant reminder that they'd been left behind. Or rather, that they had chosen to stay while so many others had fled. A decision Libby had convinced her mother to make. One she doubted more and more each day.

Mama straightened, attention fixed on the growing flames as they leaped higher. Lines etched her face, and the strands of gray nearly outnumbered those of blond in her simply styled hair. Guilt gnawed at Libby's stomach, even stronger than the ever-present hunger. This weight on Mama's shoulders was her fault. All because she couldn't let go. Of both the past and her selfish, misguided hopes for the future.

"'Come unto me, all ye that labor and are heavy laden, and I will give you rest.'" Mama spoke with quiet conviction, turning to face her. "Matthew...?"

"Chapter eleven, verse twenty-eight." Libby filled in where her mother left off.

Mama didn't need help in finishing the verse, of course. She knew more of the Bible by memory than anyone Libby had ever met. But from the time Libby was able to speak, Mama had been instilling as much Scripture as possible into her daughter's mind this way. Clearly, her efforts had been a success. Still...knowing the words and truly taking them to heart were two different matters. And lately, Libby had been struggling with the latter.

A gentle smile eased the weariness on Mama's face. "Indeed. A reminder we both needed this morning, I believe."

Libby nodded, forcing herself to match her mother's smile. It seemed she required quite a few reminders, and the day had hardly begun. Would any of them manage to stick?

She reached for the ladle hanging from the rough-hewn mantel, intent upon stirring the meager serving of porridge that had begun to bubble in the pot. An anguished shout echoed from the direction of Lieutenant Harrison's quarters, and she startled, the spoon clattering to the floor.

"What was that?" Mama's eyes were wide, her face ashen.

"I do not know." Libby's heart pounded. "But I'll find out."

She spun away and dashed toward the parlor, ignoring Mama's call to wait and once more silencing the voice in her head that warned her to keep her distance from Lieutenant Harrison.

≈

Isaac Harrison bolted upright in bed, gasping for breath. His heart raced, and cold sweat beaded on the back of his neck. The bedclothes twisted around him as though he had wrestled them all night. Perhaps he had. Struggling to break free, he swung his legs over the side of the mattress and hung his head in his hands.

Breathe in slowly. Hold it. Exhale. Repeat.

His heart slowed to a regular rhythm, well-accustomed to such training after nearly a decade in the military.

If only he could train the nightmare away just as easily. But even now, when he closed his eyes, the images were still there. Flashes in his mind like bolts of lightning that jolted him to the core. Fire and smoke and blood.

He pushed off the bed and stalked to the wooden chair beside the hearth where he'd draped his uniform last night.

The crimson coat taunted him. A reminder of who he was. The man he had never wanted to be.

But he'd had no choice nine years ago, and he had no choice now.

Tugging on his wool breeches, he shoved his linen tunic into the waist and fastened the buttons. He reached for his stockings, but before he could pull them over his bare feet, a knock sounded on the door separating his chamber from the parlor.

"Lieutenant Harrison?" A tentative voice called from the other side. Miss Caldwell's voice. "Are you well?"

Why would she ask such a thing, unless... He grimaced. Had he cried out in his sleep? Heat crept up the back of his neck.

"I am." The words came out gruffer than he intended, but all the better. He couldn't have her hovering outside his door worrying over him. 'Twas in her best interest not to think much of him at all. To act as though he wasn't there.

If only he weren't.

Would that he could escape this city. But after the fighting that broke out in Lexington and Concord in April, thousands of colonial militiamen had surrounded Boston, cutting off the peninsula from the mainland and effectively laying siege to the entire town. Admiral Graves's fleet of ships still held control of the harbor, but beyond that, Isaac and the over six thousand other soldiers stationed there were trapped.

Over a month had passed, and the men under his command were growing restless. Morale would continue to deteriorate, along with the conditions of Boston, the longer they were contained within its bounds. Without access to the rest of the colony, food and supplies would decrease further with each passing day. Already, shops were closed, and in May, an accidental spark had started a fire in Dock Square, burning thirty warehouses to the ground before it was contained. What necessary goods had been lost to that blaze?

The once-thriving town was a skeleton of its former self, emptied of citizens who had fled while they had the chance. Why had Miss Caldwell and her mother chosen to stay?

"Are you certain there is nothing that I...that my mother and I can do for you?" Miss Caldwell cleared her throat. "We have porridge to break your fast."

"Thank you, but I am well." The rumble of his stomach belied his words, but he'd not take their food. Not when he had noticed how carefully they were rationing it.

He stared at the door, willing her to listen. To leave him be. But the shifting hint of shadow between the thin gap where the door met the floorboards declared that she still lingered on the other side.

She could wait if she wished, but he couldn't go speak with her in this state of dress. Surely, by the time he was presentable, she'd have left. And if not, he'd simply slip out the side door and make his way to the Common for morning drills.

Sighing, he sank to the chair and pulled on his stockings. Miss Caldwell was too kind, too sweet and innocent for her own good. How could she continue to extend him such grace and generosity? Did she not know the things he had done as a lieutenant in The King's Own? He was an officer of the grenadiers, the elite company of soldiers purposed to be first in all attacks. If she had seen him in battle, watched him load his musket, raise it to his shoulder, and train his sights upon another man, a fellow human...

The scenes of the nightmare returned in full force, and his fingers fumbled with the leather garter buckle.

If only his past friendship with Miss Caldwell's father had not placed upon her some sense of obligation toward him.

A fresh wave of grief tightened his chest at the thought of his friend. Strange, how a man he'd known for only a year could leave such sorrow behind at his passing. But in truth, the late Dr. Caldwell had been more like a father than a friend. The kind of father Isaac had longed for since boyhood. The one his real father had never been.

A rustle of petticoats drew his head up. The shadow disappeared from beneath the door. Miss Caldwell had given up waiting, just as he'd hoped she would. Why then the odd prick of disappointment?

Shaking it away, he stood and reached for his waistcoat. He worked his regimental buttons closed, each one a reminder of who he was and of the duty he'd sworn to fulfill. After securing his stock, he lifted his coat from the chair, staring at the bright red fabric.

His men needed a strong leader. His king demanded allegiance. His family expected a son they could be proud of. And surely, his betrothed waiting in England wished for a heroic man as her future husband, even if they'd never met.

Donning his uniform, Isaac squared his shoulders. He would continue to serve honorably, just as he had striven to do since the moment his father handed him his commission. There was no escape from this life that had been chosen for him, but perhaps soon, they would find a way to escape Boston and quell the rising tide of revolution for good.

CHAPTER 2

A mild June breeze tugged at Libby's curls as she knelt beside Hannah's garden on Wednesday afternoon. She pulled another weed out from where it encroached upon a bed of lavender. How strange it seemed to be there without her childhood friend, and how much Libby longed to share a conversation with her. But Hannah had been forced to flee Boston in April when her father was wrongfully arrested. Who could say now when Libby and her friend would be reunited?

Until then, she was determined to tend the garden that Hannah had so carefully nurtured for years, instead of allowing everything to fall into disarray. It seemed a hopeful thing to do. A sort of promise that Hannah's home would be ready and waiting for her when she returned. Libby had hoped it might also help her feel closer to her friend, but instead, an all-too-familiar loneliness pricked at her spirit.

Pushing the feeling away, she glanced at the other end of the garden, where Mama knelt, pruning a patch of horehound. "Thank you for coming with me. I couldn't bear the thought of letting Hannah's garden grow completely wild."

And the task helped take her mind off Lieutenant Harrison,

who had never given an explanation for his shouted cry two mornings ago, though she dared not voice that thought aloud.

"I understand. I am glad to help." Her mother looked up with a soft smile that faded when her gaze drifted to the road behind them. "Nor is it safe for you to go about unaccompanied with all these soldiers roaming the streets."

Libby pressed her lips together. Mama was right, but her words stung, a reminder of how much her hometown had changed. Everywhere businesses sat vacant and silent. Grass grew between the cobbles of the once-bustling roads, and wooden boards barred the windows and doors of homes abandoned by their owners who sought refuge elsewhere.

Leaning back on her heels, Libby peered at Hannah's empty house. "Do you think Hannah will even return to live here, now that she and Will are married?" Her dear friend had wed Libby's stepbrother last month.

"I cannot say. They may decide not to come back to Boston at all."

She hadn't considered that. But 'twas a possibility. Her stepsister, Patience, had already settled outside of the city with her husband over a year ago. Libby had not seen her since.

And what of those who had been parted from her, not by distance but by death? First, her father, then her stepfather. So much had happened the past two years, so many unexpected changes sweeping the people she loved out of her life like a relentless current.

"Do you regret that we stayed?" Libby held her breath as she risked a glance at her mother.

Mama stood, moving to a new patch of the garden where chives sprouted bright green from the dark soil. "Mayhap we should have left, but there is nothing to gain from considering what should or could have been, for we've no power to turn back and change it now."

Libby sighed. Despite the truth of Mama's words, she found

little comfort in them. Her mother possessed the gift of being content no matter her circumstances. Although Mama would say 'twas not a gift but a discipline. An act of faith in God, who instructed His children to give thanks in all things and promised to keep them in perfect peace.

Libby trusted in God. She had for as long as she could remember. Why then did she not experience the same thankfulness and peace? The same contentedness?

There was a time when she had felt it. Before Papa's death. Before she realized that her faith did not protect her from loss and grief. That the same God she begged to save her beloved father had chosen to take him instead.

Was there still comfort to be found in such a God?

Frowning, she yanked at a particularly large weed. The leaves tore off in her hand, but the roots stayed firmly embedded in the ground. She felt much the same, still clinging to the foundation of her faith, but broken in ways that had yet to mend.

She tossed the leaves aside, squeezing her eyes shut against the sting of tears. It wouldn't do for Mama to see her cry. To wonder what was wrong. Tilting her head back, she tried to focus instead on the welcome warmth of sunshine on her face and the fresh scent of spring drifting in the air.

As she opened her eyes, a fleeting movement in the upstairs window of Hannah's house snagged her gaze. She blinked. Perhaps she'd imagined it. Or simply caught the reflection of a bird or a drifting cloud in the glass panes.

She pushed to her feet, staring hard. There it was again. The slightest rustle of the curtains. The faintest shifting shadow. "Did you see that?"

Mama frowned. "What?"

"There, in the Pierces' house. I thought I saw something. Or someone."

"Are you certain?" Her mother squinted at the window.

Was she? "I do not know, but I thought—"

"We'd best leave. If a soldier has taken up quarter there..."

Disgust churned in Libby's gut to think that some Redcoat might have taken advantage of the Pierces' absence to invade their home. She'd heard rumors of soldiers plundering the deserted houses and shops throughout town, as though all that had been left behind was theirs for the taking. Was some stranger riffling through their belongings this very moment? Stealing food or clothing or anything of value? Anger welled inside her, along with a maddening sense of helplessness that she could do nothing to stop the intruder.

Clenching her jaw, Libby spun away and followed Mama out the gate. As they hurried down the street, she cast one more glance over her shoulder. Her heart froze, for this time there was no mistaking it.

A face peered out after them.

～

A pounding headache and a long list of unsolved problems were all Isaac had to show for his day as he pushed through the door to his quarters Wednesday evening. He slammed it shut behind him with a little too much force, wincing at the sound that jarred his throbbing head. And likely alerted the women of the house to his return as well, something he typically tried to avoid.

It wasn't that he disliked them. Quite the opposite. He had the utmost respect for Dr. Caldwell's widow and daughter, and 'twas for that reason that he kept his distance. Isaac had been more willing to share the occasional meal or conversation with the family when the widow's stepson still dwelt with them. But now that the two women lived alone, he was hesitant to accept such offers, determined to do all he could to honor their privacy. Indeed, he wouldn't have imposed upon them at all were it not for Sergeant Jackson.

Even the thought of the man's name made Isaac scowl. He pressed his fingers to his temples and rubbed a slow circle, though it did little to reduce the ache.

Jackson's habits with drink and women, not to mention his temper, made him someone Isaac tried to associate with as little as possible, and someone to keep far away from Dr. Caldwell's family. When the sergeant had expressed interest in quartering in their home last fall, Isaac had done the only thing he could think of to prevent such a disaster—he'd quartered there himself instead.

Shrugging out of his coat, he hung it and his hat on a peg jutting out of the wall. This room was once Dr. Caldwell's office, purposed for attending to patients, storing medical supplies, and keeping his books. What would the doctor think if he could see Isaac now? Hopefully, he would understand Isaac's heart behind such an imposition upon his home and family.

A knock sounded on the door separating his room from the parlor. "Lieutenant Harrison? Might I offer you something to eat?" Mrs. Abbott's words drifted toward him. It still startled him sometimes, to think of her by the name of her second husband instead of *Mrs. Caldwell* as he'd known her before.

Crossing the room, he opened the door and was greeted by a gentle smile and the savory smell of fried fish. His mouth watered, but how could he take their food when it was already so hard to come by and would only grow worse the longer the siege lasted?

"I thank you, but I cannot accept such an offering—"

"Indeed you can. A neighbor boy brought us some of his catch as a generous gift, and we've more than enough." She held out the plate. "'Twould be better with a bit of lemon, but…"

But of course there was none to be had. Even without a single garnish, the meal was sure to be better than his typical fare of late. He accepted the offering with a dip of his head.

"You are welcome to eat in the kitchen if you'd prefer."

"Thank you, but I think I'll remain here for the night. I've a bit of a headache and would make for poor company."

Concern etched her brow. "I have a soothing tea to help with the pain. I'll have Elizabeth steep some for you."

"You needn't worry about—"

"Please." She pressed a hand to his arm in a motherly gesture. "'Tis not wrong to accept help from a friend."

Was that how she saw him? As a friend, despite the circumstances?

He swallowed and nodded. "Aye, thank you, I will take some tea, then."

"Very good. I'll send her when it's ready."

Leaving the door ajar, Isaac sank onto his wooden chair and balanced the plate on his lap. The food was warm and tasty, but the silence of his chamber settled uneasily over his shoulders. He glanced at the novel laying on his bedside table. *The Vicar of Wakefield*, borrowed from Dr. Caldwell's collection. It was an engaging story, but his pounding head made the thought of reading unappealing.

Perhaps he should have accepted Mrs. Abbott's offer to dine in the kitchen, simply for the distraction of a bit of pleasant conversation. Something better than the discussion he'd had with Sergeant Jackson this afternoon.

Scooping another bite into his mouth, he chewed slowly as he recalled Jackson's report. Or rather, his endless complaints.

The sergeant had been tracking a rebel spy by the name of James Lawrence for months. Jackson's preoccupation with the man had begun to hinder his already questionable judgment, and his inability to stop the spy festered like a wound.

"I've brought your tea." A soft voice startled Isaac out of his thoughts.

Standing, he turned to see Miss Caldwell in the doorway, cup and saucer in hand.

"Papa always recommended this blend for a headache. That and a good night's rest." Her gaze flicked to his bed, then quickly back to him. A hint of pink colored her cheeks.

Where were his manners? Of course, she was uneasy, hovering there at the entrance to his room. He crossed the floor in a few long strides and took the tea she extended to him. His fingers brushed over her much smaller ones, and the color in her cheeks deepened.

Strange, that. Miss Caldwell had always seemed at ease with him in the past, possessing a cheerful openness and ready smile whenever they spoke. Had his purposeful reticence of late made her uncomfortable?

Perhaps the distance he'd placed between himself and the women had been perceived not as respect, but as hurtful disregard toward people who had only ever treated him with kindness.

He bit back a twinge of regret, and before he could reconsider the idea, gestured to the parlor behind her. "Would you like to join me for a few minutes?"

Her eyes widened, emphasizing their bright blue, the color of a summer sky. The look of surprise only deepened his guilt. Clearly, his actions over the past month had appeared harsher than he meant. A fact he'd try to rectify now.

She preceded him into the parlor, and he waited until she'd taken her seat in front of the hearth before claiming the other high-backed chair beside her.

Despite sharing her home these past ten months, he'd rarely been alone with Miss Caldwell before, and on most occasions found her to be the one to start conversation. But she was quiet now, peering at him expectantly, as though he must have something particular to say. Not surprising, given he'd been the one to invite her to sit with him, but his mind seemed suddenly and frustratingly blank. How was it he could command the attention of a company of soldiers, but not know what to say to one young woman?

Was this how he would feel when he finally met his betrothed, Miss Victoria Bradbury? No, that was likely to be infinitely worse. What did one say to the woman he was intended to marry when he'd never seen, spoken to, or even exchanged a letter with her? Isaac clenched his teeth. Better to save that concern for another day. With all the trouble in Boston of late, who knew when his regiment would even return to England.

He sipped his tea, buying time and drawing his focus back to the woman who sat beside him. Tea. There was that. A rather bland start to a conversation, but it would have to do.

"What is in your father's special blend?"

"White willow bark, lavender, and chamomile." She ticked off the ingredients with an easy smile. "He may have been the one to recommend it, but Mama was always the one to make it. She never stopped, even after..." She faltered, smile fading.

Even after her father died. The unspoken words echoed in his mind.

He frowned. "Forgive me. I didn't mean to trouble you with difficult memories."

She shook her head. "Not at all. I like to remember Papa. To talk about him. It makes me feel closer to him again."

"I remember fondly many a conversation with your father in just this spot. He challenged me to think deeply on questions of politics, life, and faith. And he listened well, even if we did not always agree."

Dr. Caldwell had treated Isaac as though he mattered, not for the duty he could perform or the honor he could bring, but for who he was as a person. A sense of worth that Isaac had never received from his own parents.

"He was the same with me. I always knew that he truly cared what I thought, what I believed. He taught me so much, oftentimes without me even realizing such a lesson was taking place, for 'twas such a natural part of who he was." Her voice dropped to a whisper. "Papa even offered me some medical training over the years, though Mama was rather opposed. I think he knew me better than anyone else. Perhaps that's why I still miss him so, these two years later. I think I'll always miss him."

His heart squeezed at her bittersweet admission. "There is no shame in missing your father. He was the best man I've ever known."

"That he was." She shifted in her seat. "He always spoke very highly of you, even after you'd departed. He would have been glad to see you again."

Glad to see him, aye. But not glad over the reason he had returned. While the doctor had made a point not to speak publicly about his political views, Isaac had gotten to know him well enough to recognize where the doctor stood. And 'twas not on the side of the army that now encamped upon his city, nor of the soldier that dwelt in his house.

Isaac hid a grimace behind another sip of tea.

"I recall the first time you came here." Mischief glinted in Miss Caldwell's eyes. "You'd accidentally cut yourself with... what was it? Your bayonet or your shaving razor?"

He chuckled, even as heat crept up his neck. "I confess, that is one memory I wish you had not recalled."

Laughter spilled out of her, as bright and free as birdsong, and warmth of a different kind bloomed in his chest. When was the last time he'd heard such a beautiful laugh or enjoyed a similarly carefree moment of his own?

"'Twas a straight razor, and not even mine but that of a

fellow soldier who'd not stored it properly. Though I doubt that fact makes it any less embarrassing." He rolled up his sleeve, exposing the faint scar on his forearm. "Your father stitched it well."

Leaning close, she eyed the pale line.

A subtle floral scent wafted in the space between them. Was it the tea, or Miss Caldwell? He stifled the desire to breathe more deeply and find out.

She lifted her hand, and for a moment, he thought she might trace the slightly raised scar. His skin prickled with strange awareness, and he tugged his sleeve back into place.

Miss Caldwell had been but four and ten when he'd first met her, the day he'd come to Dr. Caldwell seeking medical care. He'd been a sergeant then, all of two and twenty years, determined to prove himself worthy of the rank his father had purchased. To him, she'd seemed hardly more than a girl. The young daughter of a man he came to respect and call friend.

But she was not a girl any longer.

He'd noticed the first time he saw her again last summer, when he came hoping for a reunion with Dr. Caldwell, only to learn his friend had died. 'Twas impossible to deny that she had grown into a lovely young woman.

Impossible to deny, yet imperative to ignore. For he had no right to admire the long lashes framing her eyes and the soft curve of her lips. Nor to notice how the last hues of sunset filtering through the windows made her honey-blond locks shine like polished gold. Or the way a few curls brushed her high cheekbones and trailed down the nape of her neck. He forced his gaze away.

Draining the last of his tea, he shot to his feet. "I'd best follow the rest of your father's instructions for a headache and get some sleep."

Miss Caldwell stared at him, brows furrowed, likely confused by his hasty desire to depart. But depart he must.

"Good night, Miss Caldwell." He returned the empty teacup with a curt nod, then retreated to his room and yanked the door closed behind him.

Exhaling, he scrubbed a hand down his face. There must be a better way to show the women of the house that he appreciated their kindness, for spending time alone with Miss Caldwell was not something he dared repeat.

CHAPTER 3

*L*ibby spread her apron on the round table beside the parlor window and examined the tear in the morning sunlight. It had snagged on the edge of the Pierces' fence yesterday in their swift departure from the garden, but would be easy to mend. Across the table, Mama threaded her needle, an overly worn pair of stockings awaiting her care. Boston Harbor had been closed to imports for a year now, part of Parliament's response to the destruction of the tea in 1773. Already, certain supplies had been more difficult to obtain, and 'twas nearly impossible now. But they would make do. What other choice did they have?

As her fingers set to work, her mind wandered beyond the row of neat stitches. She couldn't stop thinking about the face that had watched them from the upstairs window of Hannah's home. Wasn't there something she could do about the trespasser?

She peeked at her mother. "I keep worrying about the Pierces' house."

Mama nodded but said nothing, attention fixed on her task.

It was her way. She'd always been quiet, more prone to silent consideration of a matter than lengthy discussion.

"I wish there was a way to ensure it was protected."

Mama did look up then. "What matters most is that Hannah and her father are safe."

Libby sighed. True. And yet... "I should have asked Lieutenant Harrison to look in on things when we spoke last night."

She had hoped to do just that, before his sudden exit. She couldn't forget the lieutenant's odd expression as he made his hurried escape. Try as she might to convince herself his headache was to blame, the truth was clear—he was uncomfortable in her presence. Why, exactly, she could not say, but the sting of it lingered still this morning.

The door to Lieutenant Harrison's quarters swung open, and Libby startled, sending the sharp point of her needle into the soft pad of her index finger. She hissed out a breath.

The lieutenant's tall frame filled the doorway, gaze straying toward Libby for a moment before resting on her mother instead. "Forgive me. I did not mean to eavesdrop but couldn't help hearing. Was there some way I can assist you?"

Mama explained what had happened at the Pierces' house the day before.

Lieutenant Harrison's brows knit together as he listened. "The Pierces...is that the young woman who was betrothed to your stepson? The one whose father was wrongfully arrested?"

"Aye," Mama said. "They're married now and safe, thank the Lord."

His attention cut to Libby, gaze intense. Was he remembering the night she'd asked him to help Will, Hannah, and Mr. Pierce get safely out of Boston? He'd done as she requested, and his act of compassion had made her wonder if he might feel something for her, after all. But days later, he'd marched off to Lexington and Concord, and when he returned, he'd been more distant than ever.

A muscle in his jaw twitched. "And you're certain you saw a person?"

Libby nodded. "I am."

"It could very well have been a soldier. These abandoned homes are"—his lips flattened into a hard line—"rather tempting to many of the men."

She frowned. "Hannah was forced to leave so much behind. I hate to think of her belongings being used or stolen."

"I understand. I cannot promise I've the power to protect your friend's home, but I will go to survey the premises if it would ease your mind."

"Thank you. It would, indeed." Libby set the apron aside and pushed to her feet. "Might I come along? I could point out what I saw and—"

"I'm not certain that is wise." Mama's voice held a hint of censure, but Libby couldn't quell the need to do something more than sit here and wait for the lieutenant's report.

She turned to face her mother. "I know the Pierces' home as well as our own. I could tell if something were missing, might even be able to rescue a few belongings and bring them here for safekeeping."

Mama said nothing, but Libby could see she was considering the idea.

She pressed on. "It won't take long. And I'll be safe with Lieutenant Harrison." She glanced his way. He blinked, but his stoic expression remained unchanged.

"If the lieutenant is in agreement, then you may go. But"—Mama rose and fixed her with a look that would bear no arguments— "you are to respect his wishes and not interfere with his decisions. I know you care about Hannah and her father, but 'tis not up to you to protect their home. That is in God's hands."

Libby dipped her head to hide the heat creeping into her cheeks. Mama was right, but she wished Lieutenant Harrison needn't have witnessed such a warning. She peeked at the lieutenant, whose broad shoulders seemed even stiffer than usual. Would he reject the idea?

Finally, he nodded. "Aye, we can go together."

Together. She pushed aside the absurd flicker of hope sparked by that word as she donned her flat-brimmed straw hat and wrapped a light shawl around her shoulders.

Lieutenant Harrison held the door open, and she stepped outside. Dew dotted the grass, and a hint of last night's chill lingered, but the air smelled fresh, and the sunshine promised a pleasant day.

"The Pierces' house is behind the apothecary at the corner of Cornhill and School Street." She started in that direction, and he fell in step beside her.

He measured his pace, shortening his long strides to match hers, but kept his gaze fixed firmly ahead. Silence hovered between them, and though she longed to break it, she held back. This was no leisurely stroll between friends, and she'd do well to remember that.

Still, she couldn't help but sneak a glance at him. He cut an impressive figure, the lines of his uniform emphasizing the breadth of his shoulders and his sturdy chest. Though she was rather tall for a woman, the top of her head only reached his shoulder, and his black hat, with its high crest, added more height to his stature. His dark hair was neatly plaited, his jaw freshly shaved and set in a determined expression.

He looked down at her, and she yanked her gaze away.

"Thank you for doing this." The words tumbled out when she was unable to bear the silence any longer. "I know it may seem unimportant, compared with everything else you must do, but Hannah is my dearest friend and…"

"I understand and am glad to assist if I can. After all your family has done for me, I owe much more than this."

Libby ducked her head to hide her frown. So 'twas a sense of obligation that drove him to help, nothing more.

He cleared his throat, a hint of hesitation in his voice. "May I ask you something?"

She nodded.

"I have wondered for some time why you and your mother chose to remain here. I thought you planned to join your stepbrother. What made you stay?"

What made them stay, indeed? There were several reasons, and one of them was walking beside her. Selfishly, Libby had not wished to be parted from Lieutenant Harrison. She swallowed, burying that thought deep where it could not escape. She'd never confessed her feelings for him to anyone but Hannah. What would Mama think, if she learned of the desire that lingered beneath all of Libby's other excuses not to leave?

Shame heated her cheeks. Why had she stayed for a man who clearly felt nothing for her in return? And what suffering or danger might she have exposed herself and Mama to as a result?

"We did plan to go when Governor Gage made provision for citizens of the town to do so, but you may remember that my mother was ill with a megrim for several days. I thought it best to wait until she was well." She stepped around a deep rut in the road. "By the time she'd recovered enough to travel, the governor had changed his mind."

A low sound of disapproval rumbled in his throat. Did he think she spoke out of turn regarding Governor Gage, who was also his general, or was he equally disappointed with the man's decision?

The governor's original offer had been a fair one, allowing citizens to leave with as much as they could carry. But Loyalists in Boston, fearful that if all the Patriots departed there would be nothing to stop their rebellious countrymen from attacking the town, had convinced him to reconsider. In response to their demands, Governor Gage settled on a new compromise—a limited number of people would receive passes out of Boston, so long as they took no possessions with them.

"I couldn't bear the thought of leaving everything behind. 'Tis the only home I've ever known, and in it are all the things that remind me of my father..." She frowned. A building and possessions should not matter so much, yet each nook and cranny of the house seemed to hold some memory of Papa that she was loathe to let go of. "It seems foolish now. I suppose I hoped all this trouble would pass quickly. That life would soon return to normal. You must think me naive."

"I don't consider you naive or foolish." He paused, turning to face her fully, and the intensity in his gaze made Libby catch her breath. "And I understand why it would have been difficult for you to leave. But I would have taken care of your home in your absence. You could have trusted me with that."

"I know." She did trust him. More than he realized. Perhaps more than she should.

He started walking again. "I confess, I wish you and your mother had left, for your sake. Who knows how long this siege will last?"

Her chest ached at his declaration. Though it clearly came from a place of concern, his words heaped new condemnation upon the scolding she'd already given herself. How wrong she had been to stay. Lieutenant Harrison would have preferred that she was gone, even if it meant they did not see each other again.

She sighed. And he was right about the siege. 'Twas hard to imagine the thousands of British troops stationed in Boston simply waiting for the militia to either attack or starve them out. But she hated to consider the alternative—that the soldiers would stage an assault of their own upon the colonial forces in order to break out of the city.

Might they have a plan to do so even now? One that Lieutenant Harrison was privy to? Questions hovered on the tip of her tongue, but she could not ask. It was a line she would not cross.

She and the lieutenant may dwell within the same walls, but the truth was, they lived in completely different worlds. Worlds that were growing farther apart with each passing day.

Isaac followed Miss Caldwell around the side of the house, keeping a wary eye on their surroundings. Thus far, nothing seemed out of place. The house was smaller than Dr. Caldwell's home, though similar in appearance with the familiar riven siding that covered many dwellings in Boston. It sat snugly behind the brick apothecary belonging to Mr. Pierce. That building had been securely locked, and a peek through the window revealed no damage inside. If the siege continued to drag on, however, the chance of the apothecary remaining undisturbed was slim. There was more than one way around a lock, if one were desperate.

The front door did not bear the same built-in security mechanism as the apothecary, for such were complicated and expensive. But a padlock acted as some deterrent and bore no signs of tampering.

Miss Caldwell stopped before the side door and sucked in a breath. "Look. This must be how he got inside."

Isaac stepped closer. Indeed, the door was unprotected—either an omission by the family in their haste to leave, or because someone else had come since and removed it.

"What should we do?" She looked up at him. "Knock? Simply walk in?"

She studied him expectantly, as though he had some grand plan. But he did not. This entire outing was ill-conceived. What had he been thinking with his offer to help? Worse, in agreeing to let Miss Caldwell join him. But he'd found himself unable to deny her.

Much like the April night when he'd agreed to secure safe passage out of Boston for Mr. Abbott and the Pierces. How well he remembered Miss Caldwell coming to him, tears in her eyes, begging that he ensure they leave the city unharmed. And he had helped. Without question. Without hesitation.

Why?

He'd told himself it was because he felt partly responsible for their trouble, given the fact that Sergeant Jackson was part of his regiment and had been in obvious error by arresting Mr. Pierce in the first place. Not to mention, Isaac owed the Caldwell family for all that Dr. Caldwell had done for him, and for the gracious kindness the women had shown him while he occupied their home. But was duty, responsibility, and obligation really all that drove him to consent to her requests? Or was it something more? Something that lingered deeper under the surface, unnamed and forbidden?

Squaring his shoulders, he positioned himself between her and the door. "Wait here. I will check first."

The words came out too much like an order given to a soldier of lesser rank. He sensed her stiffen behind him, but she didn't protest.

He rapped on the door, listening intently for a voice or footsteps inside. Nothing. Grasping the handle, he slipped his other hand to the pistol holstered at his hip and eased the door open. Quiet emptiness greeted him.

"Is anyone here?" His raised voice echoed through the house.

Again, silence was the only reply.

He glanced over his shoulder at Miss Caldwell, who hovered just outside, watching him. Her words to her mother echoed in his mind. *I'll be safe with Lieutenant Harrison.* Despite the foolhardiness of bringing her along, he would indeed keep her safe. Better to have her at his side than leave her waiting on her own while he searched.

"You can come with me." He tipped his head to invite her in. "It seems deserted now, but we'll see what we can find."

They scoured the parlor, but everything looked untouched and in good order. The kitchen appeared similarly undisturbed, but Miss Caldwell stopped in the center of the room, brows drawn.

She sniffed, then paced to the hearth and held her hand over the black coals. "Someone had a fire here not long ago. No more than a day, I'd reckon."

"It doesn't appear lived in, nor as if someone plundered supplies." He strode to join her and extended his own fingers over the ashes. The faintest bit of heat rose from them. "Perhaps a vagrant wandered in yesterday and was scared off by your presence in the garden."

She pursed her lips, apparently dissatisfied with his answer. "Should we not still look upstairs?"

He led the way up the steps and into the first chamber, which bore enough left-behind items to indicate it belonged to her friend. Miss Caldwell circled the room, trailing her fingers over a small table which boasted a delft washbasin and pitcher.

"Dusty." She wiped her hand on her apron. "I can see no sign that someone is staying here."

The second room was equally untouched. He crossed into the third chamber and stopped so abruptly that Miss Caldwell ran into his back.

This room had been torn apart.

"Oh no." Miss Caldwell breathed out the words, stepping around him to survey the damage.

Drawers had been yanked from the bureau, their contents dumped on the floor. Clothing, books, and papers lay scattered about as though a fierce wind had swept through. A round table and pair of chairs had been overturned in one corner, and even the mattress had been shoved onto the ground.

A look of utter dismay contorted Miss Caldwell's pretty features. Isaac reached for her arm, intent upon steadying her, but she didn't seem to notice as she moved farther into the room, gingerly picking her way around the mess. She righted one of the chairs, a small attempt to restore order to the chaos.

"Why would someone do this?" Her voice wavered as she turned back to him.

Isaac frowned. He'd seen senseless destruction out of anger, hatred, or spite, but this was different. Why had nothing else in the house been damaged save for this room? Unless...

"I wonder if someone was looking for something in particular." He stooped to gather a handful of papers and eased them into a tidy stack.

"But what? There were valuables in other rooms that went untouched, and then there's this..."

"Money, perhaps. Someone may have thought this the most likely room for it to be hidden." He set the papers atop the chair. Or could Sergeant Jackson still be clinging to the absurd notion that Mr. Pierce had some hand in the spy ring and been hunting for evidence to confirm such a theory? Isaac grimaced to think that the unscrupulous soldier may have been watching Miss Caldwell and her mother, but he kept such suspicions to himself. "Was this the window in which you saw someone?"

"Aye. That is the one."

Pushing the curtain aside, he peered at the garden below. Whoever was here, his position had afforded him a clear view of the two women while they worked. Disgust and concern churned in Isaac's gut. If they'd not noticed the intruder, or if he'd had a more sinister intent... This was no place for Miss Caldwell to linger. Not now, nor in the future.

He turned back to find her staring at the open page of a leather-bound book.

She looked up at him, and his heart clenched at the sheen of tears in her eyes. "'Tis a journal. Mr. Pierce writes of his son, Elijah, who went missing. Of how he has lost hope of ever seeing him again and fears his son is already in heaven with his wife."

Gently closing the book, she cradled it against her chest.

The urge to hold her in similar fashion rose up so unexpected and strong, he clenched his teeth and stalked to the door. "I'm sorry this happened, but I fear we'll find no answer as to who caused this damage, or why. I'd best see you home."

Blinking, she opened her mouth as though to protest, then sighed and followed him down the stairs. She kept the journal tucked close, clearly upset by what they'd seen and the words she had read. Her uncharacteristic moroseness begged him for a better answer, for some sort of comfort. But what could he offer?

They exited the house, and he pulled the door shut behind them, staring at the handle for a moment. A strange awareness prickled the back of his neck. The same wariness that had sent chills down his spine as his regiment marched back to Boston in April under musket fire from unseen assailants. The disconcerting sense that someone was watching.

He spun around, instinctively stretching his arm out to block Miss Caldwell from view. But there was nothing. No one. All around them was quiet and still.

"What's wrong?" Worry tainted her voice. She moved closer, brushing against his back.

"Nothing. I..." He squinted, staring hard, but no movement caught his eye. "I thought someone was here, but I was mistaken."

"Are you certain?" She peeked around him, gaze wary. "What if whoever vandalized Mr. Pierce's room has returned?"

Certain or not, he needed to get her away from here. He cleared his throat. "I'll procure a padlock for this door. Hopefully, that will discourage any further damage to your friend's home."

A hint of a smile tipped her lips, restoring some of the light to her eyes. "Thank you, Lieutenant."

Heat swelled in his chest as her gaze held his, but the use of his title quickly doused it. He swallowed and looked away.

Lieutenant. That's what he was. Who he was. He knew his place, and it was not, nor could it ever be, with Miss Caldwell.

~

Libby dunked a dirty plate into the lukewarm basin of water, staring out the back window of the kitchen. She'd not been able to shake the odd feeling that lingered on her walk home with Lieutenant Harrison from the Pierces' house earlier. Almost as though someone was watching her again. But she and the lieutenant had searched every room thoroughly and seen no one, only the destruction left behind as evidence of whoever had been there before. It must have been her imagination.

She handed the dish to Mama, who stood at her side with a towel ready to dry, then set to washing a pair of forks. Libby had recounted their findings to her mother when they returned, after which Mama promptly insisted she not visit Hannah's house again. Libby hadn't argued, for she had no desire to go back now. She'd hated seeing Mr. Pierce's room torn apart, and his journal entry regarding Elijah had brought old sorrows to the surface.

"Your thoughts seem far away tonight." Mama reached for the utensils that Libby had been aimlessly wiping for far too long. "Are you still thinking about the Pierces?"

"About Elijah, for the most part. I remember him as a boy, always mischievous and playful." Plunging the next plate into the basin, she smiled at the recollection.

She'd known Elijah Pierce her whole life, as her father and Mr. Pierce had been friends even before she was born. He was a few years older and had teased her and Hannah with a brotherly mix of ruthlessness and affection. He'd kept that fiery spirit as a young man, turning it toward a staunch and whole-hearted dedication to the Patriot cause.

"Indeed, he was. Quite a challenge to his mother, though she loved him dearly and raised him well."

"I will never forget the day Hannah brought us the news that he was missing." Libby frowned as she scrubbed at a stubborn spot on the plate.

Elijah had departed for England in late 1773 after their mother died, intent upon bringing the news to their older brother, Andrew, in person. But he'd never arrived in London, where Andrew lived, nor had he returned home. His disappearance weighed heavily on Hannah and her father, especially as the months passed without word of any sort.

"Nor I." Mama's brow furrowed. "I prayed often for an answer that would bring some peace to our friends."

Libby handed her the plate. "So did I, even if it were bad news."

But none came. Instead, they were left to assume he had died, without ever knowing for certain what had happened. She knew well the toll it took on her friend and Mr. Pierce, and had grieved in her own way over the unexplained loss.

Grieved, too, at the added confusion it brought to her already struggling faith. Some things, like her friend's disappearance and her father's death, were hard to reconcile with her understanding of a loving and good God.

Libby dried her hands on her apron. "What a strange and lasting kind of sorrow, to not know what happened to him."

"Aye. As a parent, I can hardly imagine how Mr. Pierce must have felt." Mama stowed the forks and plates away, then turned to wipe down the table. "But we never grieve without hope, for we know that nothing is hidden from God. We can trust His sovereignty in all things, even this."

Libby nodded as she tugged open the door and dumped the tepid water from the washbasin outside. She believed the truth of Mama's words, but knowing it in her mind was different than resting on it in her heart.

"I am glad I found the journal, even if it brought back difficult memories. I'll keep it safe until I can return it to Mr. Pierce again."

Mama hung the damp towel from a hook on the mantel while Libby covered the smoldering coals in the hearth with the curfew. Chores finished, they moved to the parlor to take advantage of the extra hours of daylight that the June days brought. Libby settled into her usual chair in front of the hearth, though no fire burned there this evening, and took up the needlepoint she was working on— a sampler she hoped to give to Hannah and Will when she saw them next, as a belated gift in honor of their wedding, though when that might be she couldn't say.

Libby's gaze strayed to Lieutenant Harrison's closed door. She'd foolishly hoped he might join them for the evening meal, but he'd kept to himself again. What did he do to pass these hours when he wasn't at the encampment? Read, perhaps. He did often ask to borrow Papa's old books, and seemed curious about a variety of topics. She'd seen him with everything from medical texts to sermons to novels. He'd even requested some old newspapers that her father had deemed noteworthy to retain in his collection. What did the lieutenant think of the Patriotic printings of *The Boston Gazette*?

It would be so easy for him to join them. To share the peace of quiet company in the fading sunlight. But he'd chosen time and again to keep himself separate from them. He'd been generous to help today, but she could not allow herself to dwell on the foolish hope that it was motivated by anything more than politeness or perceived duty to the widow and daughter of his old friend.

She pulled her attention back to the stitched sprigs of lavender taking shape beneath her fingers. Better to fix her mind on that than to let it wander to the soldier on the other side of the door. So close, and yet so far.

CHAPTER 4

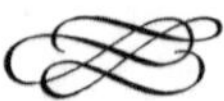

$\mathcal{I}$saac shielded his eyes against the midday sun as he watched his company complete their drills on the grassy expanse of Boston Common on Thursday afternoon. Thirty-six men, among the largest, strongest, and most skilled of the regiment, marched in formation to the rolling beat of the company drummer and the high-pitched trill of two fifers.

He should be proud to oversee such a force. Many men would envy his status as a lieutenant of the grenadiers in the 4th Regiment, The King's Own. Perhaps he would wear his title with more pride if he had in fact earned it of his own merit. Instead, it hung on him like a heavy weight, chaining him to obligations and expectations he had no desire to bear, and a faltering loyalty he dared not explore.

A memory rose up, unbidden, of his father's face, when he'd handed Isaac his papers for the 29th Regiment.

"You're to be a sergeant of the grenadiers." For the first time in Isaac's recollection, Father's stern countenance held a hint of pride, though it quickly shifted into a far more familiar expression, the one that seemed ever on the verge of reproof. "'Twas no small effort on my part to ensure such a position when you've no experience. Do not squander this opportunity. Do not give me reason to regret my efforts."

Isaac stared at the words inked on the page as though they were a prisoner's sentence. At not quite twenty years of age, with no desire to be a soldier, enlistment was its own sort of condemnation.

"Father, you know I do not wish to—"

"I'll hear no arguments." Sir Oliver's words echoed off the high ceiling of his library with cold finality. "It is already decided. We all have our own sacrifices to make for the sake of our family's honor. This is yours."

Isaac watched in silence as the man who had always been more baronet than father spun on his heel and departed. Sir Oliver had never seen him for who he truly was. Only looked at him and thought of what he might gain for himself. Although Isaac's stature exceeded that of his father's, the man still managed to make him feel small.

Shoving the regimental paperwork in his pocket, Isaac strode to the window and stared out at the expanse of land belonging to his father. Oh the hours he'd spent wandering those woods and fields as a boy, or tucked in the branches of a sturdy tree with a favorite book. Was that why his father thought he'd make a good soldier? To tame his roaming into something useful? To turn his studious mind toward the strategies of battle?

Or was it simply the logical choice in his estimation for his second son? The one that offered another chance at honor and status?

Isaac's eldest brother had inherited Father's name and personality, and would one day inherit the estate. In him, it seemed the baronet found all the familial connection he desired, or deemed necessary. Elliot, the youngest, was their mother's favorite. Charming in manners and appearance and skilled with words, he was training for the church, bringing a respectable amount of religious devotion to the family.

Then there was Isaac. Too bookish and contemplative for his father's liking, but too physically active and enthralled with the outdoors for his mother's affection. On more than one occasion, he'd watched the farmers in their fields and wondered if he'd not have been better off being born into one of their families. And yet the longing to please his parents, to earn their respect and love, was ingrained deeply within him, as though fused into his very bones.

So he had obeyed his father's wishes without another word and worked hard to be the kind of soldier Sir Oliver could boast about amongst his friends. The kind whose mother would welcome him home with a tearful embrace.

But his return to England, after the unhappy incident in 1770 when several colonists were killed by soldiers of his regiment, had only served to prove how difficult such desires would be to attain. And to show that the baronet would stop at nothing in order to mold Isaac into the man he wished him to be. Even if it meant an arranged marriage to a complete stranger in exchange for the position of lieutenant in a new regiment.

"Lieutenant Harrison." A commanding voice startled Isaac out of his sour memories.

He pivoted to greet his captain. The man was his senior both in rank and age, but also his closest friend in the army. A career soldier, his square jaw and sturdy build gave him an intimidating appearance, as fitting an officer of the grenadiers. But beneath the fierce exterior, Isaac knew him to be a dedicated leader who truly cared for the wellbeing of his soldiers.

"The men are growing impatient." Captain Merrick started in without preamble, gesturing toward the soldiers. "They go through their drills well enough, but their minds are elsewhere. They're losing their intensity and sharpness."

Isaac shifted. 'Twas good Merrick couldn't read his own thoughts, which had just been wandering far from here.

"We should have struck out again immediately after that mess at Lexington and Concord." The captain sighed. "Now we've given those rebels time to organize themselves."

"In truth, I was in favor of General Gage's decision not to attempt an attack, but I'll not argue with a higher-ranking officer." Isaac raised his brows at his friend.

Merrick chuckled. "That has never stopped you before. Come now, you know I appreciate your insight."

"The men were exhausted and in no shape to go to battle again after hours of fighting and marching, especially since the latter half of our return to Boston was under fire from men hidden along the road." Isaac crossed his arms, shoulders tensing at the memories of that April day. "Still, I agree that the longer we wait, the more opportunity we give the colonial militias to prepare a possible attack of their own."

"Indeed. We can't let them have the high ground. If they take Dorchester Heights or the hills on Charlestown Peninsula, we'll be easy targets. And if they manage to get cannon up there…"

"Aye." Isaac stared at the Charles River beyond the Common. The water stretched nearly a mile wide until it reached the verdant, forested mainland. A beautiful country, deceptively peaceful, that seemed to mock the plight of those trapped in the city. "Though I suspect they don't have enough artillery to stage such a maneuver. Would they not have attempted so already if they did?"

"Perhaps. I'd rather not find out."

"Agreed. Better to take the offensive while we can." Isaac's stomach churned at the thought of going to battle again.

"Between you and me…" The captain leaned closer and lowered his voice. "We have too many generals. Makes for too much talk and too little action."

Isaac huffed a wry laugh. General Gage had been in Boston for over a year as acting governor, but at the end of May, Generals Burgoyne, Clinton, and Howe had joined him. They arrived aboard the man-of-war *Cerberus*, and the fact that three generals sailed upon a ship named after the mythical three-headed dog had not gone without its fair share of jokes amongst the soldiers. But mayhap Merrick was right. Trying to reach a decision between four men, each used to holding command, very well may have slowed the process.

"I don't suppose we'll solve all the problems standing here, but I confess, I hope we have answers soon." The captain clapped Isaac on the shoulder. "I nearly forgot—Sergeant Jackson was looking for you."

Isaac suppressed a sigh. "Where is he?"

Merrick nodded toward a row of tents. "Eating, last I saw."

Excusing himself, Isaac made his way toward Sergeant Jackson's tent. Now that the ground was dry enough, the men had moved out of their winter barracks to encamp upon the Common once more. Perhaps he should relocate there as well, but his chest tightened at the thought of leaving Mrs. Abbott and Miss Caldwell alone. He'd had no arguments or complaints yet from his fellow officers about his current living situation. Perhaps he could remain with the women a little longer, for the sake of their safety.

Miss Caldwell's face flashed through his mind. The way she'd looked up at him with trust and gratitude yesterday. He scrubbed his palm over his face, attempting to wash the image from his mind, and focused on the regimental camp in front of him.

The canvas tents were arranged in tidy lines, every two rows facing each other to create a street between them. The sergeants' tents stood at each end, turned sideways to distinguish them from the others. Isaac made his way for the one in which Sergeant Jackson dwelt. The flap was open, allowing fresh air to circulate, and he ducked his head as he stepped inside.

Jackson glanced up from the plate of rations on his lap. "There you are." He spoke around a mouthful of food. Reaching into his pocket, he extracted a letter and handed it to Isaac. "Take a look at this."

Unfolding the page, Isaac noted the signature of Benjamin Church at the bottom. "Who is he?"

"Dr. Church has been a very useful informant these last months. He's well established amongst the inner circle of those so-called Patriot leaders, Adams, Hancock, and Warren." Jackson sneered the names. "They think him on their side, but he's been secretly reporting to General Gage all the while."

A turncoat, then. Isaac frowned. 'Twas no surprise that espionage was prevalent on both sides, but there was something particularly abhorrent about someone who claimed allegiance in one way while secretly harboring the opposite loyalties. It went beyond the typical underhanded actions and deception into more personal territory. To pretend to be an ally, and then use what you gained in your relationships to scheme against the very people you claimed were your friends was especially vile.

Isaac swallowed back his disgust as he skimmed the script. "He says he's bound for Philadelphia and vexed that he cannot write for some time. Why did you wish me to see this?"

"I'd hoped Church could assist in my search for Lawrence, but now he's away for who knows how long. I don't know what else I can do, stuck here in the city with no connection on the outside any longer." Jackson wiped the back of his hand across his mouth and stood. "I need help. I asked Captain Merrick if he was willing to assign a few more men to this task. He told me to speak with you instead. Said he'd trust your decision."

Isaac gritted his teeth. He had no desire to involve himself in this hunt for the spy and had grown weary of listening to

Jackson's complaints over his failed attempts to track the man down. Clearly, Merrick was equally disinterested and had conveniently managed to pass the problem down the line. Too bad there was no one else for Isaac to push it off to.

He handed the letter back to Jackson as he considered the soldiers under his command. "You may ask Stanton." The young man was level-headed enough to temper Jackson's moods and restless enough to benefit from some extra work. "I'll talk to him this afternoon. But you must ensure he's not taken from his usual drills."

"Anyone else?" Jackson shoved the letter back into his pocket. "I did find a couple colonists who may be willing to help. Plenty of men out of work who can be enticed to do a bit of meddling for some extra food or coin or drin—"

"Only him." Frustration edged Isaac's words. "I know this spy business is of great importance to you, but we've a larger problem to deal with. If we don't manage to break this siege..." Isaac shook his head. Jackson knew just as well as he did how things stood, but the man was obsessed.

Annoyance flashed in Jackson's pale blue eyes, but he quickly hid it beneath the shadow of his cocked hat as he dipped his head in acquiescence.

Isaac stalked out of the tent and away from the encampment, feeling again like the boy he'd once been, desperate for an open field to wander or a tree to climb. What he wouldn't give for a moment's escape from the plotting and questions. For a sliver of peace that didn't come at the cost of bloodshed.

But as he gazed over the river once more and thought of the thousands of militiamen that surrounded them on the other side, he feared such hopes were not to be.

CHAPTER 5

Libby wrapped a towel around her wet hair and squeezed the excess water into her washbasin. The smell of her rosewater soap filled the air with a pleasant sweetness, and the last muted rays of twilight lit her chamber with a soft glow. She rolled her shoulders, easing the tension that had lingered there ever since her visit to Hannah's house yesterday. Try as she might, she couldn't rid her mind of the sight of Mr. Pierce's belongings strewn senselessly about his room. Nor could she wash away the sorrow that had come over her when she read the words he'd penned in his journal.

She glanced at her trunk where she'd tucked the small leather book. She hadn't read any more of the pages, nor would she, but she would keep it safe until the time she could return it to its rightful owner.

Reaching for her comb, she began to work the knots from her hair. If only she could untangle the mystery of what had happened to Mr. Pierce's son just as easily.

"Why, God?" She whispered the question she'd asked so many times in recent years.

The words Mama had instilled in her from Matthew

chapter seven echoed in her mind...*how much more shall your Father which is in heaven give good things to them that ask him?*

How was it a good gift when a dear brother and son disappeared? Or when her own precious father died without warning? Why did God answer some prayers with a yes and others, though just as desperate and heartfelt, with a no?

Setting the comb aside, she separated her hair into three segments and wove it into a thick braid, as she forced the unsettling thoughts away. Dwelling on them would only bring more doubt, for she'd yet to find a satisfying answer.

She tied a strip of ribbon at the end of her plait to secure it, then lifted the washbasin from her bedside table and crept downstairs. Though she could wait until morning to empty it, her memories and questions had left her restless. Mayhap a breath of fresh air would ease her mind before she attempted to sleep.

Crossing through the empty kitchen, she pushed the back door open and stepped outside. She dumped the water onto a patch of grass behind the house, then stood for a long moment, soaking in the peaceful quiet.

Might God quiet her spirit as well?

"I need You, Lord." She spoke softly into the fading evening light. "I don't understand You, but I want to. Please help me."

Silence hung in the air, and she tipped her head back to gaze at the canopy of sky, the first and brightest stars just beginning to peek through the growing darkness. She felt small beneath their pinpricks of light, yet God, who had created them all, knew her. She believed it. If only she could feel His presence.

A cool breeze brushed against her linen petticoat and bedgown and swept over her damp hair. Shivering, she turned to go back inside.

A man-shaped silhouette separated itself from the shadows at the corner of the house and stalked toward her. She gasped, dropping her washbasin. It shattered at her feet. Jumping out of the way of the sharp pieces and the approaching figure, she dashed for the door. An arm shot out to block her, another hand clasping her wrist. A scream lodged in her throat. She stumbled backward, struggling to yank herself free.

"Shhh, don't be afraid." The man's voice was calm, gentle, and strangely familiar. "Elizabeth, it's me."

He knew her name? Libby froze, peering into the darkness at a face she recognized. A face she thought she'd never see again.

Her pulse stuttered. "Elijah?"

"Aye." He released her arm. "I'm sorry I frightened you. I didn't want to call out and alert anyone else in the house, but when I saw you, I couldn't miss the opportunity to talk to you and—"

"What...how are you...?" Libby pressed a hand to her racing heart. "You're alive?"

A half grin pulled at his lips, hinting at the mischievous young man she'd known, but there was a shadow in his gaze that could not be blamed on the darkness. "I am, indeed."

"I cannot believe it." She exhaled a shaky breath, battling against the pounding in her chest and the strange numbness seeping through her arms and legs.

Elijah was not dead. He was standing before her, in the flesh, alive and whole. God's answer had not been a no, after all.

She studied him, trying to tame her whirling thoughts into some semblance of order. He looked much the same as she remembered. Angled jaw, straight nose, green eyes so like his sister's, small scar above his left brow. Yet there was a tension in his face, in his stance, as though he were ready to sprint away at a moment's notice. Where had he been all this time? And why hadn't he returned until now?

So many questions, but she could only speak the thought foremost in her mind. "Your father and Hannah will be overjoyed. Have you been looking for them? They're not in Boston any longer. They went to—"

"I know." He interrupted her rambling. "I've seen them."

"You have?" Libby furrowed her brow. "But when? How?"

"In April, here in Boston." He grimaced, as though the admission pained him. "And again last month in their new home. I shouldn't say more. The less you know, the better. For your sake...and mine."

"I don't understand. Hannah never told me."

"Then it seems she and William kept their secrets well." Elijah's voice was barely a whisper, but a note of pride clung to his words. "I'm glad of it and hope you'll forgive both them and me for the deception."

A shiver crept down her spine. Deception? What did he mean? "You're not making sense. Why would such wonderful news be kept hidden? Everyone thought you had died. Your return is cause for celebration, not secrecy." Libby couldn't contain her frustration over his cryptic answers, nor could she silence the growing panic inside. Her dearest friend and her stepbrother had both known something this significant, but they'd kept it from her? "I'm not a child, nor so fragile that I must be sheltered from the truth. Whatever Will and Hannah knew, can I not know it as well?"

He frowned. "Forgive me. I realize how confusing this must be, but 'twas already my fault that my father was arrested, and I cannot put anyone else in danger."

His words swirled and crashed in her mind like waves on the harbor shore in the middle of a storm. Her chest clenched, breath catching as though she were drowning. Elijah was the reason Mr. Pierce had been detained by the British soldiers? How could that be? What was it that he refused to tell her, and why had the people she loved and trusted kept her from the truth?

The ache in her chest spread, burning through her limbs,

desperate for escape. She wanted to run. Wanted to scream. Wanted to shake the man standing in front of her with a look of pity in his eyes.

Her legs trembled, and she leaned against the house, dropping her gaze to the dirt. "Why did you even come here, then, if you will say nothing more?"

"I came to scout." He stepped closer. "I saw you at my father's house with that soldier and—"

"You saw me with Lieutenant Harrison yesterday?" She snapped her gaze back to his face.

He nodded. "Why did you bring him there?"

"Because I was concerned, and he was willing to help." Straightening, she crossed her arms. "Mama and I had gone to tend Hannah's garden two days ago, and I thought I saw someone in the upstairs window. Lieutenant Harrison agreed to return with me to try to determine what was happening."

"That was me you saw." He tugged off his hat and raked a hand through his tousled hair. "I was careless. I'm glad it was only you that noticed."

She gaped at him. "But surely, you didn't destroy your father's chamber."

"Of course not. 'Twas that way when I arrived. I have my suspicions as to why." He pressed his lips into a hard line, making no attempt to hide his disgust. "I watched you leave with the officer, and I followed you home."

"You what?" The same uncomfortable prickle she'd felt yesterday made her bristle again. So it was Elijah who had made her feel that way? "But why?"

"I wanted to talk to you. To warn you. I would have tried then, but that soldier refused to leave."

Libby arched her brows. "That soldier, as you call him, is still here now. He is quartering with us."

Elijah stiffened, glancing furtively at the door. "You've a British officer living in your house?"

She nodded, then stepped closer. "What are you doing here tonight? You could not have known you would find me outside at such a time."

"I didn't. I planned to leave a letter." He patted his pocket. "But this is far better...and safer." His brows drew low, and the little scar on his forehead puckered. "Please tell me there is nothing between you and the lieutenant."

Libby blinked. Of all the things he could say, and in light of all the questions he refused to answer, that was his most pressing concern?

"Lieutenant Harrison was stationed here six years ago and knew my father. They became good friends. He's always been kind and respectful toward me, but that is all. There is nothing more between us." Saying it aloud pinched her heart anew. But it was the truth, and perhaps one she needed to hear even more than Elijah did.

"I'm glad to hear it. You must be careful around him. Old friendships do not guarantee anything in the present. Be cautious who you trust. For your sake and for the sake of others you care about."

Libby bit her lip. She wanted to defend Lieutenant Harrison, wanted to beg Elijah to explain, but she held back.

He leaned in, voice low. "Did the lieutenant say anything about a man named James Lawrence?"

She shook her head. "I've never heard that name before."

"Good." Elijah's shoulders sagged, as though a great weight had fallen off.

Libby waited for him to explain more, but he fell silent. She bit back another wave of frustration. Why should she have to defend her actions when they were done for the good of his family, especially if he would admit so little to her? But her anger faded as she remembered the shaky scrawl of Mr. Pierce's journal. Whatever the reason for Elijah's strange behavior, she was glad for Mr. Pierce's sake that his son was alive.

He rested a hand on her shoulder. "Please promise me that you'll tell no one, not even your mother, that you've seen me. It's better for everyone that way. And take care around that soldier."

"Are you in danger?" Or was he part of something that would endanger someone else? Could she truly promise not to say anything when she knew so little?

"I'll say this—I am part of something important, something that matters deeply to me and many others. It requires the utmost caution, or else...aye, I could be in danger."

"I'll not speak of this meeting." Libby frowned, torn between concern for his wellbeing and discomfort at the thought of keeping this news to herself. "I wish I understood better..."

"I know. I am truly sorry for all the secrecy. And for scaring you. And for any other things you're likely disappointed in me over. I just want you to be safe." A wistful smile softened Elijah's expression. "'Twas good to see you, Elizabeth. I'm on my way out of Boston soon. I hope we'll see each other again someday."

He turned away, ready to slip back into the shadows, which had deepened significantly, but Libby reached for his arm to stop him.

"Will you see Hannah and Will? Might I send you with a letter for them?"

He pursed his lips, and for a moment, she was certain he would refuse her request. Then he nodded. "I've some other business to tend to, but if you have one ready by Monday evening..." He glanced around, gaze settling on the woodpile stacked next to the back door. "Hide it there, under the logs. I'll make sure it gets to them."

Without another word, he was gone, fading into the blackness of night. Disappearing much as he had before, and leaving even more questions in his wake.

With a sigh, Libby stooped to pick up several bits of her broken washbasin, her thoughts equally messy and scattered. She pushed the door open and stepped into the kitchen, nearly colliding with Lieutenant Harrison.

She sucked in a breath. Was everyone intent upon startling her tonight?

"Miss Caldwell?" His brows rose in surprise as he glanced at the broken fragments in her hands. "Is something wrong?"

"I was emptying my washbasin and..." Elijah's words of warning rang in her mind. She didn't wish to lie, but she wouldn't reveal what had happened. A sliver of truth would have to do. Stepping past him, she set the shards on the table. "Unfortunately, I dropped it. 'Tis quite ruined I fear, but I want to pick up the pieces, nonetheless."

"Allow me to help."

Libby darted a glance into the darkness, but there was no sign of Elijah. How long had Lieutenant Harrison been in the kitchen? And why? He rarely wandered the house on his own, seemingly intent upon keeping to his small chamber. Had he heard her and Elijah talking outside and come in search of the noise? Her heart beat faster. What should she say if he questioned her?

But he said nothing as he stooped to retrieve a handful of the shattered basin. He wore only his linen shirt tucked into his breeches, and Libby tried to ignore the way the fabric pulled taut against his back. Her shoulder brushed his as she bent to gather the rest of the broken pieces. A rush of heat spread through her arm. She caught her breath, ashamed at such a reaction to his nearness. Especially now, so soon after Elijah's warnings and her own adamant denial of any deeper connection between her and the lieutenant. Why would her foolish heart not listen?

They moved back inside in silence and piled the last of her broken washbasin on the table. She'd have to tell Mama in the morning, and the thought of withholding the whole truth made her stomach churn.

Turning away from the mess, she looked up at Lieutenant Harrison, forcing a pleasant expression. "Was there something you needed in the kitchen?"

"Your mother told me there was some hot water left in the kettle. I'd thought to make myself a cup of tea, but…" He glanced at the hearth where the kettle hung.

"Then you found it empty." She smiled sheepishly. "I'm sorry. I used it to wash my hair."

His eyes widened, as though noticing for the first time the thick braid that trailed down her back and the damp curls framing her face that refused to be tamed.

She ducked her head at the intensity of his gaze and turned toward the shelf that held the tea tins. "Do you have a headache again? I would be glad to fix you some of Papa's blend."

"I'm fine. No headache."

She glanced back at him over her shoulder. "I'd likely have one every day if I were out there on the Common listening to the drums hour upon hour."

The corners of his mouth tipped up, and the slightest hint of laughter rumbled low in his chest. It sparked a swell of warmth in her own.

Had she ever heard him truly laugh? And how long had it been since she'd seen a genuine smile upon his face? He'd always seemed a stoic sort, but these past months had made him even more so. The desire to make him smile, to hear his laughter, welled up inside, and her pulse tripped faster.

She crossed to the hearth. "I'd be glad to fetch more water if you'd like. It won't take long to—"

"Please don't." The gruffness in his voice halted her steps. He cleared his throat, and when he spoke again, his tone was gentler. "You shouldn't go out alone. I need…I want you to be safe."

Safe. Two men had issued the same warning tonight, yet they felt so different. Elijah's words brought confusion, but Lieutenant Harrison's wrapped around her like an embrace.

She stared at him, candlelight flickering across the strong planes of his face and illuminating the depths of his brown eyes. The kitchen felt suddenly smaller, their closeness in the dim light more intimate. Could he hear her heart beating? She forced her feet to stay grounded in place, despite the longing to move nearer. The desire to experience the kind of safety she believed she would find in his arms.

A muscle ticked in his jaw. He dipped his chin, breaking the connection. "Good night, Miss Caldwell."

He strode out of the kitchen before she could respond.

She watched him leave, then leaned against the rough bricks of the fireplace with a shuddered sigh. Her whole body trembled, the shock of Elijah's reappearance and his evasive conversation mingling with the rush of emotions she felt in Lieutenant Harrison's presence.

Her gaze fell once more on the jagged fragments of pottery on the table. This night had broken more than her washbasin. It had shattered what she thought she knew about Elijah and put cracks of doubt into her relationship with Hannah and Will. There was so much she didn't understand. About her friends, her family, even her own heart. Could she fit the pieces back together into something whole, or was the brokenness here to stay?

CHAPTER 6

Isaac settled into his chair at the kitchen table on Sunday afternoon as Mrs. Abbott placed a steaming bowl of baked beans in front of him with a gracious smile. She'd insisted upon him joining her and Miss Caldwell for the Sabbath meal, and he'd found it impossible to refuse without appearing rude. Miss Caldwell took the seat across from him, her own dish in hand, smile a bit more hesitant than her mother's. Was she remembering how they'd stood in this room two days ago, in the quiet dark of evening? Had his bumbling admission that he cared about her safety discomforted her?

"Lieutenant, would you like to offer the blessing?" Mrs. Abbott looked at him expectantly.

Him? He'd not spoken to God since…'twas too long to recall. Unbidden, his gaze drifted to the empty chair at the head of the table. If only Dr. Caldwell were still here. His words had always held a mix of humility and boldness as he approached the Lord. Much better than anything Isaac could offer.

Still, he bowed his head and cleared his throat. "Lord, for this food and for the hands that prepared it, we give thanks. Amen."

Quiet *amens* from the women followed his brief and stilted prayer. He reached for his spoon, glad for the excuse of the meal to keep his head down. Lifting a bite into his mouth, he savored the smoky flavor with just a hint of sweetness.

"I fear 'tis not as tasty as usual." Miss Caldwell frowned. "We must use our molasses sparingly."

"I don't mind the change." He scooped another spoonful as proof.

Baked beans were their traditional meal each Sunday, easy to prepare the day before and keep warm in the brick oven so as to allow the women to honor the Sabbath with rest. Even with the adjusted recipe, the beans were comforting in their familiarity, reminding him of past Sabbath meals shared with the family, before Dr. Caldwell's chair was empty.

"Did you enjoy Reverend Caner's sermon this morning?" Mrs. Abbott drew his attention.

Isaac looked up to find her regarding him. He hesitated, spoon hovering over his bowl. In truth, he'd missed much of the reverend's message, his mind drifting more than the June breeze outside.

First, he'd spotted Captain Merrick, seated not far from him in King's Chapel, which turned his thoughts to the discussion they expected to have tomorrow regarding a strategy to break the siege. Then, when he attempted to wrestle his focus back to the man at the pulpit, his gaze had caught upon Miss Caldwell instead. Her gown complemented her feminine curves, and she'd styled her hair differently, with several ringlets draped over one shoulder. His attention had lingered far longer than it should.

"I regret to admit that I was distracted during the service." He purposefully avoided a glance at Miss Caldwell.

"It happens to all of us now and again, whether we admit it or not." Mrs. Abbott's eyes crinkled at the corners. "I always knew when Dr. Caldwell's mind had wandered, for he had a habit of drumming his fingers atop his knee."

"He did, didn't he?" Miss Caldwell giggled. "But he always went still when you reached out to squeeze his hand and bring his focus back again."

The two women shared a tender look, and Isaac's heart ached anew at their loss. His own parents had shown little outward affection to each other, or to their three sons. What would it have been like, to grow up as Miss Caldwell did, with parents who so clearly cared for one another? Who knew each other deeply enough to read each little movement and respond to a wordless message through the simplest touch?

Did he have any hope of such a connection in his own marriage one day? It seemed difficult to imagine, having never met the woman his father had promised him to. More likely, his future relationship with Miss Bradbury would be as decorous and impersonal as his parents'.

The thought made the food turn sour in his stomach. Guilt over his silent admiration of Miss Caldwell's appearance only worsened the churning in his gut. The sooner they ended this siege, the better. The women needed protection, but increasingly, Isaac needed distance.

"I wonder what Papa would have thought of Reverend Caner's words." Miss Caldwell pursed her lips. "He did love the fifty-fifth chapter of Isaiah, but today's message was…"

Isaac felt her gaze upon him as her words trailed off. Had there been a political bend to the reverend's sermon? The man made no attempt to hide his loyalty to the Crown, though he preached to a congregation with mixed allegiance. Including Dr. Caldwell's wife and daughter, who had clearly sided with those that called themselves Patriots.

"He would have held to the truth spoken from God's Word and not worried himself overmuch with the rest." Bittersweet fondness tinted Mrs. Abbott's voice.

Miss Caldwell accepted her mother's response in silence, but her expression hinted at the thoughts she kept at bay. Evidently, she had taken exception to some of the reverend's words. Curiosity niggled at Isaac, a pressing desire to know her opinion. Would that he might discuss it with her, as he once had all manner of topics with her father. He suppressed the strange longing.

"And as to your distraction, Lieutenant"—Mrs. Abbott eyed him kindly— "if my late husband were here, he would reassure you that church is not the only place to meet with God. God is just as present with you in your everyday life as He is within those walls. Wherever you go, in all that you do, He is always near, always attentive to the needs and cares of His children. Indeed, Dr. Caldwell often said that he felt God closest in the moments that seemed the least sacred—while he mended a broken bone or stitched a wound or kept vigil beside an ill child—for 'twas in those moments he most clearly recognized his own weakness and dependence upon the Lord."

Isaac swallowed hard, a bite of beans sticking in his throat as her words prodded at his spirit.

Growing up, he'd viewed God much like his own father—stern, detached, and difficult to please. But Dr. Caldwell had challenged Isaac to think differently. To understand God as a good father, who knew each of His children in a deeply personal way, and loved them enough to offer His Son as a ransom for their sins. Many of Isaac's discussions with the doctor had touched on such topics, always pushing Isaac to move beyond shallow ritual or duty to a trusting dependence upon God that was as real and vital as the air he breathed. That was how Dr. Caldwell lived, and for a time, Isaac thought he, too, could have such faith. One equally alive and unshakable.

But the disappointments of the past five years had torn holes in his fledgling faith, like musket balls piercing a target made of straw. It had been a long time since God felt near, be it inside a church or anywhere else.

He attempted a smile, though it fell short. "Your husband was a wise man."

"That he was." Mrs. Abbott nodded. "But more importantly, he was a man who trusted God fully for all of his days."

The women's conversation drifted to other matters, which Isaac attempted to follow with enough interest to be polite. But his conscience stung to think of his old friend, and how disappointed the faithful Dr. Caldwell would be if he knew that Isaac's association with God had once more fallen into a place of mere duty. He was glad when the meal came to an end and Mrs. Abbott began to clear the table.

Miss Caldwell rose to help, but paused, attention fixed on him. "Did you know you've a button loose on your coat?"

He glanced down and frowned. Indeed, one of the buttons of his uniform was hanging by a thread. "I did not. I'll have our company's tailor mend it tomorrow."

"Nonsense. I'll see to it now. It will take me but a few minutes." She wiped her hands on her apron. "Bring it into the parlor. I shall get my sewing things."

Mrs. Abbott remained behind to wash the dishes as Isaac followed Miss Caldwell into the parlor. She placed her box of needles and thread upon the small table and opened it. Shedding his coat, he handed it to her. She settled into the chair beside the window, where afternoon sunlight slanted through to illuminate her work.

Should he sit as well? Or perhaps that was presumptuous and he'd do better to leave her alone while she mended the button. He started toward his chamber.

"You can stay if you'd like." Miss Caldwell's voice halted his steps. "I'll make quick work of this. Besides, I cannot help asking..."A hint of teasing glinted in her eyes. "Did you truly hear none of the sermon?"

Isaac grimaced as he turned back. "Not enough to recall."

Fitting the thread through the tiny eye of the needle, she recited the passage from the morning service. "'Let the wicked forsake his way, and the unrighteous man his thoughts: and let him return unto the Lord, and he will have mercy upon him; and to our God, for he will abundantly pardon.'" She glanced up, a wry smile on her lips. "I suppose Mama and I are among the wicked."

His frown deepened. "What do you mean?"

"The reverend did not say so directly, but the implication was clear. Those who rebel against the king are straying from God and must return for His mercy and pardon."

Isaac shifted, apprehensive and uncertain how to reply. Miss Caldwell spoke so freely, as though completely unconcerned that his position as an officer of the army stood in direct opposition to her views. Did she feel no discomfort in it? Or was she able to see beyond their differences, just as her father had years prior?

She turned his coat to examine the button from a different angle, her slim fingers deftly weaving the thread in tiny, neat stitches. Such a simple act, yet he couldn't look away. How could she mend the uniform of the army that occupied her town without hesitation, while also speaking so candidly and unapologetically of her opposing beliefs?

"Do you think we are the wicked ones, then?" The question slipped out before Isaac could stop it.

Her gaze shot to his. "Of course not. I am not so naive as to declare any man wicked simply for the uniform he wears or the allegiance he has sworn. I think we should not use that verse in such a way. Without the Lord, we are all unrighteous, for all have sinned and come short of God's glory. But thankfully, He is rich in mercy and abounding in love."

He was quiet for a moment, digesting her words. He was familiar enough with Scripture to recognize the way she'd drawn from it to form her response. Was it so ingrained within her heart that she could call it to mind to answer in such a way? Did she believe it with the same conviction and strength that her father had? She certainly spoke with the same confidence. A confidence he ached to have for himself.

She studied him, brows pulling low. "Forgive me if I overstepped."

"You needn't apologize." It was not her fault that the words left him so unsettled. In truth, he appreciated her open nature, which echoed that of the man he'd so admired and appreciated. "You remind me of your father."

"Do I?" Her expression was half flattered, half skeptical.

"Well, not in looks certainly." He shocked himself with the jesting remark, and her wide-eyed expression revealed matching surprise.

But then she laughed, and the sound shot warmth through his belly. "I should hope not. I'd rather like to keep my hair."

A rare grin tugged at his lips. Though Dr. Caldwell had worn a simple wig in public, in the comfort of his own home, he'd had no qualms about his balding head.

He sobered. "I meant that you are unafraid to say what you think, and to do so with confidence, despite our obvious differences. Your father was the same, and I always appreciated him for it."

She ducked her head, but not before he spotted the color rising on her cheeks.

Whether she was embarrassed or pleased by his remarks, Isaac could not say, but he pressed on. "How is it that you and your mother have graced me with such kindness and generosity, even though..." He gestured to the coat in her hands, uncertain of how to finish.

"Because this alone is not who you are."

How he wanted her words to be true, that he would be defined not by his position in the army but by who he was as a man. Yet his father's voice echoed in his head, louder than Miss Caldwell's, repeating a message he'd heard for all of his eight-and-twenty years. A message sometimes spoken, always implied. His worth was only as much as the honor and status he brought to the family. A noble officer was worthy, indeed, but a dishonored soldier, or a misunderstood son was a hindrance, a problem to be solved.

Miss Caldwell knotted the thread and stood. "You say I remind you of my father. He treated you the same way. Did you think that strange?"

"I confess that I did at first. But then he became my friend, and the other aspects of our individual lives did not seem to matter as much."

"Can you and I not be friends as well?" Her voice grew quieter, and for the first time in their conversation, he sensed a hint of uncertainty in her tone. "I know 'tis not the same, and yet..." She held out his coat, the garment and her words extended like an offering, an invitation.

No, friendship with Miss Caldwell was not the same as friendship with her father. Was it even possible for him to share such a relationship with her? He'd purposefully kept her at arm's length, a young woman to be protected, one that deserved respect and kindness. But something more personal? It seemed a dangerous territory to tread.

He accepted the proffered uniform, his fingers brushing over hers as he did. Isaac swallowed. Dangerous, indeed. The warning to keep his distance rattled in his head like a drum beating the signal to retreat, but as he held her gaze, hope flick-ered within her blue eyes, and he could not say no. Nor did he wish to.

"Aye, Miss Caldwell." He draped his coat over one arm, ignoring the weight that settled over him as he nodded. "We can."

The rising sun was just beginning to filter through Libby's bedchamber window on Monday morning as she creased her second letter closed and carefully scribed *Hannah* on the back of the page. She had filled two sheets of parchment, and still there was so much more she wished she could say to her friend. Blowing on the ink to help it dry, she set it next to the other missive, labeled *Patience*. A bittersweet ache settled in her chest at seeing their names side by side. Glad as she was that the two women had each other, she dearly missed them both.

She had decided against asking Hannah anything more about her brother and his mysterious return. Nor had she penned a letter to Will to press him for more information, much as she'd been tempted to. The knowledge that they'd kept Elijah's reappearance from her still nagged, like a sliver just beneath the skin, but how could she expect an answer through writing if they'd not even spoken openly with her in person? Indeed, she had no hopes for a reply of any sort, given the current state of the siege and the difficulty it posed for communication. 'Twas a gift that Elijah could even take her letters out of Boston. She would be content with that. She must.

Rising from the desk that had once been her father's, she crept to the trunk at the end of her bed. She winced at the creak of the hinges as she opened it. The sound echoed accusingly in her quiet room, scolding her for sneaking around to prepare these letters without her mother's knowledge. What a hypocrite she was, bemoaning her disappointment over Elijah, Will, and Hannah's secrets, while hiding this from Mama.

She lifted Mr. Pierce's journal from beneath the clothing where she'd stowed it. She would leave this with the letters, too, so Elijah could return it to his father. Her fingers skimmed over a pair of stockings she'd embroidered with a curling vine adorned with flowers. If only she had some extra fabric, she could stitch a lovely little gown for Patience in anticipation of her baby's arrival, and send that with Elijah as well.

Mrs. Barker, the mantua maker, had remained in Boston. Perhaps Libby could venture to her shop and purchase a bit of linen. But what would she tell Mama? Guilt pricked, stinging more than an errant needle. She pushed the idea, and the awful feeling, away as she dressed. Tucking the letters into the front cover of the journal, she wrapped everything in her apron and tiptoed downstairs. Best hide them now, before anyone else in the house was awake.

Once her delivery was well concealed within the woodpile, Libby set to work preparing breakfast. By the time Mama came in, the porridge was warm and ready to serve.

"Good morning." Her mother smiled, but it didn't reach her eyes.

Weariness lingered there, the kind born from something more than restless sleep. What was it that troubled her most? There were certainly a myriad of things that could. Worry for their safety. Concerns about their dwindling food and resources. Fear over how long the siege would last.

Libby bit her lip, the all-too-familiar shame flaring hot within her. She should not have convinced Mama to stay in Boston. Her foolish infatuation with Lieutenant Harrison would never come to anything, even if he had reluctantly agreed to call her a friend. Why had she allowed her misguided feelings for him to influence her so much?

Perhaps Elijah was right in thinking her incapable of knowing the things he knew. The things he'd evidently entrusted to Hannah and Will. Perhaps she was too easily swayed by emotions, too prone to rash decisions.

The thought heated her cheeks, and she turned away so her mother would not see, busying herself in serving porridge into their bowls. They ate together in silence, a sense of gloom hovering despite the clear sky outside.

Perhaps Mama felt as confined as Libby did, forced to forgo the freedom to move about town as they had always before. Might it do them both good to get away from the house, even if only for a short time?

Mrs. Barker came to mind again. Libby would refrain from making a gown to pass along with Elijah, as she had no desire to deceive her mother more than she already was, but a trip to the mantua maker might still be a welcome diversion.

"What do you say to paying Mrs. Barker a call?" She peeked at Mama to ascertain her reaction. "I am certain she would be glad to see you, and perhaps we might work on some things to set aside for when Patience's baby arrives."

"I think it a lovely idea." Mama's face brightened for a moment, then fell. "Though, who can say that we will be able to deliver it in a timely manner?"

"I know. But it would give us something hopeful to look forward to, would it not?"

"That it would." A genuine smile finally lifted her mother's expression. "Aye. We shall go."

Once the breakfast things had been cleaned, Libby and her

mother set off for Mrs. Barker's shop on Leverets Lane. It was a short walk, and the early-morning sun offered a welcome cheer that chased Libby's troublesome thoughts into the shadows. In the absence of the usual bustle of crowds, the cry of sea birds rang clearer, and Libby tipped her head back to watch them swoop through the cloudless sky. She breathed deeply of the salt-tinged air, her spirit lighter already. This was just what she needed.

Reaching the shop, Mama stepped inside first. The bright tinkling of a bell chimed overhead, welcoming them. Mrs. Barker turned from the back wall where she stood arranging bolts of silk upon a shelf. A broad smile broke across her round face.

"Mrs. Abbott. Miss Caldwell. How good it is to see you both." She ushered them farther in with a wave of both hands. "To what do I owe the pleasure of this visit?"

"My stepdaughter is with child, and Elizabeth and I would like to work on some things for when the babe arrives." Mama crossed the room and placed a hand on her friend's arm. "And I suspect we all could use a bit of company."

"Indeed." Mrs. Barker bobbed her head. "Much too quiet lately, and much too idle. I need busy hands, else my mind becomes occupied with worries better left to the Lord."

Was that part of the reason for Libby's troubled thoughts of late? With little to do aside from the mundane chores of everyday life, was there too much space in her mind to dwell upon things she had no control over?

"Well, come, then, Miss Caldwell." Mrs. Barker gestured toward the stacks of fabric brightening the rows of shelves. "You may look as you wish. Find something that suits your fancy for your coming niece or nephew."

As Mama and Mrs. Barker talked, Libby meandered along the wall, eying first one pattern, then the next. Something simple would do best for the baby, but she couldn't help admiring the swaths that would make a fine gown or petticoat of her own. She paused at a rich burgundy chintz printed with a winding fig leaf pattern in white and pale blues. How lovely it would look as a *robe a l'anglaise.* But what need had she for a new gown of that sort? And what means to purchase one? Suppressing a sigh, she moved on, her gaze landing on a cream-colored linen. Simple but soft, and sturdy enough to bear frequent washings. It would make for a good little gown, and she could embroider a design along the hem to embellish it a bit.

She lifted the fabric from the shelf and joined her mother and Mrs. Barker where they stood beside the worktable.

"Ah, a perfect choice for a new little one," Mrs. Barker said with approval. "When is the babe expected to come?"

"September." Libby set the linen on the wooden surface. "Although Patience and her husband are in Watertown, so we can't be certain of when we will see them."

"'Tis better that they are out of the city, for it would be an unfortunate time to welcome a child to Boston." A smattering of wrinkles lined Mrs. Barker's pursed lips. "Let us hope this trouble is sorted by then, else you may not even be able to receive word. My daughter left in April with her husband and young ones, and I've heard nothing since. I pray they are safe, but it pains me to know so little."

Mama nodded. "'Tis difficult, indeed. I pray for God's protection over our loved ones day and night, and for His hand over us."

Libby grimaced. Thankful as she was for the opportunity to send letters with Elijah, he'd said nothing about returning. And even if he did come back bearing news from their family, would he expect Libby to keep that hidden from her mother as well? She couldn't do that to Mama.

Mrs. Barker measured out a length of the chosen linen, cutting it deftly with the shears hanging from her chatelaine.

Mama reached into her pocket to extract some coins for payment, but Mrs. Barker stilled her with a raised hand. "No payment necessary."

"But Mrs. Barker—"

"I'll take no arguments." The older woman's voice was firm, but her hazel eyes held a warm affection and a hint of concern. "You've no husband to provide for you, and these are hard enough times as is. I reckon I can spare the shillings. Not as charity, mind, but out of love for a friend."

Mama dipped her chin but made no protest.

Libby's chest tightened. Did it pain her mother to accept such a gift? Did it trouble her to depend upon the benevolence of others?

A memory flashed, as clear as though it were yesterday. Libby could still see the look on Mama's face the moment she told Libby she had accepted Mr. Abbott's offer of marriage.

"I know your father has not been gone long. If I could, I would wait before I..." Mama's voice had faltered as she struggled to regain her composure. "But your papa, he was so generous in his care of his patients, always willing to provide medical attention, even when those he treated could not pay him fully in return. And as a result...well, Mr. Abbott has generously stepped in to offer us protection and provision. We can stay in this house, and you'll have all you need."

Mama's face had held such a strange mix of resignation and determination. Pain and hope. Her mother had sacrificed much for Libby's sake. Marrying again, despite her grief over losing the husband she loved so deeply, to ensure they were taken care of. Hot tears pricked Libby's eyes, as they had that November morning two years ago. She blinked them away, along with the memory.

"Miss Caldwell." Mrs. Barker's voice caught Libby's attention. "I daresay, I recall that you are quite good with a needle."

Libby forced a pleasant expression. "I am."

"I've taken on some mending, to make up for the lack of new commissions of late. There are a number of men who remained in town, while sending their wives and children elsewhere, and they've come to depend upon my sewing skills. It isn't much, but every bit helps." She crossed her arms over her ample waist. "Might you be interested in taking work with me? Only if your mother allows, mind you."

"Here in the shop?" Libby glanced between Mama and Mrs. Barker as a thread of excitement wove through her. After all that her mother had done, might this be the chance for Libby to finally be the one to take care of her? To prove herself as capable as Papa had always believed her to be?

"If you like. I'd be glad for this place not to feel so empty and quiet." Mrs. Barker's gaze roamed the shop before landing on Mama. "But if your mother would prefer to have you at home, 'tis easy enough for you to work there instead."

Mama was quiet for a long moment, and Libby held her breath as she awaited the answer.

"I think it a very kind offer." Her mother smiled at Mrs. Barker, then turned to Libby. "I am in favor of the idea, but the choice is yours."

Libby's heart swelled, and she grinned back at Mama, hoping she could see the fullness of her gratitude. Not only for the permission to accept the offer, but the freedom to choose the terms. "I'd like that very much, Mrs. Barker. Perhaps I can work here with you twice a week, and complete any other requests from home so as to be available to help my mother as well."

"Aye. A responsible and wise choice." Mrs. Barker's eyes crinkled with obvious approval. "You've raised a fine young woman, Mrs. Abbott."

"She is, indeed." The softness in Mama's voice drew Libby's gaze to her face. The pride and love in her eyes warmed Libby to the core. But there was trust also, and that sent a sharp pang of guilt stabbing through her middle.

What would happen if Mama knew the truth? If she knew the real reason Libby had wanted to stay in Boston, or discovered what Libby was hiding about Elijah? What would she see in Mama's gaze then?

~

A peaceful quiet lay over the parlor as dusk fell Monday evening. Libby sat at the round table with her mother, both of them busy stitching baby clothes. Mama's head bent closer and closer to her work as the sun sank lower in the sky. After returning from the mantua maker, they'd spent much of the afternoon sewing, and it had indeed seemed to spark a bit of hope for them both. Or at least given them a new task to take their mind off other matters for a while.

Narrowing her eyes, Mama stared at the row of stitches forming the arm of a tiny gown, then blinked and sat back in her chair. "'Tis too dim for me to see well enough any longer. I think I shall retire for the night." She rose, leaving her work on the table, then glanced over her shoulder at the closed door that led to the lieutenant's chamber. "You'd best move upstairs now as well."

Libby stood and stretched, pressing a hand to the small of her back. Mama was right. Though they'd not seen, nor heard, Lieutenant Harrison return this evening, it would do no good for Libby to be alone with him, should he venture beyond the confines of his room. For propriety...and for the sake of her heart.

Still, she was not quite ready to put aside her work yet, so she gathered the small gown and her sewing box and followed Mama to the upper level of the house. They bid each other goodnight and went to their separate chambers, Libby easing the door closed behind her. She lifted the tiny garment to examine her progress, and her breath hitched at the thought of holding a person so small. Was there any hope of meeting Patience and Josiah's wee one when he or she arrived, or would the siege keep them all apart?

She pulled her wooden chair beside the window and returned to the intricate pattern of flowers and birds she was embroidering along the bottom hem of the gown. There would be enough linen left for her to make a matching bonnet, and she planned to decorate that with Hollie Point lace in a similar design. Libby was halfway through the next bird's wing when she realized that, like Mama, her head was dipping closer to the fabric to make out the tiny stitches. She rose, frowning at the candle perched on the desk. Or what was left of it. She had let it burn too low this morning while she wrote her letters.

Determined to complete the bird before going to bed, she crept downstairs to fetch a fresh candle but froze at the sound of voices coming from the direction of Lieutenant Harrison's quarters. He had returned and evidently was not alone.

She paused at the doorway of the parlor. Who was with him? She shouldn't linger, and yet curiosity held her in place.

"What did you hear of the plan?" An unfamiliar male voice, muffled but clear enough for her to make out the words in the otherwise-silent house, drifted toward her. "I was called away at the last minute and missed much of the discussion."

"They plan to strike on the eighteenth, while most of the provincial forces are attending services for the Sabbath." She recognized the lieutenant's voice immediately, but her heart froze at his words.

Plan to strike? Was the army preparing to attack the militia? Were they going to try to break out of Boston?

She slipped farther into the room, padding softly on her toes and barely breathing as she listened.

"A sound strategy," the other man replied. "And where exactly will they target?"

"Multiple locations, if all goes as planned. General Burgoyne is to be stationed at Boston Neck, where his troops will be responsible for cannonading Roxbury. At the same time, General Howe will lead a detachment to Dorchester Heights to attack from the east while General Clinton leads an assault to the center."

The low rumble of Lieutenant Harrison's voice held a note of authority she'd heard several times in the past. Before, it had always inspired a sort of awe in her, but now it sent a chill down her spine. 'Twas so calm, almost detached, as if he spoke of the weather instead of a battle that could bring all manner of death and destruction.

"Good." The other man huffed. "The rebels in Roxbury will have no choice but to retreat."

"Perhaps." Lieutenant Harrison did not sound as confident. "We've seen them fight, though. You know as well as I how persistent they were on our march back to Boston after the skirmishes at Lexington and Concord—the way they surrounded the road, firing from all sides. We cannot underestimate their tenacity."

"Tenacity only goes so far. What are untrained farmers against the king's army?"

Libby's pulse throbbed in her temples. What, indeed? She'd seen the troops practicing drills on the Common. Watched their lines move with precision, a terrifyingly powerful force. How could the colonial militia stand against such an attack?

"What about Charlestown?" The second soldier pressed on. "We need to secure those heights if we're to hold full control."

"They plan to send General Howe there after the Dorchester is taken," Lieutenant Harrison answered. "Once he has possession of those hills, he can move into Cambridge."

"And thus, we'll have control over all the high ground and

the provincial headquarters." The other man spoke as though it were already completed. "We'll be free of this city in a sennight."

Libby pressed a hand to her racing heart as she backed out of the room. There were thousands of soldiers in Boston and multiple generals to lead them. What chance did the militia have against such a foe?

Will and Josiah could be out there somewhere. The thought rushed over her like a frigid ocean wave, and her whole body began to tremble. If only she could protect them somehow, could warn them...

She sucked in a breath. Elijah. It wasn't fully dark yet. He wouldn't come for her letters until the cover of night, would he?

Scurrying back upstairs as quietly as she could, she ducked into her room and pulled another sheet of paper from the desk. She dipped the quill, splattering drips of black ink on the page in her haste, and scrawled a desperate note.

Elijah—I heard the lieutenant talking about a plan to attack the militia. They will send troops against Roxbury and Charlestown this Sunday, the eighteenth, while church services are in session. Please try to find Will and make sure he is safe. Josiah Wagner, too—my stepsister's husband. Be careful.

Libby sprinkled a hefty pinch of pounce over the ink to make it dry faster, then tucked the missive deep into her pocket and snuck down to the kitchen. Inching the back door open, she stepped outside into the deepening night. The seconds stretched long as she searched for her hiding spot in the pile of wood, silently praying that everything was still there. Her hand landed on the smooth leather of the journal, and she exhaled in relief. She tucked the letter into the book, unfolded, so Elijah would see the words.

Dear God, please let him see them. Please keep them safe.

Stuffing the bundle back into its hiding place, she hurried to her room and sagged against the solid wood of her door, breath coming in short gasps. Her palms were damp, her hands shaking as she clasped them together and pressed them against her churning stomach.

Only the moon lit her room now, and its pale silvery glow cast looming shadows that stretched across the wide-planked floor, as though threatening to engulf her. She shivered. Hopefully, the soldier visiting Lieutenant Harrison would be gone before Elijah arrived.

That thought sent a new stab of fear through her heart. What if Elijah was intercepted with the words she had written? By reporting what she'd heard to him, could she be accused of committing some act of treason against the king's forces? Had her rash decision put them both at risk?

CHAPTER 8

Steady rain dampened Isaac's uniform and dripped from the brim of his cocked hat on Tuesday afternoon. He tucked the bundled cloak he carried under the edge of his coat, attempting to protect it from the weather and to lessen the distractingly feminine rosewater scent that clung to it, though he failed miserably at both.

He had ended drills early for his men when the dark clouds rolled in, threatening a storm. Discipline was imperative, but health was of equal importance, and it would do none of the soldiers good to spend the day soaked through. Not when they needed to be ready to make their attack come Sunday.

His conversation with Captain Merrick last night had settled uncomfortably in his thoughts, nagging him long after the other officer departed. Merrick had much more confidence in the success of their plans than Isaac did. And more enthusiasm as well.

Isaac scowled as he dodged a muddy puddle. He knew the necessity of breaking the siege as well as any other soldier, but he disliked the thought of what it would take to do so. Of the lives that might be lost in the process. Water sluiced off the back of his hat and slipped behind his collar, sending a chill down his neck.

He had returned to the house after dismissing his men and found Mrs. Abbott about to depart, despite the increasingly foul weather. She'd been intent upon fetching her daughter from the mantua maker, explaining that Miss Caldwell had left home while it was still clear that morning and had brought nothing to protect her from the rain. Wanting to spare Mrs. Abbott, Isaac had offered to go in her stead.

He reached the shop that she'd directed him to and rapped on the door, hesitant to intrude upon a space intended for the fairer sex.

A stout woman opened the door, her brows lifting until they nearly touched the wisps of gray hair that edged her forehead. Her attention fell to his uniform, and she narrowed her eyes, a hint of suspicion creeping into her gaze. "May I help you, sir?"

"I came for Miss Caldwell, on behalf of her mother." He held out the folded cloak. "I'm to give her this, to protect against the rain on the walk home."

"Lieutenant Harrison?" Miss Caldwell joined the older woman at the entryway, her smile a much more pleasant greeting than the distrustful look of her companion. "Mrs. Barker, this is Lieutenant Isaac Harrison. He was a friend of my father's."

Isaac. He tried to ignore the way his given name sounded from her lips. 'Twas only an introduction, after all. Still, she said it with a softness that made him wish he could grant her permission to call him that always. He cleared his throat, willing the absurd thought away.

"Pleased to meet you, ma'am." He dipped his chin, which only served to splatter more water that had gathered in the folded corners of his hat.

Mrs. Barker shuffled back a step.

"Come in." Miss Caldwell waved a hand to usher him indoors. "Dry off a bit."

The offer tempted him, but Mrs. Barker's watchful gaze made him unwilling to risk dirtying her floors. "Thank you, but I'll only turn around and get wet again in a few minutes."

Miss Caldwell chuckled. "I suppose you're right." Tilting her head, she peered up at the cloudy sky. Thick gray hovered above them, but blacker clouds hung low over the sea, the wind pushing them farther inland by the minute. She turned back to the owner of the shop. "Perhaps I should leave as well, before the storm grows even heavier."

Mrs. Barker wrinkled her nose, likely debating which was worse—letting her charge return home with a British officer now, or sending her out in a raging gale later. With a sigh, she nodded. "Best go, and no need to take anything with you. The work will keep until Thursday."

Miss Caldwell swung her cloak around her shoulders and tied it closed, then tugged her hood over her head. She bid her friend farewell and followed him outside, sending him a grin that seemed to suggest she saw the rain as more of an adventure than a nuisance.

They traipsed down the muddy road at a quick pace but had not made it far before the rain began to pour in earnest, and thunder rumbled far too close for comfort. Isaac squinted through the torrential downpour, spotting an abandoned house where the upper story had been built in such a way that it jutted out a couple of feet further than the lower level. Just enough to provide a bit of cover.

Grasping Miss Caldwell's elbow, he leaned down so as to be heard over the next thunderclap. "We'd best take shelter until this passes."

She didn't protest, instead pressing closer to his side as he led her off the road. They ducked beneath the overhang, and he released her.

She tipped her face up to look at him, blinking back the drops that splattered her cheeks and clung to her long lashes. But there was no dismay or fear in the depths of her eyes. Instead, they sparkled with...humor?

Indeed, laughter broke free from her lips as they curved into a smile. "I believe I may have been better off waiting with Mrs. Barker, after all."

"So it seems." His own answering chuckle surprised him. "I am sorry."

"Whatever for? You may be capable of a good many things, Lieutenant, but even you cannot lay claim over the weather."

Something in her voice as she said those words stirred a swell of heat in his belly. What was it? Admiration? Pride?

He was used to respect from his soldiers. Even accustomed to the esteem of his fellow officers. But this? This was more. Meant more, because it came from her.

He tugged his gaze away and stared at the sheet of rain streaming off the edge of the house like a curtain in front of them. Closing them together in a private sanctuary. Far too near to her for his good.

"I did not realize you'd taken work at the mantua maker." His tone was a bit too gruff, but all the better. Perhaps if he kept her talking about impersonal things, he could manage to ignore her nearness.

"Aye. Today was my first day." Enthusiasm brightened her words as she explained how Mrs. Barker had begun taking in mending and had invited her to join the endeavor. "I suspect there was some sense of charity involved in her offer, but I am glad of it, nonetheless. I cannot help but hope this work will give me a new sense of purpose and distract me from feeling so..."—she waved a hand in a small circle, as if to encompass their surroundings— "trapped. Boston is the only home I've ever known, but now it feels like a cage."

A cage, indeed. He felt much the same. Would she be

relieved if she knew they were planning a way to break the siege? Or would her loyalty to the Patriot cause outweigh the discomfort of her current circumstances?

He couldn't ask. Could say nothing, for he would not reveal the army's secret plans.

"I also hope this work will allow me to contribute to the care of our family in some small way. Mama has sacrificed so much for me already, what with her marriage to Mr. Abbott, and..." Her voice dropped into a sigh.

Isaac frowned. "Was that union an unhappy one?"

"Oh, no." She shook her head. "That is...well, my mother was still grieving Papa's death, so it was a marriage born of necessity more than anything else. But he was good to us, and through him, I gained a stepsister and stepbrother whom I love dearly, so I will forever be grateful in that regard. Still..." She paused, her expression pensive and sober. "I cannot help but feel as though I've done so little. Except convince Mama to stay in Boston, which was clearly a mistake, as you yourself noted."

"I didn't mean to place blame upon you—"

"I know." She pushed her hood off her head, revealing several errant curls that had escaped during their brisk walk. "I blame myself enough as it is. But now I've a chance to atone for my mistake and give back to Mama, who has selflessly cared for me all my life."

Isaac propped one foot against the wooden planks of the house's exterior and crossed his arms over his chest, at a loss as to how to respond. In a way, he understood, for he had been striving to prove himself worthy of his father's expectations and his mother's love since he was a boy. Yet the idea of admitting that aloud to her was nearly as terrifying as staring down the barrel of an enemy's musket.

"Forgive me for prattling on." He felt her gaze upon him and shifted to meet her earnest stare. "I am certain you did not wish to hear all my troublesome thoughts."

"I do not mind."

It was the truth. Listening to her was no difficulty. 'Twas the talking in return that gave him pause. Why was it so easy for her to lay her inner thoughts and feelings bare but so difficult for him to do the same?

Still, her words tugged at his heart, begging for some encouragement or comfort. He could offer that at least, could he not?

He pushed off the wall and turned to face her fully. "Knowing what I do of your mother, I have no doubt she would sacrifice time and again for your wellbeing and happiness."

She peered up at him for a long moment, then a soft smile tipped her lips. "Thank you."

He nodded, pulling his attention back to the storm, which showed no sign of lessening. Quiet settled between them. It was not an uncomfortable silence, yet from the corner of his eye, he could see Miss Caldwell fidgeting, as though she was as full of more words to say as the clouds were laden with rain.

"What about your family?" Her voice was quiet, but he startled at the question.

Of all the conversations, this was one he would rather avoid. He forced a neutral expression, despite the impulse to clench his jaw.

"I recall a little of what you had said of them before." She pressed on, clearly oblivious to his unease. "Your father is a baronet, is he not? And you've two brothers?"

"You remember correctly."

"Do you miss them? Miss home?"

Such simple questions, yet they struck as harsh as lightning. Would she be shocked if he admitted that he did not? Or that he missed something that had never existed in the first place?

"I suppose I've become accustomed to being away. And my family is..." His fingers balled into fists at his sides. He flexed them open. "You have been blessed, Miss Caldwell, to know such love and closeness as you share with your mother, and as you had with your father. Even with the step-siblings you spoke of. I never did."

"I am sorry." Pity laced her words.

Isaac cringed. He did not want her pity. Such was the reward for matching her honest openness with some of his own.

Yet her gentle kindness loosed something in him, and he found he could not stop the torrent. "My father is a proud man, whose regard for the members of his family hinges upon what they can contribute, rather than on any affectionate feelings. That is why I am a soldier. He purchased the commission, intent upon the honor it could bring to our name."

Miss Caldwell gasped, but he refused to turn to look at her. Her slender hand pressed upon his forearm, and his muscle jumped in response to her tender touch. Her fingers fell away.

"I always assumed you wanted to be a soldier. You seem so well suited to it."

"Do I?" He slanted a look at her.

"Well, you've quite an imposing stature and commanding presence. And you're always so serious, which seems fitting in a profession where such discipline is necessary."

Isaac pressed his lips together to hide the amusement that rose at her description. He fixed her with a solemn expression to match her assessment. "Imposing, commanding, and serious. I cannot determine if those are compliments or not."

She ducked her chin, but not fast enough to hide the rosy hue rising in her cheeks. "I meant them as good qualities."

He couldn't suppress a low laugh.

Her gaze shot back to his, eyes wide. "Are you teasing me?"

Was he? It felt so natural, so unexpectedly enjoyable. And so dangerous. He needed to be more careful not to breach the barrier he'd erected between them.

He sobered. "Forgive me, Miss Caldwell, I should not have."

"I don't mind." Her voice was hardly more than a whisper, and her gaze held his with a vulnerability he'd never seen before.

Swallowing, he turned away. The rain had yet to lessen, but perhaps they should brave the storm, after all. A solid drenching might do him good.

She cleared her throat. "So, if not soldiering, what would you have liked to pursue, if you had your will?"

Isaac furrowed his brow. When was the last time he'd allowed himself the luxury of considering a life of his own choosing? The fields near his childhood home came to mind, wheat or barley or clover rippling in the wind. He remembered the grazing lands, dotted with sheep, and the shepherd boy he'd spied on from a high perch in one of his favorite climbing trees. A child much the same age as himself, whose simple life seemed so enviable as he tagged along beside his father, a frisky dog always at his heels.

He risked a glance at Miss Caldwell. "I rather think I'd enjoy farming."

"Truly?" Her delicate brows arched high. "I confess, I cannot imagine you as a farmer."

"No? I suppose not." He tried to ignore the odd pang of disappointment that followed her admission. It always had been a foolish notion, and he was even more the fool for telling her.

He'd only ever spoken of it with one other person—her father—and the man's reply had been uncomfortably convicting. When Isaac told Dr. Caldwell of how idyllic the farms near his father's estate seemed to him as a boy, the older man had hummed deep in his throat, the same sort of sound he made when considering the ailment of a patient.

"Perhaps it is not farming you truly desire, but rather the life that your younger self built up in your mind. A life that seemed to hold the things you felt most lacking." Dr. Caldwell had offered the words slowly, each one carefully chosen. "The dependence and closeness of a family working together. The honest accomplishment of nurturing something with your own hands. The ebb and flow of a life built upon the predictably changing seasons, instead of one centered around society's fickle expectations."

Had the doctor's diagnosis been correct? And if so, perhaps his remedy had been equally true...that the only real satisfaction Isaac's soul longed for was to be found in God.

Isaac shifted his feet, the memory disquieting. Mud squelched beneath his shoes. He couldn't keep waiting here, with Miss Caldwell's conversation stirring up thoughts and feelings he would rather avoid.

"It doesn't look as if this will improve anytime soon." He nodded toward the rain, though the words settled into his chest with a weightiness of a different sort. "We may have to press on through it."

She stared at the street for a long moment, then glanced at him, her smile looking a bit forced. "Aye. We'd best go." Tucking her hood over her head, she stepped out into the storm.

He followed her, flinching as cold drops pelted his face and soaked through his clothes. But it was Miss Caldwell's silence that truly chilled him to the core.

⁓

*L*ibby eased the door of her mother's chamber closed and crept downstairs carrying her untouched plate of food. Poor Mama was plagued by another megrim, and the painful headache had left her dizzy and nauseous. Though unable to eat or even sit up, at least now she had fallen asleep. Libby prayed the rest would give her some relief, and that this spell would not linger as long as the last one in April.

Perhaps the afternoon storm had caused her mother's discomfort. Papa had noted years ago that Mama's episodes often occurred in conjunction with a severe thunderstorm, and had theorized that the heavy weather disrupted the humors in her body, setting them off balance. It seemed a plausible explanation, though Libby wondered if emotional strain also played a part. Some women fainted in the face of acute grief or fear, others due to prolonged stress. Mayhap her mother's body reacted with a debilitating headache instead. Such reasoning would better explain Mama's suffering in April, certainly.

Stepping into the kitchen, Libby set the plate on the table with a sigh. She had desperately wished to speak with Mama this evening because thoughts over the whispered plans she'd heard last night, and guilt over keeping her encounter with Elijah a secret, had plagued her all day. Her spirit felt as messy and knotted as a tangled ball of yarn, and she had determined to bare her heart, no matter the consequences.

Despite Elijah's warning, her mother deserved to know the truth. And how could Libby keep from telling Mama what she'd learned about the impending attack? What if there was something more she could or should do? She had checked the wood pile this morning and found the notebook and letters gone. Elijah had come, at least, but had he opened the journal and looked long enough to discover her hastily scrawled warning?

How she had longed to seek Mama's counsel, but now she couldn't. Not when the strain of such revelations might worsen her mother's condition. She would have to hold it all inside a little longer.

An even weightier exhale escaped her lips. Crossing to the hearth, she peered into the skillet. Another whole serving of potato and onion pie, in addition to that which Mama had not partaken of. 'Twould be impossible for her to finish it all, yet she could not let it go to waste. Should she offer some to Lieutenant Harrison?

She'd not seen him since they returned earlier, both drenched from their rainy walk home from Mrs. Barker's shop. The stiffness of his back as he disappeared into his chamber without a word had left Libby shivering more than her soaked petticoat did. Just when she thought he had begun to abide her company, mayhap even enjoy it, he had closed himself off again.

Had she pried too much with her questions about his family? Or perhaps 'twas his knowledge of the army's plans to break the siege that made him intent upon putting distance between them. Should she not feel the same, given what she knew? Lieutenant Harrison could never guess that she had overheard his conversation, and she dared not tell him. And yet, in spite of the fear his words had stirred in her, she felt no anger toward him. Especially now that she knew he had never wanted to be a soldier. He was simply following orders. She could not blame him for that.

She bit back another sigh. Whether he wished to speak with her or not, there was no harm in offering him the meal.

Libby scooped the remainder of the pie onto a fresh plate, then crossed through the parlor and rapped on the door to his quarters. A beat of silence followed, then the shuffle of footsteps. The door eased open, the lieutenant's broad shoulders filling the frame.

Her gaze snagged on his clothing, and she blinked. Instead of his uniform, Lieutenant Harrison wore dark brown breeches with a white linen shirt and blue waistcoat. The civilian clothes softened him somehow, replacing the sharp distinction of his crimson coat with an altogether too appealing sense of familiarity. As though he weren't a British soldier but just a normal man. A man she could allow herself to care for without censure.

Silently banishing such thoughts, she forced her attention to the task at hand. "My mother is unwell and unable to partake in the evening meal. Would you like some?"

"I'm sorry to hear that." His dark brows drew together in concern. "Are you certain you don't want it for yourself?"

"'Tis more than I can eat on my own." She held out the plate, stifling the desire to invite him to join her in the kitchen to share the meal together. After how their walk today had ended, no doubt he'd decline. Or accept merely out of obligation, which might be worse. She mustered a smile. "Please, I'd like you to have it."

"Thank you." He took the offering with a dip of his head but said no more.

She made a swift retreat to the kitchen and sank into the chair beside Mama's uneaten serving. Bracing her elbows against the wooden table, she rested her forehead on her clasped hands.

"Father in Heaven, thank You for Your provision." The prayer was no more than a whisper, but it seemed magnified in the quiet room. "Please bring Mama relief from her suffering and allow her to rest well this night. Watch over our family and friends that have been parted from us. I ask that You protect them, and protect our town as well. And Lord..." She fell silent, afraid to speak the last of her plea aloud, though it echoed in her soul. *If there is to be a battle, please keep Will and Josiah far from it. And preserve Lieutenant Harrison through whatever may come.*

Lifting her head, she picked up the fork and cut a piece of the pie, her appetite squelched by the lonely emptiness of the kitchen and the whirling thoughts in her head. She peered out the open window. Though gray clouds still lingered, the rain had passed, leaving a cool freshness to sweep inside. If only the breeze could blow away all the uncertainties that plagued her as well.

A low cough sounded from behind, and she jumped.

"Forgive me. I did not mean to startle you." Lieutenant Harrison hesitated at the entrance of the kitchen, plate in hand. "I thought perhaps...that is, I wondered if I might join you?"

Libby blinked and pressed her lips together to keep her mouth from dropping open in surprise.

"I thought you might wish for some company, what with your mother ill, but if you'd prefer to be alone, I—"

"Of course you may." She pushed to her feet, anxious to reassure him before he changed his mind. "Please, sit. The company is most welcome."

His shoulders relaxed ever so slightly, and he settled into the chair across from her. "What troubles your mother?"

"One of those headaches she suffers from time to time."

"Is there anything she needs that I might be able to procure for you?"

"Thank you, but it will pass. Rest is the best remedy, so I will leave her to sleep for now and prepare some tea when she wakes."

He nodded and turned his attention to the meal. Libby did the same, as silence fell between them. She tried to focus on eating, hesitant to speak out of concern that she might once more prod too far and cause him to retreat as he did earlier today. But the quiet seemed an almost palpable weight, and everything in her strained to break it.

Glancing across the table, she found him watching her, and her mouthful of food caught in her throat. His gaze flicked away.

She reached for her cider and swallowed several large gulps to force the bite down. If this was how the entire meal would progress, 'twould have been better to eat alone. Perhaps if she addressed their previous conversation, they could be rid of this awkwardness between them.

Squaring her shoulders, she fixed her attention fully upon him. "I feel I owe you an apology, Lieutenant."

His gaze snapped to her. "Whatever for?"

"I suspect I upset you somehow, in our conversation earlier. I did not mean to pry into things that you had no wish to speak of, and for that, I am sorry."

He shook his head. "'Tis I who should apologize for departing so abruptly. I am...not so accustomed to speaking on personal matters. Too often around soldiers and too rarely around young women, I suppose." A grin surfaced, so briefly she almost missed it, but enough to stir a smile of her own. "In truth, I appreciate your openness, even if I struggle to match it."

"Well, you did say I remind you of my father in some ways, and I cannot deny that I inherited his curious disposition."

"Indeed. You've been that way since first I met you." He crossed his arms against the top of the table. "I recall one evening when I came to visit not long before my regiment was shipped out of Boston. Your father and I were discussing the violence that had occurred front of the State House, and you hid just outside the parlor to listen.

Heat crept up her face. "You saw me?"

"Your father and I both did." He chuckled, a low rumble that made the warmth of her cheeks blaze all the more. "I thought he might get up and send you off, stop you from eaves-dropping and spare you the harsh realities we were speaking of. But he didn't. Later, when I was leaving, he told me he would rather have you learn such things within the safety of your home, under his care, than be left faltering in the future."

Her eyes pricked at the memory. "I remember that night as well. Papa came to my chamber, and we sat on the edge of the bed talking until the candle guttered. He answered all my questions with patience and honesty. He said that the time might come when my convictions would be tested, and he wished me to have a firm foundation and confidence in what I believed. And"— her voice quivered as she pictured her father's beloved face, his steady arm wrapped around her shoulders— "he said I never needed to hide in the shadows, but instead to come to him with every question or problem, because he loved me and would always seek the best for me. Just like my Heavenly Father did in an immeasurably greater way."

Libby ducked her chin to cover the tears welling in her eyes. Oh how she missed him. Missed his wisdom. His voice. His embrace that felt like a safe shelter no storm could breach. How right he had been to warn that her convictions would one day be tested, but could he have guessed his own death would be the cause? Some days, 'twas difficult to understand God as the loving Heavenly Father that Papa had always spoken of. Had she been hiding in the shadows now, afraid to bring her most difficult questions to the Lord? Afraid, perhaps, of His answer?

"What a treasure to have such a man for your father." Lieutenant Harrison's gentle voice drew her head back up to meet the compassion in his gaze.

He reached across the table and covered her hand with his own. The touch lasted only a moment, a reassuring squeeze before he released her again, but comfort settled deep in her chest. The lieutenant's words about his own family came to mind. He'd never had the kind of closeness with his parents that she shared with hers. Painful as it had been to lose Papa, the depth of her grief testified to how precious their relationship was, and she would rather bear that sorrow than have never known such fatherly love.

"Aye." She pushed the bittersweet thoughts back with a teasing smile. "But if you are going to recount my embarrassing moment, it only seems fair that I recall one of yours."

The tilt of his mouth dared her to continue.

"Do you recall the day you walked into my father's office, not knowing he was in the middle of extracting a woman's tooth? I don't know that I've ever seen someone's face such an odd shade as yours turned."

A sheepish smile flashed, as color crept up his neck. "'Twas a shocking sight."

"Indeed. I thought you might faint away right there in our parlor. I was preparing myself to break your fall if necessary."

He laughed. "You? Catch me?"

"Admittedly, 'twas not a well-thought-out plan. More of an emergency rescue attempt."

"I do not know what surprised me more, the procedure itself, or the fact that you were there, holding the woman's hand, as though it did not trouble you in the least."

"I confess, the grip she had on my fingers did trouble me somewhat, but I knew my presence would help calm her, so..." Libby shrugged. She'd done nothing especially grand or praiseworthy that day, but the approval shining in Lieutenant Harrison's dark eyes made her heart beat faster.

"Well, I learned my lesson and never made the mistake of entering your father's office again."

She searched his face, a question brewing that she hesitated to ask.

"You've something more to say." He raised his brows, waiting.

Could he read her so well? "Perhaps I'd better not. I don't wish to pry again—"

"Please, go on."

"I wondered how you could be so uncomfortable at witnessing an extraction when you were...are...a soldier who could face all manner of..." She fell silent, afraid to finish her thought aloud.

He leaned back in his chair, expression sobering. "I've never been at risk of fainting on the battlefield, if that is what you mean. I do what I must in the moment, but some things linger that I wish I could erase."

"You have nightmares, don't you?"

He frowned, and she wished she could take the words back. But then he dipped his head in acknowledgment. "I wondered if you had heard me."

"Only once. That morning, not a fortnight ago."

"I'm sorry if I frightened you."

"Nay. I only wished I could help."

"Thank you. Your kindness is…"—his voice grew thick, and he paused to clear his throat— "truly appreciated, Miss Caldwell."

Quiet lingered between them again, not uncomfortable this time but settled somehow, as though it drew them together rather than pushed them apart. A rather risky thought for her heart to grab hold of, especially as they sat alone in the growing darkness.

Lieutenant Harrison stood, his chair scraping on the floorboards. "I'd best retire. Thank you for the meal, and the time reminiscing."

She stood as well. "'Tis always a pleasure to revisit old memories."

"Aye." He pushed in his seat, hands resting atop the wooden back. "I was such a frequent presence in your home while my regiment was stationed in Boston, 'tis a wonder you didn't think me a nuisance."

"Of course not. I enjoyed your company."

"I suppose I was rather like a temporary older brother."

"I never thought of you that way." The confession slipped out before she could stop it, barely more than a whisper. She caught her breath. Mayhap he hadn't heard.

But his eyes widened, and his gaze held hers for the span of several heartbeats. His grip tightened on the chair. She looked away.

Had she upset him again? If only she could learn to better control her tongue. Risking a glance his way, she found him studying her, an expression on his face she'd never seen before. Not anger or discomfort as she'd feared, but a sort of curiosity and thoughtfulness, as though he were lost in the pages of a story he couldn't quite understand. Her pulse stuttered. Was it just the evening shadows that put such softness in his eyes?

He blinked, and it was gone, as quickly as a pair of shutters blocking out the sunlight. In its place was the familiar stoic facade.

Clearing his throat, he backed away. "Again, my thanks for the food, and I hope your mother recovers quickly." His words were sincere, but his voice lacked the comfortable tone they'd shared moments before. "I bid you good evening, Miss Caldwell."

She forced a smile and bobbed her head. "Good night."

Sagging against the edge of the table, she watched him leave. Heaviness seeped through her heart and her limbs. Would she never learn? She had to stop grasping at hope, for it sifted through her fingers like the sand at the ocean's edge. The shared conversations, smiles, even laughter, did not mean to Lieutenant Harrison what they meant to her. And they never would.

CHAPTER 9

The familiar beat of the company drummer summoning the men to water and wood detachments rolled across the Common as Isaac dismissed the last of his soldiers from inspection on Thursday. The late-afternoon sun was warmer than recent days, evidenced by the smell of sweat that permeated the grenadiers after they finished their drills. He'd not be surprised if many of them sought the cool waters of the Charles to bathe tonight.

He'd worked the men hard with the firelock in the morning, then focused on marching and maneuvering drills after the midday meal. Their planned attack on the Dorchester Heights grew nearer every day, and he was intent upon ensuring the men under his leadership were in top form.

Glancing toward the river, he swiped a hand over his own damp brow. There were strict rules regarding bathing hours, before seven in the morning or after six in the evening. Perhaps he would linger at the camp later than usual. Go over the strategy for Sunday with Captain Merrick once more. Share a meal with his fellow officers. Take a dip in the brackish water. Return to his quarters after dark.

Avoid an encounter with Miss Caldwell.

He trudged past the rows of tents, heading for the southern end of the encampment where Merrick stayed. Miss Caldwell had occupied far too many of his thoughts of late, ever since he'd sat across from her at the kitchen table on Tuesday evening. A foolish decision on his part to join her, but she had looked so lonely, and his conscience couldn't bear it. Or was it he who was lonely, and anxious for her company? Hoping the warmth of her smile might push aside the harshness of reality for a few precious minutes?

And indeed, it had. Their conversation and shared memories, the teasing glint in her blue eyes, the sweetness of her voice...he'd enjoyed it far too much. Allowed himself to forget who he was for a moment. Forget who she was.

He swatted at a pesky fly circling about his head, but the truth nagging his spirit could not be shooed away so easily. His feelings for her had shifted. Begun to deepen in a way he could not allow them to.

The last drumbeat faded, and he paused to watch the movement around camp. Orderly and purposeful. Every man knew his place and his duty. And those who fell out of line? Isaac grimaced, recalling the treatment of deserters and troublemakers he'd witnessed on more than one occasion. The lashings turned his stomach, and the execution of a deserter he'd been forced to watch last September had haunted his dreams for weeks.

This was the world he belonged to, a world at odds with the one Miss Caldwell hoped for. Friendship or not, they stood on opposite sides of this conflict, and they would both do well to remember it. Even if those stark differences could somehow be overcome, he was betrothed to Miss Bradbury. While not of his desire or choosing, he couldn't dishonor the commitment his father had made.

The insect returned, its buzzing as incessant as a fifer's trill.

Desperate for blood, the little beast. For a patch of unprotected skin. Thankfully, Isaac's wool uniform left little exposed. If only his emotions were equally impenetrable.

"Good, you're still here." Sergeant Jackson's voice called from behind Isaac, and he stiffened. Jackson sidled up next to him. "I've been meaning to talk to you."

Isaac glanced down, regretting his decision to stay longer at camp. "What is it?"

"Stanton's been quite helpful tracking down more leads." The sergeant slapped a hand against the haversack draped over his shoulder. "I could still use another man, though, and was hoping you might consider—"

"Not now. You know as well as I the plans for Sunday. Keep that your focus. Surely, your spy business can wait a few days."

"*My* spy business?" Jackson scowled. "You act as if this is some whim I'm chasing. Don't you realize how significant my work is? Have you even considered that the very mission you insist I focus upon could be at risk as we speak thanks to Lawrence and his web of conspirators?"

Isaac suppressed a sigh. The man was already on the defensive, so it would do no good to argue. "I recognize the importance, but I cannot spare another soldier at the moment. I want their attention to be undivided—at least until this attack is carried out."

A charged silence met him. Better that than a string of curses. Jackson might not like his reply, but he would follow orders.

"I saw that girl you live with." A hint of derision crept into Jackson's tone. "She was walking alone on Winter Street. I'm surprised you're not with her. Perhaps I should go keep her company instead."

Heat shot through Isaac's veins. Was Jackson goading him as retaliation for Isaac's refusal to grant his request, or had he really seen Miss Caldwell? He spun around to search that direction but saw nothing. "What are you talking about?"

"I was just passing by and spotted her. Almost forgot what a pretty little thing she is." A sneer curled the sergeant's lips. "I rather think I'd enjoy a long stroll with her on my arm. Find a quiet, secluded corner. Plenty of those now that—"

"Enough." Isaac clenched his jaw. Whether Jackson was telling the truth or sending him on a pointless chase, concern for Miss Caldwell's safety was of much greater importance than his own pride. He stalked away, Jackson's jeering laughter fading behind the pounding of his heart.

With swift strides, he left the grassy landscape and ducked onto Winter Street, scanning the row of houses and buildings that lined the road. There. His attention caught on a familiar figure, standing outside the open door of a narrow clapboard house. Her flat-brimmed hat hid most of her face in shadows, but he could still make out enough of her profile to be certain it was indeed Miss Caldwell. A man leaned against the doorframe, attention fixed on her, gesturing with one hand as though deep in conversation. Isaac was too far to hear them, but the interaction seemed amicable.

Who was this man, and why was Miss Caldwell alone with him? Could he possibly be a suitor that Isaac hadn't known about? A strange twinge of jealousy churned in his gut. He shook it off as he slowed his pace, tucking himself into a dim passage between two buildings. They'd not noticed him. He could observe from a distance to be certain she came to no harm.

Miss Caldwell shifted closer, nodding at something the man said. Suddenly, the stranger pitched forward, one hand shooting out to grab her arm. Isaac's breath caught as the man yanked back, pulling Miss Caldwell toward the open door. She stumbled, then tried to brace herself, but the man didn't let go.

Isaac dashed out of his hiding spot and broke into a run. "Miss Caldwell!"

She and the man both spun to face him just as Isaac pushed himself between them, shoving the stranger's arm aside and forming a protective barrier in front of Miss Caldwell. The man tripped backward, lost his footing, and crashed to the ground.

Miss Caldwell gasped. Stepping around Isaac, she crouched beside the stranger. "Mr. Gerrish, are you hurt?"

The man hissed out a breath through clenched teeth. "I'll be fine, miss. Apologies if I startled you."

"Not at all." She helped him to his feet, then aimed an accusing glare at Isaac. "Lieutenant Harrison, whatever are you doing?"

"I saw you alone and,"—he glanced at the man, who sagged against the house, watching him warily— "I wanted to ensure all was well."

"Surely, you could have done so with less force."

He'd come to her rescue and she was...upset?

Only then did Isaac notice that the man's left foot hovered inches above the ground, wrapped in bandages, clearly unable to bear any weight. Had he grasped Miss Caldwell, not with some ill intent but to keep himself from falling? Had she been trying to help, only for Isaac to sweep in and throw the man to the ground? Heat climbed his neck.

Mr. Gerrish's eyes narrowed at Isaac. "And who do you be to keep watch on this woman's comins' and goins'?" He pressed his lips together as he inched closer, sunlight catching on his rust-colored hair that hung loose around his gaunt cheeks. "Like as not, I should be protectin' her from you."

Isaac gritted his teeth at the insinuation. "I would never—"

"No need to fear on either account." Miss Caldwell broke in with a placating tone. She looked to Mr. Gerrish first. "I have known Lieutenant Harrison for years and am in no danger with him." Her gaze traveled to meet his own. "Nor am I at risk here.

I'm simply delivering some mending I completed at Mrs. Barker's shop today." She held out a folded bundle that had been tucked under her arm. "Please forgive the trouble, Mr. Gerrish. Mrs. Barker said you'd already settled the payment."

"Aye, miss." The man accepted the gray waistcoat from her outstretched hands. "These be hard days without me wife and youngins'. Yer kindness is appreciated."

"You are very welcome. I hope you can be reunited with your family soon. I will pray for your swift healing." The gentle smile she aimed at the man only increased Isaac's remorse.

She glanced back at him, expression fading into a look he couldn't quite decipher. Disappointment? Reproach? His stomach clenched.

"Are you returning to your quarters?" Her tone lacked its typical warmth.

Your quarters. Not *home*, like she usually said. Was she ashamed of their arrangement? Of him? Embarrassed to be associated with a soldier who leaped to wrong conclusions and toppled a man on the steps of his own house?

He nodded. Despite his misguided reaction to Mr. Gerrish, he still did not like the idea of Miss Caldwell traveling home alone.

"Then we can walk together." Her words were clipped. She bobbed a curtsy to Mr. Gerrish and set off down the street.

He followed, his long strides helping match her swift pace. She said nothing, attention fixed ahead, arms stiff at her sides. A gaping chasm seemed to stretch between them—the kind of separation he'd told himself he needed, but now it pierced as sharply as a bayonet blade.

They turned onto Marlbrough Street, and she stopped short, rounding on him, eyes blazing. "What were you thinking?"

A flash of frustration burned inside. Annoyance at Jackson for provoking him. Annoyance at himself for allowing his emotions to distract from making better decisions. Annoyance at her for being so upset with him when all he cared about was her good. "I was thinking you were in danger. One of the soldiers saw you walking alone, and—"

"I was simply doing my job. Something I am quite capable of on my own." She jammed her fists on her hips. "You should be grateful Mr. Gerrish didn't re-injure his foot the way you came crashing into him."

"And how was I to know? It looked as though you were about to be dragged into a stranger's house." Defensiveness edged his words. "Either that or accosted by a man you were secretly seeing."

Her mouth dropped open. "How dare you suggest such a thing? Surely, you know me better."

Did he? He'd never seen this side of her, certainly. The fiery temper that lashed out at him. And yet, was he not doing the same? Accusing and shifting blame, just to ease his own bruised conscience?

"You're right, my actions were...excessive." His shoulders sagged. "But they were born out of fear for your safety, and for that I cannot apologize."

"'Tis not your duty to protect me."

"'Duty'?" He spat out the word that had haunted him all his life. "That is not why I am concerned for your wellbeing."

He stared at her, watching the fight seep out of her expression and be replaced with something so vulnerable, he hardly dared to breathe. Hope. Tentative and raw and far more terrifying than her anger.

"Why, then?" Her voice was soft, almost fragile.

The question burrowed deep within him, stirring up answers that he could hardly comprehend and certainly could not speak. Not aloud. Not to her. Feelings and reasons that must stay buried, for both their sakes.

He swallowed against the strange tightness in his throat.

"Your father was the closest friend I've ever had, and your family means a great deal to me. I only want what is best for you, Miss Caldwell."

Like a candle beneath the smothering weight of a stopper, the light in her eyes flickered and went out. Her lips parted on a shaky inhale. She pressed them together and nodded. "I appreciate your concern and will try to take better care in the future. Good day, Lieutenant."

She whirled away and hurried home, not waiting for him to follow. He watched, unmoving, until she reached her house and ducked inside. She never looked back. He hung his head, hating the emptiness that settled in his chest.

Best return to the Common, after all. Perhaps he could even stay with Merrick tonight. And after Sunday, no matter what came of their attempt to break out of the city, he would leave the Caldwells' house for good.

~

Hot tears burned in Libby's eyes, blurring her vision. Clutching her petticoat, she ran up the stairs, heedless of the front door slamming behind her and of Mama's voice calling out in concern. She burst into her bedchamber as the first tears escaped, trailing down her cheeks.

What had come over her, arguing with Lieutenant Harrison like that? She'd spilled her emotions everywhere like a sack of flour split open. There had been so much pent up within her the past sennight. So much she had to hold inside and carry alone. Her secret encounter with Elijah, the overheard plans for the army's attack, her feelings for Isaac...

Isaac. That was how she thought of him in her heart. Not as a British lieutenant but simply a man. An honorable and admirable man whom she called friend. Whom she...loved.

Sinking onto the edge of her bed, she pressed a hand over her mouth to hold back a rising sob. She loved him. Try as she might not to, she did. More deeply now than the girlish infatuation she'd felt years ago. More sincerely than she had even last summer when he returned to Boston and stepped back into her life.

Perhaps that was why she'd been so upset today. Because when he'd stormed in and pushed Mr. Gerrish aside, she had, for the first time, truly seen him as a soldier. The ferocity in his expression, the glint of the sun against the buttons lining his crimson uniform, the broad white strap that held his pistol in place. And in that moment, she finally knew how impossible her hopes for any future with him were.

Mama's soft footfalls from the doorway drew her head up. "Oh, Libby." Her mother settled onto the mattress and wrapped an arm around her shoulders. "Tell me what happened. What is wrong?"

"So many things." Her voice quivered.

"The Lord's hands are strong enough to carry any burden you lay before Him." Mama squeezed her arm. "And my hands are right here to hold you as best I can."

Swiping at her damp cheeks, Libby rested her head against her mother's shoulder. "I've much to tell you, and I hope you'll forgive me for not speaking of it sooner."

Mama's patient silence urged Libby on. She told her everything, from Elijah's shocking return and his petition that she keep such news a secret, to the plans she'd accidentally eavesdropped upon and the letters hidden for Elijah to find. Then she hesitated, for despite the significance of all she'd already spoken of, the hardest piece to reveal was that of her own heart.

"Those are heavy cares to bear on your own." Mama's voice was gentle, if a bit weary. "'Tis no wonder you are overwhelmed."

"I nearly told you on Tuesday, but then you were ill and…"

Libby straightened, shifting to meet her mother's gaze. "I felt as though I were breaking confidence no matter what I did. If I kept it all to myself, I was deceiving you. But by telling you, I have gone against Elijah's wishes and shared the army's plans that are surely meant to be a secret." She curled her fingers into the linen fabric of her apron, still uncertain if she'd done the right thing.

"Sometimes, we are forced to make difficult decisions because our own actions lead us to that point. Other times, such decisions are foisted upon us by things outside our control. Meeting Elijah as you did and overhearing the lieutenant's conversation seem to me more the latter. However"—Mama's brows pinched, and lines furrowed around her mouth — "you did make some choices that have complicated matters."

Libby dipped her chin.

"You entangled yourself further by staying to listen to the entirety of Lieutenant Harrison's discussion, and even more so by passing that information on to Elijah. I pray no one discovers you were the source, for that could be dangerous, indeed."

The gravity of her mother's voice made Libby's heart sink. Why hadn't she considered her actions more carefully?

"Although, truth be told, I may have done the same thing."

"You would?" Libby snapped her head up.

Mama reached over and wrapped her hand around Libby's. "Aside from God, there is nothing more important to me than my family. I would go to many lengths to ensure your wellbeing, and that of Patience and William, so far as it is in my power. Let us pray that God uses your actions for their good, and your own, and that no harm comes of this. But, Elizabeth, I beg you take care in the coming days. These are matters beyond our control. 'Tis better for us to remain in our place than try to interfere. We must trust that God's will shall be done, no matter the outcome."

Libby bit her lip. Mama's council was wise, yet she could not shake the desire to do something. To take action. To help. To make a difference, instead of sitting and waiting for whatever may happen.

She had watched others step out in defense of their beliefs and for the sake of their loved ones. Will and Josiah, who had thrown the tea in the harbor. Or Patience, who warned Josiah when he was in danger and left her home behind to be with him. Hannah kept the apothecary running to protect her father when he was unable to do so on his own. And Will had helped Mr. Pierce escape Boston after he was wrongfully arrested. If they could all make an impact in some way, why not her as well?

"There's something else, isn't there?" Mama's voice broke in, all too perceptive.

She tucked her protests away, thoughts shifting back to Isaac. There was indeed something else, but did she have the courage to admit it? "'Tis Lieutenant Harrison. I..." The words stuck in her throat.

"You care for him."

Libby sucked in a breath. "How did you know?"

"I'm your mother. I know you nearly as well as I know myself. And though it may be hard to imagine, I was a young woman once too. I remember the signs well enough." Mama punctuated her teasing remark with a soft laugh.

Libby matched it with her own.

"I've been waiting, hoping you would confide in me, though I did not wish to pry."

"I thought to do so many times, and yet..." Libby sighed. "I was afraid you would disapprove. Or try to convince me of what a foolish notion it was, when all I wanted was to stubbornly cling to hope."

Mama smiled, but sadness shadowed her eyes. "Lieutenant Harrison is a good man. Your father respected him greatly and considered him a true friend, despite their differences. I do not disapprove, nor think you foolish for harboring feelings for him."

"But?"

"I fear the obstacles to a future between you and the lieutenant are too great to overcome."

There was an ache in Mama's voice that echoed the one in Libby's chest. 'Twas the same thought she'd had time and again, but to hear her mother confirm it aloud brought a true sense of finality. Tears pricked again, and Libby blinked swiftly to hold them at bay.

Mama's own eyes grew damp. "I remember the first time I held you as though it were yesterday. Red faced and wailing, you quieted the moment the midwife placed you on my chest, right against my heart. I wanted to hold you there forever, and shelter you from the hurts of this world." She raised a hand to Libby's cheek, brushing aside a wayward curl. "Of course I couldn't. Not then and not now. But oh how I wish I could spare you this heartache, my precious daughter."

Libby's tears spilled out again as her mother pulled her into a tight embrace. Mama's shoulders shuddered. How much pain she had endured, losing the man she loved and shared a life with for six-and-twenty years—a grief that dwarfed Libby's own disappointment. If Mama had found the strength to carry on after Papa's death, surely, Libby could too. She had to let go of the love she held for Isaac. A love that would never be reciprocated, and a life that could never be shared.

CHAPTER 10

Isaac stared over the Charles River in the growing light of dawn on Saturday, his heart sinking at what he beheld atop the heights of the Charlestown peninsula. From his perch on Copp's Hill at the northernmost tip of Boston, the clear skies afforded an unobstructed view of the band of militiamen at work across the water. They'd raised a redoubt on Breed's Hill, and from the look of things, they must have been building through the night to have so much of the defensive fort already in place.

Beside him, Captain Merrick crossed his arms, attention fixed on the same spot. "This certainly spoils our plan to attack the Dorchester Heights tomorrow."

Isaac nodded. The colonists had forced their hand. Now 'twas imperative that the British troops turn their attention to Charlestown instead, and they dare not wait long.

"Those rebels must have gotten word of our strategy somehow." Merrick slid him a glance. "Mayhap through that spy Sergeant Jackson always complains about?"

"Perhaps." He frowned, remembering Jackson's words two days prior. The sergeant's fixation on the notorious James

Lawrence had been a thorn in Isaac's side far too long, but what if he was right? Could Lawrence be responsible for learning the army's plans and communicating them to the colonial forces?

"Whatever the source of the leak, the response remains the same. We must face them and cut off their attempt to control the high ground. The sooner the better, I say."

"You said General Gage and the other generals are in council this morning?" Isaac glanced at his captain, and Merrick nodded. "I suspect we'll know the new plans before too long, then."

"Aye." Merrick lowered his voice. "Let us hope they feel the same urgency as you and I do."

Peering back over the water, Isaac grimaced, for while he recognized the need for a quick and decisive response, he dreaded what such action would require.

An explosion rent the air, echoing from the wide river that stretched before them and opened into the harbor. Another cannon boom followed, puffs of smoke rising from the guns lining the broadside of the *HMS Lively*. He snapped his attention to the colonial redoubt. Debris flung into the air upon impact, but as far as he could see, the men kept working, undeterred.

"Ranging rounds." Merrick crossed his arms as the guns of the *Lively* fell silent. "To set the powder charge and elevation for the target."

Not a full bombardment yet, though that was sure to come. The frigate *Lively* was equipped with twenty guns, the nearby sloop *Falcon* with fourteen, and farther off in the harbor, the command ship *Somerset* held sixty-four. Isaac eyed the twenty-four pounders lining the battery on Copp's Hill. 'Twas impossible that the militia had anywhere near the firepower to match their own, but they held the advantageous position atop the hill when it came to a battle on the ground. And an attack on foot would be necessary to clear them from their position.

Isaac clenched his jaw. How much bloodshed awaited them this day?

They watched together in silence for some time, until Merrick was summoned to receive the new orders for the day.

"Meet me back at the Common." Merrick clapped a hand on Isaac's shoulder. "I've no doubt we'll win the day. Those men are farmers and laborers. While they may have the skills to dig and pile an earthen barrier, they don't have the guns, nor training to defend such a position."

"Agreed, and yet I dare not underestimate them. We've seen how industrious and determined they are. How passionate for their cause. I do not expect they'll simply turn and run in the face of our assault."

"Nor I. There will be a fight, to be sure, but they cannot match us. Their troops are haphazardly thrown together, and they lack both leadership and supplies. I am confident. You should be as well."

As Captain Merrick departed, Isaac made his way down the hill, weaving around the stone markers of the burying ground. His skin prickled. Death seemed almost peaceful here, with grass softening the landscape and tall trees casting protective shadows over the graves. But how different death looked when it sought a man on the field of battle. Harsh and merciless. Sometimes as quick as the flash of a musket, other times agonizingly slow. If he was to meet his end in the midst of fighting, he prayed God would grant him the former.

Pausing before one arched gray slab, he frowned at the musket ball holes that marred the surface. *Daniel Malcom, true Son of Liberty,* the epitaph read. Isaac had heard of several British soldiers who used the man's grave as target practice but had hoped such rumors were false. 'Twas one thing to take to the field of battle out of duty, honor, and allegiance. 'Twas another to act out of spite. He rubbed his thumb over one of the largest markings, as though he could smooth it away, then let his hand fall to his side.

He did not lack confidence in the success of their mission, but he did despise what would come as a result. Both for his fellow soldiers, and for those he'd watched across the river.

Would the men of his regiment think him weak if they knew how deeply the deaths on both sides of the fight affected him? Or did they carry the same hidden scars? It would never feel natural to him to take up arms against another man. To march close enough to see their faces and pull the trigger.

He could stand strong for that which he had sworn to defend. He had done it before and would do it again today. But he could not harden himself to the point of viewing those across the battlefield solely as enemies. Nor did he wish to, for he feared the kind of man he would become if he allowed such cold detachment to seep into his soul.

Instead, he must brace himself for the fresh wounds that were to come, whether the physical ones that could be seen, or the invisible ones that festered far deeper inside.

~

Isaac's footsteps slowed as he approached the Caldwells' home. There was little time before he had to assemble with the other troops to parade to Long Wharf and board the barges there, but this had to be done first. He must bid the women farewell, in case the worst should happen. And seek Miss Caldwell's forgiveness, for he could not bear the thought of their last interaction being one of strife.

The companies had received their orders. Per General Howe's proposal, one thousand five hundred troops were to be ferried across the river to the Charlestown Peninsula. Once there, the grenadiers would advance toward the front of Breed's Hill, seeking to occupy the defenders in the redoubt, while the light infantry were dispatched to attack from the rear. Gage had instructed them to wait for high tide to set out, and until then, the ships would maintain intermittent fire, with a full bombardment set for just after noon in hopes of clearing the way for their arrival. It was a sound plan, a strategic one, and they held the advantage in many ways. But that did not mean they would leave this day unscathed.

He hesitated in front of the house, taking in the familiar riven siding, weathered by years and seasons, the double-hung windows, and the pair of brick chimneys. All symmetrical, save for the room that jutted out from the back of the house. His quarters for nearly ten months. Connected to the home, but not part of the original structure. An addition that didn't quite belong.

Like himself.

A sense of finality settled heavy on his shoulders. How many times had he walked this road? Crossed that threshold and been greeted as a friend? Might this be the last?

Even if he did return from the battle, how could he ask the women to accept him under their roof again? This was not like Lexington and Concord — a mission to confiscate military supplies gone awry. No. Unless the colonial forces willingly abandoned their post, this would be a battle. Surely, the women's clemency toward him would be exhausted if he came back with the blood of their countrymen on his hands.

He would not put them in such a terrible position. If he was still standing at the end of the day, he would hold to the decision he'd made after his argument with Miss Caldwell and depart his quarters in their home for good.

Squaring his shoulders, he rapped on the door. Moments later, it swung open, revealing Mrs. Abbott's gentle smile.

"Lieutenant Harrison. We'd not seen you in a couple days and began to wonder..." Her voice trailed off as her gaze swept over him, from the tall bear fur hat he wore, to the brass match case strapped to his shoulder belt and the sword hanging at his left side. Her expression fell. "What happened?"

He swept off his hat, a feeble attempt to diminish the appearance of his full accoutrement for battle. "May I come in?"

"Of course." She pulled the door wide, ushering him inside.

"Is Miss Caldwell here? I'd like to speak with both of you."

"In the kitchen." Mrs. Abbott led the way, her furrowed brow hinting at questions she left unsaid.

The scent of woodsmoke and hoecakes greeted him as he stepped into the room, along with a rush of memories he dared not dwell on. He must remain focused on his purpose. Miss Caldwell bent over the hearth, apron wrapped around one hand as she flipped the hoecake in the pan. Her golden curls were more unruly than usual today, with several escaped to frame her face and trail down the back of her neck.

She looked up, and her eyes widened. "Lieutenant, I did not realize you were here."

He dug his fingers into the edge of his hat. He'd best get this over with, for the longer he lingered, the harder it would be to carry it out. "I wish to apologize. My behavior on Thursday was rash and unwarranted. I did not mean to upset you and beg your forgiveness."

"Of course you are forgiven. And I..." She dipped her head, but not before he saw the color filling her cheeks, as deep as the rose-colored day gown she wore. "I must also apologize for overreacting as I did. I know you meant well."

He nodded, one weight lifting off his shoulders. But the next words would be even more difficult. He turned to include both women. "I also came because my regiment is to be dispatched within the half hour."

Miss Caldwell sucked in a breath. "What do you mean? Where are you going?"

"We've been ordered to advance upon the militia who have

occupied Breed's Hill." He would give no more details than necessary, but the entire town would know soon enough what was happening.

Mrs. Abbott pressed a hand to her chest, face ashen. "There's to be a battle?"

"Unless the colonial forces retreat upon our arrival, it seems unavoidable."

Miss Caldwell stepped closer. "You're leaving? Now?"

"I must." He tugged his gaze away from her to encompass her mother as well. "I wish to thank you both for the kindness you've shown me all these months, and years ago. I cannot express what your generosity has meant. Whatever happens today, I have always and will always cherish your friendship. I wish only the best for you and—"

Mrs. Abbott's soft touch on his arm stilled his carefully practiced words. "Lieutenant Harrison, may I pray for you before you go?"

Pray? She wished to pray for him? When he was about to march out against her fellow citizens? Even his own parents had not prayed over him when they sent him away. Did they ever pray for him now?

He couldn't manage any words past the tightness in his throat, so he simply bowed his head.

"Lord, we pray for peace. We entreat You, that You would stretch out Your mighty hand and bring resolution without fighting. We ask that You spare us from bloodshed. But if not..."

But if not.

Those three words lodged in Isaac's heart as scenes from April flashed across his mind. The flames and cries rising from the town of Menotomy as the soldiers left a wake of destruction in their path. The harrowing march back from Concord, never knowing when gunfire might rain down upon them from militiamen hidden along the road. The heat of his own musket as he fired in defense. The acrid, smoky scent of gunpowder mixing with the metallic smell of blood. He clenched his jaw, willing the memories away.

"Even still, we trust You. We believe Your promises are true, that You will never leave us nor forsake us." Quiet confidence filled Mrs. Abbott's words. Would that the same confidence could find its footing in his soul. "Be with those we love this day. Watch over William and Josiah and Lieutenant Harrison."

His breath trapped in his chest. Those we love included... him? It seemed impossible. But before that idea could take root, the other names she'd spoken churned in his gut. William and Josiah. How had he not considered that the men connected to the Caldwell family might be on the other side of the river even now? What would he do if he came face to face with one of them?

Her steady prayer continued, breaking through his tumultuous thoughts. "We plead for their safe return, even as we entrust them to You, knowing their days were written in Your book before one of them came to pass. We ask all this in the name of Your Son, whose death gives us life, amen."

He lifted his head and his gaze collided with Miss Caldwell's, her blue eyes damp. The prayer had already chipped away at his resolve, and her tears were nearly his undoing. He had to finish this and leave as quickly as possible.

He turned his attention to Mrs. Abbott, clearing his throat, though he couldn't rid the thickness from his voice. "Thank you." It wasn't nearly enough, but he hoped she understood. "I...I bid you both farewell."

Shoving his hat atop his head, he turned away before they could speak again and escaped out the door. He fisted his hands at his sides, feet pounding on the road as he fled, desperate to put as much space as possible between himself and the tangle of emotions the visit had stirred within him. Why did he feel no relief, no closure, from that goodbye?

"Lieutenant Harrison, wait!" Miss Caldwell's voice called after him.

He froze and turned to see her dashing down the street.

She came to a halt inches away. "Will may be out there. Josiah too. If you see them, please don't..." Her voice quivered, eyes pleading through the silence of the words she left unspoken.

Please don't hurt them. Please don't kill them. Her thoughts had traveled the same dark path as his own. Isaac swallowed against the bile rising in his throat. What promise could he give? He would recognize her stepbrother, but he'd never met the man married to her stepsister. And who could say what would happen in the frenzy of battle?

"I pray they are not there." It was the best hope he could offer.

"As do I."

Quiet hovered between them, as laden and near to bursting as a storm cloud. Her voice dropped to a whisper. "Please be careful. I cannot bear to think of something happening to you."

He could give no assurance of his own safety but couldn't keep from offering something in response to her pleading tone. "I will try."

She held his gaze a long moment, searching his face, as though cataloging every detail. His breath grew shallow under her scrutiny. What did she see when she looked at him? The soldier who had disappointed her, or the man she had asked to call friend? Did it really matter, when he had decided not to stay, even if he got out of the battle unscathed?

He tugged at the hem of his coat. Time was growing short, he couldn't delay any longer. "I am sorry, Miss Caldwell, but I really must—"

She closed the scant distance between them and threw her arms around him in a tight embrace.

His whole body stiffened in shock. Though he had seen

fragility in her face, heard it in her choked voice, she hugged him with surprising strength and ferocity, as though she was trying to protect him from what he was about to face. Yet there was undeniable softness, too, in the curves of her feminine form and the brush of her hair beneath his chin. Heat blazed through him, and with it an unquenchable longing to hold her in return.

He couldn't. Shouldn't. But oh how he wanted to cling to one final comfort before he stepped onto the field of battle.

A desperate sort of need stirred within him. Pushing all other arguments aside, he wove his arms around her waist and gave in to the tenderness of her farewell. She relaxed against him, resting her cheek on his chest, as if she had offered him every bit of her strength and now needed his in return.

When was the last time anyone had shown him such affection? He could not recall. His own mother had only offered a perfunctory peck on his cheek when he left home. His father had sent him off with even less—a stern nod and a reminder to serve the Crown and the Harrison name honorably.

This was infinitely different, this feeling that someone truly cared for him. Was it possible that Miss Caldwell, who had every reason to distance herself from him, had chosen to draw close instead? He should be the enemy in her eyes, and yet she held onto him as though afraid to let go. As though his life mattered to her as much as the lives of the family she loved. Could it be?

She fit so perfectly tucked against him. How had the girl he'd known years ago grown into the woman he held in his arms? It seemed the most natural thing in the world...and the most dangerous.

A warning drummed in his head, a caution, but he dismissed its orders and basked in her embrace. His eyes slid closed, his senses lost in the feel of her. In the rosewater smell that clung to her hair and her warmth that felt like the last ray of sunshine in the sky. He pressed one hand to the small of her back. His other hand traced upward, edging temptingly close to the bare skin at the nape of her neck and the curls resting there. What would it feel like to bury his fingers in her hair? To tip her head back and taste her lips...

She trembled beneath his grasp. His eyes shot open, and he yanked his hands away, breaking out of their embrace. What was he thinking? She had come to send him off, and what had he done in return? Nearly lost his head and taken advantage of her.

Gritting his teeth, Isaac stepped backward, forcing much-needed space between them.

Miss Caldwell stared up at him, questions pooling in her tear-rimmed eyes, her chest rising and falling with rapid breaths.

He swallowed, his words sticking in his throat. What could he say? That she'd shown him more tenderness in that moment than he'd felt in years? That her presence somehow bolstered his courage and terrified him all at once? Should he beg her forgiveness for holding her as he had? No, he couldn't do that, not when the memory of her arms around him was seared into his heart forever.

"Come home safely. Please." Her bottom lip quivered, but she squared her shoulders and held his gaze. "God be with you, Isaac."

Isaac. His pulse tripped.

He cleared his throat, but the words still came out husky. "Goodbye, Miss Caldwell."

CHAPTER 11

*L*ibby grasped the wooden frame of the open window, wincing as another round of explosions split the air. Would the ships in the Charles and the cannons in the battery never stop? Their constant barrage seemed to shake the very foundations of Mrs. Barker's house at the north end of Boston, where Mama had consented to take her to watch the battle unfold.

After Lieutenant Harrison's departure, Libby had paced their kitchen for nearly an hour, fear over what was to come driving her. And while Mama had expressed concern that seeing the fight would only make things worse, Libby was convinced it would be better to have some knowledge of what was happening than to wait in uncertainty.

She glanced over her shoulder, where her mother and Mrs. Barker sat at a small table in the opposite corner of the room. Their heads were bowed, hands clasped together. Libby worried her lip. Had she been wrong to beg Mama to bring her here, or might the two friends find comfort in each other's presence and shared prayers?

Turning back to the window, she braced herself for the next

blast. But none came. An eerie silence fell. She leaned farther out, spotting others like herself peering from windows of nearby homes, while some perched atop their roofs for a better view. The sun was high now, the air thick with warm humidity and the lingering smell of gunpowder. She lifted a hand to shade her eyes and squinted toward the heights across the river. 'Twas hard to tell for certain, but it looked as though the defensive structure the colonial forces had erected still stood.

Movement near the mouth of the river, where it opened into the sea, caught her attention. Slowly, a double column of barges came into view, each one packed with crimson-clad soldiers. Sunlight glinted off the water and caught on the gleaming edges of their bayonets. She held her breath as the two rows of boats proceeded toward the Charlestown Peninsula. Squinting, she counted them stretching onward. Twenty-eight in all. A massive force, and Lieutenant Harrison was among them somewhere.

Isaac. She hadn't been able to keep his name from escaping as she bid him farewell any better than she'd been able to hold back from embracing him. At first, she was certain her display had upset him, so rigid was his stance, but then his arms had enveloped her with an almost desperate strength, and she'd wished he would never let go.

"What is happening, dear?" Mrs. Barker's voice brought Libby back to the present. "It's so quiet. Is it over?"

Libby shook her head, crossing the room to join them. "I fear 'tis just beginning. They've sent the Regulars across on barges."

Mrs. Barker stood and hurried to the window. "So many soldiers. Can we possibly have the same number of men to face them?" She turned away, fingers twisting the knotted end of her fichu. "I cannot bear to watch. I'll fix something for us to eat."

"You needn't worry about—" Mama tried to protest, but Mrs. Barker waved her off.

"I must have something to do, else I'll wear this thin with worry." She patted the lacy fabric draped over her chest, then bustled from the room.

Libby sank into her vacated chair. "I'm so afraid that Will and Josiah might be there, among the militia gathered atop Breed's Hill. I want those men to succeed, and yet..." She felt like a seam being torn apart, stretched in two opposite directions until the stitches that held her together ripped from their place. "I want Lieutenant Harrison to come back unharmed. And while I hope we have the victory, I cannot imagine what that would bring next. If we can hold the heights of Charlestown, might the militia then move into Boston? Will the Regulars still attempt to take Dorchester tomorrow, or will they abandon their plans? What if there is a war and—"

"Elizabeth." Mama's tone stilled her spiraling thoughts. "Is any of that within your power to change?"

Chastised, Libby shook her head.

"We cannot know what the next hour will bring, let alone the next day or sennight or more. 'Take therefore no thought for the morrow: for the morrow shall take thought for the things of itself. Sufficient unto the day is the evil thereof.'"

Libby sighed, the well-known words from the sixth chapter of Matthew offering little comfort. "Evil seems more present this day."

"But God is still near, always sovereign, no matter our earthly circumstances."

"Why, then, do such terrible things happen?" The questions and doubts that had simmered inside her since Papa's death boiled to the surface. Libby pushed to her feet, unable to contain them any longer. "If God is in control, if this world is His and He loves us, why does He allow such pain? Such suffering and grief? How can this"—she flung her hand toward the window—"be part of His plan? Surely, there are men on both sides praying to Him now, fully believing their cause is the right one in this fight, the one He should award victory. But God cannot answer both prayers with a yes, for if one side is to win, the other must lose."

"It was not God's desire, when He created the world, that any of this should happen." Mama rose slowly, eyes lined with sorrow. "'Twas mankind's sin that brought evil into the world. All of these things you speak of—grief and pain and war—they are a result of that sin. Yet God, in His immeasurable love, did not leave us in our brokenness. He made a way for healing and hope and restoration through His Son. That does not mean our lives will be easy. We are bound to live in this world, and as such, we will experience its sufferings. We will have tribulation, but we must take heart, for He has overcome this world."

Another familiar scripture. All words she had known for as long as she could remember, but they had somehow lost the solace they once held. "I believe all that, truly. But I...I feel as though I cannot understand who God is anymore. And I'm afraid. Ever since Papa died, I..." Her throat tightened and her eyes burned. "Why did God take him from us when He knew how much we loved him and needed him? God's answer to my most desperate petition was no. How can I seek comfort in Him for the other trials I'll face? How can I trust Him to care for me?"

Mama took Libby's face in both hands, brushing her thumbs over the damp streaks on her cheeks. She had not even realized she was crying.

"Oh my sweet Libby, I am sorry you have carried this pain without me knowing. Forgive me for not seeing the depth of your need." Tears spilled down Mama's own cheeks, but she kept Libby in her tender hold. "And forgive me for allowing you to think that I've not asked the same questions, harbored the same doubts, in my own life."

"You have? But your faith seems so steadfast. I never thought..."

"It is, but all the more so because of the doubts and questions." Mama pressed a kiss to Libby's forehead, then released her. "I have found 'tis in the hardest times, when God has seemed utterly incomprehensible, that my faith has grown the most. For in those struggles, He has shown me that it is not my grasp of Him that matters, but rather His hold on me. Nothing can take me from His hands, no question or doubt will cause Him to turn His back on me, and no sorrow of this world will shake His promise that my soul is secure for eternity in Him."

"But are you never worried? Never afraid that more trials and sorrow will come?"

"I am. But I trust in who God is and know that my circumstances do not alter His character. And I believe His Word to be true. That is why I worked so hard to instill it in you." A small smile tugged at Mama's lips. "For while my emotions and thoughts are unsteady and changing, the truth of the Scripture is ever solid."

Was it truly so simple, and yet so challenging, as that? To trust in God's character, His Word, and His promises, and let that be enough? Knowing that her faith was not a guard against trouble, but rather an anchor that tethered her to the only One who stood beyond anything this world could hold, unchanging and eternal. To rest in who He was and be content.

"What does Second Corinthians 4:17 say?" Mama prodded softly, the same gentle way she'd done all of Libby's life.

She searched her memory, and the words came in a rush, like a wave crashing in the harbor. She exhaled. "'For our light affliction, which is but for a moment, worketh for us a far more exceeding and eternal weight of glory'."

"I am convinced of that truth. That God works in our suffering to produce something far greater. To grow us more like Christ and to fix our hearts on eternal things, teaching us not to cling to this earth but rather reach toward glory. We may see the fruit of it here on earth, but even if we do not, 'tis a reminder of where our true home lies. Jesus promised to prepare a place for us. One day we will be with Him, and on that day, all the afflictions of this world will indeed feel light when held up to the weight of His everlasting glory."

Mama's steady assurance wove deep into Libby's soul, stitching some life, some hope, into her threadbare faith. And while it did not rid her of her fears, a hint of courage flared within her.

Mrs. Barker returned with a tray of simple fare—some slices of cheese and salted ham alongside day-old biscuits topped with the barest hint of apple preserves.

Libby composed herself and accepted the cup of steaming tea that Mrs. Barker offered with a nod of thanks. They spoke of mundane things as they ate—fabrics and spring planting and the challenge of creating any variety of recipes given the shortage of supplies—as though such conversation could help them forget the enormity of what was happening outside. But when the platter was clear and the cups empty, Libby moved back to the window again.

The soldiers had landed on the shore and seemed to have arranged in different formations, but her view was incomplete, making it hard to tell where they were moving or how they planned to confront the men stationed on the hill. Time ticked on. Mrs. Barker fetched a basket of mending, and they each took a piece to keep their hands busy. Libby tried to focus, but her fingers fumbled, and the hem of the trousers she was working on grew uneven. With a huff, she pulled her stitches out to start again.

A volley of musket fire sounded. Dropping her work, Libby dashed to the window. Another volley rang out, then a third, all in quick succession, but she could not see where they came from. Lines of British troops moved slowly toward the front of Breed's Hill. It did not appear that they had fired, nor were fired upon. Were other troops advancing on the side blocked from her view? Perhaps that was where the shots came from.

Closing her eyes, she offered a silent prayer. *Lord, please help me. Despite what I cannot see or understand, I want to trust You. Give me strength to fix my eyes on You and not on the struggles of this world. Watch over Will and Josiah and Isaac. God, please—*

A massive boom rattled the windowpanes, and her eyes shot open. A second followed.

Mama and Mrs. Barker rushed to stand behind her, watching over her shoulder.

"They're cannonading Charlestown." Mrs. Barker's voice shook. "Oh Lord, save us."

An orange glow rose from the town, faint at first, but growing swiftly.

"'God is our refuge and strength, a very present help in trouble.'" Mama whispered the Psalm like a prayer. "'Therefore, will we not fear, though the earth be removed...'"

Another cannon drowned out her words, this one blazing even as it streaked across the sky. The terrible, consuming light in the town grew steadily higher. Black smoke rose from it, marring the clear blue canopy above.

Dread crept down Libby's spine and trembled through her words. "Charlestown is on fire."

CHAPTER 12

Isaac hoisted himself over another stretch of fence that ran across the army's path toward Breed's Hill. He and the other grenadiers had been instructed to deliberately advance at a slow pace, giving the light infantry companies time to envelop the hill from the side, but they'd not anticipated this many obstacles to impede their progress. Swampy stretches of land merged into tall grass, dotted with brick kilns and fences, all hindering their movement.

Sweat beaded on his brow under the hot bear fur hat and dampened the collar of his shirt beneath his stiff stock. The sun beat down on them without cover of clouds and scant trees to provide any relief. They were still out of range for the men perched behind the redoubt, but there was no denying how exposed their position would be once they drew near. And how difficult the terrain would prove to mounting a brisk assault when the time came.

Sounds of drumming, musket fire, and shouts reverberated from the eastern side of the hill, where the light infantry carried out their attack, but it was impossible to see what progress they made. He glanced over his shoulder toward

Charlestown on the other side, now engulfed in flames. A terrible sight, especially the blazing church steeples, like pyramids of fire stretching heavenward. Rumors claimed the town had already been emptied of citizens. He prayed such reports were correct and that no innocent lives would be lost.

Shoulder to shoulder in tight formation, the lines of grenadiers continued to advance. Two rows proceeded ahead of Isaac's own, where Captain Merrick tramped along beside him.

Isaac flicked his gaze to his captain. "I know we've the strength in numbers that the militia cannot match, but there's no denying they have the better position."

The defensive redoubt, built of bundles of wood, empty hogsheads, and piled-up earth, spanned the top of the hill, providing cover for the men inside and an advantageous view of their approach.

"True enough. But remember..." Merrick tapped the tin front plate on his hat.

Isaac didn't need to look to know what was stamped there. The motto of the grenadiers, alongside the royal crest. "*Nec aspera terrant*, hardships do not deter us."

"We need only hold them long enough for the light infantry to break through the weaker defenses on the flank. Once those rebels realize they are surrounded, they'll flee."

Would they? Or would they fight until the bitter end? And how many lives would be lost in the process?

He shifted the musket in his hands, gaze fixed upon their goal, but it was Miss Caldwell's tear-rimmed eyes that flashed before him. What if William and Josiah were standing behind those earthen walls? *Lord, may they be far from here.*

The silent prayer seemed a feeble attempt. After years of neglecting anything but the most perfunctory of prayers, why would God listen to him now? If only He had answered Mrs. Abbott's petition for peace. Surely, the Lord heard the pleas of one so devoted.

But peace was not to be. Not this day.

Even still, we trust You. Mrs. Abbott's words pounded through him with each beat of his heart. He wanted to draw courage from that declaration. Instead, condemnation burned in his veins. His trust in God was as unstable as the sandy shore, battered and weathered. He had tried to muster a faith worthy of God's love, but it seemed such an unattainable thing. If he fell on the field of battle today, was there any hope of earning the Lord's favor?

The drum tatted out the order to halt, and they drew to a stop about seventy yards away from the top of the hill.

"Ready, Harrison?" Captain Merrick's voice was low and steady.

Isaac drew a long breath, shutting out all other thoughts but that of their mission. "Aye."

Lieutenant Colonel James Abercrombie called for platoon volleys, and they snapped to firing position. Setting his jaw, Isaac raised his firelock, aimed it toward the redoubt, and pulled the trigger.

With the smoke of his first shot still hanging in the air, Isaac reached into his ammunition pouch and withdrew a fresh cartridge. Ripping the paper open with his teeth, he shook some of the powder into the pan, then cast the musket down to pour the remainder inside the barrel with the paper and ball. He rammed it down tightly with his ramrod, then raised the musket to ready again. Shots rang out through the battalion as each platoon fired in order, but no volleys were returned from militia men.

The drum rolled its call to march, and they resumed their ascent of the hill, each step bringing them closer to the waiting line of muskets perched atop the redoubt, trained toward them. Isaac pressed on, every sense fixed upon their goal. He breathed in deeply, held it, then exhaled, forcing his heart to maintain a steady rhythm. The world grew small around him, gaze narrowed, all noises fading save for the constant beat of the drum.

They climbed higher, but still the militia men held their ground...and their fire. Isaac clutched his gun, awaiting the order to shoot, but none came. They had to be but forty yards away now, close enough to make out the fierce determination on the faces of the colonial force as they raised their muskets and—

"Fire!" The shout echoed mere seconds before a deafening blast burst from the redoubt.

Smoke and cries rent the air as the front line of grenadiers was shattered, men tumbling to the ground as though a wave had crashed against them.

Isaac shouldered his firelock and braced himself on the uneven ground as he fired in return. Heat flashed in his face, the stench of gunpowder filling his nose and smoke burning his lungs.

"Fall back!" At Abercrombie's order, the troops retreated out of range, leaving a wake of wounded and dead covering the ground in crimson as though a gaping wound had been slashed into the hillside.

"Reload and regroup." Merrick called instructions to those closest to them.

Isaac tore his gaze away from the destruction and focused on the men at his side. His regiment, whose hands moved with swift, memorized motions. But next to Isaac, one young soldier's fingers shook, spilling black powder on his white cuffs.

"Steady, now." He clasped the man's shoulder, keeping his own voice calm but firm.

The order to march came again. They drew tight, closing the holes left by the men who had fallen, and scaled the incline. Stepping over the bodies that littered the ground, they raised to firing position and let loose upon the redoubt. But once more, they were met with a devastating volley that swept through their ranks.

A gut-wrenching cry sounded at Isaac's side, and he spun just in time to watch Captain Merrick crumple to the ground. Isaac dove to catch him as a whirling buzz blazed past his ear, clipping the top of his hat. It flew off, a musket hole blown through, just inches above his skull.

But there was little time to think of how close he'd come to death, for blood was seeping from a wound on his captain's head.

"Merrick!" Isaac knelt, grasping the man around his broad shoulders. The captain lay utterly still, eyes closed, but his chest rose and fell. Alive, then. "You there, help me," Isaac called to two soldiers who were running back down the hill.

Both dashed to his side, and together they hefted Captain Merrick off the ground, lugging him out of range.

Abercrombie ordered another retreat as men dragged wounded with them to safety. Moans filled the air, and the unmistakable smell of blood hovered around them. Isaac secured a blanket to wrap around Merrick, whose eyes fluttered open briefly before rolling shut again.

With the captain down, Isaac stepped up to organize the men left in his regiment, horrified to find their numbers greatly reduced. They scrambled to reform lines as word arrived that the light infantry had been repelled multiple times, suffering significant casualties. They, too, had fallen back, and General Howe was calling for an all-out assault of the redoubt.

So many grenadiers had fallen before them that now Isaac and his men took to the front line as they advanced for a third time.

"Charge bayonets," Abercrombie shouted.

Isaac leveled his musket, sunlight glinting off the sharp point fixed to the end, finger hovering over the trigger. Looking to the men on either side, he gritted his teeth and charged forward. Shouts, pounding feet, and explosions surrounded him. Smoke filled the air. Soldiers collapsed on every side. He fired his last shot, unable to reload while running, and braced himself for a blow in return. But none came. His feet carried him forward, faster than ever before. Regulars were scaling the walls of the redoubt now, fighting hand to hand with the colonists within.

Isaac's gaze collided with that of a man perched atop the earthen wall who held his own musket ready—not to shoot, but to defend. As others fell or fled behind him, the colonial soldier stood steady, eyes narrowed on Isaac's approach.

Isaac steeled himself for the horror of fighting against someone close enough to look full in the face.

He was nearly to the edge of the redoubt when light and smoke flashed in his periphery, followed by a searing pain that shattered his left arm and knocked him to the ground. His head snapped backward, crashing into something solid, and the world went black.

~

Darkness clung to Isaac like grasping hands, pulling him farther from the light with every passing second. Dirt pressed against his back, as though the earth was already opening itself to receive him. But he wasn't dead yet. Was he?

He willed his eyes to open, straining against the heaviness that threatened to hold them closed forever. A little crack of sunlight. A hint of blue sky. He was alive. For now.

Slowly, his other senses returned, and he immediately wished they had not. The consuming darkness was better than this pain. It radiated from his left arm and his head, throbbing through him with every heartbeat. Even his shallow breaths brought agonizing torment, waves of it coursing through every inch of his body.

An eerie silence hung in the air, replacing the piercing screams of soldiers and the thundering retorts of musket and cannon that had filled the battlefield just moments ago. Or perhaps it had been hours earlier. How long had he lain here?

He shifted his weight, leaning hard on his right arm as he attempted to push himself to sit up. Pain knifed through him. He gritted his teeth but could not contain the moan that escaped. Tilting his head, he dared a glance at his injury. His left arm hung useless, uniform and flesh torn to pieces. A wave of nausea crashed over him, and blackness spotted his vision. He collapsed back to the dirt, squeezing his eyes closed until the dizziness passed.

He'd been hit at such close range. Was there any way to repair that kind of damage? Or perhaps he'd already lost so much blood that he didn't have enough time for the surgeon to try.

His head lolled in the other direction, gaze snagging on the body of a soldier next to him, his once white waistcoat stained crimson. He tore his attention away from the fatal wound in his chest and found the man's face instead. Pale blue eyes, wide and vacant, stared back at him. Sergeant Jackson. Bile rose in his throat. Though the soldier had been a nuisance in many ways, Isaac hadn't wished him dead.

Lightness crept into his limbs, offering a strange sort of relief. An ache radiated through his head, pulse thrumming in his temples, the beat far too slow. He yanked his focus back to the sky. If this was to be his end, he didn't want his last sights on earth to be of the gruesome scene around him.

Wisps of clouds brushed the heavens, like paint strokes on a canvas of blue. His mother enjoyed painting landscapes. Had even hung one over the mantel in the drawing room—an idyllic portrayal of the sweeping property of their estate. A sight he would likely never lay eyes on again.

Would she weep, if he died here today? Would his father regret forcing Isaac into the army, or would the baronet use his loss as another mark of honor? A son who died valiantly serving his king.

A pair of sparrows darted through the air, their song clear and joyous. Isaac blinked, wishing he could drift on the breeze with them.

He shall cover thee with his feathers...

The words flitted into his mind. A Psalm, perhaps? Had he read them once? Heard them preached from the pulpit? Nay, Dr. Caldwell had prayed that verse over him the last time they spoke. A parting benediction.

Tears burned in Isaac's eyes. Was it true? Did God care for His children in such a tender and personal way? Would He welcome someone like Isaac, whose faith had never matched the level of devotion like that of Dr. Caldwell? Was there still time to atone for his shortcomings?

"God, have mercy on my soul." The plea fell from his lips in a strained whisper.

His eyelids were so heavy. He let them slide shut even as the thought gripped him that in doing so, he may never open them again. But the darkness welcomed him, offering relief from the torment.

"I found Lieutenant Harrison!" A voice crept into his consciousness. "Hurry, men—he's still breathing."

More voices joined the first. "Steady on, Lieutenant, we'll get you to the surgeon."

"We need a tourniquet. Quickly!"

They kept talking, but he hadn't the strength to answer. Hands jostled, fabric wrapping and tightening around his bicep. Fresh pain sliced through his arm.

"We'll get you home, Lieutenant. Just stay with us." The

words drifted from somewhere above him, but in his mind a different voice echoed.

Come home safely.

Miss Caldwell's goodbye settled into his heart, both a balm and a sorrow. He'd give anything to see her face again. To feel her embrace one more time. It wasn't his right to wish for such things, but he did all the same.

Why had she been so kind? So good to him? He had tried so hard to protect her. Now he would cause her grief instead.

I'm sorry. He mouthed the words, though no sound came out.

He forced his eyes open a sliver, catching a glint of blue sky swirling above. Blue like her eyes.

God be with you, Isaac.

Aye. May the Lord listen to her plea on his behalf. And perhaps, if her voice, her face, were the last things he remembered, then he could die in peace.

CHAPTER 13

*L*ibby paced to the window and peered into the late-afternoon sunlight, desperately hoping to see Isaac striding down the road. But the street lay empty, just as it had every other time she checked. She didn't even see Benjamin, the neighbor boy who had offered to scout the encampment on the Common and see what information he could garner. She pressed a hand to her stomach, but nothing could settle the unease churning there.

'Twas the Sabbath, a full day since the muskets had fallen silent across the water at Breed's Hill. Libby and her mother had watched from Mrs. Barker's home yesterday as the Redcoats took possession of the high ground, driving the colonial militia to flee. They had all cried together as Charlestown burned to ashes, and remained long enough to see the barges full of soldiers cross the river back to Boston.

But Isaac had not returned to the house. Not last night. Not this morning when Libby begged Mama to stay home from church in hopes he would arrive. And now, with every passing hour, his continued absence only increased her fears.

What if the worst had happened?

The quiet shuffle of pages drew her attention to where Mama sat in one of the chairs before the empty hearth. Bible on her lap, she had somehow managed to remain there for the last hour, quietly pouring over the Scriptures, while Libby could not sit still for more than a few minutes.

Mama looked up, a sympathetic smile on her face. "You'll not change anything by staring out the window, nor hurry Benjamin along any faster."

"I know, but I can't help it." She crossed to the vacant chair next to Mama and sank down with a sigh. "I feel so restless waiting for news."

Mama reached out and clasped Libby's hand. Libby squeezed back. Despite all the times she had missed Papa's conversations, there was something comforting about Mama's quiet steadiness. A soothing kind of silence that came from shared understanding of the heart. From the recognition that no amount of words could fully ease this burden.

A rapid knocking at the door made Libby shoot to her feet. She scurried to tug it open, hope falling at the somber expression on Benjamin's youthful face.

"There's lots of men dead or wounded, Miss Caldwell." He shook his head, and a lock of blond hair fell over his eyes. He huffed a breath to push it away. "I couldn't get near enough to ask anyone about that soldier who lived with you, but I did hear them say there's an army hospital by the harbor. The warehouse at Hunt and White's Shipping Yard."

"Thank you." Libby spoke around the lump in her throat. It was what she'd expected. Still, she'd clung to the hope that Benjamin would find Isaac safe and well. At least now she had another place to search. She forced a quick smile. "Wait here. I have something for you."

Libby ducked into the kitchen and grabbed the small bundle of strawberries wrapped in a linen cloth. She had picked them from the garden Saturday morning but never had a chance to enjoy them given the troubles that day had brought.

Returning to the entry, she held them out for her young neighbor. "In gratitude for your efforts on our behalf."

His eyes widened, and his tongue darted out to lick his lips before they parted into a gap-toothed smile. "For me? Truly?"

She chuckled at his enthusiasm, ignoring the rumble in her own stomach as he accepted the sweet-smelling fruit. The boy's reaction took away the sting of parting with such a treat, and since Mama had forbidden her from going to the Common to search out answers on her own, Benjamin's help was well worth rewarding.

He popped one of the berries into his mouth as he set off for home, an extra lilt in his step. Oh to have that childlike innocence once more. That something as simple as a bundle of fruit might take her mind off the fear that weighed on her. But how much innocence would remain, even for one as young as Benjamin? Already he had seen more of war and hardship at ten years than she had at that same age. What kind of world might he grow up in if things continued in such a way?

She turned to find Mama's gaze on her, a knowing expression in her eyes. "I suspect you want to visit the warehouse."

"If there are any more answers to be found, I must try. I know you'll not wish me to go alone, but perhaps—"

"We will go together. But, Libby..."—Mama held her gaze, concern furrowing her brow—"the inside of an army hospital will not be an easy thing to witness. You must prepare yourself for whatever we might find. As well as an answer you may not wish to hear."

"I helped Papa several times, remember? And I never minded listening to him talk of his procedures. I think I have the strength..." Her voice faltered, belying her words.

She may very well be able to stand the sights, sounds, and

smells, but could she bear the heartbreak should she learn that Isaac was dead?

⁓

The warehouse loomed large at the edge of the water on the North End, where the harbor and the Charles River mingled. Arm in arm, Libby and Mama approached the door, and Libby pressed her teeth into her bottom lip, willing herself to hold to the courage she claimed to possess.

"Should we knock?" Her words quivered, and she frowned at her own weakness.

A memory flashed. She'd spoken the same question only ten days ago, to Isaac as they stood together in front of the Pierces' house. If only she could go back in time and change what had happened since. Keep him from ever setting foot on the battlefield.

"We'd best simply enter. Stay close. We shall try to find someone to speak to without having to venture too far inside."

Mama pushed the door open, and a wave of smells assaulted Libby. The coppery scent of blood clashed with herbaceous and pungent medicinals. Other sour odors turned her stomach, and she tried hard not to consider their source. Rows of makeshift beds and pallets stretched along each wall of the open space, save for the one where they stood. On the nearest mat, stained bandages wrapped around a man's bare chest. She yanked her attention away.

Beside her, Mama's back stiffened, but she did not falter. "Look. There is a woman gathering laundry. We can speak with her."

A black-haired young woman—not much older than herself, she would guess—stooped to gather a bundle of crimson-stained sheets from the foot of a vacant bed. Libby swallowed. What had happened to the man who had lain there?

The emptiness of the mat shouted the answer. Her stomach clenched.

The woman turned toward them, and Mama lifted a hand to gain her attention.

She hurried over, weariness shadowing her dark eyes. "Good day. May I help you?"

Libby blinked, trying to pull her thoughts away from the fate of the soldier whose blood soaked the linen fabric in her hands, but she couldn't formulate a response. What if that was Isaac's bed? A strange fog descended upon her, blurring her vision and muddling her thoughts.

"We are here to inquire after a certain officer, a friend to our family." Mama tightened her grip on Libby's arm. "Lieutenant Isaac Harrison. A grenadier in the 4th Regiment."

"There are so many men, I have not learned any names." The woman's brow furrowed. "If you wait a moment, I will inquire of the surgeon."

"Thank you."

As the woman scurried toward the back of the warehouse, Libby's mother's gaze bored into her.

"Would you rather wait outside?" Mama's voice was gentle, but it stung as though an accusation of Libby's weakness.

She had thought she would be the strong one, the experienced one who had Papa's knowledge on her side, but instead 'twas her mother who faced the scene undaunted while she trembled like a coward. Her eyes burned and she shook her head.

"'Tis nothing to be ashamed of." Mama turned them away from the lines of beds to face the door where they had entered.

Crates containing whatever meager goods the warehouse was intended to store were stacked along that wall, framing the doorway and blocking the pair of windows. A much easier sight than the wounded men, but a stark reminder of the effects of the siege upon their town. This building was meant to be filled with goods, not injured Redcoats. If only the soldiers had never come to Boston in the first place. And yet, then she would never have seen Isaac again and…

Perhaps that would have been better. The thought settled cold and hard as a stone in her chest. If he'd never returned, she would have been able to move on. To keep her thoughts of him tucked far away, fond memories that would fade with time. Then her heart might not feel on the verge of breaking in pieces.

A throat cleared behind them, and Libby turned to find the surgeon, sleeves rolled above his elbows, apron dotted with all manner of stains she dared not focus on.

"Ladies." He offered a hurried bow. "Miss White said you're looking for Lieutenant Harrison."

"Is he here?" The words burst out of Libby with a desperation she could not disguise.

"Nay." Deep grooves etched his cheeks as he frowned. "He is being cared for in the Whites' home, along with two other officers. But I fear his condition is quite grave."

Libby's breath caught in her throat, and a chill stole through her veins. He was alive, but in how much danger? "May we see him?"

He glanced between her and Mama. "Are you quite certain you wish to? Miss White can take you, but none of us physicians have the time to care for a pair of fainting women in addition to all these men."

Libby nodded, her battered courage flaring with renewed strength. All the things that had discomforted her since their arrival faded behind the urgent need to be at Isaac's side. She could manage anything for his sake.

Straightening, she met the doctor's somber gaze. "I am certain. My father was a physician, so you need not worry over my constitution."

His thick brows dipped, expression relaying his doubt in

her claim, but he gestured for Miss White to join them. "Please take these women to your father's house and inform him that they wish to see Lieutenant Harrison. Dr. Reynold is there. He can assist them if necessary."

Thus dismissed, they followed Miss White outside, Libby gulping a breath of the fresh air. Her heart thumped with every footstep as they proceeded down the street. What injury had Isaac sustained? Would he even be awake to know that she had come looking for him? She steeled herself for what he might look like, praying the surgeon was somehow wrong about his prognosis. That he could be healed and well again. That God would spare his life.

"My father's house is just here, on Charter Street." Miss White tipped her head as she led them around the corner. "Forgive the lack of introductions. I am Katherine White."

"Mary Abbott," Mama supplied. "And my daughter, Elizabeth Caldwell."

"Pleased to meet you both, though I am sorry 'tis under such circumstances." The young woman stopped in front of a stately house painted in yellow ochre. Shifting the bundle in her hands, she opened the door and gestured for them to proceed ahead of her.

Libby stepped in toward the dark wooden staircase in front of them. The door to the left was closed, while the one on the right stood open, revealing an elegant parlor with intricately stenciled walls. Mr. White's shipping company may be suffering now, with the harbor closed and the town cut off by the colonial militia, but clearly, he had amassed substantial wealth over years past.

An older man emerged from the parlor, white-wigged and well-dressed. His attention dipped to the stained bedding in Miss White's arms, and he frowned. "Take those outside, please, Katherine. There's a basin of hot water for washing behind the house."

She bobbed her head. "Aye, Father, but first, I've brought these women, Mrs. Abbott and Miss Caldwell, to see Lieutenant Harrison. He is a friend to their family."

Mr. White turned to them, smile tight. "He's staying in a chamber upstairs. I will escort you, but I must warn that he is very unwell and unlikely to respond to your presence."

They followed him through the parlor and the family kitchen behind it, up the back staircase where a pair of doors stood open on either side.

He gestured to the one on the right. "In here. According to Dr. Reynold, he appears to have been hit in the arm by a musket ball at close range. The bone was shattered and much blood lost. He also seems to have injured his head when he fell. I regret to tell you that there is but small hope for his recovery."

Libby swallowed a sob.

Mama pressed a comforting hand to her back. "I am right here with you. And God is in control, no matter what happens to him."

She knew it to be true, but God had taken her father, despite Libby's desperate prayers. Would he take Isaac too?

Libby stepped into the room. Her gaze found Isaac immediately, and she gasped. He lay so still upon the bed, she feared he was already gone. Her own heart seemed to stop, but a shallow rise and fall of his chest set it racing again. She moved closer, tears welling. He'd always looked so tall and strong, but now, with the blanket pulled up to his chin, skin as pale as the sheet covering the mattress, he seemed utterly vulnerable.

She dropped to her knees at his side, not caring that her mother and Mr. White were watching. Pain etched his forehead, even in sleep. His dark hair spilled across the pillow haphazardly, and she reached out to brush a lock off his forehead. He did not stir.

"Isaac. You must get well. Please. I'll help you. I'll do

anything I can—only, you must hold on and keep fighting." Tears spilled down her cheeks.

She meant every word. She would stay by his side. Care for him. Help him heal or, may God forbid it, ensure he was not alone when he passed from this world. The thought tore through her, and she wrapped her arms around herself as though it would dull the pain.

Bowing her head, she silently offered a plea that God would save him. Mayhap this time, God would grant her request for healing and not steal another person she loved out of her life.

$\sim$

*H*e knew that voice. Isaac strained to listen through the darkness that seemed bent on consuming him. Not a soldier's harsh tone, but a woman's soft plea. Desperate. Tear-filled. Tender. A voice that knew his name.

Hold on. Keep fighting.

Why had she issued such an order? Wasn't the battle over?

If only he could open his eyes. See the face that belonged to the words. Then he would know who she was. But his body refused to obey his commands. He could not move. Could not speak. Trapped beneath the overwhelming weight of pain and a swirling haze that dulled his mind.

Another voice joined the first. Similar, a woman again, but steadier than the one who had called his name. "Our Lord, You alone are the Great Physician. You hold Lieutenant Harrison's life in Your hands."

The words washed over him, both comforting and confusing. Was she praying? For his life?

"We ask for Your provision, knowing You are able to work in ways beyond our comprehension. And we humble ourselves to Your will, even should we not understand it. Amen."

"I want to stay with him." The first voice again.

Where was he? What woman would be so concerned over his welfare as to wish to remain at his side? A memory inched into his muddled consciousness. An unexpected embrace. Soft warmth pressed against his chest. A voice, *that* voice, sending him off.

God be with you, Isaac.

Miss Caldwell. Realization broke through the suffocating fog, and relief coursed through him. She was here. With him. Had he made it home to her, after all?

But why, then, did she sound so broken?

"Libby, you cannot intrude upon the Whites' house." He recognized the second woman as Mrs. Abbott now. "They've enough skilled surgeons to care for the soldiers, so what more can you do that they cannot?"

"I'm certain I can be of help in some way. But even if not, surely, you understand why I must try." Miss Caldwell's voice dropped low.

Murky haze slithered into his mind like a snake coiling to strike, threatening to send him back to the unbearable nothingness. He had to resist somehow. He focused all his energy on attempting to open his eyes. Just a single glance of Miss Caldwell's face. A hint of assurance that this darkness would not last forever.

"This is a conversation better held elsewhere." Mrs. Abbott spoke with quiet authority. "Mr. White, we thank you for your hospitality in allowing us to visit the lieutenant."

"Of course." A male voice broke in, surprising Isaac. How many others were in the room? Helplessness choked him over the thought of countless specters he couldn't see. "You are welcome to return and look in on him again. Or I can send word should anything change."

"That's very generous. Thank you, sir." Mrs. Abbott's voice sounded farther away.

Were they leaving? Panic gripped Isaac. Their presence was

the only thing holding back the shadows. If Miss Caldwell and her mother left, what would keep them away?

Don't go! He wanted to beg, but the words were swallowed up in the encroaching blackness. Wanted to reach out, but his limbs felt chained to his sides.

"I will come back." A whisper against his ear. Miss Caldwell. "I promise."

Hope blazed for a split second, like the last ray of light before the sun set behind the waves, then he sank into the void.

CHAPTER 14

*C*horus of birdsong drifted through the window in Libby's chamber on Monday morning as she pinned the last of her curls at the nape of her neck, silently repeating what she would say to Mama when she went downstairs. The walk home from the Whites' yesterday afternoon had been filled with tense silence. Mama had overheard Libby's promise to Isaac as they left, and the rigid set of her shoulders spoke volumes as to her opinion on the matter. But when Libby had tried to speak of it last night, Mama had replied that the conversation could wait until morning, when they were both able to think more clearly.

Libby felt the censure of those words as she fell asleep, and the scolding lingered still today. She'd been too impulsive with her parting words to Isaac. She knew that. Especially since she made her promise only moments after Mama chided her for pressing to stay. But such a reaction could be forgiven, could it not? Shouldn't her mother understand? Libby had spoken openly of her feelings for him. Was it any surprise she longed to be with him?

Smoothing her hands over her petticoat, she descended the

stairs and made for the kitchen. Mama was there, back to her, staring out the window. Libby paused. Gone was the confident stance her mother had displayed in the army hospital yesterday. Instead, her shoulders drooped, as though a heavy yoke hung over them.

Guilt pricked Libby's conscience. Was she the cause? Was she once more allowing her emotions to guide her decisions, instead of thoughtful consideration? She hated the tension between her and Mama, but she could not silence her desperate concern for Isaac and the bone-deep need to be at his side.

She stepped closer, and Mama turned, the weariness in her face matching that of her posture. Had she struggled to sleep last night as much as Libby had?

Libby drew in a breath. Best say what she meant to say instead of prolonging both of their discomfort. "I realize I spoke out of turn yesterday, and for that I apologize, but I cannot change the way I—"

"Elizabeth." Mama held up a hand, cutting her prepared speech short. "You did, and I thank you for your apology. But if you think I am angry with you over something so small as words uttered from a depth of feeling, you are quite mistaken."

"What do you mean?"

"I only want to protect you. I know your heart toward Lieutenant Harrison, and I know what kind of pain it is to watch the man you love suffer. To watch him die."

"But to leave him alone in that suffering? Is that any better, for me or for him?" Libby choked on the words. "I can bear the pain, for his sake. I cannot bear being trapped here, waiting in uncertainty, and doing nothing. Would anything have kept you from Papa's side?"

"This is not the same. To stay with your husband, who you promised devotion to in sickness and in health, is quite different than sitting at the bed of a man you know you cannot share a future with."

"But what if we could?" The frayed hope that she'd secretly clung to burst out of her. "All this time, I've been telling myself it is impossible, but mayhap it is not. If he ever felt the same for me, isn't there a way?"

"Even if he should recover and return your feelings, are you willing to give up everything you have known and been devoted to for his sake? Should this become a full war, he will be called upon to fight again. Could you accept that? And should all of this end swiftly, he would return to England, or move on to whatever post his regiment was stationed next. I cannot bear to think of that kind of loneliness in life for you." Mama's voice broke.

Libby's throat tightened. She had not thought so far into the future, not with the same kind of rational consideration her mother had. She'd let herself dwell in some sort of dream instead, pretending there was a way for her heart to come out of this unscathed.

"I know you have prayed for Lieutenant Harrison's wellbeing, but have you prayed for yourself? That God would grant you wisdom regarding your own feelings and His will for you? You are not a child, and I will not treat you as one, even though I wish I could still tuck you against my apron and shelter you from danger." Mama exhaled a shaky laugh, but tears spilled down her cheeks. "You are a grown woman, and as such, you may choose to do what you deem best. But I have this request —pray first. Do not act on emotions alone, for they are not to be trusted. Seek God's guidance and listen to Him, above all else."

Libby swiped a hand over her damp face. This conversation had not gone the way she'd expected or planned, but her mother's gentle guidance was better than her anger or disappointment. "Aye, I will."

"Now, we'd best have something to eat. I'll set the water boiling. There may yet be a few strawberries if you search hard enough."

Libby nodded as she lifted her apron from the peg on the wall and tied it round her waist. It was her mother's subtle invitation for Libby to follow through with her request. A gracious opportunity for her to spend some time in quiet solitude and prayer.

Pushing the door open, she picked her way across the dew-soaked ground to the patch of bushes at the end of the kitchen garden. Mama was right. She had allowed her feelings to take priority, and she had not stopped to pray. Conviction burrowed deep.

Why had she not? Was she afraid of the answer she might receive? Another no as she had when she begged for her father's life? It was easier to follow the tug of her heart than it was to lay her life before God and trust that His plans for her were best. But easier did not mean it was right.

She crouched low and searched the plants but found only a few small berries, still white, clinging to the edges. When God searched her heart, was this what He saw? Unripe fruit, waiting, but not yet mature? She'd been longing to prove that she was as capable as the other members of her family. To make a difference, as they had. But in all her striving, had she only demonstrated the opposite? Mama said she was no longer a child, but had she not acted childishly by allowing her feelings to govern so many of her thoughts and decisions?

"God, I don't know what to say." She tucked her chin to her chest, feeling contrite and small in His presence. "I want to trust You, but I am afraid to hear Your answer. I want to be wise, but I cannot ignore the way I feel. Can You help me?"

No clear answer came, but a sense of assurance seeped into her soul. God could help her—she knew that. She need only choose to trust Him, even if life still hurt sometimes.

Reaching out, she brushed the leaves aside, checking the bushes one last time. There. Two bright red strawberries, hidden deep in the center. There was fruit, after all. She picked both berries, fingers coming away damp. It wasn't a meal, of course, but she and Mama could both savor one sweet bite.

Joy and hope swelled in her, along with the words of a verse her mother had spoken time and again.

"'Being confident of this very thing, that he which hath begun a good work in you will perform it until the day of Jesus Christ.'" Libby smiled as she recalled them aloud. "Lord, may that be true of me."

CHAPTER 15

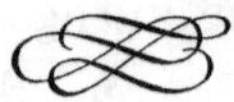

He was on fire. There could be no other explanation for the searing agony that burned through every inch of him. Charlestown had been in flames. Was he caught among them?

No. That couldn't be right. He'd been carried away from the battlefield, hadn't he? Isaac shook his head, trying to clear the delirium that billowed in his thoughts like smoke.

"Shhhh." A soft voice hushed, and blessed coolness pressed against his forehead. "Rest. You're safe."

Slender fingers wrapped around his hand. He wanted to cling to that comfort. Mustering every scrap of strength left in him, he willed his fingers to move. Slowly, reluctantly, they obeyed, closing around the smaller hand that held his.

A gasp sounded beside him. "Isaac? Can you hear me?"

If only he could reply. But he'd spent so much energy already.

"'Tis Libby. I came back, as I promised I would."

Peace settled over him. She was here. What was it about her presence that seemed to free him from the grip of darkness?

Libby. He had never called her that. Never even thought of her that way. Too intimate. A name he could not, would not, speak. But now…now he wished he had. Just once.

A sharp knock shattered the calm and ricocheted in his skull. A low voice followed. "Miss Caldwell. How does he fare this morning?"

"Feverish and unsettled." She didn't let go of his hand. "He's been thrashing about. I keep changing the cloth on his head, but I am not certain—"

"I will try another cup of willow bark tea, though 'tis difficult to say how much he truly swallows." The man's voice moved closer. The surgeon, based on his words. "I need to look at the wound now. You'd best step outside for a few minutes."

Libby squeezed his fingers, then released them. Immediately, he missed her touch. In its place, larger hands pulled the sheet off his chest. A rush of air hit his bare skin, refreshing for a moment, then he started to shake with cold. The probing fingers moved to his left arm, tugging at something there and yanking a moan from Isaac's lips. He jerked away from the pain.

"Keep still, Lieutenant. I need to remove the bandages." A discouraged grunt followed the surgeon's muttered words. "Just as I suspected."

As swiftly as he'd come, the click of shoes on the floor signaled the doctor's departure. The man had left Isaac's upper half uncovered, and he shivered uncontrollably.

Would Libby return? He longed for her comfort, but she should not see him like this. If he could find the doctor, call him back to cover him first…

He tried to speak, but his tongue felt thick, his mouth parched. Where had everyone gone? He forced his eyes open the slightest crack. They were dry and scratchy, as though full of sand, but a blurry image emerged. The surgeon and Miss Caldwell, shadowy figures, framed by the open door of a room he didn't recognize. She turned to look his way, and for a split second, he caught a glimpse of her face, but the doctor shifted, blocking her from Isaac's view.

"Don't go back in there, miss." The surgeon's voice drifted like an echo. "Fetch Dr. Hawkins at the warehouse, and send him immediately with his surgical tools."

"May God help him. Do you have to…"

Miss Caldwell's voice faded as Isaac's eyes slammed shut. He was too weary to hold them open any longer. Too weary to make sense of their words.

⁓

Nausea swelled in Libby's stomach, and she pressed a hand to her mouth as the surgeon ushered her away from Isaac's room.

"Are you certain there is no other way? You really must amputate?" She forced the word through quivering lips.

Dr. Reynold frowned. "Miss, I appreciate your concern, but please, do not question my work. I tried to save his arm, but the damage is too great, and now the wound is festering. If I wait any longer, he will most certainly lose his life. Even now, his chance of survival is slim. But I will do all I can to give him that chance."

Libby dipped her head, reminding herself to hold tightly to the reins of her emotions. "I know. Forgive me—I did not mean to imply anything about your decisions or your work. I pray for your success and for Lieutenant Harrison's recovery."

His stern features softened slightly. "Pray indeed, Miss Caldwell. But do not return here this day. A woman should not be exposed to such things. Understood?"

She nodded. She understood far more than he realized. She'd seen Papa's surgical tools laid out on the table in his office. The sickle-shaped blade of the falciform amputation knife. The retractors and saw. Her vision blurred at the thought of such instruments being used on Isaac.

Libby kept one hand on the wall, not trusting her shaky legs, as she made her way downstairs. She'd remained home on Monday and spent much of the day in thought and prayer, bent upon honoring her mother's request to seek an answer guided by more than her emotions. By nightfall, her decision was clear. She'd made a promise to Isaac, and even if it was impulsively offered, she could not break it. But she had also committed to helping Mrs. Barker at her shop every Tuesday, so much as it pained her to wait, she had held to her responsibilities at the mantua maker yesterday and waited to come today. Mama's only stipulation to accepting her choice was that she take Benjamin along so she needn't travel alone.

Their young neighbor had been happy to do so this morning, especially when offered a hoecake, fresh off the griddle and topped with the last of their honey, in thanks. Though Libby thought it a bit strange that a boy of ten could offer any sort of protection as an escort, his youthful chatter had helped lighten her spirits as they traversed the cobbled streets. But as soon as she stepped into Isaac's chamber, any cheer she held had immediately been snuffed out. His condition had worsened significantly since her visit on Sunday, and while his injury had been covered by bandages and a sheet every moment she was in the room, she'd feared the worst even before Dr. Reynold confirmed it.

When Libby ducked into the kitchen, Miss White stood at the worktable, instructing the younger girls on preparations for the midday meal. She looked up and offered a kind smile. "How fares the lieutenant?"

"Not well, I'm afraid. Dr. Reynold sent me for another surgeon to assist him as he plans..." She hesitated, eying the two girls. Leaning closer to Miss White, she lowered her voice.

"He needs to remove the injured arm. Best keep your sisters, and yourself, out of the house for a time if you can."

Miss White's dark eyes widened. "Aideen. Briana. The meal can wait. Go help my mother tend to the garden instead. Don't come back inside until I say."

The girls bobbed their heads and scurried out.

"I'll walk with you to the warehouse to find the surgeon." Miss White gestured to the door the girls had passed through. "My father is there, and I'd best inform him of what is happening."

They set off together, Libby's stomach churning. She grasped for something different to focus on. "You said, 'help *my* mother.' They're not your sisters?"

Miss White shook her head. "We took them on as indentures three years ago. Orphans, from Ireland, though they remember little of their homeland. Their father sailed for Hunt and White Shipping but fell ill and died on one of the voyages. Their mother passed not long after."

"That explains the littler one's bright hair." Libby had noticed the red hue immediately upon seeing the girl, so different than Miss White's black locks. "Do you have any siblings, then?"

"Three, but they're all quite a bit older. My eldest brother is twenty years my senior, with another brother and sister close behind him." Her lips tugged into a half smile. "My parents say I was their surprise child."

"Indeed. But a pleasant surprise, I am sure."

"I should hope so." Miss White chuckled, then sobered as they approached the warehouse. "I'll find my father. He can help us locate the surgeon you're looking for."

Libby braced herself and followed Miss White into the makeshift hospital. Prepared as she was this time, the atmosphere inside still jarred her. Thankfully, Mr. White stood near the door.

He turned and, spotting his daughter, hurried to her side. "Is something wrong?"

"Miss Caldwell was sent to find..." She paused, looking at Libby.

"Dr. Hawkins," Libby supplied. "Dr. Reynold needs his help and said to bring his amputation tools."

"That poor soldier. I do not like to see such fine men suffer for the rebellion of a handful of our citizens." Mr. White scowled, then glanced toward a short, wiry man attending one of the nearby beds. Raising his voice, he beckoned with one hand. "Dr. Hawkins. Your services are required at the house."

Libby bit her tongue as the surgeon approached. She had suspected the Whites were Tories, given their offer to keep the recovering soldiers in their warehouse and home. Likely, they assumed her to be the same since she was so concerned over Isaac's care. There'd be nothing to gain in revealing the truth of her loyalties.

Dr. Hawkins halted at Mr. White's side. His hooked nose and sharp eyes seemed to fit his name. "What's the problem?"

As Mr. White explained, the doctor's frown deepened. "I told Reynold we needed to amputate from the start. Let us hope there is still some chance of saving the lieutenant, but I have my doubts."

Libby's eyes burned, and she squeezed them shut, determined not to cry in front of these strangers.

"I wish we had more yarrow. We'll need a good styptic to dress the wound." Dr. Hawkins ran a hand over his pointed chin. "Does your wife grow any?"

"I am not certain." Mr. White looked to his daughter.

She shook her head. "I do not believe so."

Libby blinked, recalling the fern-like leaves and clustered flowers of the plant she'd seen time and again in Hannah's garden. "I know where I can find some."

"Good. Fetch it quickly." Dr. Hawkins spun away to gather his tools.

"I'll go with her." Miss White looked to her father for his approval, and he granted it with a swift nod.

Libby set off at a quick pace, sliding a glance at Miss White beside her. "I must warn you, 'tis quite a walk. All the way to School Street."

"I don't mind." Miss White kept up with no trouble. "I am sorry your lieutenant is so ill."

Libby's cheeks heated. "He's not *my* lieutenant really, he's only—"

"You are not betrothed? Or courting?"

"Nothing like that." The hot flush spread down her neck. Was that what her behavior toward him appeared like? She must set things straight. "Lieutenant Harrison is—was—a good friend of my father when his regiment was stationed here six years ago. He returned with The King's Own last summer and hoped to renew their acquaintance, but unfortunately, Papa had passed in the meantime. The lieutenant has been very good to my mother and I and..." What more could she say? She hardly knew Miss White. She couldn't pour out all her complicated feelings.

"But you do care for him, do you not?"

Libby couldn't meet her probing gaze. "He is a dear friend."

Silence settled between them as they wove through the crooked streets, but Libby's thoughts screamed in her head. She tried to pray, but it came in bits and pieces, broken by fear and horror over what was about to begin in Isaac's chamber. All she could manage was a repeated wordless plea—*save him, please save him.*

As they passed King Street, Miss White's quiet voice broke into Libby's tumultuous thoughts. "I was in love once."

Libby nearly stumbled at the confession, turning to find her companion's gaze fixed on the State House.

"He was an apprentice to an ivory-turner on Salem Street. We crossed paths quite by accident and then…" It was Miss White's turn to blush. "Perhaps I cannot rightly say that we were courting, for my parents did not approve of the connection. I was young, only six and ten, and they sought a match with higher standing. But I did hope that one day…"

"What happened?"

"He was killed five years ago, when the shooting broke out between the mob and the soldiers in March. You may have read his name in the papers—Samuel Maverick." She sighed. "Samuel never seemed interested in all the arguments over taxes and such. He certainly wasn't caught up in all that Sons of Liberty nonsense. I do not know what would have possessed him to even be there."

"I do recall the name." Libby's breath caught in her throat. She remembered it well, in fact, not because of the papers but because he'd been a good friend of Elijah Pierce. Hannah had spoken more than once of her brother's grief over his loss. "I am sorry."

Miss White forced a smile. "Thank you. I have moved on, but a part of me will always miss him. I suppose one never does forget how it feels when you first fall in love."

"I suppose not." Indeed, Libby was certain she would never forget how she felt when Isaac had wrapped his arms around her and held her close before he left for the battle.

If she lost him today, or in the days to come, would she be able to move on, as Miss White had? Or if he was taken from her, not by death but by the stark differences in their two worlds, could she tuck her feelings away and allow them to become simply a fond remembrance of a friend?

They rounded the corner, and Libby stopped in front of the fence that enclosed the Pierces' property. She glanced at the house, the hairs at her nape prickling. What if someone had broken in again and was there, this very moment, watching them? Best be quick about it.

She pushed open the gate and led Miss White to Hannah's garden, which had grown rather wild in the absence of her care. "My friend lived here. Her father was the apothecary, but they left Boston in April. I know she would not mind us using her plants for such a purpose."

Together they searched the overgrown plot until Libby spotted the tall branching stalks topped with tiny bunches of white flowers. "Here. This is it."

Miss White crouched beside her. "I should have thought to bring shears, but we were in such a hurry."

"No matter. We'll make do." Libby reached for the bottom of one plant and tugged hard, pulling it up by the roots. "I do not know what quantity they need, so let's gather as much as we can carry."

Miss White joined her. They tucked their aprons up at the corners and filled them until leaves and dirt were spilling out on both sides.

Standing, Libby peeked over her shoulder at the apothecary. A pity it was securely locked, for there might be helpful ingredients inside. But she'd not damage the Pierces' building to obtain any.

Movement passed behind one of the apothecary windows, and Libby gasped.

"What's wrong?" Miss White followed her gaze.

"I thought I saw..." Not again. It couldn't be. She backed up slowly. "We should leave. Now."

The back door of the apothecary swung open, and a figure emerged, cloaked in shadows. Libby's mouth went dry. They shouldn't have come, but Isaac needed this. She grabbed Miss White's arm, tugging her away. Her feet tangled in her petticoat, and she nearly tripped as she spun toward the gate.

"Elizabeth?" The voice halted her in place.

She turned as the man stepped just past the corner of the brick wall, still mostly shrouded in the shade cast by the building. A swath of sunlight cut across one side of his face, and recognition sent a wave of relief coursing through her. "Elijah? What are you…"

Miss White sucked in a breath. Her face drained of all color. She stared wide-eyed at Elijah as though she were looking at a ghost. A shudder ran through her, then she crumpled.

Libby tried to break her fall, crashing hard onto her own knees as she did. Elijah dashed from the shadows and dove, catching Miss White's head before it could slam against the ground. He cradled her gently for a moment, searching her face with a look of remorse and…longing?

Questions swirled in Libby's mind, begging for release. What had caused Miss White, who braved the army hospital without flinching, to faint at the sight of Elijah? And why did he stare at her the way he did? What was he doing here, anyway? Had he never left Boston, after all?

Before she could find her voice, Elijah shifted Miss White fully onto Libby's bent legs and stood. "I need to leave, and you do, too, as quickly as you're able." He darted to the garden and broke off a handful of mint leaves from the sprawling herb. "Here. These will help her wake up. Hold them in front of her nose so she breathes the scent, then have her chew the leaves to revive her energy."

"But what is—"

"We cannot speak now. Not here in the open." He glanced over his shoulder as though expecting someone to accost them at any moment. "I'll come to your house again tonight. Meet me outside after dark. Ten of the clock."

He turned and ran, leaving Libby with the unconscious Miss White on her lap, a bundle of yarrow she desperately needed to get back to the surgeons, and a jumble of unanswered questions.

CHAPTER 16

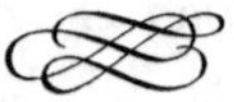

$\mathcal{A}$ half moon peeked out of the black sky, casting pale light on Libby's surroundings as she crept outside to wait for Elijah. She dared not bring a candle and risk catching Mama's attention, even though she'd gone to bed over an hour ago. Leaning against the worn shingles of the back of the house, she peered into the darkness. This time, she would not be caught off guard by Elijah's approach, nor would she allow him to leave until he'd answered her questions. Like it or not, he owed her that much.

Poor Miss White had traipsed home from the Pierces' in a silent stupor, hardly speaking a word even when Libby tried to draw her out. She'd plastered on a weak smile when they delivered the yarrow to her father, making the excuse that the thought of the procedure happening upstairs had left her feeling out of sorts. Libby didn't dare speak otherwise and, terrified of what she might hear should she remain at the house, had hurried home. She had finally given in to tears when she recounted Isaac's condition to Mama, though she'd left out the trip to Hannah's garden and all that happened there.

She squinted as a dark shape rounded the corner of the house. Silent as an owl's wing, Elijah neared, his face hard to make out in the dim moonlight.

"You have much to explain." She fixed him with a stern glare, even if he couldn't see it.

A low laugh emerged, edged more in shame than humor. "Aye. But first, how is Miss White?"

"So you do know her. I wondered, given the way she responded to your presence. Likely, she thought you dead, as I once did." Libby huffed. Did he find some pleasure in returning from the grave, as it were, to his family and friends? "She will recover but was much shaken. How are you acquainted with her?"

"I knew her through Samuel. He was taken with her. We all spent some time together before his death." Elijah sighed. "I am sorry for frightening her. I suppose this simply adds to the ways I've wronged her."

"Whatever do you mean?"

"'Twas my fault Samuel was even there at the State House. If it weren't for me, he'd still be alive. They could be married by now, building a life together as they'd hoped."

Libby frowned, recalling Miss White's words. *I do not know what would have possessed him to even be there.* Was Elijah truly at fault for his friend's death? What a burden to carry all these years.

Elijah shifted on his feet. "Will you see her again?"

"I will." Libby intended to return early tomorrow to see how Isaac fared, before she fulfilled her Thursday commitments to Mrs. Barker.

"Then please give her my apology, and tell her that I will be certain not to upset her again."

"Perhaps it would be better coming directly from you."

He stepped closer, and with her eyes more adjusted to the night, she could see the slash of his lowered brows. "I cannot. I must leave Boston, and I plan to stay far away for the foreseeable future."

"Why are you here, anyway? I thought you'd left."

"I did. I picked up your letters, and when I saw what you'd written about the army's plans, I made for the Massachusetts Committee of Safety immediately." He grasped her shoulder with an affectionate squeeze. "You do not know how vital that information was, Elizabeth. Because of what you discovered, the Committee was able to organize our militia to make the first move before the Regulars could attack. Who can say what would have happened without your message."

A chill swept over Libby that could not be blamed on the night air. "You mean, it is because of my letter that the militia moved on Breed's Hill?"

"In a way, it was." The pride in his voice did nothing to stave off the cold that settled deep in her gut.

If she hadn't overheard the plans, hadn't passed them on to Elijah, was it possible that the battle would never have taken place? That Isaac would right now be well and whole?

"We heard rumors from other sources later, but yours was the first to reach me, and thus, I could give the most credible report." He crossed his arms over his chest. "Though we had to retreat in the end, we made quite a stand on that hill. We showed those Redcoats we're not some mob to be punished as they thought the night of the massacre, but rather troops who will hold our ground and stare them in their faces."

Libby couldn't keep from trembling. She wanted to see her countrymen succeed for the cause of liberty—truly, she did— but at the cost of Isaac's life? She did not regret warning Elijah if it meant protecting her family, but had she brought harm to Isaac instead? How could she be so conflicted, tattered like a frayed thread? One strand tugging toward her homeland and the cause she'd long been dedicated to, the other pulling toward the man she loved, who stood against her country and convictions.

"I was there, with Colonel Prescott." Elijah carried on, unaware of her inner turmoil. "Though you'll be glad to know that William and Josiah were not."

Relief coursed through her, followed by startling realization. "You...you fought at Breed's Hill?"

"I did. I held my place in the redoubt until the very end, when the Lobsterbacks came crawling over the wall with their bayonets. We ran out of ammunition. Otherwise, we could have fought longer. During the hand-to-hand combat, I was knocked unconscious by the butt of a musket. When I woke, they'd taken me prisoner."

Libby gasped. "But how are you free now?"

"I escaped." His voice dropped low. "'Twas not the first time."

Libby furrowed her brow, a whole new storm of questions raging in her mind. "I do not understand. What have you been doing?"

"I did not want to burden you with this, but it seems I have no choice any longer, for you are part of it now, whether you wished to be or not." He ran a hand over the back of his neck. "Do you remember, last we spoke, that I asked if you'd ever heard of James Lawrence?"

She nodded.

"Lawrence is the name I took on, nearly two years ago, when I began organizing a group of spies in and around Boston. I've worked under that alias ever since, only revealing my true identity to Hannah last April, when I came to see her and my father."

"You're...a spy?"

"I am. And a good one." There was pride and defensiveness in his tone. "Your stepbrother and my sister were part of the ring as well."

"Will and Hannah? But...but how?" Libby sputtered the words, disbelief tangling her tongue.

Elijah explained how he had recruited both of them to help gather and spread information for the spy ring. How letters were encrypted and coded and passed by a series of signals and drop locations. Hurt crashed against Libby's muddled thoughts at the realization that two people she had loved and trusted had kept such a significant secret from her.

"I told you I was responsible for my father's arrest." Elijah dipped his chin. "I...I got complacent. I should not have dared to visit them. There was a soldier, one of several men who have been intent upon capturing me for a while now, who tracked me down. My father was in the wrong place at the wrong time, and the soldier arrested both of us. I thank God your step-brother was able to rescue him."

"Hannah and Will never said anything about you. I don't understand how..." Her throat tightened against the words. How could they keep all of this from her? Did they not trust her? Did they think she was incapable of keeping the same secrets they had? Of handling the same responsibilities? "Will helped you escape, too, then?"

Elijah shook his head. "I couldn't get away, not without compromising my father's safety. But I have other connections, and I was able to break out of the prison not long after."

"How did you manage to escape this time? Once you were taken from the battlefield?"

"I swam." His smile flashed white against his shadowed features. "They stuck me in one of their barges, amongst a load of injured men. When they neared the shore this side of the river and everyone was either engaged in rowing, tending to the wounded, or in such condition as to be incapable of stopping me, I leaped off the side. Kept my head underwater and swam until I'd found a spot among the tall marshes to come up for air. I heard them shouting, but they couldn't trouble themselves enough to turn the bulky boat and search. Not with so many of their men in need of the surgeons' care. I got to safety, but my head ached something fierce, so I spent a few days in my father's house to recover. That's why you spotted me in the apothecary, searching out remedies for the lingering effects."

His words hovered in the air as silence fell between them. She could hardly grasp all that he'd revealed. So many things she hadn't known. Things kept hidden from her. They seemed to seep into her skin, leaving her hands clammy and her arms prickling.

"Why?" The question slipped out on a shaky exhale. Such a small word to capture all of her confusion and pain. "What drove you to do this in the first place?

"I did it for our country. For our liberties. No citizen should live under the thumb of a government that refuses to give them a voice. A king and Parliament who think they can take away our rights with the stroke of a quill, and send their laws across the ocean without ever stepping foot among the people they claim to rule. We are more than capable of governing ourselves. 'Tis time we fought for the freedom to do so." His voice sliced through the darkness, as hard and sharp as a knife. "And for Samuel. No young man should be cut down in the streets of his own town. Justice must be served."

"Justice? Or revenge?" She leaned closer. "You speak well of our rights, and I do not disagree. But it seems this is a personal quest for you, as though it will help you heal the grief of your friend's death. Elijah, it will not."

He looked away, jawline edged in moonlight as he stared into the darkness. "Your affection for that soldier has blinded you."

Libby jerked back at the harshness of his tone.

"But he will never return it." Elijah looked back to her, and she saw in his face a man she no longer recognized. Determination and regret swirled across his features in a haunting dance, like dark clouds before a storm. "You must understand this—you, too, have been a spy. When you listened to his conversation and passed it on to me, you used his very words against him for our cause. And it was the right thing to do. Ours is the side upon which you belong. How could he ever forgive you, ever care for you, if he learned what you had done?"

The accusation stabbed through her, the final cut that would sever any fragile hope she'd clung to of a future with Isaac. What would he think of her if he knew?

Tears burned and she clenched her teeth to hold them at bay. "I did not want this. I only wished to protect my family. I had no idea what I was—"

"I know." Elijah's voice softened again. "I did not wish this for you either. I am sorry you were pulled into such a knotted web. I am sorry that I ever sought you out in the first place." He scrubbed both hands over his face, and when he looked at her again, she caught a glimpse of the boy she had once known. "It seems I am bound to hurt the people I care for. That is why I must remove myself again. Far from anyone who could suffer for my choices."

Libby shuddered, both at the weight he bore and the deception she'd unwittingly become entangled in.

"There is one more thing." His chest heaved with an unsteady breath. "I lost my haversack when I was captured. I pray it did not fall into the wrong hands because my father's journal was in it."

Libby's legs grew weak. "My letter to you? The one that told of the army's plans?"

"Still tucked inside the cover." He hung his head. "I...I don't know what I was thinking. Why I didn't burn it immediately like I always did the others. There was so little time. I passed the news to the Committee and then rushed off to join the militia at Breed's Hill, and I..." He grasped her arms. "You must be careful. That is why I did not want you to be seen with me.

To have any chance of being connected to me. You mustn't speak of me. Not at all. Keep yourself as far from this as you can."

"But even if the soldiers found the journal, surely, there is no way they could know it was me. I did not sign it. How could they…" Her words faded as a memory crashed over her. "Isaac."

"What?" Elijah searched her face. "What are you saying?"

"Lieutenant Harrison saw me with your father's journal. I even read a page of it to him. If he were to see it, he would know where it came from. Who it came from."

"And the lieutenant, he survived the battle?"

"He did, but he was badly wounded and may yet…" She couldn't manage to finish the thought aloud.

"Then let us hope he never has the chance—"

"No." She shook her head. "I will pray for his healing. I will still do all I can to help him get well. But I will also pray that he never sees that journal and that letter. That no one does."

Elijah stared at her a long moment. Did he no longer recognize the woman she had become, just as she had seen such a stranger in his eyes? She'd not be surprised, for right now, she hardly recognized herself — an accidental spy, in love with the one man who could condemn her as such.

CHAPTER 17

Light flickered against his eyelids, as soft as the sunrise beckoning him to wake. A gentle breeze brushed across his face, reminding Isaac of boyhood days long gone, when he perched amongst the branches of his favorite tree, the leaves rustling with the summer wind. And a hand held his. Small against his palm, but grasping him with tender strength.

He pried his eyes open, heavy and dry as they were, and stared at the swath of white overhead, dappled with sunlight. Blinking, he tried to make sense of it. To remember where he was and why he was there. He lay on his back, not in the dirt of the battlefield but on a soft mattress and pillow. Snatches of memories darted through his mind. Whispered prayers in the darkness. Unquenchable heat. And agony like he'd never experienced before. A pain so terrible it tore a scream from the depths of his gut before it sent him into blessed oblivion.

But it was gone now. Had it somehow been banished forever?

"Isaac?" A breathless voice drew his attention.

He shifted his head, neck stiff and protesting at even the slight movement, and his gaze caught on a familiar face.

"Miss Caldwell?" Her name scraped against his parched throat.

Her blue eyes lit with joyful tears as they held his. "Praise God, you're awake."

For a long moment, he stared at her, at the face that had swirled like mist in his thoughts for countless days. Or were they nights? Had he dreamt her? Imagined her?

She was very real now. Rosewater scent. Blond curls that escaped her cap and brushed against her shoulders. Broad smile.

He traced his gaze down to where her fingers entwined with his atop the coverlet at the edge of the bed. They tightened around his own before she released him and lifted her hand to his forehead instead. His breath trapped in his chest as she trailed it across his brow.

Her smile only grew. "Your fever has broken. I'll alert the surgeon and ask the girls to bring something for you to eat and drink." She started to rise from her chair beside his bed.

"Wait." His weak voice cracked, but it was enough, for she stayed at his side. "Where am I?"

"You're in the home of Mr. White, recovering from the injuries you sustained in battle." Her attention flicked to his left side, and a shadow fell over her expression. "Do you remember anything of what happened?"

"I was...was climbing...almost at the top of the hill." The scene flashed back in sudden, blinding clarity. The fallen soldiers all around him. Blasts of musket fire and clashes of bayonets. A shooting pain that threw him to the ground. "I was hit in the arm and fell. I must have been knocked unconscious. Some soldiers carried me off but then..." The rest was a murky blur. Snippets of memories that he couldn't be sure were real or delusions. "How long have I...?"

"'Tis Friday, the twenty-third of June now."

Nearly a sennight since the battle. He frowned. "I've not been awake all that time?"

"Not fully. Or at least, not enough that you seemed aware of anything. Your wound was very bad and you took ill." She worried her lip. "Isaac, do you know about your arm?"

The hesitation and sorrow in her voice sent a chill down his spine. He knew his arm had been hit. Had been bleeding badly. Had looked as though it might be beyond repair.

A horrifying realization slammed into him, and nausea made his vision speckle with black. He did know. The pain that seemed too excruciating to be real had not been a nightmare, after all. He did not want to look but couldn't keep from turning his head to his left side. He pushed back the blanket draped over him and there, where his arm had once been, a thick wad of dressings and bandages covered a stump that ended just below his shoulder. His arm was gone.

Rolling away, he heaved, again and again, but there was nothing in his stomach to lose.

"I'm so sorry." Miss Caldwell's voice broke into a sob as she slipped an arm around his back and pressed his head to her shoulder. "It was all they could do to save your life."

He fell out of her embrace, sinking onto the bed, wishing it could swallow him whole. "You should not be here. Should not see me this way."

"I don't mind. Not your arm nor your grief. I am so thankful that you are alive. That is what matters." She reached for his face and smoothed back a hunk of hair that had fallen over his brow.

He turned away, shutting his eyes so he need not see his ruined arm again. "You should go now. Fetch the doctor as you said. And"—he gritted his teeth, knowing his words would hurt her—"please do not come back."

She sucked in a breath, and for a few stretched seconds, he

was certain she would argue. Foolishly hoped she would, though he knew his decision was for the best.

But she said nothing.

Only once her soft footfalls had disappeared out of the room did he dare to open his eyes again. He stared at the ligature that held together what remained of his arm. Miss Caldwell claimed that all that mattered was that he still lived, but what kind of life would he have now? He could not be a soldier. Even though he'd never wished for such a position, it was all he knew. His livelihood and purpose. What future did he have? To return to his father as a disgrace and disappointment once more?

He shifted his gaze to the empty chair at his bedside. Why had Miss Caldwell been there when he woke? Why had she comforted him, instead of turning away, repulsed? He should never have agreed to be her friend. Never have allowed himself to hold her or savor the sound of his name from her lips.

Thoughts of her had been a comfort when he believed he was dying, but now...now he must become nothing to her. And if the sight of him like this was not enough to drive her away, then he would have to do so of his own accord.

~

Isaac stared at the window on Sunday morning, watching the raindrops wind in twisting paths down the panes. Still confined to bed, he was sitting up at least, propped against the headboard for support. It was an improvement from when he'd first woken on Friday afternoon with Miss Caldwell at his side.

She'd gone for the surgeon and not come back. Much to his relief...and regret. Dr. Reynold had explained all that had happened while Isaac was barely conscious, changed the dressings on his arm, and warned Isaac that he was not yet safe from all harm. There was still danger that the surgical site could fester. With that cheerful thought, the physician had departed, leaving two young girls in his wake who came bearing a tray of tea and porridge. He'd managed the meal rather poorly, disgraced by his own weakness and glad that Miss Caldwell had not been there to witness his struggle. Then again, if she had, likely, she would have helped...

He shook his head to banish the thought. She'd tried to visit yesterday, but Isaac had requested that Mr. White keep her informed of his condition without allowing her access to his chamber. The older man had complied, but the loneliness as the day stretched on had left Isaac doubting his decision.

Now the storm was likely to keep her at bay, if his treatment of her had not already done enough.

A knock on the door pulled him from his gloomy thoughts. Isaac looked over and blinked upon spotting a man he had feared he'd never see again. "Merrick? You're alive?"

"And I have you to thank for it, I reckon." His captain shuffled inside. A strip of white cloth wrapped around his head, and he moved a bit stiffly, but otherwise seemed hale.

Isaac grimaced as he shifted to sit up straighter, annoyed by his inability to stand at his captain's approach.

Merrick did not seem to mind. Instead, he laid a hand on Isaac's good shoulder with a smile of relief. "You had me worried that I'd never get the chance to express my gratitude to you. 'Tis good to see you awake, my friend."

"I'm glad to see you as well. How do you fare?"

"I've been better." He chuckled as he settled into the chair next to Isaac's bed. "The ball only grazed my head, but the surgeon did have to cut open my skull to relieve the pressure building there. Dr. Hawkins was kind enough to indulge my curiosity and fixed a pair of looking glasses so that I might catch a glimpse of my own brain. Least now, everyone shall be convinced that I possess such a thing."

Isaac widened his eyes at the captain's story—and his apparent delight in recounting it.

"I've been recovering in the other upstairs room ever since, and keeping abreast of your progress. I was sorry to hear about your arm."

"Seems it could not be avoided, but…" Isaac sighed. What more was there to say? The captain understood the depth of his loss, even if Isaac did not put it into words. "What news on the rest of the company?"

Merrick sobered. "I hear tell we lost nine grenadiers and four light infantrymen from The King's Own. Thirty-one wounded from both flank companies."

"So many."

"Aye. At least eighteen grenadier officers were wounded or killed, along with five officers from the light infantry."

"What of Lieutenant Colonel Abercrobmie?"

Merrick firmed his lips and shook his head. "Gone, I'm afraid. He sustained an injury to his thigh and succumbed three days ago."

Isaac scrubbed a hand over the bristles of his short beard, which had come in while he lay ill. So much suffering and loss. "I saw Sergeant Jackson on the battlefield."

Merrick nodded. "He's buried now, amongst many others. I suppose someone else will be tasked with picking up where he left off in the search for that spy, Lawrence." He leaned closer, voice low. "I heard we captured a man matching Lawrence's description before leaving Breed's Hill, but the scoundrel managed to escape somehow during the transport back to Boston."

"If it was Lawrence, then he is one lucky fellow."

"His luck will run out eventually." Merrick crossed his arms over his chest. "But enough of that. You've had an attentive young woman here caring for you. Where is she now?"

Isaac swallowed. This topic was no more welcome than talk of spies. "I thought it better for her to keep away."

"The surgeon said she was quite a help. Even found some herbs he had run out of to aid in your recovery. Seemed Dr. Reynold valued her assistance."

"I appreciate her kindness, but she does not owe me such attention. I've built somewhat of a friendship with her and her mother, and suspect she feels some obligation because of my connection to her father, but—"

"Obligation?" Merrick's brows arched. "Have you not considered that she is driven by something more than friendship or obligation?"

He had considered it. And swiftly set such thoughts aside. He could not dwell on the idea that Miss Caldwell might hold deeper feelings for him. Their worlds were an ocean apart. Always had been, even when they shared the same roof. And his future was not his to decide. The army still held his commission, and his father still held the terms of his betrothal. Isaac was bound by both until forces outside his control determined what he should do next.

Such thoughts had been trying enough to accept when he was of full strength and at least possessed some authority over his daily life. Could find some meaning in fulfilling his duties. But now? Now the realization of how helpless he truly was gripped him in a suffocating chokehold of despair.

"If I were you, I'd not spurn such help while you are recovering, whatever the motivation behind it." Captain Merrick broke into his morose thoughts. "She would certainly be a more pleasant caretaker than the surgeon."

Isaac could not argue with that, especially when he compared Dr. Reynold's grim expression to Miss Caldwell's hopeful smile. But while his healing might be aided by her presence, his heart was not strong enough to come out unscathed.

CHAPTER 18

Sweat beaded on the back of Libby's neck, dampening her floral print fichu, as she and Benjamin approached the Whites' house on Friday afternoon. 'Twas the last day of June, and the month seemed determined to depart in a wave of humid heat that settled between the cramped buildings lining the narrow streets. She'd wanted to visit earlier, but Benjamin had been occupied with chores for his parents, and Mama had been unwilling to relent on her stipulation that Libby not walk alone.

A whole sennight had passed since she'd last seen Isaac, though not for lack of trying. Despite Elijah's warning that Isaac would never forgive her should he learn of her involvement in passing on the army's confidential plans, she could not convince herself to stay away. She'd visited the house three times since Isaac dismissed her, but was turned back on each occasion with an apologetic smile from Mr. White. The older man was kind enough to keep her informed of Isaac's condition, so she knew that he had not fallen ill again since the surgery. But Mr. White was insistent upon honoring Isaac's request for privacy, which, despite the passage of days, had not seemed to change.

Libby's young neighbor had rolled his shirtsleeves to his elbows and unbuttoned the top of his waistcoat. His trousers looked a bit too short. Had he grown a lot recently? Perhaps she could let down the hem for his mother, as a token of thanks for all the trips he'd made with her of late. Though he didn't seem to mind, especially since young Aideen often greeted him with a dipper of water or something tasty from the kitchen. The girl stepped out of the house as they drew near, and Benjamin's cheeks, already rosy from the heat, grew a deeper shade of red. Libby suppressed a smile.

With a giggled promise of a freshly baked roll, the two scurried inside, nearly crashing into Miss White. She pulled away just in time, shaking her head even as her lips tipped into an indulgent grin.

"I'd begun to wonder if you had decided not to come today." Miss White joined Libby on the back step.

"I had to wait for my escort." Libby nodded toward the boy, his mouth full with an oversize bite. "How is the lieutenant?"

"The surgeon seemed pleased when he visited earlier. Briana said he was sitting at the table when she brought up his breakfast, and that his plate was so clean when she fetched it later, she wondered if he had licked off every last bite." Miss White's eyes crinkled at the corners, mirth over the young girl's words evident.

"I do not doubt it. Likely, he is fed better here than he would be amongst his regiment." Or at Libby's home, though she refrained from saying so.

"Dr. Reynold recommended beef for his meals if we can manage, to help regain his strength, but 'tis so hard to come by these days."

Libby nodded. The siege was wearing on everyone, even a family as well-to-do as the Whites.

She hesitated, afraid to ask if Miss White knew whether Isaac was willing to see her or not. Perhaps it was better to linger in the unknown a bit longer, since it left room for hope. Her heart was already bruised from days of refusals. Could she bear it if he continued to deny her? If he closed himself off from her for good?

Miss White dipped her head, voice barely a whisper. "Have you seen Elijah again?"

The unexpected question interrupted Libby's thoughts. She shook her head, matching Miss White's hushed tone. "I have not."

She had passed along Elijah's apology last week, as he'd requested, and said simply that he expected to be away from Boston for quite some time. Miss White had looked as though she wanted to ask more, but they'd been interrupted by her mother and not had a moment to discuss it again since.

"I am sorry for causing such a fuss when he appeared. I could not believe it was him, and—"

"You need not apologize. I nearly screamed the first time I saw him."

"That does make me feel a bit better." Miss White chuckled, then gestured toward their gardens. "Walk with me a moment?"

Libby fell in step beside her, curious as to what more Miss White wished to say but equally worried over misspeaking in regard to Elijah. She must tread carefully and not reveal anything that would put him, or herself, in danger.

"I must confess, I am rather angry with him." Miss White paused beside the garden and flicked a beetle off a winding bean plant. "This is not the first time he has passed in and out of my life with little explanation."

"He seems to have an uncanny, and rather undesired, skill in that area." Libby shared Miss White's frustration, especially knowing how Elijah's disappearance had impacted Hannah and Mr. Pierce.

"He was so upset when Samuel died. He came to our house to tell me in person, before the rumors spread or the news was printed in the papers. I burst into tears when he explained what had happened and..." She pressed her lips together to collect herself. "He wrapped his arms around me and let me cry as long as I needed. When I pulled away, there were tears on his face too. I'd never seen a man cry before, and it broke my heart afresh to know how much he grieved the death of his friend."

Libby's own eyes pricked. "He was heartbroken over the loss."

"I know. I thought we might offer some comfort or encouragement to each other. But then I hardly saw him again after that, and I felt...I do not know exactly. Betrayed, I suppose? I could not mourn Samuel openly with my parents, as they had never been in favor of our association in the first place, and I did not wish to reveal how dear he was to me. Elijah was the one person who truly understood my grief, but it seemed as though he had abandoned me." Miss White crossed her arms over her chest and sighed. "I'm sorry. I don't know why I'm telling you all of this, except that...well, I've never had anyone else to talk to about it all."

"I don't mind." Libby understood far too well what it was to hold onto things she was not free to speak of, and right now, as Miss White spilled her heart, the weight of all that Elijah had revealed felt even heavier than before.

"I suppose seeing him again brought everything back, and I cannot help but wish he had stayed long enough for me to tell him how his silence, his disappearance, only compounded my grief. Though, 'tis unlikely I'd have the courage to say it so bluntly, even if given the chance." Miss White frowned. "I know he is your friend and beg your pardon for speaking thus about him."

"No pardon necessary. I was hurt by his actions too." In more ways than she dared name. But she'd realized something about Elijah, when they'd spoken last week under cover of darkness. 'Twas not sheer recklessness that drove him, but something deeper. She ran her fingers over a golden cluster of flowers blooming atop a clump of tansy, as she contemplated how to put her thoughts into words. "We all grieve in different ways. I lost my father two years ago, and I think I've been searching ever since for something to fill the hole his absence has left in my life. My mother mourned so quietly, I regret to admit that sometimes I missed how much she was hurting. And Elijah...I think he ran from his sorrow—or tried to, at least. Perhaps he is running still."

"Rather like your lieutenant."

Libby snapped her attention back to Miss White's face. "What do you mean?"

"It has not escaped my notice how little time you've spent with him since his surgery, and I heard my father say that Lieutenant Harrison had requested his privacy. He may not be able to run, but he can hide. 'Tis his own sort of attempt to escape the pain, I reckon."

"Perhaps you're right. I was so relieved when the surgery was a success, and so determined to see him well again...I suppose I did not consider how difficult this is for him. Mayhap I should stop trying to visit and give him the space he evidently desires. I've been rather selfish, I fear."

"I would not call it selfish to want to be near the man you love."

"I never said I—"

A soft laugh interrupted her protest. "You denied it before, I remember. But it seems plain enough to me. Does he know?"

Libby's face heated as she resigned herself to Miss White's astute observation. No sense attempting to protest again. "I hope not. I spoke true when I said we are friends. I believe that's all he thinks."

"But why not let him see the truth of your feelings? Perhaps that would give him some comfort through these trying days."

"Because there is no..." She wrestled with the words that had spun 'round her head countless times. "I do not see a way for a future between us, so I am determined to be content to care for him as I can for now. And when the time comes that we must inevitably part, I will force my heart to accept it."

"But why are you so sure that you must be parted? What if he feels the same?"

"I am certain he does not. He knew me when I was but a girl, and I believe a part of him still thinks of me as the young daughter of his friend, not a woman full grown." Even as she said it, Libby couldn't help but remember the way he'd embraced her before the battle. Was it possible his feelings toward her had changed? No, it could not be, and there was nothing to gain by hoping. She shoved such thoughts aside, mind straying instead to the stark difference between their loyalties. Did she dare speak of that to Miss White? "There are other reasons. Other things to stand between us."

Miss White narrowed her eyes, quiet for a long moment. "You're a Patriot, aren't you?"

Libby blinked at her intuitive guess. Perhaps she'd not done as well at hiding her beliefs as she thought. She dipped her head in silent confirmation.

"I had begun to wonder." There was no condemnation in her tone. Instead, a note of sympathy softened her voice. "I see, then, why you believe there will never be anything more between you and the lieutenant. Forgive me for teasing so."

"There's nothing to forgive." Libby searched Miss White's face for a hint of disapproval or anger but found none. "I hope you'll not think differently of me now, for I have enjoyed getting to know you these past days."

"And I you. You need not fear any change in our friendship.

May I consider it that? With all that has happened in Boston lately, I am dearly in need of a friend."

Relief tugged Libby's mouth into a smile. "As am I."

Despite their differences, Libby had come to look forward to seeing Miss White and sharing a sense of camaraderie with another young woman equally trapped in this town that increasingly felt less like home.

"Call me Katherine, then?"

"Aye. And you may call me Libby if you wish."

"I am inspired by your courage, Libby. I do not know if I would have the strength to take care of a man I loved while knowing I must keep that love forever hidden away." She grasped Libby's hands. "And you give me hope that one day this town will not be so torn apart. For if you can overcome the divide between your ideals and those of a British officer, then surely, one day there can be peace amongst our neighbors again."

Libby squeezed Katherine's fingers in return. Peace seemed as fragile and fleeting as a morning mist on the harbor, but Libby could not deny that she longed for the same. The path to reach it, however, might be quite different in her eyes than in those of her new friend.

"I've delayed you far too long." Katherine released her and gestured toward the house. "Go on. I hope for your sake that the lieutenant has had a change of heart today."

Libby's pulse stuttered. Swallowing, she turned and forced her feet toward the back door, grasping for a scrap of the courage Katherine claimed she had.

Mr. White met her in the kitchen, the apologetic look in his eyes speaking the answer before she even said a word. "Good day to you, Miss Caldwell. I regret to say that the lieutenant is sleeping and has asked not to be disturbed."

"I understand." She plastered on a smile, unwilling to let

Mr. White see her disappointment. Why was Isaac so intent upon keeping her away?

Her facade must have been weak, though, given the pity etched in Mr. White's forehead. "I am sorry, Miss Caldwell. I will tell him you called."

She nodded, not trusting her voice, then turned to Benjamin, who waited in the doorway, unspoken questions swirling in his wide eyes.

She crossed to his side and squeezed his shoulder. "Ready to go home?"

He opened his mouth as though to speak, then promptly shut it and followed her outside. Libby's gaze snagged on Katherine, stooped beside her garden. Katherine peeked up, face falling when she saw Libby. She lifted a hand in a parting wave, and Libby returned the gesture, blinking against the sting of tears.

She would come again tomorrow morning. One final attempt. If Isaac still wished her to stay away then, she would respect his decision, even though it would break her heart.

CHAPTER 19

The rich scent of coffee and the lilt of girlish chatter greeted Libby as she stepped into the Whites' kitchen on Saturday morning. Aideen and Briana bobbed their heads at Libby as she approached, Aideen's gaze straying behind her to where Benjamin hovered in the doorway. Steam rose from four cups lined along the table, and a stack of empty plates waited to be filled with the eggs and ham that sizzled over the fire under the girls' watchful eyes. No one else was in sight.

"Is some of that food for Lieutenant Harrison?" Libby peeked over the girls' shoulders.

"Aye, miss. Nearly done now." Briana, the older sister, deftly flipped a slab of ham. "We're to bring his tray up soon as it's ready."

"I'll take it for you," Libby hurried to offer. She'd been considering how she might convince Mr. White to let her see Isaac. She needed to see him, speak to him face to face, instead of hearing his refusal through someone else. Delivering his breakfast was the perfect excuse.

Once the plate had been filled with hearty fare that made

her own meager bowl of porridge seem rather pitiful, Libby balanced the tray in her arms and made for the back stairs.

As she climbed, she considered Katherine's words from the previous afternoon about courage and hope. The compliments felt undeserved. Rather, it was a sense of inadequacy and guilt that had been her constant companions of late, heaping blame upon her conscience with their accusing whispers. Sometimes it felt as though they'd become stitched into the very fabric of her being.

With each step, another mistake, secret, or poor decision flashed through her mind. She'd been so desperate to stay in Boston near Isaac, but now he could turn her away with a single word. She had ached for something significant to contribute to her family or the Patriot cause, but the news she'd spread to Elijah had entangled her in a dangerous spy ring. She claimed to miss the openness of Papa's conversations, but had chosen to keep secrets from Mama. She'd told herself she could maintain a friendship with Isaac and still be able to move on, but it was clearly a lie, for whether he turned her away now or at some other point, there was no ending that would spare her the pain of goodbye.

Her breath grew shallow as she reached the top of the stairs, trapped in her chest much like she was trapped in this city and in the muddle of emotions and choices she'd made. She paused, willing her pulse to resume a normal pace, then crept forward and peered through the open door of Isaac's chamber. His bed was empty. Her heart seemed to stop for a moment, even though the girls had assured her he was well and expecting his morning meal. At the far corner of the room, a small table had been moved next to the window. A single chair perched beside it, and there, to her relief, sat Isaac.

Dressed in a linen shirt and breeches, his back was to her, and he seemed unaware of her presence. Sunlight slanted through the window, glinting off the shaving blade he ran along his cheek. She'd noticed his beard coming in when she was here last and been curiously tempted to trace her fingers over the dark stubble, so different from his normally clean-shaven jaw. But she'd forced herself to refrain.

Not wanting to startle him into accidentally cutting himself, she waited until he pulled the razor away from his face to dip it clean in the basin before she rapped softly on the door.

The blade clattered against the porcelain edge of the bowl as he spun to face her. His eyes widened, and she steeled herself for a rebuke, but he simply stared.

"Good morning." She ventured inside, hovering near the threshold. "I brought your breakfast."

Reaching for the towel, he scrubbed his face dry. "Miss Caldwell. I did not expect to see you."

"I wonder why." She forced a note of teasing into her voice to hide the hurt.

Still, he seemed to understand her message, for he turned away. "You've caught me at a rather inopportune moment."

"I did wait until that sharp razor was nowhere near your face. I've not forgotten what brought you to my father's care years ago." She hoped the lighthearted recollection would draw him out, but his back only stiffened even more. Though her heart sank, she pressed on. "It is good to see you out of bed."

"If you'd seen how difficult it was for me to get here, you'd think differently." Frustration simmered in his muttered retort.

"You have been through so much, 'tis no wonder your body needs time to recover." How strange and discouraging it must be for him, who had long been stronger and more physically capable than most other men, to now be weak and reliant upon the help of others. "I know it is hard, but try to be patient with yourself. You will regain your strength soon enough."

"Do you forget that I no longer have one of my arms?" He shook his head, and his unbound hair tumbled around his shoulders. "I will never recover fully. Never be whole again."

A lump swelled in her throat. His physical suffering had been painful enough, but now he faced another kind of torment, one hidden and perhaps even more difficult to heal.

Lord, help Isaac see that he is so much more than what this injury has taken from him. Swallowing, she crossed the room to set the tray on the table and forced herself into his line of vision.

He dipped his head, refusing to meet her eye. A tangle of dark locks spilled forward, shadowing his face. She buried her fingers in the folds of her petticoat to keep from reaching out and tucking the strands behind his ear. Had no one thought to help him tie it back? He could not do so on his own. Not with only one hand.

The thought sucked the air from her lungs. He'd not only lost an arm, he'd lost his independence. He was no longer capable of doing something as simple as plaiting his own hair. She'd been so relieved that he survived, and so determined to encourage him, she'd failed to recognize the depth of what he would need to overcome. The challenges that he would face for the rest of his days. No wonder he was grieving.

"Thank you for breakfast." His words came out gruff. "The girls could have seen to it."

She tried to ignore the sting of his comment. "I know, but I wanted to see you, and I thought—"

"I'm told you visited often while I was ill, and I appreciate your kindness." He swiped the hair out of his face but did not look at her. "You and your mother have been more than generous these past months, but you do not owe me anything more."

Another barb lodged in her heart. Did he really believe that was why she was here? Why she had kept vigil at his bedside every moment she was able?

"That is not why I've come. Surely, you know better. I want to be here. I want to help, because..." She bit her lip, holding back the words that begged release. With a sigh, she settled on a safer choice. "Did we not agree that we are friends?"

A muscle in his jaw twitched. "I cannot see why you should wish to continue such a friendship. Not after..." He finally lifted his gaze to hers, regret etching lines in his brow. "Everyone in this house is loyal to the Crown. They have good reason to nurse our wounded men back to health. But you, do you not wish to distance yourself from me now?"

"Is that it, then? Why you're intent upon pushing me away? Because my patriotic leanings are in opposition to your obligation as a soldier?" She planted her palms on the edge of the table. "That did not hinder our friendship in the past. I have always seen you as more than the uniform you wear. I told you that. Did you think I was lying?"

"Of course not. But that was before all of this."

"All of what? The battle? I did not despise you after what happened at Lexington and Concord. How is this any different? If you think me so fickle in my friendship as to turn my back because you fulfilled the duty you are bound to, then you think quite poorly of me."

The truth settled deep inside, even as Elijah's words taunted her. She could look beyond Isaac's actions as a soldier to the man she'd come to know and admire, but would he do the same for her if he found out what she had done?

"That is not what I meant. I..." He shoved his hand through his hair. "I think too highly of you and your mother to hold you to a connection that will only bring you pain. It is better this way. For both of us."

"You're wrong." Her voice quivered.

"What do you want with a broken man like me, anyway?" Anger flashed in his eyes before they dimmed with resignation. "Look at me."

She did. For a long moment, she let her gaze roam his face, noticing the sunken contours after days of illness and little food. Taking in the spot of stubble he'd missed while shaving and the knotted hair in need of a good combing. She let her attention fall to his left shoulder and the empty sleeve that hung there. He twitched under her scrutiny.

Was that the real reason he'd kept her away? Was he ashamed of the injury that had stolen his arm? Did he think she saw him as weak because of it? As less of a man? Nothing could be further from the truth.

Emboldened by the need to make him understand, she reached out and brushed her fingers over the rough patch on his cheek. "You missed a spot." Her voice came out far too breathy, but she could not turn back now. She let her hand fall to rest on his left shoulder, feeling him tense beneath her gentle touch. "And this will never change how I look at you."

He swallowed, gaze searching hers, then dipping ever so briefly to her lips before he pulled away to stare out the window.

Libby exhaled a ragged breath. For a moment, it had looked as though he wanted to... No, she must have imagined it. "I'll leave you to your meal. If you wish me to return, say so. Otherwise, I will not bother you anymore. Not today and"—she sucked in a breath, forcing out the painful words—"not again."

Silence hung thick in the air, palpable and tense. She swallowed but could summon nothing to break it. Nor would she try. She had left that to him.

He shifted to look at her again, weariness shadowing his face. "Thank you for your concern for me, Miss Caldwell. I will always remember your kindness, and I wish you well."

She stared at him, his words hardly making sense. Was that all? Gratitude and a...goodbye? *Please, Lord, let there be more.* "Is that your answer?"

"Aye." Resignation and determination mingled in his brown eyes.

Her hands shook. She tucked them beneath her apron to

hide the trembling. Her eyes welled with tears, but she refused to let him see. Spinning away, she fled from the room, one hand pressed to her chest, as though doing so could keep her heart from shattering into a thousand pieces.

As swift and sharp as a pair of shears slicing a strand of thread from a spool, their relationship, whatever it had been, was severed for good.

~

Isaac stared out the window as Libby's retreating form passed beneath the shadow of a tree. He should not think of her by that name, yet it burrowed deep, and while he could still force his tongue to address her as Miss Caldwell, she was Libby in his heart. And that was the danger.

She picked her way around the stone markers of Copp's Hill burying ground, a spot of color and feminine beauty amidst the cold gray slabs. He'd almost laughed when he first realized that his chamber in the Whites' home overlooked the cemetery. A reminder of all his fellow soldiers who now lay beneath the dirt. Why had he been spared? A breeze pushed through the open widow, rustling the dangling fabric of his empty sleeve. And for what purpose had his life been saved, now that he would never be the same man again?

He held Libby in his sight until she passed over the top of the hill and out of view. Everything in him wanted to call her back. To keep her close. To soak up the light and hope that she brought into the dreariness and despair that hung over him. His shoulder burned where she had touched him, but not with pain. He lifted his hand to his cheek and could almost feel her fingers brushing his skin. She'd nearly done him in with her touch and those searching blue eyes. Had she seen enough to know the real reason he kept her away?

His excuses held truth. It seemed impossible that she

should still bear his company, after he'd stormed into battle more than once against her countrymen. And equally impossible to understand why she would trouble herself to help take care of a man so broken. He did not want her to see his weakness. The way he'd been forced to cling to the surgeon for support simply to take five steps across the floor. Or how he'd struggled to don his clothing with just one arm, as though he were a mere child.

But it was more than all of that. It was his heart that he must keep locked away. She'd become too precious to him, her presence like fresh air in his stale sickroom. Like sunlight piercing through an endless night. A promise that he would one day be well...and, oh, how he wanted to believe it.

He knew, without a doubt, that she could help him heal. That her care would aid his recovery. But it was selfish of him to want her near when he could offer nothing in return.

Turning from the window, he eyed his untouched breakfast. His stomach growled, loud in the empty room. Strange, he'd never thought himself someone who needed the company of others to be content. But perhaps he'd been wrong. Or mayhap his brush with death made him crave companionship more than before. Loneliness seemed a heavier weight than usual, compounding the lingering pain in his body and the aching grief over his uncertain future.

The indentured servant girls had flitted in and out of his room these past days, delivering food or, to his dismay, emptying his chamber pot. But they spoke no more than the slightest of greetings. Dr. Reynold stopped by at least twice a day, but his visits were brief and focused on changing bandages or inquiring as to Isaac's pain. Captain Merrick was the only one who had come simply to keep Isaac company, but he'd since been deemed well enough to return to the encampment on the Common and resume most of his responsibilities there.

Doubt assailed him. Perhaps he should have allowed Libby

to return so that he would feel less alone. But did he have the strength to hold his feelings in check if she came again? He'd barely held himself together this morning.

He'd been strong enough to march up Breed's Hill and face the militia's muskets head on. To step over the bodies of his fallen men on the way. To push all fear and sorrow into a place where it could not escape, and fulfill the duty he'd sworn to carry out. Why, if he could stand firm in battle, could he not do the same in her presence?

He slid his shaving kit out of the way and pulled the tray of food near. There was a knife and fork beside his plate, but he could not manage both at once. Frowning, he stabbed his fork into the center of the slice of ham and bit off a chunk.

Isaac had just finished his breakfast when Dr. Reynold's firm footsteps drew his attention to the doorway.

"Good. You're eating well." The surgeon nodded at Isaac's empty plate as he entered. "Glad to move on from broths and porridge, I imagine."

"Aye." Isaac huffed. Indeed, he was, given how helpless he'd felt in his first days of healing, attempting to manage the prescribed liquid meals while half propped against the headboard.

The two servant girls hurried into the room, one with a pile of clean bandages, the other balancing a basin of water.

"Clear the lieutenant's food and leave those things on the table." The doctor doled out his orders with naught but a passing glance in their direction.

They did as they were told, peeking at Isaac when they drew near.

He offered them a smile. "Thank you. Breakfast was delicious."

That drew a blush from the red-headed girl and a timid smile from the older one. They bobbed matching curtsies and left as quickly as they'd come.

Dr. Reynold stepped closer. "Let's have a look at that wound now. I'll help you back to the bed."

Gripping the edge of the table, Isaac pushed himself out of the chair. His vision swam, and he closed his eyes for a moment as Dr. Reynold looped an arm around his back.

Though shorter than Isaac, the surgeon was a solid man and did not strain under Isaac's weight as he released his hold on the table to shuffle forward. His legs felt heavy and unsteady, and his heart thumped in his chest at even so slight an exertion. He sank onto the mattress, winded and ready to sleep.

He didn't protest when Dr. Reynold helped him remove his shirt, even though the assistance left him feeling as helpless as a baby. Nor did he flinch when the surgeon unwound the wrappings and examined the stump that remained of his arm.

Dr. Reynold graced him with a rare and fleeting smile. "I'm very pleased. It's healing nicely. The yarrow helped immensely to staunch the bleeding, which was of utmost importance, given how much you had lost from the initial injury."

Crossing to the table where the girls had left his supplies, Dr. Reynold proceeded to cleanse the wound with a wet strip of linen. Isaac gritted his teeth at the surgeon's ministrations. Next came the ointment, an herbaceous-smelling paste that clung to his nose long after it had been applied.

"I'll call for more willow bark tea for the pain. Best stay abed for the remainder of the day and rest as much as possible." The surgeon wrapped fresh linen around Isaac's arm. "Once more granulations have formed at the site, we can draw the edges of the wound together with adhesive plasters."

"How long do you think?"

"Another few days, perhaps, until we can move to the next stage. 'Tis hard to say for certain. Every case proceeds in different manners."

"I meant until it is fully healed." Isaac grimaced as the doctor knotted the final bandage in place.

Dr. Reynold hummed low in his throat. "Some surgeons say as little as three to four weeks. Others have observed patients for nearly two months before the cure is complete."

Two months? Isaac couldn't suppress a sigh. "I do not need to be confined to bed all that time, do I?"

"Certainly not. As your strength builds, you may move about more freely. But for now, once a day at the table is a good start. Keep up your spirits, Lieutenant. Things are proceeding better than I had hoped." Dr. Reynold faced him with a stern expression that seemed an odd match to his attempted encouragement. "I'll send the servants to clean up and bring you the tea."

Isaac eased back onto his pillow as the surgeon departed. Drained of energy, he let his eyes slide closed. The girls may bring his tea, but 'twas unlikely he'd be awake to drink it.

He remembered the patch of stubble he'd never gotten around to shaving. Too late now. He rubbed his thumb over the rough spot, thoughts drifting once more to Libby.

Be it weeks or months, the thought of passing these slow days of healing in empty loneliness was too hard to bear. Perhaps Libby's cheerful spirit and steady prayers would have helped his recovery proceed faster. Couldn't he have held his feelings in check? Hidden them deep inside so she would never know. So that perhaps he might even forget them.

But he had sent her away.

She'd only ever shown him kindness, and he'd met it with rejection. He'd seen the tears in her eyes. Heard the quiver in her voice. All his fault.

Guilt churned his stomach. He had wanted to protect her from the dangers of a town under siege and the harsh realities of war, but he'd been the one to hurt her in the end.

Thunder rumbled in the distance, and dark clouds threatened to burst at any second as Libby yanked the last of the laundry off the line and hurried toward the back door that Mama held open. She ducked inside as the first fat raindrops began to fall.

"Just in time." Mama smiled. "Come, I'll help you fold."

Libby could not manage to return her mother's smile. Nearly a week had passed since Isaac turned her away, and she felt as gloomy as the storm outside. Each day when she woke, there was one moment of peace, when the haze of sleep still lingered, wrapping her broken heart in a sheltered cocoon and blocking out the truth. But it lasted only a few seconds before the painful reality crashed over her once more. Isaac had rejected her, fully and finally, and no amount of preparation could have protected her from the crushing blow.

She traipsed upstairs behind Mama, following her into her chamber where she deposited the armful of clothing onto Mama's bed. The blue-and-white floral bedcurtains were drawn back, the coverlet neatly tucked 'round the mattress without a wrinkle. Libby had left her own bed unmade. Simple tasks seemed to require more energy than she could muster. Every day this week, she had forced herself through the motions, determined not to let all the household chores fall on Mama, or to neglect her duty to Mrs. Barker, but even the smallest things left her exhausted. She felt as hollowed out as the empty clam shells that washed up along the harbor shore.

Reaching for a shift, she shook the garment to ensure no insects were hidden inside the fabric before she folded it into a tidy square. She moved to grab another, but Mama's hand closed over hers, stilling her motion.

"'Tis time we talked about this, Libby." Her voice was soft but firm.

Libby pulled her hand free, taking a wadded-up fichu with it. "I already told you what happened."

"You did. But now you are holding all your hurt inside. That is no way to heal. Trust me, for I tried to do the same."

Libby peered at her mother. She understood. Indeed, she had grieved an even greater loss. Had she ever wished to stay in bed all day? To pull the blankets over her head and pretend the world did not exist? That each day did not keep moving on as usual when she felt like her life had come to an abrupt halt?

She dropped her attention back to the swath of fabric in her hands. "It is not as though he died. Or that he ever cared for me as I did for him. I should not be struggling so much. I told myself I would be stronger, that I would not—"

"There is no shame in your sorrow over the lieutenant's decision. You need not add to your pain by punishing yourself for feeling as you do."

"But I am ashamed. If you knew..." Libby's throat closed over the words.

"Then tell me. Tell me what I should know so I can help you."

"I've been so foolish. I could have spared myself, and you, so much trouble and pain if I'd only let go of my stubborn feelings for Isaac earlier." Libby sank to the edge of the bed, burying her face in her hands, unable to meet Mama's probing gaze. "He was the reason I wanted to stay in Boston. I convinced you that we should remain here because I couldn't bear the thought of being separated from him, and look what happened. I'm separated from him by his own choosing, which hurts even more. Now we're stuck here, and I've put you through so much suffering because of my selfishness."

"Elizabeth, do you think I did not know why you wished to stay? You may not have said it then, but I have known the truth all along."

Libby's hands fell to her lap. "You have?"

She laughed softly. "Do not doubt a mother's instincts. You are not a child any longer, but you are still *my* child. I knew he was the reason, just as I knew how much you cared for him even before you told me." Mama pushed the laundry aside and settled next to her, wrapping an arm around her shoulders. "If you believe you alone are responsible for convincing me to remain here, then you misremember all that happened. Do not blame yourself for the circumstances we are in. We both came to this decision together, and my part in it, at least, was well covered in prayer."

"Mine was not." The confession leaked out.

Mama didn't scold. Instead, she pulled Libby closer. "The book of Proverbs teaches that 'A man's heart deviseth his way: but the Lord directeth his steps.' Your choices cannot thwart His plans. I say this not to excuse rash actions, but rather to remind you that nothing can stand in the way of God's purpose. He will use all things for His glory, and I am convinced that God has a reason for us to be here, whether we understand it fully now or not."

Libby pressed her lips together. Could it be true? That despite her mistakes, God could use her right where she was for something good? That even the hardest things could be part of His greater plan for her life?

"It is not wrong to grieve, Libby, but I will not stand by and allow you to lose hope." Mama brushed a kiss to her forehead. "Fix your eyes on God. Allow Him to use even your sorrow to draw you closer to Himself and trust that His ways, while beyond our comprehension, are always best."

Libby nodded. It would not be easy, but there was comfort in knowing she could lay aside her own strivings and failures and rest in God's hands. She remembered Mama's words the day of the battle, that all the troubles of earth would feel light compared with God's eternal glory. That He was enough, always enough, no matter what else happened in her life. If she could hold to that truth, might her heart feel a little less empty? Her days a bit more hopeful?

Mama pushed off the bed and lifted a pair of stockings from the pile. Libby stood to join her as the rain drummed harder on the roof. Another sound, a pounding noise, echoed from downstairs, bringing both of their hands to a halt.

Her mother frowned. "Is someone at the door?"

"I will go look."

Libby hurried down as the knocking grew louder and more persistent. She tugged open the door. Katherine stared back at her, pale-faced, dark strands of hair plastered to her cheeks. A carriage stood in the street behind her, the driver hunched in the seat and the horses tossing their heads with obvious displeasure over being put to work in such weather. Why would Katherine come here in the middle of a storm, unless...

Libby's heart froze. "Is it Isaac? Has something happened? Has he taken ill again?"

She shook her head, water droplets splattering off the brim of her bonnet. "Not in body, at least. But he has hardly slept all week, and when he does, he wakes up crying out as though in terror. He just had one of the worst episodes yet, and we are at a loss as to how to help. I thought if anyone might be able to encourage or soothe him, it would be you."

Libby's chest ached at the thought of Isaac's suffering. Everything in her longed to be at his side. But he'd sent her away. The ache spread through her limbs, and she clasped her arms over her stomach in attempt to quell it. "He did not want me to come back. He said—"

The stairs creaked behind Libby, and she turned to see Mama descending. "I agree with Miss White. Your presence will help him. You should go."

But what if she made things worse? Only upset him more and exposed her heart to a fresh barrage of hurt?

God, what do I do?

The prayer was swift and silent, made almost without thinking, as though her soul formed the words her mind could not. But, to her surprise, peace followed it. Just as swiftly. Just as silently. It enveloped her in warm assurance and confidence. If there was any way she could bring Isaac comfort, she must try.

"Aye. I'll go."

"Good. Let's hurry." Katherine rushed back outside.

Libby dashed after her toward the waiting carriage. It jerked into motion, clattering over the rutted street. She gripped the edge of the seat to keep from falling and clung even more tightly to Mama's words of confidence in God's purpose for them.

Perhaps loving Isaac would never bring Libby the future she had longed for, but might it still be part of God's plan, for her life and his? Not born of selfish desire, but offered as a selfless act for a man in desperate need of hope.

~

*I*saac stumbled to the window and pressed his forehead against the smooth pane. His shirt clung to his back, slick with cold sweat, and his heart raced faster than a cavalry horse charging into battle.

Battle. It was all he saw when he fell asleep. Fire and gunshots and blood invaded the darkness. Phantom pain pulsed through an arm that was no longer there. The visions and sensations terrified him, and the terror left him weak and ashamed.

Rain streamed down the glass, and thunder rumbled overhead. He braced himself against the wall with his good shoulder, his body so weary he feared he could collapse at any moment. He desperately needed sleep, but there was no rest to be found when he closed his eyes.

His breath came in short gasps that, try as he might, he could not steady. He'd hoped that attempting to sleep during the afternoon would be better somehow. That the daylight would hold the horror at bay. How wrong he had been.

This nightmare had been the worst yet. It started the same as the others, with his climb toward the redoubt, but when he reached the top 'twas not a stranger that stared back at him, but William Abbott, hand clasped to his chest, blood seeping from between his fingers. And then a scream. Not of a soldier but a woman. Libby. She had run past him, sobbing as she threw her arms around her stepbrother. She'd turned to look at Isaac, William's blood staining her gown, betrayal swimming in the depths of her gaze. Only then did Isaac realize his musket was pressed to his shoulder, smoke rising from his fatal shot.

He'd jolted awake, trembling, his own cries summoning Miss White, who stared at him wide-eyed before he sent her away with an apology, but no explanation. What could he say? He'd sought help from the surgeon earlier in the week, but Dr. Reynold's only answer was to offer a dose of laudanum. Isaac had refused. He'd lost too much of himself already. He would not lose more to a numbed stupor.

He shoved a hand through his hair, which had come loose from the queue little Briana had arranged for him. The two girls tiptoed around him whenever they came to his room now, always giving him a wide berth as they delivered his food or tidied the space. Likely, they'd heard his screams and were afraid. He did not blame them. He was beginning to be afraid of himself. Afraid that he would never escape the prison his mind had created.

A soft knock at the door made him jump. He straightened, turning to see who it was, but the door remained closed. Another knock sounded.

He cleared his throat. "You may come in."

Slowly, the door pushed open and a familiar face peeked around the corner. A face he'd seen in his nightmare, but this time, it bore a tentative smile instead of an accusing glare. His breath left in a heavy exhale. "Miss Caldwell? What are you...?"

"Miss White was concerned about you. She thought you would benefit from the presence of a friend. I hope you do not mind that she sought me out." She stepped into the room but hovered with one hand on the latch. "We were friends once, were we not?"

Her words stung, despite the gentle manner in which they were offered. *We were friends once.* How he hated to think that their friendship would forever be in the past, even though he'd tried to convince himself such a separation was necessary.

He stared at her a long moment. Several damp curls clung to her cheeks, and the hem of her petticoat was soaked several inches high. She'd come out in this storm...for him.

He had shut her out and pushed her away. He was broken in body and mind. He had nothing to offer her and yet...she'd not given up on him. He swallowed against the sudden urge to cross the room, pull her against his chest, and weep.

"We are friends still, I hope." His voice came out rough. "If you'll forgive me for the way I treated you."

"Of course I do." Her smile bloomed, full and bright, the most beautiful sight he'd seen in days. She moved to stand before him and peered up with a searching gaze that seemed to see into the depths of his soul. Her expression sobered. "I will not pretend to fully understand what you are going through, or how you are feeling. But I will stay and offer whatever I can to help ease your burden, if you'll let me."

Her forgiveness washed over him, as cleansing and free as the rain falling outside. He nodded, not trusting his voice.

"You're having nightmares again?" Her attention flicked to his bed and the tangle of sheets hanging off the side before returning to his face.

Another nod. Miss White must have informed her. What did she think of him, to see his weakness so exposed?

"I'm sorry. You must be exhausted." There was no judgment in her eyes. She lifted a hand as though she might reach for him, but pulled back, tucking a stray curl behind her ear instead. "My father always touted the importance of sleep when one was healing. What does Dr. Reynold say?"

"He suggested laudanum, but I'll not resort to that."

"That is a good choice. Papa was quite opposed to its use, except in the most dire of circumstances."

Her affirmation of his decision shouldn't matter so much, yet it brought a sense of relief to know she supported him. 'Twas a welcome change compared to the surgeon's dismissive grunts.

"I was plagued by nightmares for a time when I was young. Not to suggest that your situation is similar to mine as a child, only that..." She hesitated, and a hint of pink filled her cheeks. "Well, Mama always said that if I spoke what I had dreamed aloud to her, then those thoughts needn't linger in my head anymore. It helped, as I recall. Along with a prayer and a hug, but..." The color in her cheeks deepened.

A hug sounded far more appealing than it should. "I would hate to trouble you by recounting the images that invade my mind." He could not tell her his most recent nightmare, certainly. But if there was any chance it would help him rest, he was anxious to try nearly anything.

"You needn't give all the details. Are you reliving the battle? Or does it have to do with your..." Her gaze trailed to the sleeve dangling loose at his left side.

"The battle. I see it again and again, but sometimes the events are...twisted." He shifted to brace himself against the back of the chair next to him for support. Standing this long was beginning to take a toll.

She glanced at his white-knuckled grip. "You should sit."

"There's only one chair." He'd lost most of his dignity. Surely, he could maintain some sense of respect and not force her to stand alone.

"Then I'll take the chair, and you"—she stepped to his bed and made quick work of straightening the covers and fluffing the pillow—"may sit right here."

Returning to his side, she offered her arm as though it did not bother her in the least that their roles were reversed. Another reminder of his weakness. He should be the strong one, extending his arm to support her. It rankled. And yet, there was such sincerity in her expression that he found himself releasing his grasp to slip his hand around her arm instead.

Warmth seeped into his fingers and spread through his chest. Walking so close to her side, he could breathe in her rosewater scent and the fresh air that clung to her. How he longed to move beyond the confines of this room. To set foot outside again and feel sunlight on his skin. Even today's rain would be a welcome change from the same four walls that held him captive. But such a trip required more energy than he could manage. He needed sleep. Desperately.

Isaac sank to the edge of his bed. Libby—he could not help but think of her as such—pulled the chair over and settled beside him.

"What if we talked of something else, something to replace the images of battle with a fond memory instead?" She offered the idea with a hopeful smile. "Tell me of a place you loved when you were young."

He furrowed his brow, thankful she'd not pressed him to describe his nightmare any more, but struggling to catch up with her shift to this new topic. The manicured gardens behind their house came to mind first, the view he'd seen from his bedroom window throughout his growing up years. That had been his mother's pride, her favorite place to retreat to paint. But the squared hedgerows and mosaic of flower beds never felt very welcoming to him.

He recalled the sprawling fields that surrounded his father's estate, stretching toward the forest that marked the edge of their property like a majestic wall. Both had been an escape to him, a place of open freedom. But they were also a reminder of who he was and the boundaries of the life he led.

The memories of each place were tainted by the knowledge that he'd never quite belonged there, and yet he'd not had the power to leave without denying his family entirely. And now, the thought that he must eventually return and once more be seen as a failure in his father's eyes stole any hint of comfort from their recollection.

There was one place, however... One memory that brought the slightest tug of a smile to his lips. "When I was a boy—I could not have been more than twelve—my family made the journey to Derbyshire to honor the passing of a distant relative who lived there. I cannot remember who it was, nor why we traveled to such lengths, given my father's overall lack of familial warmth. Perhaps he stood to gain something in an inheritance and desired to be present." Isaac huffed, then winced when he caught sight of Libby's sympathetic frown. "Whatever the reason, it seemed a grand adventure to me as a child. I recall little of the estate where we stayed, but there was a governess there who was entrusted with my care for any of the events in which I was deemed too young to join with the adults and my elder brothers. She had a fierce look about her but was one of the kindest women I'd ever met." Until he'd come to know Libby and her mother, but he kept that thought to himself. "One afternoon, she took me walking amongst the peaks. I'd never seen anything like it, nor have I found its rival since."

"What was it like?" She scooted to the edge of her seat, rapt attention fixed on him. "I've not been outside of Boston my whole life. I've seen plenty of the sea, of course, and the forests and rolling hills across the river, but never mountains."

"The peaks are not mountains, really. They are hills as well, though different from the ones surrounding Boston. Craggy, with moorlands covered in grass and wildflowers, and steep cliffs that drop away to sprawling valleys. We took a picnic to a rocky summit, and I scrambled atop the largest boulder I'd ever seen. The view seemed to stretch forever in front of me, unhindered."

He closed his eyes, and for a moment, he could see it again, as clear as though he stood there now. Could feel the way the wind had tugged at his shirt and whipped his hair against his cheeks. Could almost smell the wild freshness of the air and hear the cry of the hawk that soared above them.

"It sounds beautiful."

Blinking back to the present, he stared at her. Beautiful. Aye, she was.

He dropped his gaze to his lap, where his hand rested, palm

up and empty. Strange to think he'd never look down to see two hands again. He drew his fingers into a fist.

"I was just a boy, so you must excuse my rambling descriptions."

"Excuse them? I relish them. If I've no hope of seeing such a place with my own eyes, I am glad to envision it through yours."

He dared another glance at her, and his chest tightened with unexpected desire. Why should she have no hope of seeing it herself? He could bring her there. Show her the splendor. Let her experience it fully. The sights and sounds and smells. What if he could climb by her side and perch atop that rocky cliff together? Watch the wind loose her curls and the sun sparkle in her eyes. Fill the emptiness of his hand with the warmth of hers.

But such a journey would span the ocean, and…steal her away from everything she'd ever known. Everyone she'd ever loved.

He wouldn't do that. Couldn't do that. And why should he think she'd ever consider such an offer? Even if he refused to honor the betrothal his father had arranged. Even if he pursued Libby instead. Even if she came to return his feelings one day. He refused to ask her to make such a sacrifice when he had so little to give her in return.

Though he'd yet to receive an official discharge from the army, surely, that was to come. How could he remain a soldier when he was no longer capable of holding a musket? But if he turned against his father's wishes in regards to Miss Bradbury, he could expect no help from the baronet in finding a new living. Indeed, would he even be welcomed back to the house he'd been raised in? Or would he be turned out as an utter disappointment and disgrace to the family?

He gritted his teeth. What a fool he was to allow himself to dwell on such impossibilities, even for a moment.

"Are you in pain?" Libby's voice broke through his tumultuous thoughts.

Relieved she could not read what was on his mind, he shrugged. "Only a little."

"Tired, then, I am sure."

The yawn he could not suppress was his answer.

"I'll leave, and let you sleep." She hesitated, shifting in her seat.

He met her earnest gaze and nodded. Part of him wanted to ask her to stay, as though her presence might ward off the nightmare. But he knew better. 'Twas one thing for her to attend him while he was in the throes of fever, but now that he was conscious...

"Perhaps I might pray for you first?"

He blinked at the gentle offer but bowed his head. Her words of petition on his behalf surrounded him like a warm summer breeze. She prayed for healing and rest. For peace in his mind and soul. Her voice drifted into a quiet "amen," then the scraping of her chair on the floorboards pulled his head up.

She stood, and he did as well, unwilling to forgo all etiquette despite the way his vision swam at the sudden movement.

She pressed a hand to his arm, soft and steadying. "I can return tomorrow, but only if you wish it."

"I would like that." The words seemed to catch in his throat. Simple, and yet they hid so much more beneath the surface. A stark statement of his weakness and need. A confession that he no longer cared to hide either of those things from her. And an unspoken declaration of the depth of his feelings for the woman he could never share his life with, but did not wish to spend another a day without.

CHAPTER 21

Friday's rain had dissipated overnight, leaving the air fresh and the sky clear as Libby and Benjamin arrived at the Whites' house Saturday morning. The boy dashed through the back door immediately, bound for whatever treat Aideen might have, or simply excited for her company. Libby followed at a slower pace, peeking up at the window of Isaac's chamber. Was he sitting there now with his breakfast, waiting for her?

Her heart picked up tempo, and she shifted the books in her hands. She'd brought two theological works from Papa's collection with hopes they might encourage Isaac and serve to fill the quiet hours of his recovery.

Ducking into the house, she waved a greeting to the girls. "Do you need me to bring anything to Lieutenant Harrison?"

"Nay, miss. I took his tray." Briana glanced up from kneading a ball of dough. "He's waiting for you."

Libby couldn't suppress a smile, the words warming her all the way through. She looked to Benjamin. "I'll stay until the midday meal. Can you return then?"

He nodded, mouth too full to speak. Potato fritters, if the smell in the kitchen were any indication.

Lifting her petticoats, Libby climbed the steep staircase and peered into Isaac's room. He sat tall at the table next to the window, back to her, dark hair tied in a simple queue. His broad shoulders still stretched the fabric of his linen shirt, despite the arm he'd lost, and the sunlight slipping through the window made his color look a bit improved.

"Good morning." She stepped inside as she offered the greeting.

He stood and turned toward her, the familiar stoic slant of his mouth tilting into something that resembled a grin. "Come in. I petitioned for another chair so we could sit together."

Together. There was a tenderness to that word, a closeness that she had so long desired. Did he feel it, too, or was she imagining far more than he meant? She joined him at the table, accepting the offered seat across from his. He waited for her to be settled before he retook his own spot.

"I brought some books for you. I know how much you like to read, and I thought you might appreciate some of my father's favorites." She set the pair down, sliding them apart so he could see both titles. "*The Method of Grace* and *A Treatise Concerning Religious Affections.* Have you read them before?"

He scanned the covers. "I have not, though I recognize the names. George Whitefield and Jonathan Edwards. I believe your father spoke of them."

"I'd not be surprised. These were well-loved. You'll discover he underlined some passages and made notes in the margins."

"Thank you. 'Twas very kind of you to loan me something so precious." He reached for Edwards's book and leafed through, pausing at a spot where Papa's tidy handwriting filled the edge of the page. His voice dropped low. "Almost like discussing theology with him again."

Libby swallowed the lump that rose in her throat.

He closed the book gently and returned to his meal. "I must thank you also, for your visit yesterday. I slept better than I have in a sennight."

"I'm glad to hear it, though I cannot take all the credit. God's peace is far greater than any words I can offer."

He scooped a bite into his mouth, neither confirming nor denying her statement. Did he not believe what she'd said? Had the battle and all that followed shaken his faith? Perhaps, if he was wrestling with his beliefs, Papa's books would make a difference.

Plate cleared, he reached for his tea, the dainty porcelain cup dwarfed by his large hand. "I spoke with Dr. Reynold early this morning and asked if I might venture out of the room for a walk. He advised a trip to the parlor, but I had something else in mind."

Libby raised her brows, waiting.

"I sorely miss the fresh air. What do you say to ignoring the surgeon's advice and venturing outside instead?"

"I'm in favor. If my father were here, I am certain he would recommend just that. Sunshine, he said, is good medicine." Her gaze drifted out the window. She could almost picture the reassuring look Papa would offer alongside such advice. A smile that would turn far more affectionate when aimed at her. *My Sunshine.*

"What is it?" The concern in Isaac's voice drew her attention back to his solemn face. "You look upset. If you'd rather not go, I—"

"No, I would very much like to accompany you. Forgive me. My mind was wandering. I was thinking of Papa. He used to call me his sunshine, and I miss that."

He stared at her, quiet a moment. "A fitting name, what with your golden hair and ready smile. But 'tis your heart that is brightest of all. Your kindness toward me, even when I least deserved it, has been..." A muscle in his jaw twitched, though his expression remained soft. "Aye, Miss Caldwell, you have been like sunlight to me."

Her breath caught, the air growing thick between them. In the stillness, it felt as though all the pains of the past and all the uncertainties of the future did not matter. As though every doubt and obstacle could fade, making room for that stubborn hope of hers to resurface. Her pulse thrummed. Her fingers ached to reach across the table. To take his hand. To lean closer and—

A knock at the door yanked her back to reality. Blinking, she swung her attention to where Briana hovered at the threshold.

"I've come for your tray, Lieutenant." The girl kept her pert chin dipped as she padded into the room.

Isaac swigged the last of his tea, looking more like a soldier at a tavern than a man in his sickroom, then placed it on the tray. "Thank you, Briana."

She brightened at his gratitude, bobbed a curtsy, and slipped out.

Isaac rose from his seat, his movements steadier than yesterday, though still slower than normal. "Shall we attempt our escape?"

Libby giggled at the hint of mischief in his tone and pointed to his stockinged feet. "Aye, but you may wish for some shoes."

He chuckled. "I suppose so. It has been too long."

Too long, indeed. Too long since she'd seen his smile or heard his laugh. Too long since his voice was threaded with happiness instead of pain or despair.

Thank You, Lord. She offered the silent prayer as Isaac worked the buckles of his shoes. He perched on the edge of the bed, one leg crossed over the other at the knee, a bit clumsy in his one-handed attempt. It would be much easier for her to help. She was about to offer, but something about the firm set of his mouth held her back. Not anger or frustration as she had seen before. Not even self-pity, though such a feeling would be understandable. Instead, there was determination in the sharp lines of his jaw, and she would not deny him the chance to prove—to himself and to her—that he was still capable.

When his shoes were securely in place, they made their way carefully down the narrow stairs and turned into the kitchen. Briana's dough sat rising in a bowl on the table, but otherwise, the room was empty.

Isaac crossed to the back door and pushed it open. "Ladies first."

"You've earned your freedom, so I think you should go ahead."

He hesitated a moment, then extended his arm. "Perhaps we should go together?"

"I like that idea." So much more than she could say. She slipped her hand into the crook of his elbow, a rush of heat seeping through her fingers at the feel of his firm muscle beneath her touch.

Side by side, they crossed the threshold. A warm breeze swept over them, bringing with it the lingering smell of rain. Libby tipped her head to watch as Isaac closed his eyes and breathed deeply. When he opened them again, there was a light in their depths, as though a heavy burden had finally lifted.

She smiled up at him. "Where would you like to go?"

"Honestly? If I had my will, I would…" He stared at her, pensive, then shook his head. "What I want and what I can actually do are two distinctly different things."

Libby's pulse stuttered. Why did it feel as though there were another layer to what he'd said? Was he speaking only of his physical capabilities, or was there something more behind his words? A deeper meaning that involved…her?

He nodded toward the sprawling oak at the far edge of the property. "That tree looks like a good spot."

She pushed aside her swirling thoughts and matched his pace as they strolled away from the house. Birdsong filled the quiet between them, and the scent of fresh herbs and flowers rose as they neared Mrs. White's garden.

Isaac paused beside the plot, where bees hovered over the blossoms and crops grew in varying stages of readiness for harvest. "I heard you were able to procure an herb essential to my healing. Was this where you found it?"

"'Twas in Hannah's garden, at the Pierces' house."

He frowned. "I wish you needn't have gone there again, not knowing who it was that broke in before, or if he might have returned."

She looked away, afraid her face would reveal too much. "It was important. I knew you needed it."

"Thank you. Seems I cannot say that enough to express my gratitude for all you've done." The sincerity in his low voice drew her gaze back to his. "You didn't go there alone, did you?"

"Miss White accompanied me."

"Good." He started walking again, and she fell into step beside him. "What about when you visit me here? 'Tis a long way from your home. Tell me you don't come by yourself."

She shook her head. "No. I have Benjamin."

His brows dipped. "Who is he?"

Was that a hint of jealousy? Surely not. "Benjamin is a neighbor. He's ten."

"Ah. I am glad."

Libby chuckled, unable to silence the curiosity that spurred her on. "Glad that he is ten? Or that I've not ventured all this way alone?"

A hint of red crept up his neck. "The latter."

"He is quite a bit more talkative than you, though I am certain you'd be better equipped to offer protection, should the need arise."

The color on his neck deepened.

Interesting, indeed. She tucked her teasing aside as they arrived at their destination and stepped under the shade of the outstretched branches. "I long for the day when I can travel more freely again. I feel nearly as trapped within this town as you must have felt in your chamber."

"I understand. Though I cannot say when, or how, such a day will come."

"Do you think…" She hesitated, unsure whether or not to broach such a subject.

"What?"

"We don't have to speak of it, if you'd prefer not to, but I am curious as to your opinion."

"Please, go on." He released her arm, turning to face her fully, and immediately, she missed his solid presence at her side.

"I do not see how we can remain here in Boston forever, cut off by land and sea. I must assume either your troops will attempt to break out, or the militia will try to move in. Either way, I feel as though I'm bracing myself for more trouble."

"Aye." He peered toward the slope of Copp's Hill that rose behind them. "I think you are correct, unless those responsible for the decisions of the colonists drastically change course, although even then—"

"What sort of change do you mean?"

"To yield to the king's authority and follow the acts Parliament bestowed upon them."

Libby raised her brows. "I do not think that is bound to happen."

"Nor I."

"But you believe it should?"

"I believe…" He sighed, and fixed her with a probing gaze. "I should have a ready answer, but I confess I find it a rather complicated question. Consider this—you know that my father purchased my commission and, in doing so, determined the course of my life, despite my protests. Does that sound familiar? Mayhap similar to the situation here?"

She stared back at him. "You mean to suggest that King George and Parliament have done likewise? Sought control over our lives and ignored our voices of protest? 'Tis a bold statement, especially coming from a soldier."

"I did not say it. You did." A barely perceptible glint of teasing passed across his eyes before he sobered again. "But, for my part, I did not rebel against my father. I accepted his choice and have done all I can to serve with honor ever since."

"As we should have, you mean." Libby frowned.

"That I cannot say."

She stepped closer, desperate to understand what lay behind the stoic facade he'd worn for so long. It seemed it was beginning to break, and, like a piece of embroidery, the more she grew to know him, the more she realized that the neat lines on the outside hid a much more complicated tangle of who he truly was. "Why did you agree to the path your father chose for you? If you had no desire for it, why not choose differently?"

"Because he is my father. 'Twas my duty to my family, and..." A muscle ticked in his jaw and he looked away.

"Forgive me, I should not have—"

He shook his head, cutting her short. "You're right. I could have gone my own way. But in doing so, I would have lost all connection to my family. I would have had no one and nothing. Don't you see? 'Tis a sacrifice of some sort with either decision. Be it duty or rebellion, in both there is something to gain, and something to lose."

His words knotted in her mind. She furrowed her brow as she tried to unravel them. "So duty preserves connection as British citizens at the sacrifice of our rights, but rebellion brings freedom at the sacrifice of our peace and the cost of men's lives?"

"Believe me, I wish that were a cost that need never be paid."

So did she, and yet there were thousands of men willing to take that risk to defend the rights they deemed had been infringed upon. Men ready to choose rebellion in hopes of freedom, despite the sacrifice. Did they ever regret it? Ever fear they'd made the wrong choice?

Did Isaac?

A cardinal's cheerful whistle broke through the silence that had settled between them, and Libby tipped her head back to spot his bright red feathers hidden amongst the leaves. Another call answered. The male cardinal cocked his head, searching for his mate, before lifting from the branch and fluttering away.

Her gaze dropped back to Isaac, absent of the uniform that would have matched the bird's crimson color. What if this injury, despite the suffering it brought, offered him the opportunity to make a new choice? Would he take it? She pressed her lips together to keep such questions from bursting out. To hold back the stubborn thread of hope that mayhap he would choose a different life, one that stood a chance of entwining with hers.

CHAPTER 22

Isaac sat at the base of the tree where he and Libby had walked two days prior, one of Dr. Caldwell's books open on his lap. The rough bark rubbed against the back of his linen shirt, but it was the words in front of him that scratched deeper, prodding uncomfortably at his soul.

He ran a finger over the lines from Whitefield's sermon, re-reading them aloud. "'...if you know Christ keep close by Him; if God has spoken peace, O keep that peace by looking up to Jesus Christ every moment.'"

Did he know Christ, truly? He certainly had not been looking to Jesus every moment. There was his desperate prayer on the battlefield, when he thought himself minutes away from standing before God's throne to be held to account, but before then? He'd done little to keep close to God these past years. Why should he expect any peace in return?

And yet how desperately he longed for it.

He paused at a carefully underlined sentence. "'Such as have got peace with God, if you are under trials, fear not, all things shall work for your good...'"

Dr. Caldwell had marked these words. Had believed them

fully, given what Isaac knew of the man. Could Isaac hope for good to come from this trial?

Sighing, he closed the book and rolled his left shoulder. There was little pain now, but the movement felt strange. A tightening of what muscles remained mixed with an unsettling lightness because of what was lost. Would he ever grow accustomed to the odd tug? To the emptiness?

He had partaken in the afternoon Sabbath meal with the White family yesterday, his first time dining with others since his injury. They were gracious hosts, but he found himself missing the Caldwells' humble kitchen table and easy conversation.

Missing Libby's smile.

He leaned back, gaze snagging on the owner of that smile as she approached with her young companion at her side. The boy's animated chatter carried toward Isaac, but it was the delight in Libby's face that truly held him captive. Delight aimed in his direction.

She waved Benjamin toward the house, where Aideen peeked out the back door, then came to a stop before him. "Good morning. This is a pleasant surprise. I'm glad to see you're reading under the tree instead of in it."

"Good morning, Miss Caldwell." He grinned as he pushed to his feet, then tipped his head back to stare at the branches. "It would make for a good climbing tree, though."

"You cannot be serious."

"Hold this." Handing off the book, he grasped the lowest branch. He had not scrambled his way into a tree since he was a boy on his father's estate in England, and clearly had no ability to do so any longer, but he couldn't resist raising his brows in silent challenge as he kept his gaze fixed on her.

"Isaac, no. You'll hurt yourself." She lunged forward to grab his arm.

He sidestepped, avoiding her. "You'll have to be quicker than that."

A laugh, half amused, half annoyed, escaped Libby as she reached for his arm again, barely missing when he dodged the other way. "Just because you're taller than me doesn't mean I cannot—"

He shifted toward her at the same moment she sprang for him. They collided, and he immediately released the branch to wrap his arm around her and keep them both from tumbling to the ground. A corner of the book she held jabbed him in his ribs, but he hardly noticed, with her other palm pressed flat against his chest. Heat bloomed beneath her touch, spreading as her breathy exhale brushed his neck.

"I was only teasing." Was that his voice, all low and rough? He cleared his throat and released her. "But thank you for looking out for my safety."

"You've barely been out of the house. You're meant to be more careful." There was no real scolding behind her words. Not when her full lips tipped up at the corners like that.

Don't look at her lips. That was a scolding he must heed. He tugged his gaze away, but it snagged on her riotous curls instead. Her flat-brimmed straw hat had been knocked askew, and blond tendrils spilled around her rosy cheeks. Before he could think better of it, he lifted his fingers to tuck one errant strand behind her ear.

Her blue eyes widened, and he stepped back, putting much-needed space between them.

She dropped her gaze. "Were you enjoying this?"

Now it was his turn to stare wide-eyed. Enjoying this? Their teasing? The feel of her pressed to his chest? Aye, he was enjoying it. Far too much.

She held out the book. "Whitefield can be rather fiery, but I find his words convicting."

Ah, that was what she meant. Clearly, she was able to set

aside the moment they had shared with more ease than he had. Best command his rebellious thoughts back in order. Swallowing, he accepted it back from her outstretched hand. "I've not finished yet, but he does give one much to think on."

Libby righted her hat, tucking the wayward curls back in place. "I did not expect to find you outside already. If you'd like to read more, I'm happy to sit with you while you do."

A tempting thought, to stay hidden here in the shade with her at his side. Too tempting. "Perhaps we should try another walk."

"It's not far to the water, if you'd like a change of scenery."

"I would, indeed."

After returning the book to the house, he offered his arm, and she slipped her hand around it. They strolled in amiable silence toward Hunt and White's Shipping Yard, where a merchant vessel sat empty at the dock. Waves lapped the wooden hull, and the briny scent of saltwater hung in the air, bringing with it a sense of melancholy. He felt oddly like the abandoned ship...waiting, stripped of his purpose, uncertain of the future.

They paused at the water's edge. To the left, Charlestown Peninsula jutted toward the sea. To the right, the ocean stretched out in its seemingly endless expanse. But he'd sailed that vast sea more than once. He knew what lay on the other side.

As though sensing his thoughts, Libby peered up at him. "Are you going to return home now?"

"I've not yet discussed it with my superior officers, but I assume I'll receive my discharge. Then, when the next ship sails for England, I could..." His stomach twisted. The thought of going back to his father's house had never been appealing, but now, with Libby beside him, it seemed even less so. And yet, how could he stay?

Even if he wrote to his father and asked for a dissolution of his betrothal to the woman he'd never met, what would he do then? Pursue a courtship with Libby, if she would have him, though he had no occupation and no prospects to gain one? Live in this town under siege, striving to reconcile her commitment to the Patriot cause with his former life as a British officer?

Gulls swooped overhead, their raucous calls mocking his questions. As they should. The future he was trying to imagine was impossible.

"What is it like, crossing the ocean?" Libby clapped her free hand to her hat as a breeze swept over them. "My stepsister Patience was sick nearly her entire voyage here, but I always thought it would be exciting."

"I would say it falls somewhere in the middle. There is a rather wild quality to the sea, which can bring both adventure and discomfort." He watched one of the gulls alight atop the mast of the empty ship. "I suspect you'd find it entertaining at first, then come to feel as trapped on board as you do here in Boston."

"Perhaps you're right."

"Do you regret staying? In town, I mean."

"Sometimes." She frowned. "I've wondered what would have happened if we'd left Boston with Will. But Mama reminded me that God uses each of us where we are, for His purposes, so I must choose to rest in that."

"And can you?" The words of the sermon he'd read earlier filled his mind again. "Do you have peace in such belief?"

"I do. It isn't always a feeling, mind, but rather a deeper conviction. I am still learning to trust, but God's character is unchanging, even if my faith should falter. I have come to understand that better now." She peeked up at him. "Might you need that encouragement too? To know who God is and rest in His love, instead of your current circumstances?"

Her words stung like salty water in a wound. A wound that

had been open in his soul for far too long. He'd been striving for years, imagining God to be like his father, instead of seeing His true character. Could he finally throw off the lies and trust in who God really was? Could he accept a love so freely given? Could he find peace for his uncertain future in the hands of an unchanging God?

"You sound much like the passage I was reading this morning. One your father had underlined. That if we have peace with God, we need not fear our trials. That everything can work toward our good."

Libby smiled. "It is true. Certainly not always easy to see or understand, but true all the same."

"Even this?" He shrugged his left shoulder.

"Even that." The settled confidence in her voice washed over him like the waves breaking against the shore. "We all bear scars of some sort, whether visible or hidden far beneath the surface. But instead of seeing the loss and sorrow in them, what if there is good that comes as a result? What if your scars have brought you exactly where God wants you to be?"

He peered out over the vast sea, her words echoing in his mind.

What if your scars have brought you exactly where God wants you to be?

Was it possible? How he longed to believe it.

CHAPTER 23

$\mathscr{L}$ate-afternoon sun filtered through the leaves of the tall maple tree, casting shadows that danced with the mid-July breeze as Libby stood with Isaac on Copp's Hill. Ten days had passed since Katherine came seeking her help, and Libby had spent more than half of them at Isaac's side. His nightmares, while not gone completely, had lessened enough that he was able to sleep for longer stretches most nights, and the difference in his recovery was immense. His strength and energy had improved so much so that they'd taken to lengthening their walks every time she visited.

This was the farthest they had ventured yet, having circled around Ferry Way, Prince's Street, and Salem Street before climbing the hill. Out of the corner of her eye, Libby could see the trip had taxed him. She would not let on that she had noticed, for it was clear that Isaac was still wrestling with his inability to do everything he used to be capable of. She had assured him she did not mind the leisurely pace of their walks, nor the frequent stops, but her words did not quite seem to stick. Actions, she hoped, would speak louder.

In truth, she'd never admired him more than she did now.

He might think himself weak, but she saw only strength as she watched him face the challenges of his healing, both physical and mental, with tenacity and determination. He'd opened up to her, too, in the conversations they shared over the past days. Facing his own mortality seemed to have loosed something inside him, and whether he realized it or not, he was vulnerable now with his thoughts and feelings in a way that helped her to understand his heart better than ever before. In a way that made her love him even more.

She buried that idea deep where it could not escape.

"It has been one month to the day since the battle on Breed's Hill." Isaac's words were solemn, attention fixed across the water at the spot where they'd fought.

Libby followed his gaze. It was still jarring to look over the river and see the blackened remains that had once been Charlestown.

Isaac reached up to rub his left shoulder, just above where the surgeon had secured plasters for the final stage of healing. She caught a slight grimace that he hurried to hide. He never complained of pain, though he clearly suffered at times. Nor had she heard him grumble over his limitations, though she knew he depended upon the assistance of the surgeon or Mr. White to dress each morning. But perhaps it was not physical pain that assailed him now, and rather the ache of memories as he stared at the battlefield.

"Perhaps I should not have brought you here." She shifted to peer up at him.

"I do not mind. It helps, actually, to see it like this. When the dreams come, the fighting repeats again and again. This reminds me that it is truly over."

"That battle is, but I fear more are to come." As soon as the words were out, Libby wished them back. "Forgive me. I shouldn't trouble you with such thoughts."

"I've already considered the same." He huffed a humorless

laugh. "Though I'm in no state to go charging into any of them. I suppose that is one mercy to come out of all this."

"If only there were another way forward." She recalled his comment over a sennight earlier about submitting to the king and Parliament. Something she could not envision happening now.

"I suspect the time for reconciliation through other means has passed. Though I do wonder...if the men who sit in Parliament were required to march onto the battlefield themselves, perhaps they would have responded differently to what has happened in this colony. Would have tried harder to restore the peace in another way."

"Some did attempt to. I remember Will reading Lord Mayor's speech that was printed in the *Gazette*. He posited that our actions could be deemed rebellion, or could be seen as proper resistance to unlawful acts of power. I know you and I may hold opposing views on such a statement, but—"

"Not so opposing as you may think."

Libby blinked. "What do you mean?"

He scrubbed his hand over his chin, quiet for so long that she feared he had fallen into his old habit of ending a conversation before it delved too deep. How she wished to know his true thoughts on the matter. She did not want to hope too much, and yet it flared up all the same. For if there was a possibility of bridging the gap between their beliefs, what might that mean for their future?

"I agree with Lord Mayor that there is more than one way to view what has happened here in recent years. Indeed, I wonder if the truth lies somewhere in the middle." A beam of sunlight pierced through the branches overhead, highlighting the firm set of his jaw. "Take the destruction of the tea, for instance. Would you deem that an act of rebellion or of proper resistance?"

"'Twas a last resort, when all other options had been exhausted."

"So it began as resistance and strayed into rebellion?"

"Perhaps." She pursed her lips. "But what if Parliament had not passed such harsh acts in response? Might some of this"—she swept her hand toward the destruction in Charlestown—"have been prevented?"

"I have wondered the same. Though I must also consider how events might have unfolded if the colonists were not stockpiling munitions or besieging us here in Boston."

Libby crossed her arms over her chest, heat climbing her neck and sharpening her tone. "Mayhap if our town had not already been occupied by thousands of soldiers, we wouldn't have the need to—"

"Aye. You may be right." He turned to face her, and the rest of her defense caught in her throat at the sincerity in his brown eyes. "Unfortunately, we're not granted the ability to see what would have been if different decisions were made. I did not mean to argue with you. I was trying to prove that, despite the allegiance I've sworn to the Crown, I am able to consider more than one point of view."

She dipped her chin. "I've no wish to quarrel either. I'm sorry. I felt compelled to defend my countrymen and..."

And what? She'd been unable to repress the growing disappointment when she realized they could find a way to disagree at every turn. Frustrated to find truth in his words that muddled the lines of loyalties and held both sides accountable for the current upheaval.

Reaching out, he gently tipped her chin up with his thumb and forefinger until her gaze clashed with his. Surely, her face must be blazing, for sparks seemed to spread from every point of contact.

"Do not apologize. The depth with which you care is one of

the things I admire most about you." The low rumble of his voice sent her heart racing.

He...admired her?

She stared up at him, unsure how to reply, and then...was it a passing shadow, or did his gaze flick to her lips? She inhaled sharply. The world seemed to still. Even the breeze settled, holding its breath, as she did hers.

His hand fell to his side, and he backed away, the summer wind and her shaky exhale filling the space between them.

Clearing his throat, he turned from her to peer across the gravestones to where the hill sloped toward the road. "I cannot help thinking of your stepbrother when I'm here."

Libby furrowed her brow at the odd shift in conversation. "About Will? Whatever for?"

"We crossed paths here once. Shared some tense words before we came to an understanding of sorts." He glanced at her with a wry smile that faded quickly. "I wish for your sake there was some way to know if he is safe."

"I..." Libby hesitated. She did know, but could she risk revealing that to Isaac when the source of her information must be kept secret?

"Forgive me, I've upset you."

She shook her head, guilt burrowing deeper into her conscience. How had Will and Hannah kept their involvement in the spy ring hidden for so long? Had it tormented them to hold onto their secrets as it did her? Perhaps she should be grateful to have been excluded from their work, for she hated this forced deception.

"I dreamed once that I saw him on the battlefield." Isaac's voice was ragged. "It was terrible, but the worst part was realizing I had failed you. That I'd hurt him when you begged me not to."

"But it wasn't real." Libby clasped his hand with both of hers, heart aching at the sorrow and regret in his eyes. If she could bring him some comfort by revealing what she knew, perhaps it was worth the risk. "'Twas only a dream, and I can assure you that he was not there."

"You cannot know that."

"I do. Will is safe. Josiah as well. Neither of them were at Breed's Hill."

"But how can you...?" Confusion etched his brow. "I thought it nearly impossible for letters to travel into the city."

"Someone was able to ensure the news reached me."

"Why did you not tell me before?"

"I...I did not think..." What could she say to avoid an outright lie?

Isaac peered at her, his expression far too astute. She scrambled to think of some excuse. Something truthful to say without revealing everything. She had long wished for him to be more open with her, but now she was the one closing herself off.

"Well, then, I am glad to hear it." He did not press further, but his demeanor shifted ever so slightly. There was a formality in his voice. A stiffness to his posture. A purposeful distance in his eyes.

Libby's heart sank.

He offered his arm. "I think it best we return to the house now."

Libby managed a nod as she slipped her hand into the crook of his elbow and began the slow trek back to the Whites' home. The invisible wall stood between them again, every brick of it built by her secrets.

*L*ibby stepped into the mantua maker's shop Tuesday morning for her usual day of work with Mrs. Barker, thoughts full of Isaac and the uncomfortable way they'd parted yesterday. Things had been going so well between them. If only he'd not mentioned Will. Or, better yet, that she had never gotten entangled with Elijah's spy work at all. Then she could speak freely, without fear of repercussions. For herself or anyone else.

She pushed the worries aside and pasted on a smile, preparing to greet Mrs. Barker, but stopped short when she saw the older woman standing in the middle of the shop, arms full of billowing pink fabric. A frown marred her typically pleasant expression.

"What is wrong?" Libby hurried to her side, gaze bouncing between the folds of what must be a gown and the downward slant of Mrs. Barker's brows.

"Miss Hollis. She returned this not long before you arrived." Mrs. Barker draped the gown over her worktable, spreading it out so Libby could see the creation in its entirety.

"It is stunning." Libby brushed her fingers over the exquisite double-layered lace adorning the sleeve. The bodice, complete with pink silk ribbons that criss-crossed the white stomacher, dipped to a V where it met the voluminous petticoat. "Why would anyone return such a gown?"

"She was betrothed to one of the Regulars and meant to be married in it." The edge to Mrs. Barker's voice hinted at how she felt about such an arrangement. "The soldier was killed at Breed's Hill, and she claims she cannot bear to look at it any longer, for it brings her too much sorrow."

"Oh, I am sorry."

"As am I, though perhaps you are more sympathetic, what with your friendship with that officer. I do feel for the girl but cannot help thinking she would have been better off if she'd never become involved with a Redcoat in the first place."

Libby winced at the not-so-subtle hint. She knew Mrs. Barker disapproved of her association with Isaac. What would the older woman think if she knew the depth of Libby's feelings toward him?

"I'll not complain. She did not demand that her payment be returned, and looked quite heartbroken. Still, I do hate to see so much work stored away, and who knows for how long, with matters as they are in town."

Libby's focus drifted to the gown again. She did not know Miss Hollis, but her heart ached for the loss she'd experienced.

"I wonder..." Mrs. Barker's voice drew her attention. Libby turned to find the woman examining her. "You are quite similar in size to Miss Hollis, and I know how much you favor this color."

"Oh, I couldn't—"

"Indulge me a moment and let me at least look." Mrs. Barker lifted the dress up in front of Libby.

Libby held her breath as the soft fabric swished against her own plain petticoat. How might it feel to wear such a beautiful creation?

Mrs. Barker's cheeks rose with a satisfied smile. "It would look quite perfect on you."

"I've no occasion for such finery, and—"

"Nonsense. A lovely young woman like you? One day, all this trouble will pass, and a man will come courting." A teasing glint sparkled in Mrs. Barker's eyes as she set the gown aside again. "I would be glad to give this dress a happier ending."

Libby pressed her lips together. Was Mrs. Barker right? Would there come a time when she could move on, set aside her feelings for Isaac once and for all, and be ready to love again? 'Twas hard to consider a happier ending now, when her heart felt so fragile.

"Think on it, my dear." Mrs. Barker patted her arm. "Now, we'd best get to work. I've a waistcoat for Mr. Gerrish that must be delivered today."

Libby furrowed her brow as Mrs. Barker hurried to the basket in the corner and lifted a familiar-looking garment. It appeared to be the same one she'd taken to the man last month. Why would it need mending again so soon?

Mrs. Barker folded the waistcoat over her arm, and Libby frowned, for every button was missing. "How did that happen? Is this not the same waistcoat we mended in June? I am certain all the buttons were securely in place then."

"Is it? I did not realize." Mrs. Barker ducked her head and fished around in her pocket, drawing out a handful of wooden buttons covered in gray fabric to match that of the waistcoat. "He must have wished to change them. A fashionable practice, as you well know."

Libby stared at Mrs. Barker, but the woman turned away and busied herself with fetching some thread. Strange. While many men did decorate their buttons in such a way, Mr. Gerrish hadn't struck her as one to concern himself with such things. Nor had he seemed to have money to spare for frivolities. And how could Mrs. Barker, who was so fastidious in her work, not recognize the garment?

Libby did not press her, though the questions lingered as she lifted a worn pair of breeches from the basket and settled into her chair by the window. Why did it seem that her employer had something to hide?

Mrs. Barker sank onto her favorite seat, spreading the waistcoat across her lap, but in place of her usual chatter, silence hovered between them. Minutes passed, as time and again, Libby wove her needle through the woolen pants, stitching a new straight hem. Still, the older woman did not speak.

Libby ventured a peek at her companion and startled to

find Mrs. Barker's gaze assessing her. Not measuring her to fit a gown, but rather as though she were trying to evaluate her on the inside, to the core of her thoughts, feelings, and beliefs.

"May I ask you something, Miss Caldwell?" Mrs. Barker tipped her head, stare unyielding.

A strange sense of nervousness prickled her neck. "Aye."

"How is it that you can hold a friendship with that lieutenant whilst maintaining your patriotic convictions?"

Libby blinked. Was that the reason for her reticence today? Did Mrs. Barker think Libby too much like Miss Hollis, infatuated with a man she should not be involved with?

She hesitated, cheeks heating under Mrs. Barker's scrutiny. "I…I believe it possible to care…that is, to consider the well-being of others, and share a friendship, even if we disagree in some ways. My father believed so."

"You mean well, I've no doubt. And I remember enough of your father to know he made a point to treat everyone with equal consideration, no matter the difference in their stance. But things are different now, can't you see? This has gone beyond neighbors disagreeing over taxes and laws. Men have been killed. Our town invaded and our livelihoods threatened. Do you not think it better to end such connections? People may begin to wonder where your loyalty truly lies."

Cold clamminess dampened her palms. "Lieutenant Harrison has known our family for years. I assure you, my loyalty has not changed, but I cannot desert a friend in his greatest time of need."

Mrs. Barker pursed her lips. "Still, I do caution you. I'm certain your mother has done the same. Only for your protection, mind. Your mother has been a good friend to me, and I've watched you grow into a fine young woman. I only wish the best for you, Miss Caldwell. I hope you know that."

Libby forced a smile. "I know, and I thank you."

They returned to their work, but their conversation remained more stifled than usual, and Libby could not shake the sense that there was something else behind Mrs. Barker's warning.

A fly buzzed through the open window and hovered around the older woman's head. With a huff, she shooed it away, knocking one of the buttons she'd not yet stitched in place onto the floor. It skittered across the boards and rolled to a stop at Libby's feet.

She bent to retrieve it, noticing the fabric cover had pulled up slightly on one edge. "You may need to repair this one before—"

"No matter. Easy to mend." Mrs. Barker cut in sharply, holding out her hand.

Libby frowned. Why was she so out of sorts today? She started to return the button, then froze when a tiny slip of white caught her eye. "There is something stuck under the fabric. Perhaps that is why—"

"I'll see to it." The edge to Mrs. Barker's tone sounded strangely like...fear?

Libby looked up and saw that very emotion mirrored in her drawn expression. "Mrs. Barker, whatever is the matter?"

"There are some questions better left unanswered, my dear." Her hand, still extended, quivered. "Please, it is best you do not know."

Libby's thoughts flashed to Elijah, who had claimed much the same about his role as a spy, then brought her trouble all the more because he'd not been open about his work from the start. She was tired of people keeping things from her. Frustration bubbled inside, like a pot ready to boil over.

"Miss Caldwell, I beg you..."

Ignoring Mrs. Barker's plea, she peeled back the fabric and tugged out a folded piece of parchment, hardly bigger than her thumbnail. Why would anyone hide paper inside a button? Unless it was a message meant for very few eyes to see.

A warning whispered in her mind. If she opened this, was she willing to carry whatever it revealed, just as she bore the burden of Elijah's secret? But, then, if she did not look, could she handle the weight of never knowing?

Libby shook her head, decision made, and unfolded the scrap of paper. Handwriting filled the page, the letters so small she had to bend closer to read it.

22,40,44,45 regt arr. end June

Miniature words, but they hit her with the force of a thunderclap. Regimental numbers, those of the new troops who had landed at the end of last month.

She snapped her gaze back to Mrs. Barker, whose face had gone ashen. "Are you reporting to someone about the Regulars?"

Mrs. Barker bobbed her head almost imperceptibly.

"Are all the buttons like this one? With hidden messages underneath?"

Another nod. "I will not apologize for what I've done, for it is in service to my home and her citizens." Color rose in Mrs. Barker's cheeks, but her expression was resolute. "Do you not wish to see us free from this...this cage that Boston has become?"

"I do, but..." Libby stared at the incriminating slip in her palm. "This is dangerous, Mrs. Barker. If you were caught, they could accuse you of espionage. Of treason."

"I am well aware. That is why I did not wish you to discover this. I wanted to protect you."

Libby closed her fingers around the button so tightly that it dug into her skin. "Tell me the truth—was I unknowingly the courier of such messages when I delivered that waistcoat to Mr. Gerrish?"

"No, I assure you. I have taken the utmost care not to involve you in any way. While I cannot regret my actions, I do regret deceiving you. Please forgive me." Mrs. Barker stood, wringing her hands. "I must ask that you vow not to tell a soul what you saw. What you now know."

"Your secret is secure with me." Another one to keep. Her stomach sank, but she offered the button and its hidden message back to Mrs. Barker, along with her promise. She could not endanger this woman who had been so good to her and Mama.

"I think it best for you to halt your work here, at least for a time. If something should happen to me, I would not want you to be in danger." Libby opened her mouth to protest, but Mrs. Barker held up a hand. "No arguments. I only care about your safety."

Safety. Wasn't that what Elijah had claimed as well? That he wished her to be safe. And yet both he and Mrs. Barker had placed her in harm's way, despite their attempts otherwise. It was Isaac that she truly felt safe with. But would she be, if he knew the secrets she carried?

"I want you to have the dress." Mrs. Barker's voice was soft and thick with emotion. "As a thank you."

"I already promised not to speak of what you're doing. You needn't give me something to ensure I keep that promise."

"I know that. I meant it as thanks for the help you've given me. Not only for your skill with the needle, but even more so for your company. Your conversation and cheerful disposition have given me hope whenever I felt overcome by the sorrows and hardships these past months have brought. You are a spot of light in the midst of the darkness, Miss Caldwell. If this gift can give you even a sliver of the joy you have brought me, I will be glad."

"Then I will accept it, and cherish it, as I have my time with you."

Tears welled in Mrs. Barker's eyes, and Libby wrapped the older woman in an embrace. She would miss her days here with the mantua maker, miss the sense of purpose it gave her. Another change, another loss, when she'd lost so much already.

CHAPTER 24

*I*saac slid his right arm through the sleeve of his crimson coat, then stiffened as Captain Merrick helped drape it across his back and ease the other sleeve over what little remained of his left arm. The last time he wore his uniform, he'd been lying in the dirt on Breed's Hill, waiting to die. And while this coat was new, to replace the one he'd ruined that day, the memories still felt as though they were embedded in the fabric, like a bloodstain that would not wash out.

Merrick stepped back and surveyed him from top to bottom. "'Tis good to see you like this again."

Isaac wished he could say the same. He glanced down at the row of buttons lining his white waistcoat. Merrick had fastened every single one, for it would have taken Isaac an age to accomplish on his own.

He straightened, the black stock round his neck squeezing tighter than he remembered. "I feel rather the impostor. I should have kept to the simple black coat."

"Nonsense. The Whites have opened their home and warehouse to our men, and now they've generously invited us to join them for what is certain to be the best fare we've had in months. The least we can do is honor them by dressing as the soldiers we are."

"I may be a soldier for now, but it cannot last much longer."

"To that regard, I've something to discuss with you. But we shall save it for after the meal. We cannot keep our hosts waiting."

Isaac wanted to pry further, but Merrick had already started for the stairs. As they descended, savory smells from the kitchen coaxed a growl from Isaac's stomach. When Mr. White first extended the invitation for what he deemed a celebratory feast, Isaac had been tempted to decline. The thought of muddling his way through various dishes with one hand was bad enough, but the idea of celebrating brought even more discomfort. Mr. White claimed they needed an evening of levity to honor their victory at Breed's Hill and Isaac and Merrick's subsequent recovery. But it did not feel much like a victory when Isaac knew how many men, Regulars and colonists alike, now lay buried beneath the dirt. Nor did his recovery seem like something to rejoice over, for glad as he was to be alive and regaining his strength every day, he would never fully heal. Never again be the man he'd been before.

Still, Mr. White had insisted, and what's more, invited Libby to join them as well. Much as Isaac relished the thought of sharing an evening with her, he hated to let her see another level of his weakness and dependence.

He followed Merrick into the parlor, where Mr. White greeted them with a warm smile, impeccably dressed as always. "Welcome, gentlemen. My wife and daughter will join us shortly, and I've sent a carriage for Miss Caldwell. May I offer you a glass of Madeira while we wait?"

As Mr. White poured, Isaac let his gaze wander the room. The oval dining table toward the front of the room was set with ornate porcelain plates, a branching silver candelabra, and far more cutlery than he would be able to make use of. The other side of the room featured a pair of Windsor chairs arranged in front of the brick fireplace. A large painting hung over the carved wooden hearth, portraying a sloop at sea, waves cresting before its prow. Isaac knew enough about art from his mother's interest to recognize the quality, and thus the high cost, of such a piece. Portraits of Mr. and Mrs. White in their younger days, equally impressive in their artistry, hung on another wall, and a spinet occupied the final corner of the space.

He was not unfamiliar with such displays of wealth. Indeed, he had grown up surrounded by it. But he'd become accustomed to a simpler life. To sleeping in a canvas tent and cooking over a fire, or to the humble accommodations of the Caldwell home.

"This is a night long overdue." Mr. White handed Isaac a cup of wine, then lifted his own in a toast. "To two fine officers of The King's Own, for your bravery, dedication, and conviction."

"Hear, hear." Merrick raised his glass.

Isaac could not muster the same enthusiasm, but he dutifully matched their salute, before sipping the rich amber-colored wine.

Mr. White adjusted his pristine white stock. "Captain Merrick, what news on the fortifications?"

"The Charlestown heights were immediately secured following our victory, as you may have heard. We've maintained a rigorous rotation of duties since then, and have thoroughly taken command of Charlestown Neck. Over the past month, we erected a redoubt and outworks, dug trenches, and built platforms and gun emplacements. Those rebels would be fools to attempt another assault."

Isaac's friend explained the shifts the troops had been taking between guard duty and manual labor, as well as the rearranging of companies to replace those men lost in the fight. Strange, to be on the outside of such doings, when for so long that had been his life. If not for his injury, Isaac would be among them now, building the defensive works and keeping watch should the colonial militia try to advance. He felt no desire to do so, no pull back toward the role he could no longer play, and yet...there was an odd emptiness in its place, much like the phantom pains that sometimes plagued him where his arm had once been.

The rustling of petticoats drew Isaac's attention to the door as Mrs. White and their daughter entered the room. In his scarce interaction with Mrs. White, Isaac had deemed her to be a poised and stately woman, and her appearance this evening matched his assessment well. Not a single strand of her silvery-gray hair was out of place, nor was a wrinkle to be found on her floral print gown. Miss White looked equally elegant in a yellow *robe a l'anglaise* that set off her black hair. Isaac slanted a glance at Merrick, whose admiring gaze was firmly fixed on the young woman.

Mr. White crossed the room and pressed a kiss to his daughter's cheek, before offering his arm to his wife. "How am I so blessed to have the two most enchanting women in Boston under my roof?"

Isaac eyed the door. He would argue that the most enchanting of all had yet to arrive, but kept that thought to himself.

Mrs. White swept into the kitchen to speak to the servant girls regarding the meal, and Captain Merrick commandeered Miss White's attention, leaving Isaac alone with Mr. White.

Isaac cleared his throat. "I must thank you, sir, for your generosity in allowing me to recover here in your home. You have my sincere gratitude."

The older man clasped his good shoulder. "You are welcome. I am glad I could be of service in this way. 'Tis nothing in comparison to the sacrifices you have made. I would do more if I..." His words trailed off as he lifted a hand in greeting toward someone behind Isaac. "Ah, Miss Caldwell, you've arrived."

Isaac turned, and for a moment, he forgot how to breathe.

Libby stood in the doorway, dressed in a stunning pink gown that fit her to perfection and brought out the blush rising on her cheeks. He took in the white lace that draped from the sleeves at her elbows, brushing her fair skin in a way he was far too tempted to imitate. She had pinned some of her blond hair up, while leaving other curls free to spill over both shoulders. Another temptation. His fingers twitched. He was staring like a fool but could not convince himself to stop.

She dipped a curtsy. "Thank you, Mr. White, for your invitation, and for the carriage ride. 'Twas most kind of you."

"My pleasure, Miss Caldwell. You have been far better medicine for our lieutenant here than anything the surgeon prescribed." He ushered her in. "You look lovely this evening."

"Thank you." Her words were for Mr. White, but her gaze flicked to Isaac.

Did she seek his approval? She had it, and more. She was utterly radiant. Dare he tell her so?

He stepped closer. "Miss Caldwell, you look—"

"We are ready." Mrs. White's genteel declaration halted his words. "Please, do be seated."

Isaac held Libby's chair for her, and the smile she aimed at him in thanks set his heart racing. He took his place to her left, with Merrick and Miss White across from them and their host and hostess at either end. Briana and Aideen bustled in, carrying bowls of green pea soup which they placed before each person. Mr. White offered a brief prayer of gratitude, and they began their first course.

Polite conversation flowed around the table, but Isaac struggled to focus with Libby so close beside him. It had been quite some time since he sat down for such a formal meal, let alone with a distractingly beautiful woman mere inches away. He dipped his spoon carefully, intent upon not embarrassing himself and spilling all over his white waistcoat. The soup was as vibrantly colored as it was freshly flavored, as though summer itself were captured in each mouthful.

A steaming platter of boiled skate and stewed spinach followed, and was passed around the table. When it reached Isaac, he hesitated, unable to balance the dish and serve himself with one hand.

"Let me hold that." Libby's voice was soft, for his ears only.

She steadied the platter in both hands as he served himself, then scooped a helping onto her plate. Her gaze met his, candlelight flickering in her blue eyes, and his throat grew thick at the expression there. No judgment over his inability. No pity, even. Simply understanding and kindness.

"Thank you." He kept his words equally low, hoping she would comprehend that the depth of their meaning went far beyond her assistance with the meal.

Turning back to his food, Isaac caught Merrick's eye. The captain's brows rose in a knowing expression. He ducked his head and shoved a bite of skate in his mouth.

"Lieutenant?" Mrs. White's cultured tone brought his head up quickly. "I must ask, have you had the opportunity to write to your family and inform them of your injury?"

The fish stuck in his throat as he swallowed. He washed it down with a swig of wine. "I have not yet done so."

"Oh, then please, you may avail yourself of my husband's writing desk whenever you wish. I am certain they would desire to know of your condition."

He forced a smile. "Thank you. I will, indeed."

If she knew the relationship, or lack thereof, he shared with his family, she would not be so certain. Still, she was right. He couldn't put it off forever. And yet a letter seemed an unnecessary formality if he planned to sail back to England himself.

He slid a glance at Libby. Did he plan to return to his home? The thought held no appeal.

"What are your plans now?" Mr. White joined his wife's discomforting line of questions. "Have you spoken to your superiors, other than Captain Merrick, about your future with the army?"

Libby stiffened at his side, and the same tension tightened Isaac's jaw. "I've not had the opportunity."

Merrick dabbed his mouth with his napkin. "I was only just telling Harrison that I have some news for him on that front."

"Good news, I hope." Mr. White lifted his thick brows.

"I should not speak more of it until we've had the opportunity to discuss arrangements in private." Merrick cast a look at Isaac. "But I hope he will see it as such."

Isaac furrowed his brow. What would Merrick consider good news for Isaac to receive? Somehow, he doubted the captain would place discharge papers in that category. Yet how could he continue to serve the army in any capacity? His stomach churned with the realization that he had fully expected, even depended upon, being invalided out of service. And he had, perhaps subconsciously, begun to consider a sort of freedom for his future that he'd not imagined in years.

This conversation was bound to ruin his meal, and given that it was the most delicious food he'd had in as long as he could remember, that was a rather disappointing prospect.

As though she sensed his discomfort, Libby turned to Mrs. White. "I cannot help but admire the fine instrument you have. Do you play?"

"Only a little." Lines creased the older woman's eyes as she smiled. "Though my Katherine is quite the musical talent. Perhaps she will indulge us with a performance after the meal."

Captain Merrick aimed an exaggerated pleading look at Miss White. "Please do. It has been far too long since I've heard any music save the fife and drum."

She dipped her chin, as though unsure how to respond to his flirtation. "I would be glad to."

The discussion shifted to which of Bach's Weimar concertos Miss White preferred most, and Isaac's shoulders relaxed.

He leaned closer to Libby. "It appears I must thank you again."

"Whatever do you mean?" She tipped her head in a look of wide-eyed innocence, but a teasing smile tugged at the corner of her lips.

He chuckled softly and returned to his meal, finally able to enjoy the mild fish drenched in buttery sauce.

A haunch of mutton followed, accompanied by carrots and mashed potatoes. Isaac was tempted to inquire how the Whites had managed to come by such an abundance, given the scarcity in town, but etiquette did not condone such curiosity.

Lifting his fork, he eyed the mutton. Might it be tender enough to manage without a knife? He attempted a piece, dismayed to realize it was not.

Libby shifted in her seat and gestured toward his plate with her knife. "May I?"

Was she really offering to cut his food as though he were a child in leading strings? And yet, did he not need just that? Swallowing what was left of his pride, he inched his plate toward her.

She made quick work of it, so much so that no one seemed to notice, then slid the plate back in front of him.

He waited for a flash of embarrassment to burn his neck. For bitterness at his limitations to tighten his fist in his lap. But neither came. Instead, a much stronger emotion wrapped around his chest, pulling tight. One so intense and true that it both terrified and delighted him all at once.

Love.

Did he love Libby? He couldn't...and yet, it washed over him with utter certainty. He did love her. Not only as a friend but as something much deeper. In a way he had never loved anyone else.

How had he allowed this to happen?

~

*L*ibby dipped her spoon in the bowl of gooseberry fool in front of her, so full she could hardly imagine taking another bite but loathe to offend Mrs. White by refusing the dessert. She could not remember the last time she had eaten this well...or this much. Mr. White was correct in calling it a feast when he invited her to share the meal. She tasted a scoop of the creamy treat and couldn't hold back a hum of appreciation at the sweet and tart tastes that filled her mouth. Perhaps she could find room for dessert, after all.

"This is, without a doubt, the finest meal I've had in years." Captain Merrick smiled broadly at Mrs. White. "And the best company."

His gaze strayed back to Katherine, who had been the focus of his attention much of the evening. Libby attempted to gauge her friend's reaction, but Katherine kept her head dipped, demurely finishing her serving.

Libby had been rather pleased with the company herself, particularly the man seated beside her. Though, if she had her way, she would have gladly shared a far less elaborate meal across the worn table in her kitchen if it meant she could spend it with him alone. 'Twas good no one could read such scandalous thoughts, but she'd become so accustomed to her walks with Isaac and the freedom of conversation they shared during such times, it was difficult to silence them completely.

"I must agree." Mr. White leaned back in his chair and clasped his hands over his belly. "A triumph, my dear Mrs. White, especially in the midst of such difficult times."

A triumph, indeed. Libby could not imagine what this meal

had cost their host, but clearly, Mr. White had no qualms about it. She peeked at Isaac, posture straight in his crimson coat. She'd been taken aback to see him dressed in his uniform again. He looked handsome, as always, but there was a formality, an almost detached quality, that made her miss his simpler clothing of late. Captain Merrick had hinted at a new role for Isaac. Did he mean within the army? She bristled at the thought, which pierced holes in her newly stitched hope that his injury could lead him to a different path, one that might possibly include her.

How many times did she have to learn the same lesson? 'Twas silly to expect anything more than friendship from him. Absurd to hope he could be part of her future. Still, the way he'd looked at her tonight…

"Shall we have some of that music now?" Mr. White gestured toward the spinet in the corner. "What do you say, Katherine?"

"Aye, Father, I'm happy to." She rose from her seat, with the help of Captain Merrick who quickly stood to pull back her chair. Smoothing her hands down her silk gown, the color of a candied lemon, Katherine smiled her thanks to the officer and moved to take her place at the instrument.

She lifted the lid of the spinet and propped it open with the lid stick, then settled onto the painted wooden stool in front of the keyboard. Delicate notes filled the room as Katherine began to play, her fingers flying over the keys in an intricate dance. The piece grew, ascending to high trills, then descending to lower chords.

Mr. White leaned toward Libby, voice low so as not to interrupt. "She's quite talented, isn't she?"

Libby nodded, awed by the beautiful music and Katherine's effortless manner of playing. "Indeed. 'Tis a lovely instrument."

"Crafted by Thomas Hitchcock in London, one of the most prolific spinet makers in England. I brought it here aboard one of my ships years ago, when Katherine stood but this high." He held his hand to his waist.

"That must have been quite a task to transport such an instrument safely across the Atlantic."

"Aye, but 'twas worth it. I've always been determined to provide the very best for my girl."

Libby smiled, but as he turned back to watch his daughter play, the gentle fondness in his expression made her heart clench.

What would Papa think if he were here with her tonight? Would he compliment her gown? Wonder at her new connection to this Tory family? Would he be able to see through her attempts to hide her feelings for Isaac, just as Mama had? Tug one of her curls with a teasing wink and say she couldn't fall in love because he wasn't ready to let her go? She certainly hadn't been ready to say goodbye to him.

Would he be proud of the woman she had become?

She blinked back the sting of tears and reached for her napkin, but it slipped, falling to the floor between her chair and Isaac's. They both bent to retrieve it, and the backs of their hands brushed, fingers trailing over one another for the briefest second. A thrill shot up her arm. She turned to look at him, his face only inches away.

"Are you well?" Concern darkened his eyes as he searched her face.

She nodded, though it wasn't quite the truth, and straightened, thankful everyone else was too occupied with the music to notice their exchange. The concerto dipped into a melancholy minor key, and she clasped her hands in her lap, emotions swirling with missing Papa, questions about Isaac's future, and the lingering feel of his touch.

He reached over beneath the table and wrapped her hands with his larger one. Warmth and strength engulfed her. She loosened her grip, turning one palm over to entwine her fingers with his own. He didn't pull away. Instead, his thumb traced a slow pattern over her skin, dipping to the underside of her wrist where her pulse raced.

Miss White's voice joined the melody, soaring over the notes of the spinet like a bird singing mid-flight. Mr. White beamed, Mrs. White closed her eyes as though soaking it all in, and Captain Merrick stared, clearly enamored. But everything faded—the music, the people, the dancing candlelight—behind the feel of Isaac's hand holding hers.

CHAPTER 25

*L*ibby felt as though she were floating on a cloud, despite the jolts of the carriage as it bumped over the rutted streets on the way home from the Whites' house. She pressed her fingers to her lips, as though she might still be able to capture the feeling of Isaac's touch. He'd held her hand for the entirety of Katherine's performance, only releasing her when the final note faded and they all rose from the table. He had walked her out to the carriage and taken her hand once more to help her inside, lingering a moment to wish her good night. Something had shifted between them, she was certain. What exactly that was, and what may come of it, she was less sure of.

The carriage rolled to a halt in front of her house, and the driver hopped down to open the door. She thanked him, then hurried inside, anxious to recount the evening events to Mama. A soft glow emanated from the kitchen, the only room where they kept a fire burning these mid-summer days. She peeked inside and spotted Mama seated at the table, staring at the low flames in the hearth. Her hands were clasped atop her worn apron, and the shadows seemed to settle on her face, making it look drawn and weary.

"Mama?" Libby eased into the room, some of her excitement wavering. While she'd been away enjoying a lavish meal, music, and company, her mother sat here alone.

Mama startled, as though she'd not even heard Libby enter, and hurried to her feet. "Oh, Libby, I had begun to worry you'd been..." She pressed a hand to her chest.

Was it the firelight, or were her fingers trembling? Libby frowned. "What is wrong? I realize I am a bit later coming home than expected, but Katherine was playing the spinet for us, and I could not—"

"That is not the trouble. Come, you'd best sit. I need to tell you..." Mama's voice quivered as her words trailed to a stop.

Fear knotted Libby's stomach. She crossed to the table but did not take a chair, reaching for her mother's hands instead. Cold, damp palms pressed back against her own, and the dread twisted tighter inside. "Whatever is the matter? Are you ill? I should not have left you here. I—"

"'Tis Mrs. Barker."

Libby's heart froze. "What do you mean?" Had the woman's spy efforts been found out? *Oh Lord, let it not be so.*

"She came here with a message for you. It seems she was involved in some...some form of espionage." Mama released her hands and sank into her chair. The disbelief in her voice bruised Libby's conscience, but it was the piercing look in her eyes that hurt most. "She told me that you discovered her work earlier this week."

"I did." Libby sighed, settling onto the wooden seat next to hers. "I am sorry to have kept another secret from you, but I promised not to speak of it."

"Mrs. Barker said she made you pledge not to tell anyone, and that if I were to be upset, it should be with her, not you."

"And...are you upset?"

The tight set of Mama's jaw spoke a silent answer to Libby's question.

"Believe me, I did not want to deceive you. I never would have known if I'd not seen that button, and now I wish I had silenced my curiosity before I discovered..." Libby shook her head. "But why did she tell you now, if just days ago she was adamant that I not share anything with you?"

"Because she had no other choice. She came to speak to you, but as you were not here, she felt it necessary to tell me instead. The news could not wait. She had to warn you."

"Warn me?"

"Mr. Gerrish was arrested." Mama's shoulders sank. "He was imprisoned today on charges of espionage."

A chill slithered down Libby's spine. How had he been caught? Was it the notes hidden behind the buttons? Had they somehow been discovered?

"Elizabeth, you must tell me the truth—did you have any part in this spy work?" Mama braced herself against the table, searching her face.

"None at all. I promise. But...Mr. Gerrish. I did deliver mending to him once. Mrs. Barker vowed it held no secret messages, though it is the same waistcoat she was stitching the buttons onto."

"Then your words match what she recounted to me."

"Surely, I cannot be in danger, can I? I've done nothing wrong, only associated with people who were involved in matters I had no knowledge of at the time."

"I do not know." The uncertainty and worry in Mama's voice made Libby shiver. "I want to believe you are safe, but think of your meeting with Elijah and the information you shared with him. Accidental or not, I am fearful of your connections with these people."

"Mr. Gerrish would never speak against me. He knows I had

no role in all of that. As for Elijah, he's far from Boston now." Or so he had claimed, but could he be trusted? Libby infused her voice with a confidence she did not feel, desperate to reassure Mama, even if she could not reassure herself. "It would be nearly impossible for someone to trace my words to him."

It was true—her message would be nearly impossible to trace...but not completely. Not now that Elijah had lost his father's journal, with her letter still inside.

$\sim$

Isaac set the punched tin lantern Mrs. White had given him on the table in his chamber and spun to face Captain Merrick. "What is it you wished to discuss?" He tempered his tone, trying to hide his annoyance. Merrick was a friend, but he was also a superior officer. For now, at least. Still, frustration and exhaustion simmered close to the surface.

"A bit impatient, are you?" Merrick chuckled.

Clearly, he'd not hidden his feelings as well as he thought. "Can you blame me? You said you had news regarding my future, then kept me in suspense all evening."

"Not enough suspense to distract you from your beautiful Miss Caldwell, though. I could see that much."

"You should not call her that."

"What? Beautiful? Or yours?"

Isaac scowled, kneading the taut muscles at the back of his neck.

"Fine. I'll not tease. But she is good for you, Harrison, anyone can see that. And believe it or not, I'd like to see you happy. Which brings me to my offer." He squared his shoulders, easily trading his role as jesting friend for that of an officer in the king's army. "With Sergeant Jackson's death, we've need of a new man to assume his responsibility."

Isaac frowned. "You mean tracking down James Lawrence?"

"Not only him. Jackson was rather obsessive on that point, but we need someone to go beyond hunting for a single rebel spy and take command of the larger issue. It appears, for all intents and purposes, that we are at war with this colony, and espionage is not something to be taken lightly. Intelligence gained, or lost, can change the course of action. Can make the difference between victory and defeat. The generals need someone capable and level-headed to manage this effort, and I took the liberty of recommending you."

"Capable?" Isaac huffed, gesturing to his left sleeve. "You consider this capable?"

"I consider this"—Merrick pointed to Isaac's forehead—"far more capable than most men I know. You may not be as physically able as you once were, but your mind is an asset we'd be loath to lose. I cannot think of anyone better suited for the job."

"I've had nothing to do with the spy efforts thus far, other than providing Stanton as an extra soldier to assist the sergeant. Jackson spoke with me of his findings from time to time, but mostly to complain about what had gone wrong. I have little extra knowledge of his work."

"That is of no import, for he left detailed notes. Stanton is willing to continue in his role, and I have every reason to believe that a request from you for additional soldiers would be favorably received. I know 'tis not the same as leading our men on the battlefield, but this is still an honorable position. And it would keep you in Boston near a certain young woman."

Honorable? What honor was there in such a role? One that would entrench him in lies and deceit as he sought to expose the colonists' secrets and hide the Regulars' own. He would despise such work. But did he have any choice in the matter, or would he be commanded to take this new post, should he wish it or not?

"I know you had likely resigned yourself to being

discharged, so this may take some time to adjust to, but can't you see what a good offer it is?"

Isaac fixed his captain with a questioning look. "Is it an offer? Or is it an assignment?"

"General Gage agreed with my recommendation. You are to begin as soon as you are able."

Isaac's chest tightened as Merrick's words wrapped around him like shackles. He paced to the window, but only blackness greeted him. Night had descended fully, and the darkness seemed to reach for him again, as it had after he was injured at Breed's Hill, dragging him back into a world he had no desire to be part of.

That truth crashed into him with the force of a cannonball. It wasn't only the spy work that he was desperate to stay out of. He didn't want to be a soldier at all. He never had, though he'd done his best to accept his role and serve with honor and integrity. But he couldn't any longer. Not when it meant going against his own conscience.

He'd been afraid to admit it, even to himself, but his convictions had been shifting for months now. Perhaps even years, when he considered the numerous discussions he had shared with Dr. Caldwell. His weeks of recovery, the long, quiet hours to think, and the conversations with Libby on their walks had only strengthened his resolve.

And his love for Libby...

He should be thankful for the opportunity to remain near her. But wouldn't their worlds still be forced apart? Perhaps even farther than if the entire Atlantic stretched between them, for she would never agree to share her life with a British officer.

The thought hit him like the recoil of a musket. He could not deny that was what he most desired. To love her fully. To claim her as his own, give her his name, and spend the rest of his life with her. If he had a choice, one without restrictions and duty and limitations, he would choose Libby.

This evening, sitting at her side, whispering over their meal, taking her hand... He had let himself pretend, for a few precious, reckless hours, that he could live a different life. A life where he was truly free to love her.

How he had deceived himself.

He squared his shoulders, turning back to face his captain. "Dr. Reynold will be here on Monday to assess my progress. With his consent, I will return on Tuesday. Who should I report to?"

Merrick stared at him a long moment, expression inscrutable. "You can meet me at the encampment on the Common. We will discuss the details then."

"I will be there."

Captain Merrick bid him good night and departed, his footsteps on the stairs echoing in the quiet that had descended upon the house. With some difficulty, Isaac shucked his coat, his fingers clenching into a fist around a handful of crimson fabric.

His father's words pounded in his head—*Bring honor to the Crown and the Harrison family name.* The baronet's decisions still held Isaac captive now, to the army and the betrothal, even an ocean away. Barely suppressing a growl, he hurled the uniform to the ground.

He sank to the bed, gaze snagging on the books Libby had lent him. He wanted to have a faith like hers. A peace like that described in the pages. He bowed his head low, daring to believe in the kind of love that Libby and her father had spoken of. A love not earned but freely given.

"God, I want to trust that You will use this, but I cannot see how." His voice broke. "Please help me, Lord. Forgive me for my doubts. Strengthen my faith. Show me the way."

He sat back, feeling less alone than before. More at peace, despite the uncertainty of his future. He stared at the wall, dappled with alternating shadows and light that glowed from the lantern. Like ink on parchment.

A letter.

The thought came swift and clear. Mrs. White had encouraged him to write to his parents, and he would. He would write and petition his father for a dissolution of his betrothal. He couldn't allow it to continue when his heart belonged so completely to someone else.

CHAPTER 26

Clouds hovered low, and the air felt thick with the threat of an afternoon thunderstorm as Libby and her mother made their way home from church on Sunday. Libby had struggled to attend to the reverend's words today, capturing more than one yawn behind her hand during the sermon. She'd lain awake far too long last night, thoughts ricocheting between her evening with Isaac and Mrs. Barker's disconcerting news, until she finally drifted into uneasy dreams. A glance at the dark shadows under Mama's eyes suggested she had passed a similarly restless night.

They turned onto Rawsons Street, and Libby suppressed yet another yawn.

Mama matched it with one of her own. "Perhaps we could both do with a nap this afternoon."

"Indeed. I am sorry if all the trouble of yesterday evening kept you awake with worry."

"It was a rather sleepless night, but 'twas prayer that filled those hours."

Libby frowned. She should have been doing the same. "I never imagined something as simple as working with Mrs.

Barker could…" She let the thought hang unfinished. The streets were quiet, but it seemed too dangerous a thing to speak of openly.

"Nor I."

"I thought that taking a position with her would help us. I felt so guilty for insisting we stay in Boston, I only wanted to do something worthwhile and useful. To give something back to you, after all you have sacrificed for me. But now I've caused more trouble."

Mama stopped and faced her. "Oh Libby, you do not have to repay me. Everything that I have done, all that you consider sacrifice, has, for me, been an honor. It is a privilege to be a mother, a precious gift I hope you one day experience for yourself. God has blessed me richly. Raising you was one of the greatest joys in my life. 'Tis a joy still now, though you're a woman full grown and do not need me in the same way."

"I'll always need you, Mama." Libby's throat tightened around the words.

"I hope so." A tender smile lifted her mother's lips. "I am so proud of who you have become. Your father would be, too, I know."

"I was thinking of him last night, when I saw Mr. White with Katherine. I couldn't help wondering…" She swallowed, blinking away the tears. "I still miss him very much, and I want to believe he'd be proud of me, but I feel as though I've made so many mistakes of late. First, Elijah, now all this with Mrs. Barker."

"I would not call those mistakes. You had no prior knowledge of Elijah's or Mrs. Barker's work, nor did you try to participate in it. I see nothing there to be ashamed of."

"I know, but…" The thoughts she'd wrestled with in the late hours of the night came rushing back. "As I watched Isaac grieving his injury, I realized something about my own grief over Papa's death. I think that I have been seeking some purpose to fill the void left behind by his absence. I wonder if I've even been attempting to be like him, to have an impact like he did, as a way to keep his memory alive. My work with Mrs. Barker and the way I rushed into communicating with Elijah grew in part from a desire to do something worthwhile. To keep from feeling as though I was left behind and fading into the background." Libby crossed her arms against her chest, a feeble barrier to the ache rising there. "Why could I not have been more like you instead?"

"More like me?" Mama arched her brows.

"You always seem content with your place in life. Prayerful in your decisions and actions. Willing to be still and wait."

Mama exhaled a soft laugh. "I shall take those as compliments and be glad you see such qualities in me, but know that they come from God, not of myself, nor were they what they are now when I was your age."

"Truly? There is hope for me yet?" Libby lightened her words with a grin, though the question clenched her stomach with unexpected desperation. She did want that kind of contentment and faith, but was she willing and able to sacrifice her own emotions and desires, even at times her own nature, to gain it?

Mama's laughter grew, rich and warm as an embrace. "Aye. There is nothing wrong with seeking purpose. Indeed, I would suggest that the opposite is true—'tis wrong to attempt to live without it. But do not be deceived into thinking that the only things that are worthwhile, as you say, are those which are seen and recognized or praised by others." She looped her arm through Libby's and gently tugged her back into a slow stroll. "It is not weak or insignificant to live a simple life, marked by everyday tasks that often go unnoticed, yet would be sorely missed should they cease to be done. Why do you think your father was able to dedicate such time and attention to his patients? 'Twas because he knew his home was well cared for and in good hands. Laundry and cooking and mending may seem mundane, but who would your father have been without clothing on his back and food in his belly? Who comforted him when he grieved over the loss of a sick child? Who prayed for him, that God would give him wisdom and skill every time he cared for someone in need? There is honor and purpose in a life of humble service. In the sacrificial love and work of being a wife, a mother, a keeper of your home. To be meek is not weakness. Quite the opposite. 'Tis strength under control, and strength is no less strong because it is quiet."

Libby's heart swelled at the conviction that rang in Mama's words and the confidence that shown in her eyes.

"And you needn't worry about keeping your father's memory alive, my sweet Libby. I see him every time I look at you. He was an excellent physician and an even better man, but I promise, nothing he achieved was more important to him than you."

Libby tightened her grasp on her mother's arm, unable to speak around the lump in her throat.

Mama reached over and covered Libby's hand with her own. "Do you know how many years we prayed for a child? How many tears I shed over my empty womb and empty arms? Your very life is a miracle. You have innate and immeasurable worth because God chose to create you. He placed you in this world right where and when He did for a reason. No matter what you accomplish, or what anyone else thinks of you, you are precious in His eyes, and in mine. Make it your purpose to live a life to His glory. That is how you find true contentment."

A flash of lightning illuminated the edges of the dark clouds, but it was the truth of Mama's words that struck deep in Libby's soul. Could she rest in knowing that her worth came not through what she did, but who she was? Uniquely created and loved by God. And if that same God had placed her when and where He did for a reason, was it possible He was already using her to accomplish far more than she imagined? In all the things she too often deemed small or insignificant, might He have been working, even then? The quiet moments at Isaac's bedside and the thoughtful conversations they shared on their walks. The clothing she hemmed and mended for those in need. The friendship she built with Katherine despite their differing opinions.

Could it be that those things—her words of encouragement, her care for others, and the simple work of her hands—were just as important as throwing tea in the harbor or storming the battlefield or passing secrets through a spy ring?

Thunder rumbled in the distance, and reassurance echoed in her heart as though God Himself had whispered *yes* in answer. Peace seeped through her.

Thank You, Lord. She lifted the silent prayer heavenward, then turned a grateful smile toward her mother. "Thank you, Mama."

Her words seemed paltry in comparison to all she felt, but the softness in her mother's eyes said she understood.

A drizzling rain began to fall, and they picked up their pace as they rounded the corner of Marlbrough Street toward home. But a flash of red in front of their house drew Libby up short, shattering the peace of only moments before.

A British soldier was pounding on their door.

Mama gasped, and Libby's heart froze in her chest. Grabbing Mama's arm, she tugged her off the road, ducking behind the edge of an abandoned house. She pressed her back against the damp siding, thoughts of Mr. Gerrish's arrest flashing through her mind like lightning. Had this man come for her?

"It could be nothing. A simple mistake." Mama's pale face belied her words.

"I pray that is all it is." Libby peeked around the corner.

The soldier had moved from the door to peer into the

window instead. She shuddered. It did not appear to be a mistake.

Thunder rolled again. Closer this time. The man stepped back, staring at the house for a moment longer, then turned and hurried down the road in the opposite direction. Libby clasped her hands around her waist, but nothing could stop the chill that settled deep inside. Clearly, the soldier had been looking for something, or someone, and she could not help fearing it was her he was after.

CHAPTER 27

*L*ibby cringed as her fingers hit another wrong note on the spinet, the dissonant sound resonating in the Whites' parlor. She had arrived not long before for her usual Monday morning visit with Isaac, only to be met by Katherine, who explained that he was occupied with the surgeon. When Libby expressed how much she enjoyed Katherine's performance, her friend had offered to teach her a bit of music while she waited—a prospect that sounded much more entertaining before Libby actually attempted it.

"I do not understand how my hands know exactly what to do with a needle and thread but refuse to obey when tasked to strike a few simple keys." She shook her head, looking up at Katherine, who stood beside her. "You made it look so easy."

The glint in Katherine's dark eyes spoke to suppressed laughter, but her voice was patient and kind. "It isn't easy, by any means. Do not be so hard on yourself. I've been practicing for years. Try again, like this." She reached over and effortlessly played the line Libby's fingers had tripped over.

Libby rested her hand on the keys, just as Katherine had shown her, pressing her teeth into her bottom lip as she focused. The notes plunked out correctly this time, but at a far slower and choppier pace than Katherine had demonstrated.

Katherine clapped. "Bravo, that was it."

"Just barely." She rose from the stool with a laugh. "I think I'd best keep to listening and leave the music in your far more capable hands. Though I do appreciate the attempted lesson."

"My pleasure. I'm glad to share a few minutes together before your lieutenant steals you away." Katherine turned to close the spinet, but not quickly enough to hide the teasing grin on her face.

"Not mine, remember?" Libby's own smile belied the scolding tone of her words.

"Not yet, perhaps, but I saw the way he looked at you on Saturday evening."

So there had been something different in his eyes. Libby had not imagined it that night.

She glanced at the door to ensure no one else was nearby. "Shhh, what if he came downstairs and heard you?"

Katherine's voice dropped to a whisper. "Would that be so bad? Perhaps he needs a bit of encouragement."

"What about Captain Merrick?" Libby shifted the focus away from herself. "He seemed quite attentive."

Katherine wrinkled her nose. "He was, wasn't he? I believe my parents noticed as well and were quite pleased by it."

"But you're not?"

"I enjoy his company, and I spoke with him several times over the course of his recovery here, but I cannot say I hold any particular feelings for him beyond that of an amiable acquaintance." She dipped her head closer with a conspiratorial wink. "And he's not as handsome as another soldier we know."

They both giggled.

How good it felt to tease and laugh with a friend. What a welcome relief from the worry over Mr. Gerrish and the fear that lingered from the soldier's appearance at their house yesterday afternoon. But that was something she could not speak of with Katherine.

The creak of the stairs and the rumble of male voices drew Libby's attention. She ducked through the parlor doorway into the kitchen, straining to make out their conversation. Katherine followed close behind.

Dr. Reynold's voice grew louder as he reached the bottom of the back staircase. "I am still uncomfortable with the idea of you staying at the encampment. Why not continue here? I suspect Mr. White would be glad to carry on as your host." He rounded the corner and caught sight of her. "Ah, Miss Caldwell. Might you convince the lieutenant for me? He seems inclined to listen to you."

Isaac stepped into the kitchen after the doctor, his tall stature placing him a head above the older man. His gaze immediately found hers, expression hard to decipher. He seemed glad to see her, but there was a hesitance in his eyes, a tension in the set of his jaw, that made her stomach lurch.

"You must forgive us for eavesdropping"—Katherine dipped her head—"but I did hear you mention my father. I can attest that he would be more than happy to have you stay here as long as you wish, Lieutenant."

"Thank you. I appreciate it." Isaac glanced at her with a polite smile, then his attention fixed on Libby again. "But as I was telling Dr. Reynold, I've been assigned a new role in the army, and 'tis necessary that I am stationed closer to the rest of my men."

Libby furrowed her brow. "You're not being discharged?"

"I am not."

"But I thought..." What did she think? That he'd no longer be a soldier and if he were not bound to the army, he might change his mind about his allegiances? Might be free to live a life that could include her?

"I planned to tell you today." His voice was strained. "I will explain when we—"

"What concerns me is your continued healing." Dr. Reynold broke in, attention shifting to Isaac's left side. "Things are progressing very well, but you would still benefit from another fortnight or so of these living conditions, which are better than you'll find in the camp, I assure you."

"I understand your concern, Doctor, and appreciate the hospitality of your family, Miss White, but I will be more effective in my work if I am with my regiment."

"You could stay with us again." The offer escaped before Libby could think twice, but once said, she had no desire to take it back. "Our house is nearer to the Common, so you'd have easy access to your duties there, but also a restful place to finish your recovery."

"A perfect solution." Dr. Reynold shouldered his bag and fixed a stern look at Isaac. "As your surgeon, I strongly recommend you accept this invitation, at least until I've removed the last of the plasters."

Isaac stared at her a long moment, indecision swirling in his dark eyes.

Libby tamped down her disappointment. Why was he so hesitant? Did he dislike the thought of being near her again? Had she been completely mistaken in how she read his recent actions and conversations?

Finally, he nodded. "Aye, I will do that. Thank you, Miss Caldwell."

As he turned to bid farewell to the surgeon, Katherine leaned close to Libby's ear, voice low. "So you took my advice, after all, and gave him a bit of encouragement."

Libby swatted at her friend, but Katherine just chuckled as she turned back to the parlor, leaving Libby alone with Isaac.

"I'm sorry. I did plan to tell you about Merrick's offer. I

didn't mean for you to learn of it like that." He stepped closer, holding out his arm. "Walk with me? I'll explain all that I can."

She slipped her hand into the crook of his elbow, relishing the feel of his nearness, even as she steeled herself for his news.

They wandered past Mrs. White's garden, the earthy scent of soil, still damp from yesterday's storm, filling the air. Isaac was quiet, but Libby let the silence linger instead of trying to fill it as she once would have. He steered them toward Hudson's Point, stopping when they reached the water's edge.

Libby stared across the river to the Charlestown Peninsula, now firmly under British control. The Regulars had secured and expanded upon the defenses built by the colonists over a month before. Her heart still ached to see emptiness where the town once stood, the clear sky unbroken by the roofs of houses or the tall steeples of churches. So much devastation. So much loss.

She glanced up at Isaac and found him watching her. He released her arm, shifting to face her fully, and her gaze dropped to his left sleeve. Much loss, indeed.

Isaac's broad chest rose and fell in a heavy sigh before he finally broke the quiet between them. "Captain Merrick spoke to me on Saturday evening, after you returned home. I fully expected to be discharged. I did not imagine there was any way for me to remain in the army. Not like this."

"But he ordered you otherwise?"

"The generals were looking for someone to fill a specific role, one that I can still assist in, despite my injury. Merrick recommended me for the position."

She turned away to hide the sorrow that shot through her. Why had she allowed herself to think there might be another path forward? One that wouldn't keep them forever on opposite sides? She stared at the ripples on the dark water as it lapped at the shore. The ocean tides filtered into the Charles, raising and lowering the river in cycles every day. Constantly moving and changing, but predictable in its patterns. Why could the ebb and flow of her own life not be equally steady and reliable? She had let herself drift on her rising hopes for too long, only to have them sink without warning.

"Are you angry?" Isaac's words were so soft, she almost didn't hear them.

She shook her head, forcing the pain deep where she prayed he could not see. "I am surprised. I did not think this would happen. What is your new assignment?"

"'Tis best that I not speak of the details."

Libby clasped her arms against her stomach, hating the distance that seemed to rapidly expand between them. What kind of work would he be intent to keep to himself? Did he not trust her? Guilt niggled at her conscience. Perhaps he was right to hold back, for she had betrayed his confidence already, even if she had not meant to.

"There's something more you should know." Tension corded his neck. "When my father arranged for me to leave the 29th Regiment and join The King's Own, he secured my new position by entering into an agreement with an officer he had become acquainted with. Major Bradbury was willing to help ensure my commission in exchange for the opportunity to raise his family's standing through a connection by marriage."

Libby's skin prickled. "What do you mean?"

"My father contracted a betrothal between myself and the major's daughter."

Cold numbness gripped Libby's chest and spread through her whole body. "You are engaged?"

He nodded. "But I—"

She stumbled backward, tears burning her eyes and clogging her throat. "I must go. I should not be here alone with you. What would your betrothed say? What would she think? I should never have been—"

"Wait." He clasped her wrist, gently but firm enough to halt her retreat. "I wrote to my father yesterday and requested the dissolution of the agreement. I do not know when I will be able to send the missive, nor how he will respond, but I had to try."

"Why?" The question cracked her voice. Cracked her heart.

Why had he kept this from her for so long? Was it because he never thought of her as anything more than a friend? But if so, why was he seeking to end the engagement now?

"I've never met Miss Bradbury. Never even exchanged a single letter. I had no say in the pledge that was made on my behalf, and I cannot in good conscience continue with it when…" He sighed, releasing her arm.

He searched her face, a tumult of emotions swirling in his brown eyes.

Libby's breath lodged in her chest. What more had he held back from saying? She wanted to ask, but the words wouldn't come.

A muscle in his jaw twitched. "I wanted you to know the truth, so far as I am free to give it. And if, knowing this, you would rather rescind your offer that I stay in your home, I understand."

"Of course not. You are still welcome. You always will be." Libby forced a smile, despite the questions that buffeted her.

He had said so much, yet he left much more unsaid. Still, her answer was sincere. She would always welcome him, difficult as it might be for her bruised heart. Would he do the same, if she laid bare the secrets she held?

CHAPTER 28

*I*saac braced himself on the deck of the ship and reached toward the shore where Libby stood, hair whipping in the wind, arms stretched toward him. She was calling, but he couldn't make out the words. Waves thrashed at the prow. He grappled for the railing, but it was slick with rain, and he couldn't find purchase with only one hand. His feet slid out from under him. He crashed hard against the wooden boards, slamming his head.

Blackness invaded his vision. He fought against it as the vessel dipped low, sending him careening into a cannon mounted on one side. He slung his arm around it, trying to regain his balance, but the fuse lit beneath his grasp. The ship lurched wildly in the raging gale. The cannonball shot out, blazing like a streak of fire through the sky, aimed directly at Libby. A scream tore from his throat, and he tumbled off the edge of the ship into the angry sea below.

The impact of the floorboards ripped Isaac from the nightmare. Cold sweat soaked his tunic, and the sheets twisted around his legs. Kicking them off, he struggled to sit upright. He leaned against the side of the bed, breath coming in short gasps. Slowly, the horrifying scene his mind had created dissipated like fog and the familiar surroundings of his chamber at the Caldwell home took shape under the pale light of dawn. Even still, his body shook uncontrollably.

"Isaac?" Libby's voice, soft but urgent, called from behind his closed door. "Are you hurt?"

Suppressing a moan, he pushed off the floor. "I'm fine." His voice came out rough and unconvincing.

"Another nightmare?"

"Aye." He reached for the breeches he'd slung over the back of the chair last night and wrestled them on, leaving his shirt untucked and hanging long over top. He shuffled for the door and cracked it open just enough to peek out.

Libby stared back at him, a candle in her hand, its flickering light illuminating the worry in her eyes. "I heard you shout and then there was a loud thump."

"I fell out of bed." He grimaced. "I'm sorry I woke you."

"Is there anything I can do?"

Her presence had certainly helped him before, when she sat by his side in the Whites' house, but those circumstances were vastly different than now. He couldn't very well have her do that here, in this quiet half darkness, with her curls spilling loose around her shoulders and her father's old banyan wrapped around her shift. She looked altogether too soft and tempting. It would be so easy to reach out and bury his fingers in her hair. To slide his arm around her waist and pull her close. His grip on the handle of the door tightened.

He shook his head. "You needn't worry about me. I am well. 'Tis early. You should get some more sleep."

She searched his face for a long moment, as though assessing the truth of his words. Her gaze dropped to the open v at the top of his shirt, then snapped upward. She stepped back, wide-eyed. "I...I suppose you are right. Good night. Or... good morning."

She spun away, nearly tripping over the long hem of the oversized banyan, and scurried from the room. He slid the door shut, thankful for the barrier it had provided against doing something he would regret. Prying his fingers from the handle, Isaac traipsed back to bed and sank onto the mattress. He eyed the tangled sheets that lay in a heap on the floor but did not bother to pick them up. There was little chance he would sleep again.

Had he made a mistake in returning here? He'd not been plagued by such awful dreams in over a sennight, but one night at the Caldwell house left him battling one of the worst yet. Perhaps it was his nearness to Libby that dragged her into the nightmare. Or mayhap it was his own conscience that haunted him.

He had almost told her everything yesterday. Almost confessed how deeply he cared for her. But something held him back. The familiar tug of duty that bound him. The painful awareness of the differences that pushed them apart. Now this, another night of weakness, lost in terrors his mind invented. He rubbed his left shoulder, letting his hand drift down to the stump that remained. An ever-present reminder of his brokenness.

So much stood between them. Things that seemed far more difficult to surmount than even the defensive fortress upon Breed's Hill. That attempt had taken his arm and nearly cost him his life. What would the price be if he tried to pursue Libby?

He rubbed at his bleary eyes but could not wipe away the sight of her. Not the way she looked standing outside his door, nor the way she'd appeared in his terrible dream. The nightmare lingered like smoke after a musket shot, an eerie warning that he was bound to hurt her in the end.

～

*B*right sunlight streamed into Isaac's chamber, and he squinted as he sat up in bed. He must have fallen asleep again, after all, and in a rather uncomfortable position, judging by the stiffness in his neck. He kneaded the muscles there as he stood and moved to the window. The sun had climbed quite high. It was even later than he'd first thought. Merrick would be expecting him. Best be quick about it, which was easier said than done these days.

He shoved his shirt into the breeches he still wore, then lifted one of the strings on the top of his tunic and grasped it between his teeth. He'd discovered this method for tying his shirt closed that, while awkward, was better than depending on someone else to help him dress. Looping the other string over the first, he was able to pull the neckline together and secure a knot to hold it in place.

His hair was another matter, one he'd yet to attempt on his own. He raked his fingers through, wincing when they caught on a snarled knot. Frustration twisted just as tightly in his gut. He should have thought of this when he accepted the offer to return to the Caldwells' home. 'Twas humbling enough to have young Briana or Aideen assist him. What would he do here?

With a huff, he abandoned the problem of his hair for a moment and turned to his waistcoat instead. Not much better, what with all the buttons that were maddeningly tedious. He'd only managed to secure two of the long row when a knock halted his fumbling efforts.

"Isaac, are you still there?" Libby's voice.

"I am." He set to work on the next button, barely holding in a growl when it refused to slide into place.

"I thought perhaps you'd left through the side door. We set aside some breakfast for you."

Forgoing his attempts, he strode to the door that connected his room to the parlor and yanked it open. Libby startled backward at the abrupt movement. Or perhaps it was his scowl that sent her retreating.

She glanced from his face to his waistcoat, then back again. "Do you...need help?"

Not from her. That was a terrible idea. Embarrassing and far too intimate a task. Yet he found himself nodding. "This is rather troublesome with one hand."

"Well, then, allow me."

He stood still in the threshold as she stepped near and reached for the first button. Her subtle rosewater scent drifted toward him, the top of her head just below his chin. Her hair was pinned up now, her father's banyan replaced by a blue linen short gown and gray petticoat, but still, her closeness made his pulse quicken. Every brush of her slim fingers on his chest sent sparks through him as she eased the last of the buttons into place.

"What else?" She peeked up, attention drifting to his unruly hair. A hint of color filled her cheeks, and hesitation crept into her tone. "Shall I tie it back for you?"

He swallowed. What choice did he have? "There's a ribbon on the table. And a comb."

She ducked around him, and he followed her into his chamber, careful to leave the door to the parlor wide open.

She lifted the ribbon from the small table beside his bed, then gestured toward the chair. "You'd best sit. You're too tall for me to reach otherwise."

He did so, gritting his teeth as she gently combed the knots loose, not out of pain but in a desperate attempt to resist the longing stirred by her touch.

As soon as she had finished plaiting his hair and secured it with the ribbon, he bolted out of his seat and stalked to the bed where he'd left his coat. "I can manage the rest."

She returned the comb to his table and reached for the wide black band he'd also left there. "What about your stock?"

He faced her, gaze snagging on her pursed lips. "Leave it be." The words sounded rougher than he meant, but he had to deter her somehow. His self-control was but a thin thread.

She dismissed his protest with a little huff. "You'll need help. Surely, I can manage this."

Standing on tiptoes, she looped the stock around his neck. Her soft fingers grazed his skin as she worked the brass buckle into place, and his breath caught in his chest.

"There. Finished." She stepped back just enough to survey her work. "You look…"

Her words faltered as she lifted her gaze to meet his. Admiration sparked in the blue depths of her eyes. Admiration and something more he dared not name. Something that snapped his last grasp on restraint.

"Libby." Her name rasped out on a shuddered exhale a second before he captured her mouth with his own.

It was as if a dam broke, releasing all his pent-up emotion and pouring every last drop into their kiss. He wrapped his arm around her waist, anchoring her to him, just as she'd been his anchor these past weeks.

Hers the voice calling his name after he was rescued from the battlefield. Hers the whispered prayers that were his only tether to the world during those feverish days that followed. Hers the smile mingled with tears that greeted him when he woke. Hers the hope that refused to dim, refused to let him sink into despair.

She matched his kiss with equal fervor, hands grasping his waistcoat, and he lost himself to her touch.

He tried to lift his other arm to cup her cheek, but an aching emptiness pierced through him, as sharp and devastating as a bayonet blade. Stumbling back, he gasped for air. He had no other arm to hold her. He never would. He'd never be a whole man again. Never be the kind of man she deserved.

"Isaac?" Libby's voice trembled as she peered up at him, confusion etched on her beautiful face.

She lifted her fingers to her lips, swollen from his kiss, and guilt pummeled him like a fist to the gut.

"I'm so sorry." Shaking his head, he stepped farther away. "I should not have..."

She blinked, the sheen of tears in her eyes heaping more blame upon his conscience.

"Please forgive me." Isaac choked on the plea as he turned away, grabbed his coat from the bed, and staggered for the side door.

Yanking it open, he escaped into the blinding morning light, not daring to look back.

CHAPTER 29

*I*saac ducked through the canvas flaps that served as the door to Captain Merrick's tent, following his superior officer inside. Stale air, tainted by the smell of dirt and sweat, greeted him. Merrick stooped to open a chest at the foot of his cot as Isaac swiped his brow, beaded with sweat from his swift walk to the encampment on the Common. He'd forgotten his hat in his hurried retreat from the Caldwell home but had not dared to turn back. He couldn't face Libby again. Not yet. If he did, he was bound to repeat that kiss, and that was something he couldn't risk, no matter how much he wanted to.

Merrick cleared his throat, and Isaac turned to find the captain eying him, brows raised. "Did you hear anything I said?"

A different kind of heat crept up his neck. "I'm sorry. I was distracted."

"So I can see." The captain eyed him curiously. "I was saying that this is for you." He held out a worn haversack that Isaac immediately recognized as having belonged to Sergeant Jackson. "You'll find copious notes inside. That is the best place to begin. You may use my table to review them here. I know 'tis not an ideal working space, but we must keep this information away from any other eyes. Even pretty blue ones."

Merrick softened his warning with a teasing grin, but the message was clear. Isaac could not bring such sensitive material back to the Caldwell house, nor could he speak of what he was doing here, because no one, not even Libby, was to be trusted.

He took the bag, surprised by its weight, and plunked it atop the small wooden table on the other side of Merrick's tent. A single chair sat next to it, and a quill and bottle of ink perched on one corner of the worn surface.

"You'll find some parchment in here, if you need to make notes of your own." Captain Merrick tapped his trunk with the toe of his shoe. "I'll send Stanton by later so you can discuss matters with him as necessary."

"Thank you."

"Well..." Merrick adjusted the broad strap across his chest. "Best of luck. I have much more faith in you than I had in Jackson. I know this is in good hands."

"Good *hand*, you mean." Isaac jested, though he kept his expression stoic.

Merrick blinked, then let out a burst of laughter. "Aye, I suppose so." He clapped Isaac on his right shoulder. "I'm glad to have you back."

Isaac couldn't rightly declare that he was glad to be back, so he said nothing as his captain departed, leaving him alone in the stuffy tent. He shrugged out of his coat and draped it over the back of the chair, then sat with a heavy exhale.

Opening the bag, he pulled out a stack of papers, bound together by a thin leather cord. He loosed the tie and skimmed the first page, noting the date in the top corner—the third of August, 1774. Nearly a year ago. Jackson's script was heavily slanted but easy to decipher. He had recorded basic information regarding the suspicions over an active spy ring in and around Boston and listed names of people to watch.

The notes on the following pages were much the same. Dates, names, lists. Observations made, information collected. Slowly, the records grew more detailed as Jackson had clearly gained a better understanding of the situation, as well as formed connections with men who were willing to act the part of a Patriot while passing information on to him instead.

The initials, *J.L.,* first appeared in early September. Jackson had underlined them and written, *Suspect this man to be the primary organizer of spy activity within the confines of Boston, perhaps beyond.*

Isaac frowned. The infamous J.L. James Lawrence, as Jackson had later determined. The man Jackson had become obsessed with hunting down. Now Isaac's responsibility to track. He rolled his neck, wincing at the stiffness that lingered from last night and had only grown worse as he hunched over the desk. Pressing on, he paused at a page from mid-September last year that bore his name.

Two cannons stolen from the new gun house. This in addition to those already taken from the old gun house. Reported the theft to Lt. Harrison. Suspect J.L. to be involved.

A blot of ink marred the edge of the paper at the end of his sentence, as though to emphasize the sergeant's anger. Isaac frowned, remembering that day clearly. Jackson had come to the Caldwells' home with the news, spewing curses and ogling Libby. His jaw clenched at the recollection.

A pattern of drumbeats echoed through the camp. Setting aside the papers and the disconcerting memory, Isaac rose to peer out of the tent at the soldiers in their drills. Lines of crimson, moving in tight formation, following orders. The rolling snare, the steps of their march, every polished musket and regimental hat...it was all so familiar, something that had been a part of him for years, and yet he felt like a spectator. Though he was still in the army, it wasn't the same now, and it was not only his new role that made him feel so removed.

It was the shift in his own allegiance. He could no longer bear to fight against the people of this colony. He'd lived among them. Listened to them speak. Read their words. He had watched them bravely stand in defense of their homes, their families, and their rights. Had watched them die for their beliefs.

Stalking back to the table, he shoved his treasonous thoughts into the recesses of his mind. He didn't sit but instead picked up the next page and read it while pacing the small confines of the tent.

Slowly, the stack of unread papers diminished as Isaac worked his way into pages labeled with the early months of 1775. A new name continued to surface—Benjamin Church— and Isaac furrowed his brow, trying to discern why the man sounded familiar. He stopped walking to mull over one paragraph in particular.

Dr. Church is a member of the Sons of Liberty and holds close ties to Adams, Hancock, and Warren, but he has recently taken up secret correspondence with Gen. Gage. Church is an exceedingly valuable asset, and I have hopes he can help expose J.L. and others involved in his circle.

Realization dawned. Sergeant Jackson had spoken to Isaac about Dr. Church back in early June. Isaac had found himself particularly disgusted by the thought of a man who would turn against his friends in such a way. The sentiment remained just as strong now. He slapped the paper onto the table, annoyance churning in his gut. He had never held any desire to involve himself in this underhanded world of espionage, but it had been foisted upon him, nonetheless.

Slouching onto the chair, he scrubbed his hand down his

face. Was he any better than Benjamin Church? He'd resigned himself to continued service in the army while he harbored doubts as to the justice of their actions.

He tipped his head back and stared at the shadows that drifted across the cream-colored canvas tent, an ever-changing pattern cast by the clouds outside. But his mind saw a different scene. Shadows dancing on Dr. Caldwell's face as they talked late into the evening beside the parlor hearth. It was days after the shooting that broke out in the front of the State House, and Isaac was wrestling with the deaths of innocent citizens at the hands of his fellow soldiers while also recognizing the duty he and the other Regulars were required to fulfill.

Isaac lamented aloud about how his task should be one of protection and order, of ensuring laws were kept and peace maintained.

Dr. Caldwell fixed that familiar piercing gaze upon Isaac, the one that seemed to assess the condition of his heart. "But is it protection of peace and order when the laws you are sent to enforce are unwanted, or even seen as oppressive, to the people?"

The question, spoken without accusation, took him aback. He stared at the doctor, uncertain how to respond. Unsure even of his own thoughts.

Dr. Caldwell propped his elbows on his knees and leaned closer. "Is it wrong for people to desire representation in their government? If we are citizens of Britain, why should we not have some voice in Parliament? And if such representation be denied, if laws be passed that impact our daily lives, should we keep silent? When our rights are encroached upon, why should we not have the ability to defend and speak out for ourselves?"

Isaac blinked, pulling himself back to the present. Dr. Caldwell's challenge had lingered in his thoughts long after, perhaps more than Isaac had even realized, or dared admit. Until now.

What would his friend think, were he still here today? If he'd taken such a stance five years ago, surely his conviction would be equal, if not stronger, under the current circumstances. Would he be pleased to learn that his passionate and thoughtful debates had brought Isaac to an understanding, even an acceptance of, his ideals?

And what would Dr. Caldwell think if he knew the way Isaac felt about his daughter?

He needed to get out of here. Needed to distance himself from the rows of tents and the lines of soldiers. From Jackson's notes and the way they clashed with his memories of Dr. Caldwell's words. From the aching desire to run back to Libby's house. To hold her and never let go.

The need for escape pulsed through every heartbeat, each fiber of his being desperate for space, just like when he was a boy, fleeing the confines of his parents' expectations and disappointment in him for the freedom he found in the branches of a tree.

He shoved back from the desk, scattering the stack of papers. Growling, he bent to retrieve them from the trampled grass, then froze. A date stared back at him, and the words at the top of the page sent a chill down his spine.

April 17th, 1775 - Arrested James Lawrence and one of his conspirators, an elderly man by the name of Ephraim Pierce.

Mr. Pierce. The apothecary. The father of Libby's dearest friend. The one Isaac had helped flee Boston at Libby's request.

No one had ever mentioned that another man was arrested alongside Mr. Pierce that day. Had they been unaware? Or did they purposefully choose to hide that information from Isaac?

Had it all been a lie? Was it possible that Mr. Pierce had deceived them all and secretly been part of Lawrence's spy ring? Or could it be that everyone Isaac had trusted and respected knew the truth?

Had he assisted the escape of a spy without knowing it?

All thoughts of leaving the tent disappeared as Isaac regathered the pages, searching for answers with new vigor. He lost track of time, poring over Sergeant Jackson's script, desperate for something that would silence the growing fear inside.

When Private Stanton entered, Isaac startled.

The soldier offered a brisk bow, focus resting on Isaac's left side for a lingering moment before snapping back to his face. "Lieutenant Harrison, I am glad to see you again."

Isaac rose and dipped his head, trying to clear his muddled thoughts enough to converse normally with the man. "Thank you."

"I see you've been reading Sergeant Jackson's notes." Stanton gestured to the papers now strewn across the desk.

"I've not gotten through them all, but I have a general sense of where things stand."

"I have some more recent news to share with you that won't be found in those pages. I must inform you that a man was arrested a few days ago. He was found in possession of sensitive material tucked beneath the buttons of his waistcoat, of all things." Stanton raised his brows. "He's being held in the jail for the time being, should you desire an audience with him."

A surprisingly creative method—Isaac had to give the man credit for that. "Do you have the waistcoat?"

"I believe it was passed on to General Gage."

Isaac nodded. "And the man's name?"

"Mr. Gerrish. Puts up on Winter Street."

A tremor shot through him. *Mr. Gerrish? Winter Street?* The very man Libby had been meeting with. The one she had delivered mending to. A waistcoat, if his memory served correct. Was it only mending, or was it this? A secret message hidden directly beneath his own nose?

No. It couldn't be. And yet, twice now she had been associated with men accused of espionage. First, in her insistence upon helping Mr. Pierce, and now this? Nausea swelled in his stomach.

Private Stanton peered at him. "Are you unwell, Lieutenant?"

Isaac clenched his jaw. He had to hold himself together. "I'm fine. Is there anything else you wish to discuss today?"

"One more thing likely to be of interest. Captain Merrick may have informed you already, but we did capture a man at Breed's Hill who matched the description of James Lawrence. He managed to escape as the barge arrived in Boston, but this was left behind." He flipped open the haversack slung over his shoulder and reached inside, pulling out a leather journal. "You'll find the letter hidden within the pages to be of particular importance."

Dread seeped through Isaac's veins as he accepted the outstretched journal. He recognized this book. Had seen it once before, in Libby's hands when they searched the Pierces' house. It was the one thing she had taken with her when they left.

Cold sweat dampened his palm, and he turned his back to place the journal on the table, hoping Private Stanton hadn't noticed the way his fingers shook. He opened the cover, and his heart seemed to stop beating as his gaze fell on the slip of paper tucked inside. He skimmed the letter, words blurring, breath leaking out of him with each new sentence.

I heard the lieutenant talking... They will send troops... Please try to find Will... Josiah Wagner too...

His vision turned spotty. There was only one person who could have written this message and placed it in this journal.

Libby.

He had fallen in love with a spy.

CHAPTER 30

*L*ibby paced the kitchen in the waning evening light, the smell of woodsmoke and salted pork lingering in the air. A breeze wafted in through the open windows, carrying with it the night sounds of crickets and the lone cry of a whippoorwill. She wanted to run outside and add her own searching call to the bird's melody. To shout Isaac's name into the growing darkness, as though that might summon him home.

Where was he? Why had he not yet returned? And why had he apologized for that kiss?

That question had been plaguing her all day. She'd been so distracted after he left this morning, she nearly burned her hand on the kettle while fixing breakfast. Mama had eyed her askance but refrained from asking anything, for which Libby was grateful. How could she explain to her mother what had happened when she could hardly comprehend it herself?

One moment, he was holding her, kissing her with a desperate sort of hunger that had stolen her breath and blazed through her very bones. The next, he was running away, begging her forgiveness. His kiss had filled her with incomprehensible joy, but his abrupt departure had drained every bit, leaving her hollow and confused. If he regretted kissing her so much, why had he done so at all?

The worn floorboards creaked under her feet, and a weary sigh escaped. She strayed to the front window and peered out at the shadowed street. Silhouettes of buildings and trees stood black against the last gray light that hovered in the sky, but no tall figure strode toward her house. She should give up and go to bed. Mama had retired already, with a knowing look in her eyes and a warning not to stay awake too late.

Perhaps Isaac wasn't coming back. And what would she do if he did? Confront him? Confess her love and assure him there was no need to apologize for what happened this morning?

She shook her head and turned away. No. She'd not make a fool of herself. Not bare her heart so openly, only to have him refuse her. Hot tears burned, but she gritted her teeth, refusing to let them fall. Her fingers fumbled with the knot in her apron ties. She yanked it free and threw her apron on the table, then spun away and traipsed to the stairs.

She was halfway up when the sound of footsteps coming from the direction of Isaac's chamber halted her. Pausing, she listened. There, the scrape of chair legs on the floor. He must have entered through the side door straight into his room. She hurried back down and turned toward the parlor, then hesitated in the threshold, doubting the wisdom of her actions. It was better to leave him alone, even if she felt as though she might burst with the need to speak with him. To understand what had passed between them.

The door connecting Isaac's chamber to the parlor swung open, and his broad shoulders filled the doorway. Libby froze as his gaze collided with hers. Candlelight from the lantern he held flashed against the regimental buttons of his coat and cast

harsh shadows on his face. A face lined with sorrow and...
anger?

"Come to see what other secrets you can discover?" Bitterness edged his tone, and his question sucked the breath from her lungs.

Secrets? Her hands trembled. What had happened? She clasped her fingers together and tried to steady her voice. "What do you mean?"

"I know everything, Libby."

It was the second time he'd said her name, but instead of filling her with a rush of pleasure as it had this morning, the raw pain in his words sent a chill down her spine. She crept into the parlor, steps unsteady, and stopped beside the chairs in front of the hearth. "I do not know what you think, but—"

"What I think?" Discarding the lantern on the parlor table, he strode closer, until they were mere inches apart. He kept his voice low, but hurt and accusation laced through his rough whisper. "I think you've been claiming to desire my friendship while turning against me at every chance. Somehow you convinced me that you might even..." A muscle jumped in his jaw, and misery pooled in his dark eyes. "I allowed myself to believe you might feel something more for me. I trusted you. Depended on you. And all along, you were using me for your own gain, just as my father has all my life. At least he never hid his intentions. You deceived me at every turn. Was it all a lie? I cared about you, but you...you've been taking advantage of your connection with me to garner information to pass on to your fellow spies."

She stumbled back, his words shredding her heart. He thought she was a spy. Worse, he thought she had purposefully betrayed him. "Isaac, I promise I never did anything to hurt you. Whatever you have heard or seen, you must believe me."

"Believe you? How?" He raked his hand through his hair, pulling strands free from the queue she'd plaited earlier in the day. "I know about Mr. Pierce. About Mr. Gerrish. I saw the journal with your letter. What more evidence do I need?"

Terror coursed through Libby, leaving her limbs numb and her heart racing. She grasped the back of the chair to keep from collapsing. "It is not what you think. I never meant…"

"I should arrest you." His voice dropped to the barest whisper. There was no conviction in his tone. No threat. Only utter resignation and grief. "'Tis my role with the army now, to seek out the Patriot spies and bring them to justice. But I cannot…" He scrubbed his hand down his face and turned away.

Libby struggled to breathe, his words tightening around her chest like a noose. "Please, Isaac, let me explain."

He didn't move. Didn't speak. She stared at his broad back, his strength evident despite the loss of his arm and his weeks of recovery. But his shoulders stooped, as though they bore a weight no man should have to carry. She had put that weight there. Not on purpose, but she had all the same.

Might she be able to relieve his burden while also clearing her name? Would he listen long enough to allow her the chance to try? Tentatively, she reached out and brushed her fingers over his back. His muscles stiffened in response, and she tugged her hand away.

Libby drew a steadying breath. "I did send that letter."

Isaac spun back, expression fixed into a stoic mask to hide whatever he was thinking or feeling.

"I wrote it to a friend out of concern for my family. I did not mean to overhear you speaking about the army's plans that night, nor did I think my message would matter to anyone beyond the people I know and love. I wanted to protect Will and Josiah. I never imagined…" She stuttered to a halt. How could she explain without revealing too much about Elijah and endangering him?

"What of Mr. Gerrish? I saw you giving him that waistcoat.

Were you handing him stolen information right in front of me?"

"No. It was only mending, I assure you. I knew nothing of the hidden messages until after..."

A frown marred his detached facade. "I want to believe you, but how can I when you're clearly still hiding things?"

"And how can I reveal the full truth after you explained your role and admitted that you should arrest me?" Desperation made her voice quiver. "I want to tell you everything. I want you to trust me, and I want to be able to trust you in return."

"I am not certain that will ever be possible again." There was a cold finality in his voice that struck more fear into her heart than even his accusations had.

"Isaac, please, there must be a way."

He stepped back, and the space that gaped between them felt like the severing of a cord that had once bound them together. Night had fallen fully, and as he moved away, shadows swallowed him, hiding his face. "I will not turn you in. For the sake of your late father and for the...for whatever it was we once shared. It was real to me, even if it never was for you."

"It was real for me. It is real." Tears spilled down her cheeks, though she doubted he could see them in the meager light cast by the lantern. "I love you, Isaac."

The confession slipped out before she could stop it. Isaac drew a sharp breath, but he said nothing, nor did he move toward her. Thick silence fell, hovering for a long, tense moment. She waited, mouth dry, cheeks damp, certain the pounding of her heart was loud enough for him to hear.

Isaac's low voice cut through the quiet. "I will move out in the morning. I suggest you leave Boston if at all possible, Miss Caldwell. I can only protect you so much. If any of the other men working with me should discover your involvement on their own, they will not have the same motivation as I do to spare you harm."

She stepped forward, desperate to see his face, to touch him, but he snatched the light from the table and disappeared into his chamber, closing the door behind him. Darkness engulfed the room and seeped into her very soul. Libby stifled a sob as she fled, leaving the shattered pieces of her heart behind.

CHAPTER 31

$\mathcal{M}$orning light filled Isaac's chamber, but his heart felt trapped in darkness. He'd barely slept last night after his encounter with Libby, her parting words to him repeating like a ceaseless echo.

I love you, Isaac.

Her confession, one that should have brought unspeakable joy, had burst through him with all the fiery destruction of a musket ball. She loved him. Had anyone ever said that to him before? He could not recall his parents even once declaring such deep affection, and while he had shared a closeness and camaraderie with some of his fellow soldiers, *love* was certainly not a word they'd ever used.

Libby loved him, and oh how he loved her. But it didn't matter. Now more than ever, the chasm between them stretched wide and impassable.

Isaac slouched onto his bed, staring at the crimson coat splayed across the coverlet beside him. It may as well have been his own blood staining the fabric for how much pain he felt. A hurt far deeper than he'd suffered on the battlefield, and one that no surgeon could mend.

Propping his elbow on his thigh, he bowed his head into his hand, closing his eyes as he covered them with his open palm. "Lord, I need You." He choked out the prayer, his voice as raw as his aching soul. "I don't know what to do."

Silence met him.

A lock of hair drooped into his face, and he straightened, shoving it away. His plait from yesterday morning was tousled from restless sleep, and he'd only bothered to don his breeches and tunic so far. He lacked the patience to attempt the buttons of his waistcoat and couldn't bring himself to put on his uniform.

He'd seen Libby's tears as she pleaded with him last night, a glint on her cheeks in the dim candlelight that almost broke his resolve. Almost dragged him back to her side so he could wipe them away and pull her close. So he could kiss her as if nothing else mattered.

But it did matter. The lies and deceit. The role he held that directly opposed the one she'd evidently chosen. So he had clenched his jaw, steeled his spine, and forced his feet away from her instead. She could claim she loved him, but her actions told a very different story.

Isaac pushed off the bed. Captain Merrick would be expecting him soon. He glanced at the door, then back at his discarded coat. He had to choose. Face Libby again and give her another chance to explain, or put on his uniform and not look back.

He reached for the coat but stopped, fingers inches away. He balled his hand into a fist and spun from the bed, grasping the latch and tugging open the door. His heart pounded as he made his way to the kitchen where he was sure to find the women at this hour.

Pausing at the threshold, he peered in but saw only Mrs. Abbott.

She looked up from the hearth where she bent to push

some glowing coals beneath the trivet. "Good morning, Lieutenant. I'll soon have some eggs prepared if you're hungry."

"Thank you, but I was looking for Lib—for Miss Caldwell."

"She's not come down yet. I believe she retired late last night." Mrs. Abbott straightened, gaze assessing.

He shifted, looking away, uncomfortable under her discerning watch. "We did speak. Or rather, argue."

"May I inquire as to why?"

The motherly protectiveness in her tone drew his attention back to her. "I regret that my new position with the army uncovered some..." He frowned. "Some condemning information about Miss Caldwell."

"Of what sort?" Mrs. Abbott's gaze sharpened, but he did not miss the flicker of fear in her eyes.

Was it possible Mrs. Abbott was aware of her daughter's actions? Might she even have taken part in them alongside her? Or had Libby deceived her mother as well?

"I have been entrusted with the task of uncovering those involved in espionage against the Crown, and yesterday I found several pieces of evidence pointing to—"

"It is not what it seems. She told you, did she not?"

"You knew?" Isaac's gut clenched. Another betrayal. Had their kindness and generosity meant nothing? Had it all been a ruse? What if even Dr. Caldwell's friendship had been a falsehood?

"I know that my daughter is not a spy, whatever you may have discovered." She stepped closer, pale but determined. "And I am certain she would have explained that to you, if given the opportunity."

Isaac's shoulders tensed. "That is why I am looking for her. I would like to offer the opportunity now."

Mrs. Abbott stared at him a long moment, blue eyes so much like her daughter's. He faltered under her assessment, which seemed to see beyond the unflinching expression he'd mastered as an officer to the man he was beneath.

"I will fetch Libby, but only if you promise to listen, truly listen, to her. My daughter cares for you a great deal, and I will not allow you to hurt her."

Isaac nodded. He would listen, and he would bear the pain of it, for he would rather shoulder it himself than do anything more to hurt her, even if all he suspected was true. "I promise."

She slipped around him. He waited, every muscle tense, listening to the stairs creak as she climbed.

"Libby?" Mrs. Abbott's gasp sent a bolt of dread straight down Isaac's spine.

He sprinted up the stairs, halting as Mrs. Abbott turned, face pale. "She's gone."

His heart seemed to cease beating. "What do you mean, gone?"

"She is not there. I don't know where she could be." Mrs. Abbott pressed a shaky hand to her chest.

Isaac slumped against the wall. Libby had fled. Because she was guilty or because his words had chased her away? Whatever the case, she was not safe wandering alone in a city teeming with soldiers.

He straightened. "I'll find her. I'll not let any harm come to her."

∽

*D*ew soaked Libby's petticoat as she knelt beside her father's grave in Granary Burying Ground. She pressed a kiss to her fingertips, then brushed them over the grooved letters that spelled his name. Cold stone, the stark opposite of her father, who'd been all warmth and kindness.

"I miss you, Papa. I wish I could talk to you. Wish you could step in and fix this mess."

She longed to bury her head against her father's chest as she had when she was a little girl. What would he say to her now, if he knew all that had happened between herself and Isaac?

Isaac. Could she ever forget the way he'd looked at her last night? The words he'd said. What he thought of her? She swiped the back of her hand over her damp cheeks. How did she have any tears left, when she'd spent most of the night crying into her pillow?

She tipped her head back and peered at the sky. Unable to sleep for more than a few restless hours, she had given up trying and crept out at dawn's first light. She couldn't bear the thought of being at home when Isaac left for the last time, and his warning that she should depart Boston lingered heavy in her thoughts. Perhaps he was right, but could she figure out a way? Mrs. Barker might be able to help, if she had connections with those she had secretly been communicating with. Libby shuddered at the thought of sneaking out of the city, as though she really were as deceptive and entrenched in espionage as Isaac assumed her to be. Would they be forced to leave everything behind? To abandon their home to the risk of looters and soldiers?

"I have to go, Papa. I do not know when I will return." She stared at the etched stone, missing the sound of his voice, the brightness of his smile, the comfort of his embrace.

It was silly to talk to him when he wasn't there. She knew well enough that the body buried beneath the ground was only that—a body. The man she'd loved and respected as her father was now in heaven. That assurance gave her hope but did not fully ease the ache inside.

Standing, she brushed the dirt from her petticoat. Enough tears. 'Twas impossible to change what had happened, but she could be strong for Mama's sake. Her mother would be awake now and sure to worry if she noticed Libby was not home. Best hurry back and explain everything.

She turned and froze at the sight of a soldier hovering near the edge of the burying ground. He leaned against a tree, one leg crossed over the other, watching her. Her pulse notched higher. What was he doing? She'd not been thinking clearly this morning. Otherwise, she wouldn't have strayed here alone. Mayhap if she ignored him and walked the other way, he'd leave her be. Keeping him in her peripheral vision, she headed for Common Street.

The soldier pushed off the trunk and started toward her.

Libby clutched a handful of her petticoat and strode faster, but he moved closer. A chill raced down her spine. He angled across her path, cutting her off. She drew up short as he blocked her way.

"Beg your pardon, miss, but I could not help noticing you were in some distress." He tipped his head, voice congenial, though his eyes held an interest that made her mouth go dry. He tugged a kerchief out of his pocket and extended it to her. "Might I be of assistance?"

"Thank you, but I am well. If you'll excuse me…" She forced a confidence she did not feel and attempted to slip past him, but he sidled over to match her.

"Who was it, the one you're mourning? A husband, perhaps?"

She swallowed. "My father."

"Ah. I offer my condolences." The sympathetic smile that curved his lips would seem genuine if not for the way he inched nearer.

She backed up, squaring her shoulders. "Your sentiment is appreciated, but I must return home now."

He frowned as he leaned in, close enough for her to notice his pitted face, likely from surviving a bout of smallpox. "'Tis a pity to grieve alone. I would be more than willing to escort you—"

"There is no need. Please excuse me." She kept her voice and expression firm, stepping around him.

His hand shot out and wrapped around her wrist. Libby tried to yank free, but his grip only tightened.

He bent to whisper in her ear, his breath sour and hot against her cheek. "I think you'd best reconsider my offer, Miss Caldwell."

She gasped. How did he know her name? Was he one of the other soldiers hunting for Patriot spies? But surely Isaac hadn't revealed his suspicions to anyone else. Had he? Her heart pounded in her chest. Whether he was intent upon her arrest or accosting her for other nefarious reasons, she had to get away from this man.

"Unhand me this instant!" Libby kicked his shin, startling him enough that she could wrench her arm loose. The force sent her reeling backward. Her heel caught on a root, and she tumbled to the ground. She flung out her hands to break the fall, smashing her palms onto the hard earth. Pain rattled through her arms and back, but it was the soldier's scoffing laughter that shook her to the core.

He planted one foot on the hem of her petticoat and crouched low. A mocking smirk replaced any false attempt at civility. "Looks to me as though you do need some help, after all."

She tried to scream but couldn't force a sound past the choking tightness in her throat. Could hardly breathe. She struggled, fingers clawing at the dirt, but his foot held her forcibly in place. Blackness dotted her vision.

"Get away from her, soldier!" A commanding voice shouted the order with such ferocity, the man nearly toppled over in his haste to stand.

She knew that voice. A rush of air filled her lungs as she looked up to see Isaac.

He shoved the other soldier away and knelt beside her, slipping his arm beneath her shoulders to pull her against him. "Libby, are you hurt?"

She shook her head, then pressed her face to his solid chest. He wore no coat or waistcoat, and she could hear his heart pounding against her ear, nearly as fast as her own.

"Thank You, God." His voice was a rough whisper. A tremble ran through him as he held her close. "Can you stand?"

"Aye." The word, and her legs, wobbled as he helped her to her feet.

Keeping his arm firmly around her waist, Isaac glared at the soldier. "Who are you? What is your regiment?"

"What business is it of yours?" The soldier sneered. "I do not answer to rebel colonists."

"I'm Lieutenant Harrison of The King's Own. You will answer to me."

Libby startled. She'd never heard such stern authority and power in Isaac's voice before. His palm pressed against the small of her back, and she leaned into him, thankful for his steady strength and protection.

The soldier's eyes narrowed. "Private Danes. 43rd Regiment of Foot, sir. And if you are Lieutenant Harrison, then you should know that I was ordered to detain this woman."

A chill ran down Libby's spine. What was he talking about?

Isaac's posture stiffened. "Explain yourself, Private Danes."

"Miss Caldwell is charged with espionage. Treason against the Crown."

Her breathing grew fast and shallow, mind spinning. What was happening? She'd thought only Isaac knew of the journal and her letter. She stared up at him, disbelieving.

The look in his eyes was as shocked and confused as her

own. He shook his head ever so slightly, then turned back to the soldier. "On what evidence?"

The man's jaw hardened. "Better to discuss that without her, Lieutenant. I've my orders from General Gage to hold her under house arrest. Unless you think the jail a better place."

Jail? A wave of dizziness made Libby's legs buckle. Isaac tightened his grip on her, holding her up.

"Of course not." Isaac's reply was swift and sharp. "I'll see that she is safely and properly detained. Tell Private Stanton he is needed at my quarters on Marlborough Street. I will meet with you at the encampment for a full explanation shortly."

The soldier's attention dropped to Isaac's arm still clasped around her waist. "Beg your pardon, Lieutenant, but you seem a bit too close to the situation. Perhaps I should—"

"Too close? Claims the man who looked about to accost her. No. I will manage this." Isaac's voice left no room for argument. "Fetch Stanton, then wait at Captain Merrick's tent. Tell him I sent you."

Disdain curled the soldier's lip, but he obeyed, turning swiftly and stalking away.

Libby slumped against Isaac, her entire body quivering. He tucked her close, unmoving for a long, silent moment, then shifted back just enough to look at her. "I'll fix this. I promise. I won't let you be—"

"How?" Her voice shook. If Isaac himself still thought her guilty, what could he do to protect her?

"I'll find a way. I must." He searched her face, and the worry in his eyes only made her own fear clench tighter. "Your mother is anxious. I will see you home."

Home. And yet now, it was to become her prison.

CHAPTER 32

Isaac kicked at an errant stone in the road as he traipsed to the encampment. It skittered down the rutted street, churning up a trail of dust to match the cloud of anger and confusion swirling in his mind. He'd left Stanton at the Caldwell home to act as guard, much as he was loath to do so. He couldn't bear making Libby feel like a prisoner in her own house, but what choice did he have? The orders had come from General Gage himself. Isaac had to obey.

Libby, clearly shaken, hadn't spoken a word on their walk home from the burying ground, and Mrs. Abbott had been similarly shocked when they recounted what happened. He hated leaving them, but he had to confront Private Danes and sort out what the man knew. If someone else had discovered what Isaac had found… No, he couldn't think that way. Couldn't allow himself to imagine what would happen to her.

He turned onto the Common and made straight for Captain Merrick's tent. Shoving the canvas flap out of the way, he ducked inside, finding both the captain and the private waiting.

Captain Merrick eyed Isaac with raised brows. "Private

Danes claims you need to speak with him. Do you require my assistance with this matter?"

"Thank you, but no." He'd talk more with his friend later, for now he had to face Private Danes without giving in to the desire to punch the man.

Merrick excused himself, and Isaac addressed the soldier, gritting his teeth at the smug expression on Danes's face. "First, you should know that I am going to report your actions to your captain and to General Gage. I cannot imagine your behavior toward Miss Caldwell is what the general had in mind."

"And yours is? Cavorting with a rebel spy, are we, Lieutenant?"

Heat blazed up Isaac's neck. "You will not speak to a superior officer that way. Understand me—you are on dangerous ground, Private. Do not try my patience, for it is nearly spent."

Danes crossed his arms but held his tongue.

"What reason do you have for detaining Miss Caldwell?"

"She is suspected of espionage, as I already said." The man seemed intent upon goading him.

Isaac met his insolent stare. "On what grounds?"

"For passing information through a spy ring under the guise of mending clothing for the citizens of Boston."

The accusation turned Isaac's stomach, for it mirrored what he had uncovered and suspected, but he maintained his stoic expression as he pressed the soldier further. "Who gave you this duty?"

"Sergeant Jackson. Nearly two months ago, he tasked me with infiltrating the spies by acting as one of them myself."

Isaac furrowed his brow. "I never assigned another soldier to work with him."

"From what I gathered, he thought you did not take his work as seriously as you should. His words, not mine, Lieutenant." Danes sneered his title. "He asked me directly, and as my work was especially sensitive, he did not inform anyone. It took some time, but eventually, I discovered suspicious activity centered around a man by the name of Gerrish. I arrested him several days ago. He kept quiet about his accomplices at first but gave them up when I threatened to track down his wife and children."

Bile rose in Isaac's throat. "And he named Miss Caldwell?"

"Not directly. He confessed that information had been passed through a mantua maker's shop. Once I knew that, 'twas easy to garner the names of the women who worked there. What cowards these so-called Patriots are, using women to carry out their underhanded schemes."

A flicker of hope flared in Isaac's chest. If Mr. Gerrish had not given Libby's name in particular, perhaps there was a better chance of clearing the charges. "How did you know to find her at the burying ground this morning?"

"I didn't. I planned to arrest her at her house. Tried to find her there several days ago, in fact. Providence must have been in my favor. I spotted her walking this morning and noticed she matched the description I'd been given. Quite a beauty, is she not?" He smiled tauntingly, and it took all of Isaac's self-control not to lash out in return. "I followed. It helped that she was crying at the grave of a man with the same surname."

Isaac's fingers curled into a fist. "And General Gage ordered her arrest?"

Danes shifted, scratching at his pocked cheek. "The general had granted Sergeant Jackson the right to arrest suspected spies as needed."

Isaac edged closer, narrowing his gaze. "But did he directly instruct you to detain Miss Caldwell?"

Danes was silent.

"I need an answer, Private."

The man's nostrils flared. "He did not."

Relief coursed through Isaac, but he kept his expression neutral. "That is enough. You are dismissed."

The soldier flung the tent open and stomped away without another word. Isaac slumped against the table. If he kept his own discoveries about Libby to himself and used Danes's abhorrent behavior against him, he might have a chance to see Libby safely freed from this accusation. But nothing could erase what he knew, and the questions that remained unanswered. Was he truly willing to defy the army, even General Gage himself, for the sake of the woman he loved, but might never be able to trust again?

Libby peeked into the parlor where Isaac stood staring out the window, his back to her. He'd returned late in the afternoon and immediately shut himself away in his chamber with Private Stanton, the soldier he'd put in place to guard the house. She had kept her distance, not wanting to appear as though she were attempting to eavesdrop, despite her desperate need for answers. Now that the private was gone, she could not wait any longer to talk to Isaac. To find out what he had learned about the charges against her and to attempt to explain the truth.

And yet, she hovered on the threshold, afraid to take the next step. Terrified of what he might say and unsure of what to tell him in return. If she revealed everything, she might help her own defense, perhaps restore their trust, but at what cost? The safety, even the lives, of Elijah and others? But if she held back, would he believe that awful soldier's condemnation of her? What of Isaac's own accusations last night that implied the same?

Still, he had come to her defense this morning, in more ways than one. That gave her hope, slim though it may be.

She drew a fortifying breath, though it did little to calm her churning stomach. She'd felt sick with worry all day, and Mama had taken to bed with a megrim that set in soon after she learned of all that had happened. Libby couldn't help wishing for her mother's quiet strength at her side right now. But this trouble was her own, and she needed to face it alone.

No, not alone. God was with her, and He knew the end from the beginning. Silently, she prayed that His will be done, and that she would hold fast to her trust in Him, no matter the outcome. Clasping her hands tightly to keep them from shaking, she stepped into the room.

Isaac turned, his brows drawn low as though she'd caught him deep in thought. His expression softened as his gaze collided with hers.

She swallowed and crossed the parlor to stand before him. "Before you say anything, I must thank you for coming to my rescue this morning. How did you know where to find me?"

"I didn't. I...prayed when I left the house. I begged God to show me where you had gone and..." A mix of confusion and wonder passed over his face. "I immediately thought of the burying ground."

Warmth swelled in Libby's chest. Clearly, Isaac had needed that answer to prayer just as much as she had. "Then I am grateful for His merciful provision."

"As am I. I only wish I'd gotten there sooner. When I saw that soldier with you, I..." A muscle in his jaw twitched.

"I am safe now, and Private Stanton was all politeness, just as you promised he would be."

His lips pressed into a sad smile. "I'm glad. I am sorry, for all of this."

"You are not at fault."

"Are you?" His question was a mere whisper, and the vulnerability in his brown eyes made her breath catch. "I want to believe what you said last night. That this is all a misunderstanding. But how did the most notorious spy come to be in possession of the journal you took from Mr. Pierce's room, with your letter revealing the army's plans inside?"

Libby exhaled a tremulous breath. "I realize I have lost your trust, and for that I am deeply sorry. I never wished to deceive you, and hope you know me well enough to believe that. But I don't know how to explain everything without endangering others."

"But what about yourself? Your own safety? Will you not tell me, for that alone?" He stepped closer and reached for her hand. The strength and warmth of his fingers wrapped around her own and sent heat rushing up her arm. "I believe I can see this charge against you dismissed, and I will do all in my power to ensure it is. I will tell no one of my own suspicions. I will protect you. But I beg you, for the sake of our...friendship, please, Libby, tell me the truth."

She stared down at their clasped hands for a long moment, then met his searching gaze. "I am not a spy. You may choose to accept my word or not, but that is the truth. The letter is mine, but when I sent it, it was into the keeping of a friend, nothing more. I overheard you speaking of the plans, and I feared for the safety of my family. I only thought to protect them. I never guessed anyone else would see that message."

"So James Lawrence is your friend?"

"There is no James Lawrence. That is only a name, assumed for secrecy."

His eyes widened. "But you know who he really is?"

"Aye."

Dropping her hand, he stepped back. "I never guessed it was an alias. Neither did Sergeant Jackson. All this time..."

She held her breath, waiting for him to press further, to demand the real identity. What could she say? Elijah was no longer in Boston, or so he'd told her, but if she revealed him as the leader of the spies, wouldn't Isaac be forced to hunt him down?

He stared at her a long moment, mouth pressed into a hard line, then shook his head. The air seeped from her lungs. He wasn't going to ask?

"What of Mr. Pierce?" Isaac shifted, assessing her. "I did not realize, until reading Sergeant Jackson's notes, that he was arrested alongside James Lawrence. That night, when you asked me to help him escape Boston with William and your friend, were you aware that a known spy had been captured with him?"

"I was not. Hannah and Will never told me. But I assure you, Mr. Pierce was incapable of espionage. His mental health was declining quite severely. He could not even manage the apothecary any longer. He must have been so frightened and confused when he was arrested, and—"

"I saw him myself. I believe you are right, and I despised the way Sergeant Jackson treated him." Isaac dipped his chin. "But you must understand how all of this looked to me, as I began to put the pieces together. Why I began to doubt."

"I do, and I don't blame you."

He sighed, rubbing his left shoulder with a barely suppressed grimace. "And Mr. Gerrish? That is the charge Private Danes has put upon you. That you were involved in passing information through the mantua maker. What explanation can you give?"

"Did Mr. Gerrish say that?"

"He did not state your name in particular, but upon threat of harm to his family, he did reveal the shop as a source of spy efforts."

Libby's heart raced. "Is Mrs. Barker safe?"

"I cannot say for certain. I've not yet had the time to inquire about her, for I wanted to return here as quickly as possible." A scowl darkened his expression. "The private was acting on old directives from Sergeant Jackson. Given that he was never officially assigned to this work by any superior officer, I believe I can use his own actions against the case he is attempting to make. I hope that will work in your favor, and in Mrs. Barker's as well, if need be."

"I promise, I was not involved. I did not lie to you about Mr. Gerrish. I had no knowledge of the information he was passing along. It was only after I made that delivery that I realized..." She hesitated, but the desperate thread of hope in Isaac's eyes spurred her on. "I discovered, quite by accident, what was happening. But that was less than a fortnight ago, and I've not returned to work at the mantua maker since."

"Is it possible that you helped carry hidden messages without knowing?"

"No. I asked that in particular and was reassured that I had never been part of any such work."

"And you trust the person who told you this?"

Libby nodded, thoughts straying to Mrs. Barker's face, lined with concern when Libby realized what she'd been hiding. She thought of Will and Hannah and the secrets they'd kept from her. Of all of Elijah's deceptions. Each revelation had left her hurt and confused at first. Yet now, as she considered her own choices, she could better understand the complicated decisions they'd made.

"Sometimes, people do things we cannot comprehend, and it may feel like a betrayal. It can bring pain." She spoke for her own sake, as much as for Isaac's. "Perhaps they do not always choose the right path, or at least the one we think to be right, but I believe they've done what they deem best. And I am confident they've acted, not with the purpose to bring harm, but out of a desire to protect others."

"And that is what you have done?"

"I fear I've been caught in the middle, quite unintentionally." She huffed a small laugh, then sobered. "But aye, it is. I did not wish to hurt you, or anyone else." She tipped her head to look up at him, reaching for the courage to lay her heart bare. Even if he rejected her and walked away forever, she needed him to know. "I am no spy. I would never betray you, nor use my relationship with you to serve my own purposes. I meant what I told you last night, Isaac. I love—"

"You shouldn't say that." His curt reply sliced deep, but it was the pain reflected in his eyes that hurt most.

"But I want you to hear it. I love you. So very much. And I understand if you cannot forgive me or ever return my affection, but I still need you to—"

"I do, Libby." His words came out ragged.

She stared at him. "What?"

His gaze roamed her face with a desperate sort of longing that made her pulse stutter. "I do forgive you. And I..." He reached out and cupped her cheek so gently she forgot to breathe. "I love you. More than I can say. In a way I have never loved anyone else."

His declaration spread through her like the sunrise over the harbor, bringing light and warmth to every corner of her being.

He loved her.

She leaned into his palm, trembling as his thumb traced her skin, then brushed over her lips. His fingers buried into her hair, and he tilted her chin up, dipping his head until his forehead rested against hers.

"But I...I cannot." His rough whisper burned as it hit her skin. "Not while I am bound by duty to serve the Crown, nor while I am still betrothed to someone else. I should not have kissed you yesterday. I should not be holding you now, wishing I could kiss you again."

Libby shivered, wanting to protest. Aching to close the mere inches that separated them and press her lips to his. Yet what could she say? What could she do?

He pulled away, resignation written in his face. "I believe

you, and I trust you. I will see you cleared from any charges. I will make sure you are safe. But I cannot offer you more than that. I am so very sorry."

Tears blurred Libby's vision and tightened her throat. She couldn't speak, could hardly think. He loved her. But he was leaving, all the same.

CHAPTER 33

*L*ight rain drizzled as Isaac mounted the broad steps of Province House on Thursday morning. The stately three-story brick mansion had been the home of the royal governors since 1715 and was Gage's current residence as both general and governor. Isaac paused under the columned portico and tugged off his hat, slapping it on his thigh to rid it of excess water before donning it again. He lifted his hand to knock, then hesitated. God had graciously answered his prayer to find Libby yesterday morning. Might He answer another one this day?

Lord, please grant me the words to say, that Libby may be absolved of any suspicion and that the general will look favorably upon my request.

He had lain awake long into the night, carefully planning his defense for Libby's sake, as well as examining his own heart.

He loved her. There was no doubt in his mind as to the depth and conviction of his feelings. He knew now that his love for her had been growing for months. Despite the obstacles between them. Despite his best efforts to resist and distance himself. It had grown all the same. Fierce and stubborn and desperate.

A love worth fighting for.

He'd told her, a fortnight ago, that whether you chose duty or rebellion, there was something to gain and something to lose. He'd been chained by duty for far too long, but what if he made a different decision? He was not willing to lose Libby. Perhaps now was the time to choose rebellion.

Straightening, he knocked. A young soldier opened the door and ushered him into a grand room which may have, in more peaceful times, provided a place of luxurious entertaining and respite, but now had clearly been purposed as a military planning space.

"General Gage will be with you shortly, Lieutenant." The soldier removed his hat, clasping it with both hands as he sketched a bow, then departed.

A large table occupied the center of the room, surrounded by chairs and covered with a scattering of letters, maps, and books. Isaac stepped closer, noting a sketch of the Charlestown Peninsula which illustrated the defensive works the army had built there. A similar drawing of the Dorchester Heights lay beside it. Did the generals still hope to mount an attack there and capture that location as well?

Footsteps drew him up short. He turned as General Gage entered the room and quickly raised his hand to his hat, palm out, in salute.

"Good morning, Lieutenant Harrison." The general greeted him with a bob of the head and a welcoming smile. His gray hair was neatly styled, his crimson uniform immaculate, but shadows under his dark eyes spoke to a familiar weariness. The siege weighed heavy on everyone, even the most powerful among their ranks. He swept a hand toward the table. "Please be seated."

Isaac waited for the general to take his place before settling into a chair of his own.

"I recognize that you are here to discuss matters of espionage, but I must begin by thanking you for your service and sacrifice." Gage nodded toward Isaac's left sleeve. "I have heard much about you from Captain Merrick and commend your bravery and tenacity."

"Thank you, sir." If the general knew what lay on Isaac's heart, would he still offer such compliments?

"Now then, what have you to report?"

Isaac recounted the happenings of the previous day, elaborating upon Sergeant Jackson's prior work, as well as Private Danes's disrespectful behavior. Gage listened intently as Isaac provided his carefully prepared explanation as to Libby's innocence. The general frowned when Isaac disclosed what had happened to Libby, and his scowl deepened when Isaac explained that Jackson had recruited and assigned Danes without the approval of any officer.

General Gage clasped his hands atop the polished wooden table. "You are confident that the young woman in question was wrongfully detained?"

"I am. I questioned her myself and found no evidence to support Private Danes's accusation."

"Then I am satisfied. Her name is cleared. I trust your judgment far more than that of a soldier who holds no regard for orders or common civility. I will see that Private Danes is properly reprimanded."

"Thank you, General." Isaac suppressed the smile that threatened to break free and offered a grateful nod instead.

"Before you leave, there is something I should like to discuss." The general tapped his fingers atop a folded paper on the table beside him. "I am quite pleased with all that I have heard regarding your service to the Crown, and can see that you are a capable and competent soldier, even now. However, a ship arrived two days ago carrying fresh troops. Among them, an officer of my acquaintance brought with him express instructions from London that he is to be established in the role of managing our espionage efforts. I know him to be highly qualified for the position, having experience with such matters during the Seven Years' War. Please understand that this in no way reflects upon your work or character. I do respect Captain Merrick's recommendation and all that you have done thus far."

Isaac caught his breath. If this new soldier was to take his place, what did that mean for his future? Might this be the opportunity he needed to break free of his bonds to the army?

"I would like to introduce you to him, if I may, and ascertain his thoughts as to a new position for you under his authority." General Gage rose from his chair. "If you will wait a moment, I'll bring Major Bradbury in."

Bradbury? The father of the woman he was betrothed to? Isaac's stomach clenched. Surely not. There must be more than one man with such a name. Still... "Does the major perchance have a daughter named Victoria?"

Gage's thick brows rose. "Indeed. Are you acquainted with the young woman?"

"I am not." It was the truth. He knew nothing about her, save her name, despite the agreement bound between their families. "However, my father has...connections with the major."

"Very good, then. Perhaps that connection will bode well for his decision."

Isaac's pulse quickened as he watched General Gage depart. The letter he had penned to his father still waited amongst his belongings. No ship had yet left port for him to send it. Dare he make the request of Miss Bradbury's father directly? But how could he, if he might be forced to serve under the man's authority?

Isaac stared at the doorway as though it were the barrel of a cannon, every muscle tense and braced for impact.

Gage rounded the corner, a tall, lean man at his side. The major bore the familiar straight posture of an officer, despite a slight limp. He had a narrow face, accentuated by the three rolled curls on both sides of his powdered wig.

"Major Bradbury, may I present Lieutenant Harrison?" General Gage made the introductions with a sweep of his hand.

"Lieutenant Harrison, 'tis a pleasure to meet you at last." The major's smile appeared genuine.

"And you, Major Bradbury." Isaac forced a pleasant expression as he returned the greeting.

When the major's assessing gaze landed on Isaac's left side, his countenance faltered and his thin brows drew together. "What is this?"

Isaac cleared his throat. "I was injured in the battle at Breed's Hill last month, sir. The surgeon removed my arm in order to preserve my life."

"A tragic loss, indeed. You have my sympathy." He stepped closer, attention still fixed on Isaac's left sleeve. "Does your father know?"

Isaac's neck heated under his scrutiny. "He does not. I have written but have not yet been provided with the opportunity to send the letter."

Major Bradbury's mouth twitched, and he finally raised his focus to Isaac's face. "I am sorry for what you have endured. I have my own battle wound that plagues me still." He tapped his right leg. "But I fear this will not do."

"Excuse me?"

"This." He gestured toward what remained of Isaac's arm, then turned to General Gage. "I would prefer to select men who can serve in a whole capacity. With due respect, General, I suggest you allow Lieutenant Harrison to resign his commission and be invalided out of service."

Isaac flinched at the major's curt dismissal, but then the full force of his words took root. Resign his commission. Leave the service. Might the injury that had cost him his arm earn him his freedom?

Gage's brows lowered, as though he was taken aback by Major Bradbury's swift and critical decision. "Lieutenant?"

Isaac squared his shoulders. "I agree with Major Bradbury's assessment, General Gage. I am no longer capable of serving as I once was." In body and in spirit, though he would not confess such to the general. "If you are willing to grant my discharge, I am honored to accept."

"Then it shall be done," Gage said. "I will draw up the papers and ensure you receive passage home on the first ship to depart."

"To that point"—Major Bradbury glanced at Isaac before turning his attention to the general—"might I have a private word with the lieutenant?"

"Indeed." General Gage turned his attention to Isaac. "If you'll return tomorrow, Lieutenant, I will have your discharge in order."

"Thank you, sir." Isaac exhaled, hardly able to believe what had happened. It was more than he had dared to hope for. Now to address the major and pray for an equally favorable outcome. *Lord, if it be Your will...*

Isaac turned to face him. "Major Bradbury, might I suggest that my discharge from the army impacts our agreement as well?"

"Rightly so." The major nodded sharply. "I regret that your new circumstances cause me to doubt the wisdom of continuing in our arrangement, as I do not see how you could rightly provide for my daughter. I realize that your father is not here to discuss this—"

"However, I am." Isaac squared his shoulders. His father had determined Isaac's path for his entire life, but no longer.

"Major Bradbury, I respect your concerns, and I am in full agreement. In fact, in my letter to the baronet, I already recommended the dissolution of the betrothal. I recognize that doing so means you have upheld your end, only to be denied the expected return." He cringed inwardly to think of himself—his hand in marriage—as a sort of payment for the position he'd been granted in the army. But that was exactly what his father had done when he made the agreement. "I am willing to petition my father on your behalf for some other recompense instead."

The older man stared at him a long moment, then shook his head. "That is not necessary. I appreciate your forthright manner, Lieutenant, and respect the sacrifice you have made for the Crown. I have dedicated my entire life to the army, and as such, I understand the significance of your loss far more than most. My daughter is young. There will be other prospects. I consider our contract fulfilled."

Major Bradbury extended his hand, and Isaac clasped it firmly in return, sealing their words.

The major did not know it, but he had brought the answers Isaac so desperately longed for. Answers he had hardly dared believe possible. He remembered what Libby had said, about how his scars may have brought him right where God wanted him to be. Isaac never could have imagined how true her words would be, or how graciously God would answer his prayers.

Major Bradbury accompanied him to the front door, and they bid each other farewell. Isaac strode down the steps into the street, the rain coming heavier now. He closed his eyes and tipped his head back, letting the water wash over his face.

"Thank You, Lord." He whispered the words toward the heavens, but they echoed in his heart with all the joyous exclamation of pealing church bells.

God had been working, even in the most difficult and incomprehensible of circumstances. He had taken Isaac's pain and brought healing. He had broken down the obstacles that Isaac couldn't surmount, making a way forward that was far better than anything he could have hoped.

Isaac set out for the Caldwells' house, nearly at a run, heedless of the puddles that splattered his breeches with mud. Back to the place where Dr. Caldwell's words had first convicted and challenged him to believe in a God who did not demand duty, like his own earthly father or the army he served, but offered grace and mercy for all who asked. Back to the home where Mrs. Abbott's prayers had sustained Isaac when he could offer none of his own. Back to Libby, who had been a light in his darkest hours and pointed him to the true Light of the World.

His soul had never felt so free.

CHAPTER 34

Libby hissed as the needle meant for her sampler pierced her finger instead. She yanked back, pressing her thumb to the spot of blood to staunch its flow. Captain Merrick turned from his place at the parlor window, eying her with concern. Isaac had asked his friend to stand guard while he met with General Gage this morning, since she remained under house arrest. Mama, still recovering from her headache, had risen late and was nursing a cup of willow bark, chamomile, and lavender tea in the kitchen.

Libby forced a smile in the captain's direction. "Not to worry. Only a small mishap. I am fine."

He answered with a sympathetic nod. "Lieutenant Harrison will make things right, Miss Caldwell. I have no doubt."

How she hoped he was correct. She did not doubt that Isaac would do everything he could to see the charges removed, but what if it wasn't enough?

The captain turned back to the window, and quiet fell over the room again, save for the patter of the rain. Libby stared at her needlework, but the stitches blurred as her mind raced. Even if she was freed, what next? Should she and Mama try to leave Boston, as Isaac had first suggested? Her heart ached at the thought of parting with him, but to stay would hurt just as much, knowing that he loved her yet still being unable to hope for a life together.

"He's coming, miss." Captain Merrick's voice broke through her muddled thoughts. "I see him now, down the road."

Abandoning her work, she jumped from her chair and hurried to look. 'Twas Isaac, indeed. His head was bowed, his pace swift. Her pulse raced. Was it the rain or the news he brought that drove him toward them in such a fashion? Spinning away, she ran to the door and tugged it open.

He halted several steps from the house and looked up, rain streaming from the corners of his hat. A smile broader than any she'd ever seen lit his face when his gaze tangled with hers. "You're safe, Libby. General Gage dismissed all charges."

She couldn't hold back a sob of relief, nor could she keep from dashing outside and flinging her arms around him. His right arm wrapped around her waist in return, holding her tightly, as though he'd never let go. The damp of his uniform soaked into her jacket, but she felt only the warmth of his embrace.

He pressed a kiss to her forehead, then her temple, then her cheek, leaving a trail of sparks along the way. "You're free, and so am I." His lips brushed her ear as he whispered. "The betrothal is ended."

She pulled back to stare at him, uncomprehending. "What do you mean?"

"I'll explain everything, but the agreement my father made is over. I am yours, Libby, if you will have me. I cannot say what the future will hold—I only know that I want to share it with you."

"But I thought you said you could not..." Libby blinked, breathless with wonder and joy and confusion.

"I was wrong. Thank God, I was wrong."

"What about the army?"

"I resigned my commission. General Gage is preparing my discharge." He glanced over her head. "I'll explain everything to you later, Captain."

A low chuckle sounded behind her, and Libby shifted just enough to realize that the officer stood in the threshold of the front door.

"I shall await your conversation at the encampment whenever you are ready." Captain Merrick sidled past them, clasping Isaac on the shoulder. "I am happy for you, my friend."

Libby's gaze found Isaac's again, and the love that shone in his brown eyes matched that which overflowed in her own heart.

He reached for her hand, threading his fingers through hers. "I love you, Libby." His voice was thick and husky.

"And I love you. Forever."

He lifted their joined hands, brushing a kiss over her fingers before capturing her lips with his own.

A throat cleared, and she jolted back to find Mama standing in the doorway. Heat blazed in Libby's cheeks. Mama's brows were raised, but there was hint of laughter in her eyes.

"Lieutenant Harrison?" She fixed him with a gaze that held both tenderness and a motherly rebuke. "Since my husband is no longer with us, might you have a question to ask me?"

He straightened, a bit of color rising in his face. "Indeed, Mrs. Abbott. I hope that you will grant me the honor of asking your daughter to marry me."

Mama smiled, though Libby caught the slightest quiver of her chin. "You have my blessing. And that of her father as well, for I am confident that he would have given it gladly."

"Thank you, Mama." Libby's voice broke.

Pressing a hand to her heart, Mama nodded, then eased the door closed, leaving them alone in the rain.

A low laugh rumbled in Isaac's chest. His fingers drifted to her cheek, thumb caressing away the mix of rain and tears that fell on her skin. "I know I am a broken man, but all I have, all I am, I offer to you. Will you be my wife?"

"I will, with all my heart." Libby rested her hand on his left shoulder, slowly, gently tracing along what remained of his arm. "Do not despise your scars, Isaac, for they are what brought you to me."

Pushing onto tiptoes, she pressed her lips to his. He pulled her close, returning the kiss as the rain fell, an unspoken promise that together they could withstand any storm.

EPILOGUE

The late-September sunset cast a rosy glow over Will and Hannah's crowded parlor. Libby perched on the settee, staring down at the tiny face of Patience and Josiah's infant daughter. She traced a finger over the baby's round cheek, in awe of the softness of her skin.

"Isn't she precious?" Hannah stood in front of Libby, equally enraptured by the new arrival.

"And her brother is too." Will stepped behind his wife, threading his arms around her waist and dropping a kiss to her cheek.

Libby tore her attention away from the girl to peek at Isaac, who sat beside her, cradling Patience and Josiah's baby son in his arm. Patience had been safely delivered of twins a fortnight earlier, just days before Libby, Isaac, and Mama arrived in Watertown. They'd named the little ones Anne and Daniel, after Patience's mother and Josiah's father.

Her gaze lingered on Isaac, admiring the handsome lines of his face and the way he looked so at ease holding the babe. One day, Lord willing, he would hold a child of their own.

He met her look with a warm smile. He had smiled often over the past month. So had she. The weeks after his proposal had gone by in a blur. After publishing the banns at King's Chapel, Libby and Isaac wed in mid-August. It had been a simple affair, their vows exchanged in her own parlor, in front of the hearth where she and Papa had spent so many hours together. Katherine and Captain Merrick had attended as witnesses alongside Mama, an unlikely yet precious blending of different worlds coming together to celebrate their union.

Patience bustled in from the kitchen, a plate of Shrewsbury cakes in hand. Mama followed, balancing a tray of steaming teacups. They placed both on the small round table that had been pushed to the back corner of the room to make space for all the guests—though Libby, Isaac, and Mama could not quite be counted as guests, as they were living with Will and Hannah for the time being.

Conditions in Boston had continued to worsen as the summer wore on, and at the end of August, General Gage offered Isaac passage aboard a ship bound for England as promised. Isaac declined, asking if the general might grant them departure from the city to Watertown instead. They'd traveled through Boston Neck three days later, passes from the governor in hand, and with the generous loan of a carriage from the Whites to ease their journey. Difficult as it was to leave her home, a weight had lifted as they put the confines of Boston behind.

She'd felt a little nervous as to how everyone would receive her new husband, given his previous position in the army, but her fears were unfounded. After the initial surprise of their arrival, the welcome had been hearty and joyous.

Little Anne began to fuss, and Patience hurried over, scooping her daughter up from Libby's outstretched arms. "She's hungry, I'm certain."

The baby immediately began rooting around as if to confirm her mother's words.

Libby laughed. "Shall we wait to eat until you're finished?"

"No, go on. The tea will be cold by then, for her brother is sure to want his turn as soon as she is done, if not before."

As if on cue, Daniel broke into his own cries, surprisingly strong for one so small. Josiah took the boy from Isaac, his large blacksmith hands rubbing gentle circles on his son's back to soothe him while he waited.

"Your father is asleep in his favorite spot again." Will pointed toward the chair perched beside the back window.

His words were meant for Hannah, but Libby followed his gesture, heart warmed by the sight of Mr. Pierce, peacefully at rest despite the noise of the room. Mr. Pierce asked about Elijah nearly every day, but no one had seen him since early July. Libby could tell his unpredictable comings and goings weighed on Hannah, and she prayed that he would find a way to stop running from his grief and his dangerous life as a spy.

Isaac rose and extended his hand to Libby. She stood, keeping her fingers entwined with his as they made their way to the table for a freshly baked treat. Mama stood beside it, sipping her tea and watching the room with a look of contentment. Libby felt the same settled happiness in her own heart. It was a true gift to be surrounded by the people she loved again, one she would never take for granted.

Dipping his head close to her ear, Isaac whispered, "Walk with me?"

She grinned and nodded. They still continued their habit of a daily walk, as they had while he was recovering. It had become one of her favorite parts of the day. A time for just the two of them, to talk and pray and hope together.

They ducked outside, where the sky greeted them with streaks of pink and orange. The crisp autumn breeze carried the scent of pines and woodsmoke, and Isaac tugged her closer to his side as they strolled down the street.

She leaned her head against his shoulder. "We can't go too far. 'Tis nearly dark."

"I'll keep you safe." There was a hint of teasing in his voice and a husky warmth that shot heat through her belly. "Only a little farther."

He paused in front of a white building and turned to face her.

Libby furrowed her brow. "What are we doing at the schoolhouse?"

"I don't know how much longer the siege will last, nor if we'll stay here in Watertown or return to Boston one day. But we're here for the time being, and much as I appreciate William and Hannah's generosity in opening their home to us, I'd like to provide for my wife."

Libby grinned. "Do you mean to say you're considering my idea?"

She had suggested that Isaac would make a wonderful teacher. His love of books and learning was clear, but she'd also noticed he had a way with children as she watched his kindness toward Aideen and Briana and even young Benjamin. And, should he run into any unruly students, he could always use that soldier tone to call things to order.

"More than considering. I learned earlier today that the previous teacher is serving with the newly established Continental army. I offered to take the position and was accepted."

"Oh, Isaac, that is wonderful news!" She flung her arms around his neck.

He wrapped his arm around her waist, lifting and spinning her in a circle before gently lowering her to the ground once more.

"What do you say to a new sort of adventure for us to

share?" He brushed the curls from her cheek, fingers trailing down the length of one.

"I am ready. Whatever the future holds, I'll walk it beside you. Hand in hand."

He pulled her close and pressed a tender kiss to her lips as the last rays of sunlight faded. They walked home together, the full moon illuminating their path. God had taken their hurts and stitched their lives into something beautiful.

Did you enjoy this book? We hope so!
**Would you take a quick minute to leave a review where you
purchased the book?**
It doesn't have to be long. Just a sentence or two telling what
you liked about the story!

Love Christian Historical Romance?
Looking for your next favorite book?
Become a Wild Heart Books insider and receive a FREE ebook
and get exclusive updates on new releases before anyone else.
Sign up for our newsletter now.
https://wildheartbooks.org/newsletter

Dear Reader,

I hope you enjoyed Libby and Isaac's story. It was a unique challenge for me to portray a British officer, but I sincerely appreciated the opportunity to look at the events through his eyes and consider the way he would have felt about the beginnings of what became the American Revolution.

While this book portrayed the Battle of Bunker Hill, you will have noticed that the fighting actually took place on Breed's Hill. Though the men were originally instructed to establish a redoubt on Bunker Hill, they made the decision to use Breed's Hill instead due to its closer proximity to Boston. Led by Colonel William Prescott, militiamen worked through the night to establish fortifications, which they defended with courage the following day when the Regulars arrived. The colonial troops were eventually forced to retreat, due in large part to their lack of gunpowder and ammunition, but their stand at Breed's Hill was a costly victory for the British, who sustained significant casualties. Doctor Joseph Warren, a key Patriot of the day, died in this battle, a loss which was keenly felt by the

Americans. Today, the Bunker Hill monument still marks some locations where the redoubt and breastworks stood.

Although most of my soldiers are fictional, Lieutenant Colonel James Abercrombie was a real officer present at Breed's Hill, who died as a result of injuries sustained there. Also, the story of Captain Merrick's head wound, rescue, and subsequent surgery is based on a real man—Captain George Harris of the 5th Regiment. Merrick's recounting of watching his surgery and seeing his own brain, as well as his joke that it proved he had one, is based on the real records of Captain Harris.

Other historical figures made appearances throughout this book to varying degrees. Benjamin Church was indeed a man who was closely connected to prominent Sons of Liberty, while also secretly reporting to General Gage. He was caught, court martialed, and imprisoned. In 1778, he was banished from America and his ship, bound for the Caribbean, was lost at sea.

Reverend Henry Caner was the reverend of King's Chapel in 1775, though the sermon I referred to is fictional. He began there in 1747 and held his last service on March 10th, 1776, before departing for Halifax, Nova Scotia, with other Bostonians loyal to the crown.

Daniel Malcom's grave that Isaac visits in Copp's Hill still stands in the burying ground, with the inscription and musket ball marks as described in this story. He died in 1769, and British soldiers, incensed by his epitaph, really did use his stone for target practice.

The spinet that Katherine plays was made by Thomas Hitchcock, a prolific spinet maker who is said to have produced over a thousand instruments in his lifetime. He lived in London, and the one known full-sized harpsichord he crafted is displayed in the Victoria and Albert Museum.

The unexpected and ingenious method of hiding notes under covered buttons was a real tactic used to exchange information during the American Revolution. Covering buttons with cloth to match the coat was a fashionable practice of the day, and more than one account is given of passing messages in such a manner. One such record is of fourteen-year-old John Darragh in Philadelphia, who was allowed to pass back and forth right under the eyes of British sentries with shorthand notes hidden beneath his buttons.

Much of Libby's struggle to understand God's goodness in the face of loss and hardship reflects my own faith journey through the loss of our first baby and the complex heart defect of our third child. I cried while writing Chapter 11, because the encouragement and truths that Mary speaks are ones that God taught me through those trials. Her words are true of my life— that it is "in the hardest times, when God has seemed utterly incomprehensible, that my faith has grown the most."

The Siege of Boston that began in the days following Lexington and Concord lasted until March of 1776...but the way it ended is a story for another book. One that will feature Elijah and Katherine's journey to forgiveness and love. I hope you will join me for their story in *Soul of the Revolution.* If you've not yet had the opportunity to read the first books in this series, you'll find more about Patience and Josiah, Will and Hannah, and the tumultuous events in and around Boston in *Spark of the Revolution* and *Secrets of the Revolution.*

My gratitude to the reenactors of The King's Own for their generosity in sharing their wealth of knowledge, which helped me bring Isaac to life.

Many thanks and love to the "Inklings" girls, for sharing life, motherhood, faith, and writing together. And for putting up with my brainstorming ramblings.

Thank you to the wonderful team at Wild Heart Books for giving these stories a place to shine and helping bring them to life in the best way.

As always, I could not do any of this without the support of my amazing family. Your love and encouragement mean everything to me, and it is such a joy to share this adventure with you. I love you all more than words can say.

And to the One whose grace is sufficient for all who seek Him—may these words point back to You and bring You glory.

ABOUT THE AUTHOR

Megan Soja is a multi-award-winning author who writes stories with strong faith, rich history, and sweet romance. She lives in western NY with her husband and two daughters and loves having adventures, both big and small, with her family. When she's not writing, she enjoys reading, hiking, canoeing and kayaking, and playing French Horn.

The Petticoat Spy by Elva Cobb Martin

A Southern belle turned spy and a dashing blockade runner fight a hopeless battle against the British.

When Anna Grace Laurens's parents are murdered by the British and her Charles Town plantation burned, she seizes her only option for escape—a desperate leap into the Cooper River. She'll do anything to survive...and get revenge.

John Cooper Vargas is used to danger as he sails his sloop upriver through war-torn colonies, but seeing a woman plunge into the river amidst Tory gunfire is something he wouldn't have thought possible. Until now.

Rescuing her draws him into a web of intrigue, but he can't let her fight the British on her own. As the American Revolution closes in around them, it may take a miracle for them—and their love—to survive.

~

A Courageous Betrothal by Denise Weimer

A wounded lieutenant, a woman fierce enough to protect her family, and an American Revolution with everything at stake.

Red-haired, freckle-faced, and almost six feet tall, Jenny White has resigned herself to fame over love. Possessing the courage and wits to guard her younger siblings against nature, natives, and loyalists in Georgia's "Hornet's Nest" gives life meaning until she meets scout Caylan McIntosh.

From the time Jenny nurses the young lieutenant back to health after the Battle of Kettle Creek, she can't deny her attraction to the vexing Highlander, who seems determined to dismantle her emotional armor. But when Georgia falls to the British and Caylan returns to guide Jenny's family on a harrowing exodus into the North Carolina mountains, will his secrets prove stronger than his devotion? Or will their love be courageous enough to carry them through the battles ahead?

~

Reclaiming the Spy by Lorri Dudley

How can he protect her from himself when she keeps winding up in his arms?

She never gave up hope. After ten years of prayers for her husband, presumed dead in the Peninsula Wars, Abigail Emerson is shocked to discover him alive. Yet what should be the happily ever after of fairy tales becomes a nightmare when he coldly instructs her to forget she'd ever seen him. Abigail refuses to let her beloved slip through her fingers again, and she's willing to battle for his love, despite the walls he's created to barricade his heart.

Nicholas Emerson's time as a spy for the War Office has left physical and mental battle wounds. He can never be the charming, carefree man he once was—the man his wife deserves—but when a threat to Abby's life returns him to their small Midland village, keeping her safe proves more challenging than expected. If only Abby would forget him and remarry, then he wouldn't have to face the torment of all the tender, buried feelings she evokes. The consequence of his life as a spy means he can never have her again...

www.ingramcontent.com/pod-product-compliance
Lightning Source LLC
Chambersburg PA
CBHW071233300726